THE WHISPERING YEARS

Charlie Foden is looking for lodgings. At number 8 Cooper Street he is warmly welcomed by George Parry's wife Lucy, who sees him as the answer to their financial problems. Naturally friendly and caring, Charlie soon becomes an integral part of the family. When George is made redundant, Lucy can't think how they would have managed without Charlie's support.

When George's unintentional involvement with the infamous Coley brothers threatens the Parrys' safety, Charlie finally realises the depth of his feelings for Lucy. He will do anything, even sacrifice himself, to protect her...

THE WHISPERING YEARS

by

Harry Bowling

Magna Large Print Books
Long Preston, North Yorkshire,
BD23 4ND, England.

British Library Cataloguing in Publication Data.

Bowling, Harry
    The whispering years.

    A catalogue record of this book is
    available from the British Library

    ISBN   0-7505-1511-2

First published in Great Britain by Headline Book Publishing, 1999

Copyright © 1999 by Harry Bowling

Cover illustration © Len Thurston by arrangement with
P. W. A. International

The right of Harry Bowling to be identified as the author of this work
has been asserted by him in accordance with the Copyright, Designs
and Patents Act, 1988

Published in Large Print 2000 by arrangement with
Headline Book Publishing Limited

Magna Large Print is an imprint of Library Magna Books Ltd.

Printed and bound in Great Britain by
T.J. (International) Ltd., Cornwall, PL28 8RW

PROLOGUE

November 1952

The heavy night rain had eased, but the morning air was wet with saturating mist already polluted by the sulphurous smoke from coke fires, lit against the cold of that inhospitable Saturday morning in riverside Bermondsey.

It should have been a day for huddling by the fire and brewing more tea, for staying in off the streets, but it was, after all, Saturday, when the markets beckoned and food queues had to be faced, and for Sue Parry there was a visit that had to be made, unavoidable after the letter that had filled her with trepidation and unease.

As she threw the covers back and slid her feet down on to the small rope mat by her bed she sighed sadly. A few short months ago she would have been woken with a cup of tea, and in the front room the fire would have been drawing up nicely. Her mother would be buttering the toast and Aunt Sara would be sitting by the fire, her dressing gown pulled tightly round her thin frame, her grey hair looking tortured by the metal curlers which did little if anything to enhance her appearance. Now though, on that cold Saturday morning, Sue Parry was alone.

Back in August Aunt Sara had left to find other accommodation after a bitter row, and then before the month was out Lucy Parry had suddenly been struck down with pneumonia and died two days later in the Rotherhithe infirmary. Sue was still trying to come to terms with the loss of her mother and the stark changes in her life, her days and nights filled with soul-searching and restlessness. She was getting married in early February and her mother would not be there, nor would Aunt Sara, and neither would Charlie Foden. Not now. Uncle Charlie she had called him, the man who was to have escorted her down the aisle, but now it was unthinkable and he would have to know the reason why.

The first-floor flat in Rye Buildings had been the family home for less than two years, ever since Cooper Street was emptied under a slum clearance order, and as the young woman reached for her dressing robe she thought about the forced move and how it had affected her mother. She had seemed to fade a little every day, and Aunt Sara too had become more and more morose and unreachable.

As she walked out of the bedroom Sue brushed her fingers over the framed photo of Alan. He was smiling up at her, looking smart in the navy-blue uniform of the Royal Signals. Alan Woodley, the rock she clung to, the one stable part of her life, the man she had loved and who had loved her since forever, it seemed. He had seen the letter and understood. 'Better to get it sorted once and for all,' he had agreed, 'otherwise the unanswered questions'll come back to haunt you, to haunt us both.'

There was just time for two cups of strong

sweet tea and some toast in front of an unlit fire before setting off, and as the young woman turned into the Old Kent Road, the rain started to fall heavily once more. She hurried through the dreary drizzle, tightly wrapped in a heavy black coat, the collar turned up to a chiffon scarf tied loosely round her neck. Her blonde, shoulder-length hair was partly concealed under a matching black beret, and she stepped carefully across the puddles in her wedge-heeled shoes and dark stockings. The small handbag she had tucked under her arm contained the letter, and one other, addressed to her mother and postmarked Bristol 1943.

There was no real need to use the derelict Cooper Street as a short cut to Charlie Foden's flat in Lynton Road but she found her feet taking her in that direction, and as she turned the corner Sue sighed deeply. Two years and still the houses remained, boarded up and ghostly, sounds of children long gone, the presence of women chatting on doorsteps just a memory, but the old Victorian gas lamp still there halfway along the turning. Two wasted years while the Council and the town planners argued and still there seemed to be no solution in sight. The street remained abandoned to its past.

Charlie Foden looked surprised as he answered the knock. 'Well, if it ain't young Susan. Come in, gel.'

The young woman walked into the small parlour and took off her rain-sodden beret. 'I needed ter talk ter yer, Charlie,' she said.

The older man helped her off with her coat and

hung it behind the door. 'I'm sorry I've not been round ter see yer since yer mum's funeral,' he said guiltily. 'Yer know 'ow it is, all good intentions, but I ain't bin too good lately. Nuffing bad – I just bin a bit off colour.'

Sue sat down by the fire and ran a hand over her hair. 'About the weddin', Charlie,' she began hesitantly.

'It's all right, gel, I'll be there, never fear,' he said, smiling. 'Now, can I get yer a nice cuppa?'

Sue shook her head as she slid her handbag down by her feet. 'No fanks, Charlie.'

He eased himself into his chair opposite her. He was a stocky man in his mid-sixties, with a full head of hair, white now but still inclined to wave, and a broad face with wide-spaced hazel eyes. He clasped his gnarled hands together and leaned forward slightly. 'What is it, Sue?' he asked, seeing the troubled look on her pretty face.

For a moment or two the young woman stared down at her hands, then she took up her handbag before fixing him with her pale blue eyes. 'Charlie, there's only one way ter say this,' she told him with a sigh. 'I can't let yer give me away at the weddin'.'

Charlie looked surprised and a little wounded. 'It's your choice, gel, but it'd be nice ter know what I've done ter make yer change yer mind. It must be somefing. You always called me Uncle Charlie, remember?'

Sue gave him a pale smile. 'The day before the funeral I was goin' frew Mum's fings an' I came across a bundle o' letters. They were tucked away in the back of 'er dressin'-table drawer, tied up wiv pink ribbon. Every one of 'em was postmarked Bristol, an' all from you. I've read 'em all, Charlie, but even before I did I knew the truth.'

'What did yer know, gel?' he asked quietly.

'That you an' my mum were – were lovers.'

For a few seconds Charlie's eyes fixed on hers. 'I don't deny it, an' I wouldn't try to,' he replied.

Sue lowered her head, and when she raised her eyes again to meet his they were misted. 'I was wiv Mum when she passed away, an' she called out your name. Not my dad's name, but yours. They were 'er dyin' words. I was shocked, naturally, but I thought the two of you 'ad got tergevver after me dad was killed, which would 'ave bin understandable. You was always good to us an' I know Mum leaned on you many times when fings were bad.'

'But the letters you found told you ovverwise,' Charlie prompted her.

She nodded her head slowly. 'You an' me mum were cheatin' on Dad. It was goin' on before the war started.'

'That's true, an' ter be John Blunt I don't regret it,' he said plainly. 'I don't expect you to understand, not from your position, but the fact is it wasn't some lustful, grubby affair. Me an' yer mum both fought against it 'appenin', but the mutual attraction was too strong, an' that's the gist of it.'

Sue opened her handbag and took out the more recent letter. 'I've thought of nuffing else since I 'eard your name on Mum's lips,' she said quietly.

9

'I was goin' ter say somefing at the funeral, but I just couldn't. It wasn't the right place. There was plenty o' time ter dwell on it afterwards, though. Too much time, but I did try to understand. After all, I couldn't change anyfing. My mum 'ad obviously loved you so I felt it was best ter bury the past an' get on wiv me own life. I still intended fer you ter give me away, but this week I got a letter from Aunt Sara, and as I read it all the old doubts an' questions came floodin' back.'

'Doubts? Questions? I don't understand yer, gel,' Charlie said with a frown.

'You'd better read this letter,' she answered, holding it out to him.

Dear Sue,

I hope you and Alan are keeping fit and well. As for me, I am not in the best of health. It's my heart, so the doctor tells me.

I bumped into Mrs Roach last week and she told me that you and Alan were tying the knot in February. It's good news and I wish you all the very best on the day. I will not be at the church but I'll be thinking about you both. Try not to feel too badly towards me. I was guilty of harsh words on the day I left, but your poor mum did not spare me either, God rest her soul.

Do me one favour, Sue. Get someone else to give you away. Charlie Foden doing the honours would be an insult to both your mother and your father's memory. Charlie Foden is a bad man, and I should know. He was behind the beating your father got from the Coleys. He coveted your

10

mother from the start, and nothing he ever did to help was done out of kindness. Even I was not safe from his lecherous intentions, as he made quite clear to me on numerous occasions. He despised your father, played on his weaknesses and almost got him killed. It was a bone of contention between me and your mum, but she saw no harm in him, not even when it was brutally obvious, staring her in the face.

I could say more but I don't want to upset you too much, now that your future happiness lies ahead of you. Suffice it to say that Charlie Foden will have to live with his sins the way we all have to, and one day he will be called to answer for them. I hope he will be able to face Wally Coates in the hereafter.

Think kindly of me if you can. I was very close to your mother despite what you might think.

My love to you and Alan, and may God go with you.

Aunt Sara.

Charlie's face had grown dark with anger as he read the spidery handwriting and when he had finished he handed the letter back with a shaking hand. 'The woman certainly showed her true colours,' he growled. 'Do you believe all that rubbish?'

'I don't know what ter believe any more, an' I'm all confused,' Sue sighed. 'Who was this Wally Coates? I've heard the name mentioned once or twice but it was always whispered. What did Aunt Sara mean by it?'

11

Charlie allowed himself a brief smile. 'I'll tell yer somefing, Sue. Yer muvver used ter look on the time we were tergevver as the whisperin' years, an' that just about summed it up.' He stood up slowly and reached up to the mantelshelf for his pipe and tobacco pouch. 'I understand why yer feel the way yer do,' he said quietly, 'an' I'll 'ave ter go along wiv yer wishes, but I would like ter fink that you'll keep an open mind on that woman's rantin' fer the time bein'. There's always two sides to a story an' yer've not 'eard mine yet.'

'I'm listenin', Charlie,' she said spiritedly. 'I've not planned ter go anywhere else this mornin'.'

'In that case I'll make us a cuppa, an' then you'll be able to 'ear it,' he answered.

Outside the rain beat down on the cobblestones and rattled the windowpanes. It bounded up from the pavements, ran gurgling down the swollen drains and cascaded from a broken gutter across the street. Charlie Foden sucked on his pipe as he glanced through the net curtains, then he turned and made himself comfortable in the chair facing the young woman. 'It 'ad been much like terday when I first walked into Cooper Street,' he began. 'The winter of '35 it was. I was soaked ter the skin an' it was still rainin', an' gettin' dark...'

CHAPTER 1

November 1935

For two days and nights the yellow choking fog had blanketed the mean Bermondsey streets, but on Friday morning heavy rain cleared the air and continued falling all day. Now, in the chill evening, water was coursing down the drains and the cobblestones were clean and glistening. With some relief the tired man dragged himself into the warmth of Joe's fish and chip shop in the Old Kent Road, the clothes on his back wet through and his saturated trousers sticking uncomfortably to his legs.

Two younger men were in front of him at the counter, hungrily eyeing the food as Joe the Italian scooped up a portion of chips from the stainless steel fryer into a small piece of grease-proof paper and then flipped a piece of haddock on top. 'Tenpence 'a'penny. You wanna wally?'

'Nah, that'll do,' the taller of the two answered with a momentary glance at the large jar of dill gherkins standing to one side of the counter.

Joe dropped the bundle of food on to a pile of newspaper sheets and finished the wrapping. 'You wanna fish an' chips?' he asked the second man.

'Nah, we're sharin' this,' he laughed as they left the counter.

Italian Joe stirred the vat of chips and scooped a large wire sieveful from the boiling fat before looking up enquiringly at Charlie Foden. 'It's a bad night,' he remarked.

The sodden customer nodded as he pushed his cap back from his forehead. 'Same again,' he said, reaching into his coat pocket for the coppers.

While Joe was wrapping his order Charlie glanced over at the two young men. They were standing by a table and the taller one was sprinkling salt and vinegar on to the chips. ''Ere, you 'alve the fish. Yer 'ands are cleaner than mine,' he said.

With the fish and chips carefully shared out the young men ambled out into the rain and Charlie turned to pick up his bundle. 'D'you know Cooper Street?' he asked.

Joe scratched his wiry grey hair. 'It'sa behinda Croft Street. You knowa Croft Street?'

Charlie shook his head. 'Nah.'

'Yer walka that way,' the Italian told him, jerking his thumb to the right. 'Yer see-a da big-a clothes shop. Turna da left. That'sa Croft Street. Cooper Street's da nexta street yer come to. Righta da bottom.'

Charlie thanked him, liberally sousing and salting his food before stepping out into the wet night. A deep doorway some way along the road gave him shelter while he wolfed down the fish and chips before, licking his lips, he set off again, hoping that the room had not already been taken.

At number 8 Cooper Street Lucy Parry was busy gathering up the used crockery. She was an attractive woman in her mid-thirties with fair hair and deep blue eyes set in an oval face. She wore an apron tied tightly round her waist which accentuated the curve of her hips, and as she piled up the used plates she was frowning. 'What did they actually say, then?' she asked.

George Parry looked up at her from the armchair by the fire and shrugged his shoulders. 'The manager just said that they'd 'ave ter look at the situation carefully, bearin' in mind the drop in sales.'

'What else do they expect?' Lucy said. 'Three million on the dole an' no sign of any relief. That's what it said on the wireless yesterday.'

George sighed and sagged back in his chair. He was a slightly built man just a year older than Lucy, with thinning dark hair and grey eyes which tended to widen when he spoke. He worked in the gift department of William Knight's tobacco company in Shoreditch and he had known for some time that the firm was intending to suspend its gift coupon scheme. 'It'll mean the sack fer the 'ole twenty-five of us,' he said. 'That's the long an' short of it.'

'Won't they transfer some of yer?' Lucy asked.

'Where to?' he retorted. 'There's no vacancies anywhere else in the firm. Some o' them'll be gettin' their notices as well, I shouldn't wonder.'

Lucy took up the plates. 'Well, it's not werf worryin' too much about it just yet. Fings might look up. They say one door shuts an' anuvver one opens.'

George Parry grimaced at her show of spirit. There were no doors opening in Bermondsey at the moment, he thought. All the local factories were on short time or going that way, and on the very rare occasions when a job was advertised the firm was swamped with applicants who seemed quite capable of murder to land the position.

'Daddy, I'm tired.'

George reached down and picked his four-year-old daughter up in his arms. 'It's all right, darlin', Mummy'll see ter yer soon.'

Lucy gave her husband an irritated look. 'Can't you put the child ter bed fer once? Yer know what I've got ter do ternight. There's all those clothes need darnin' an' ironin', an' I gotta sort that copper out. It's all clogged up.'

'All right, all right, don't go on about it,' he replied sharply, giving Lucy a hard look. 'Come on, sweet pea, Daddy's takin' yer up ter bed.'

Susan rested her blonde curls on her father's shoulder as he carried her out of the room and Lucy sat down at the table with a sigh. George was not normally snappy, but she knew why he was in this mood. He was worried over his job, and also not too happy about her decision to take in a lodger. He knew that the few extra shillings would come in handy but he had been angry at her for not discussing it with him first. What was the use, she asked herself? She knew what his reaction would have been. He would have ended up by saying that she should do as she saw fit. George was not the most inventive or demonstrative of men and it was always left to her to make the decisions and take the initiative.

He was a good man, it was true, and she knew he loved her and Susan above all else, but at times he could be infuriating with his indecisiveness.

'She was asleep soon as 'er 'ead touched the piller,' George said as he came back into the parlour.

'Sara's late,' Lucy remarked as she looked up at the chimer on the mantelshelf.

George followed her glance. 'Yeah, she's normally in by now.'

Lucy stifled a smile. 'I expect she's got 'erself tied up wiv some new-fangled idea at the fellowship. Last time it was patchwork quilts. Spare us anuvver quilt, please.'

George forced a smile and then his face became serious again. 'I know she can be tryin' at times, but yer gotta take fings inter consideration,' he said. 'She's not 'ad the best o' luck over the years, an' she's not too well at the moment.'

Lucy looked at him quizzically. 'I'm sure Sara's well. She just likes ter put fings on a bit. She should get out an' about a bit more instead o' sittin' in that chair from mornin' till night. The church fellowship's the only place she goes to. And it would be nice ter see 'er take a little more pride in 'erself.'

'What d'yer mean? She keeps 'erself clean an' tidy,' George said quickly.

'I'm not disputin' that,' Lucy replied. 'What I'm sayin' is she could do somefing about that 'air of 'ers. I've offered ter perm it for 'er. She could dress a bit younger, too. She looks like an old woman in those long frocks an' skimpy cardigans she wears. Christ, George, she's only

17

forty, not sixty.'

'You should 'ave anuvver word wiv 'er,' George suggested.

'I'm fed up wiv talkin' to 'er,' Lucy said, frowning. 'She's your sister, you should do it. She'd take it more kindly comin' from you.'

George leaned forward in his armchair. 'Yer don't regret us takin' 'er in, do yer?' he asked.

'Course I don't,' Lucy lied. 'I'm used to 'er ways by now. 'Ow long's it bin, four years?'

'Goin' on four,' George corrected her. 'It'll be four years next March when me mum died. Sara came to us at the end o' March. What else could we 'ave done but take 'er in? There's no way she would 'ave stayed in that old 'ouse alone, bearin' in mind 'ow nervous she is.'

Lucy nodded and reached for her sewing box. Sara's stay was only supposed to be short-term, she thought, until she could find something suitable. After nearly four years she treated the house as her own and there was no way she was even considering leaving.

The sound of a key in the lock heralded Sara's arrival and she came into the parlour with a dripping umbrella which she placed in the hearth. 'What a terrible night,' she said in greeting. 'It's absolutely pourin' down.'

'Never mind, it's got rid of the fog,' Lucy said tartly.

Sara made herself comfortable in her favourite chair by the fire. 'Mrs Phelps ain't none too good,' she remarked. 'She wasn't at the club ternight. That nice Reverend Beeney was, though. I made 'im a cup o' tea an' 'e told me 'ow nice it was. 'E liked those rock cakes I took along, too. It's nice ter be appreciated.'

Pity you don't try making the tea here some time, yer scatty mare, Lucy thought.

'I fink I'm goin' down wiv somefing,' Sara announced. 'I've got this sharp pain keeps catchin' me in me left side. I'm sure it's me kidneys.'

'There's only one that side,' Lucy pointed out. 'It could be stones, or those rock cakes yer made. You didn't eat any yerself, did yer, Sara?'

'There's nuffing wrong wiv my rock cakes,' Sara replied indignantly.

'No, nothing a sledgehammer wouldn't put right,' Lucy muttered under her breath.

'I fink I'll take me cocoa up ter bed wiv me,' Sara said. 'This side's playin' me up somefing awful. If yer wouldn't mind, Lucy.'

The younger woman put her darning down on the table and went to boil the milk, and as soon as she was out of the room Sara leant towards her brother. 'You should 'ave put yer foot down when she got the idea ter take in a lodger,' she growled. 'Yer can't be too careful these days. There was a woman murdered in 'er bed a few weeks ago over in Brixton an' it turned out it was the lodger what killed 'er.'

'Where did yer 'ear that?' George said, smiling.

'It was in the Sunday paper,' Sara replied. 'An' you shouldn't laugh about it neivver. When yer take people in yer don't know anyfing about 'em. They could be wanted by the police, or escaped prisoners.'

The sharp knock made Sara jump and she

19

frowned as George got up to answer it. 'Who could it be at this hour?' she wondered.

'We'll soon find out,' he said. 'It could be one o' those escaped convicts after a room fer the night.'

'Don't mock,' Sara implored him, her eyes wide and frightened.

George Parry opened the front door to a bedraggled figure standing in the rain. 'Yeah?'

'The name's Charlie Foden, I've come about the room. Is it still goin'?'

George nodded. 'Yeah. Come in out the rain. I'll fetch the missus.'

Lucy was standing in the scullery mixing the cocoa in a large beaker and she heard what was said. 'There we are, luv. I've put two sugars in. All right?'

Sara glanced along the dark passageway as she nodded. 'I'll go straight up. Yer don't want me in there when yer talkin' business,' she said in a low voice. 'You just be careful. It's a bit late at night fer anyone ter come askin' after a room.'

'Sara, fer goodness' sake,' Lucy sighed.

'You can make light of it, but I'm very wary o' those sort,' Sara muttered as she climbed the stairs to her back bedroom.

George offered his armchair to Charlie but the visitor declined. 'I'd better not, I'm wet frew,' he said. 'It'll make yer seat all wet.'

''Ere, take a dinin' chair, then,' George told him.

Lucy came into the parlour, smiling, and Charlie stood up quickly. 'I'm Charlie Foden an' I've called about the room.'

'I'm Lucy Parry an' this is me 'usband George.'

Charlie reached out and shook hands with him. 'Nice ter meet yer.'

'The room's still vacant, but first things first,' Lucy said cheerfully. 'You look like you could do wiv a cuppa.'

'I'd be more than grateful,' Charlie said, smiling.

'I'll do it,' George offered, wanting to let Lucy sort things out herself.

'I should begin by tellin' yer that I am in work,' Charlie said as George left the room.

'That's good,' Lucy replied. 'The room's on the bend o' the stairs an' it's quite small but cosy. There's a fire in there an' the bed's nice an' comfortable. There's a wardrobe fer yer clothes as well. The rent's as on the advertisement, twelve an' six a week wiv breakfast or fifteen shillin's if yer want the evenin' meal. Did yer see the notice yerself?'

'Yeah, in the paper shop in the Old Kent Road.'

Lucy appraised him and liked what she saw. There was a calm expression on his open face as he sat holding his saturated cap in his large hands. He was obviously a manual worker, she decided. His wet greying hair was thick and inclined to curl about his ears and his shoulders were wide, giving him a powerful appearance. 'Are you from round 'ere?' she asked.

'Walworth Road, but I've bin lodgin' in Lucas Street, off of Abbey Street,' he explained. 'The places 'ave bin condemned an' we've all 'ad ter get out. At the moment I'm stayin' at the workin' men's 'ostel in Tooley Street but it's not ideal.'

'I'm sure it's not.'

'I'm a docker.'

'I understand fings ain't too rosy in the docks neivver,' Lucy remarked.

'I get one or two days' work as a rule,' he replied. 'The rest o' the week most of us 'ave ter bomp on at the labour exchange. It's not good but we're better off than many.'

George came in with the tea and Charlie drank his down gratefully. When he had finished, Lucy led the way up to the small bedroom and lit the gas mantle. 'As you can see, it's quite 'omely.'

'It's very nice an' I'd be glad ter take it, wiv the evenin' meal,' he told her.

She glanced at his sodden garments. 'Right, then. First fing is ter get yer somefing ter put on while I dry those clothes out. You're bigger than my George but there's a large dressin' robe be'ind the door that'll fit, an' I'm sure I can find some long johns an' a vest you can squeeze into. Just leave yer wet stuff outside the door. Me an' George usually 'ave a bite o' supper before we go ter bed, cheese or a brawn sandwich wiv a cuppa. Can I get yer one?'

'That'll be smashin',' Charlie said, smiling gratefully. 'An' by the way, I do appreciate yer takin' a chance wiv me.'

'Why? Yer not some escaped convict, are yer?' Lucy said, grinning.

He looked embarrassed. 'No, I'm 'armless, I assure yer.'

As Lucy was leaving the room she stopped and turned back to him. 'By the way,' she said quickly. 'Me 'usband's sister's stayin' wiv us fer the time bein'. She's a spinster an' gets a bit ratty at times, but take no notice of 'er. I thought I'd better put yer on yer guard.'

Charlie smiled at the expression on her face. 'Fanks fer warnin' me,' he said.

George was poking the fire when Lucy came into the room. 'I noticed 'e 'ad no luggage wiv 'im,' he remarked.

'Yeah, I noticed too.'

'Don't yer fink it's a bit strange?'

'Not really. It doesn't mean anyfing.'

'Doesn't it?'

'George, what yer gettin' at?'

'Someone on the run wouldn't let 'imself be bowed down wiv luggage.'

'Nor would someone who stormed out of the 'ouse after a row,' Lucy countered.

George put down the poker and eased himself back into his chair. 'I dunno, there's somefing about the bloke I can't put me finger on an' it's bovverin' me.'

Lucy looked at him closely. 'You don't fink 'e's a criminal on the run, do yer?'

'No, but there's somefing...'

It was cosy and warm in the room on the bend of the stairs and Charlie Foden felt at ease as he reached for his pipe and tobacco pouch on the chair by the bed. The makings had stayed dry in the oilskin wrapping and once he had got the pipe glowing he picked up the tatty old wallet from the chair and opened it. There were two sepia photos inside the flaps. One looked stern and military, a picture of himself as a young fusilier taken just before he went to France in 1916, and smiling up at him from the other was a beautiful young woman with classical features and hair that hung in long ringlets over her shoulders. Charlie closed the wallet with a deep sigh and placed it back on the chair. Outside the rain was easing and he could hear the clanging sounds of metal on metal and screeching wheels from the nearby freight yards. He drew on his pipe and blew the smoke upwards to the cracked ceiling as he took stock of his situation. He was forty-eight and had taken his share of kicks, suffered loss, and made mistakes which had cost him dearly, but there had to come a time when life finally turned in an upward direction, when a man could again enjoy some of the good things in the world, live contentedly and walk tall once more. That might be some way off as yet, he thought, but it had to start somewhere. Why not here, now?

The tap on the door startled him and he wrapped the dressing robe around him as he got up from the bed.

'There's some bread an' cheese an' I 'ope yer like strong tea,' Lucy said cheerily.

'It's the only way ter make it,' he said, smiling.

The rain had finally stopped and a lone star shone down from among the driven clouds. Yes, it had to start somewhere, Charlie told himself with conviction as he sipped his tea.

CHAPTER 2

Charlie Foden stepped out of number 8 Cooper Street and stood for a moment or two looking up and down the small turning. The rain had given way to a bright Saturday morning and already he could feel the pleasant warmth of the winter sun on his face. His coat and trousers were badly creased but at least they were dry, he thought. His boots felt damp, though. The sooner he picked up his suitcase from the hostel the better.

As he stood at the front door taking his bearings, Mrs Goodwright from number 7 opposite nudged her next-door neighbour Mrs Black. 'Who's that?' she asked.

Ada Black peered through her glasses, then took them off to get a better view. 'Must be the Parrys' lodger,' she replied.

Emmie Goodwright huffed. 'Didn't take 'er long ter get fixed up, did it?' she remarked. 'She only put the ad in the shop a few days ago ter my knowledge.'

Ada folded her arms over her ample bosom and nodded. 'There's a lot movin' inter the area lately,' she said. 'It's the factories, I expect. There's always the odd job goin' in one o' them. Pearce Duff's took a couple on last week, so Mrs Reefer told me. 'Er ole man got a start there. Two years 'e's bin out o' collar.'

'My ole feller's bin out o' work more than that,'

Emmie replied stiffly. 'It knocks the stuffin' out of a man after so long. I know by 'im. So moody 'e is. I'm frightened ter talk to 'im at times. Bites me bloody 'ead off.'

'Your Bert's all right, Emm,' her neighbour remarked. 'It's nuffing a few weeks' work wouldn't put right.'

'That's what I was just sayin'.'

'Yeah, well, we know 'ow it affects 'em bein' on the dole.'

Emmie Goodwright sensed that Ada was beginning to drift off on one of her mental rambles and felt that enough was enough. 'Well, I can't stand 'ere chattin' all day. I gotta get me shoppin' done,' she said quickly.

The two watched Charlie Foden set off along the street and Emmie brushed her hands down her clean apron. ''Ow long d'yer reckon 'e'll last there?' she asked.

'What d'yer mean?' Ada replied with a frown.

'Sara Parry, that's what I mean.'

'Oh, I see. Well, it depends whevver the bloke lets 'er get to 'im or not,' Ada said. 'We all know what a miserable cow she is. If she gives 'im too much grief 'e might decide ter piss off.'

'Couldn't blame 'im, could yer?'

'Not really.'

'Oh, well.'

'I'll pop in later,' Ada told her friend.

Charlie bought a pair of socks at Cheap Jack's stall in the Tower Bridge Road market and then called into a shoe shop nearby. Wearing his new brown brogues he made his way to the hostel in

Tooley Street and was surprised at the activity going on outside. Men were milling around the entrance and the warden was trying to keep order. 'Now look 'ere, it's no good you all tryin' ter get in at once,' he growled. 'Mr Coley'll see you all in good time. Now just line up an' be patient.'

Fred Wilson spotted Charlie and pulled a face. 'They're all goin' mad 'ere this mornin',' he said, shaking his head. 'Coley's recruitin' again.'

'Who's Coley?' Charlie asked.

'Yer tellin' me yer never 'eard o' the Coley bruvvers?' Fred said disbelievingly. 'I thought everybody knew those nasty bastards.'

'Well, I've never 'eard of 'em,' Charlie told him. 'Let's pop in Ted's café an' you can put me in the picture.'

Fred Wilson was at a loose end that Saturday morning and was quite happy to oblige. The two men sat clutching huge mugs of tea inside the steamy café and when Fred had painstakingly rolled a cigarette he jerked his thumb over his shoulder. 'Those poor bastards don't know what they're lettin' themselves in for,' he began. 'Every now an' then the Coleys get a subber, an' they—'

''Ang on a minute,' Charlie interrupted. 'What's a subber?'

Fred smiled. 'Sorry. I fergot you ain't familiar wiv the buildin' game. One o' the big buildin' firms get a large contract an' they subcontract some o' the jobs. That way they don't 'ave to employ too many new workers an' people like Coley can take on casuals fer next ter nuffink. The big firms don't lose by it – they get their cut an' everyone's 'appy, 'cept the poor bleeders Coley takes on.'

'That bad, is 'e?' Charlie said, sipping his tea.

Fred Wilson shook his bald head slowly. 'Worse. I worked fer the buggers once. Never again.'

'What work is it they do?' Charlie asked.

'Pipe layin', mainly,' Fred explained. 'This contract's fer sewage pipes by all accounts, an' that can be a killer. Yer gotta go down furvver fer sewage pipe layin' an' yer diggin' clay. 'Ave you ever dug out clay?'

'No, but I can imagine.'

'Yer can't, Chas, not till yer've actually done it. A lot don't last the day, an' if yer do yer so tired an' full of aches yer just fall inter bed exhausted. Yer gotta remember too that Coley needs so much done every day an' 'e's on yer back all the time, 'im an' 'is bruvver. They're 'ard men an' they'll get their quota by 'ook or by crook, even if it means thumpin' a few 'eads.' Charlie looked unimpressed and Fred leaned forward on the marble table. 'I've seen Frank Coley drag a poor sod out the trench an' give 'im a right-'ander before tellin' 'im ter piss off. That feller 'ad worked most of the week an' was dead beat. Coley didn't pay 'im any wages an' the poor bleeder was in no position to argue. Take it from me, Frank Coley's a real bad 'un, but there's a lot'll tell yer that 'is young bruvver Ben's even worse.'

''Ow do they get away wiv it?' Charlie asked, frowning. 'Workers 'ave rights. What about the union?'

28

Fred snorted. 'Union? What union? The Coleys won't entertain any union an' they get away wiv it. They recruit casual labour from places like the 'ostels an' dole queues an' they rule by fear, an' any talk by the men o' gettin' themselves organised is likely ter get 'em sorted out good an' proper. They've got a few gangers runnin' the jobs who are as 'ard as them, so you can see it ain't no good complainin.' You eivver sign on an' do the work wiv yer mouth shut or yer give 'em a wide berf. Once was enough fer me, I can tell yer.'

Charlie drained his mug. 'Well, it's bin nice talkin' ter yer, Fred. I'm off ter pick up me suitcase. I got meself a nice little lodgin's.'

'I'm sorry ter see yer go,' Fred replied, 'but yer better out of it. There's gonna be a lot o' sad, sorry faces in the 'ostel next week.'

Charlie picked up his case from the office and saw the welter of people in the dining hall at the end of the corridor. Wanting to get the smell of the place out of his nostrils he strode briskly off into the morning sunshine.

Sara Parry sat by the fire holding a saucer under her chin while she sipped a cup of tea. Drinking tea was a refined art as far as George's older sister was concerned. The brew had to be weak and milky, with a half-teaspoon of sugar, and not too hot. Given a suitable concoction Sara would spend quite some time sipping at her cup while she expounded her opinion on whatever the current topic of conversation happened to be. It usually conflicted with Lucy's opinion, but the younger woman thought it better to ignore her silly ways than to create an atmosphere in which Sara would sulk, often for days.

''E's collectin' 'is fings at the 'ostel,' Lucy told her.

''Ostel?' Sara said with feeling. 'Is that where 'e's bin stayin'? I 'ope 'e don't bring any bugs or fleas in 'ere.'

'Workin' men's 'ostels are usually clean, not like the flop-'ouses,' Lucy answered.

'Well, I'm still worried,' Sara went on. 'It's always the way when yer take people in. We don't know anyfing about 'im. I really don't know why yer decided ter take a lodger. After all, yer not much in after the food's taken inter consideration. That sort usually eat yer out of 'ouse an' 'ome, if yer let 'em.'

Lucy bit on her tongue as her temper rose. Sara had little room to talk. She paid very little towards her keep and had been cosseted from the day she arrived. 'I fink you'll find 'e's a decent bloke, Sara,' she said. ''E seems very friendly an' 'e is workin'.'

'Well, we'll just 'ave ter wait an' see, won't we?' the older woman replied haughtily. 'I must say I'm gonna feel uncomfortable wiv 'im sittin' round the table wiv us.'

Lucy forced a smile. 'Who knows, 'e might even brighten the place up fer a change. It's not bin very cheerful lately, yer gotta admit.'

'Well, it's understandable,' Sara said sharply. 'George is naturally worried about 'is job an' 'e's the breadwinner. Some women go out office cleanin', but you can't, can yer? Not till Susan starts school.'

Lucy was tempted to suggest that Sara herself might feel a lot better if she dragged her arse out of that chair and found an office-cleaning job. She could just see her, off to work beneath a pig-filled sky. 'If George loses 'is job I'll 'ave ter go out ter work,' she said. 'George can look after Sue, an' you can pitch in, can't yer?'

Sara looked horrified. 'I wouldn't be much 'elp, not wiv my chest,' she replied with a pained expression. 'An' you can't expect George ter do all the fings you 'ave ter do.'

Lucy watched her sister-in-law slide the bottom of her cup across the edge of the saucer yet again and wanted to scream. 'D'yer want anuvver cup?' she said out of desperation.

'Presently,' Sara said. 'By the way, I'll need ter go ter the wool shop in the Old Kent Road later, once the streets 'ave aired. It's fer the church fellowship.'

'I'm sure the streets are aired by now, Sara,' Lucy said, a note of irritation stealing into her voice. 'Leave it too late an' it'll start turnin' cold.'

Sara placed the cup and saucer down on the table and held a hand to her back. 'I'm sure there's somefing wrong wiv my kidneys,' she groaned. 'Lucy, 'ave you gotta go out any more?'

'No, why?'

'You wouldn't like ter collect the wool for me, would yer? I don't fink I could make it ter the shop the way my back is this mornin'.'

'Yeah, I'll collect it, if yer tell me what it is.'

For the first time that morning Sara raised a smile. 'George should be in soon. I'll put the kettle on, shall I?'

Lucy would normally tell her that she would do it, and that was exactly what Sara expected to hear. 'All right, if yer don't mind,' she replied instead. 'I'll just slip upstairs an' sweep the lodger's room out before 'e gets back.'

Sara looked a little hesitant as she lit a match and reached for the gas tap. Lucy knew how she hated lighting gases, especially when there was air in the pipes. As the jet belched Sara shut the tap off quickly and stood back, and at that moment George walked into the house carrying Sue in his arms. 'You all right, Sara?' he asked as he put the child down and looked into the scullery.

'Yer'll 'ave ter get these pipes blown,' she declared with irritation. 'Yer know I get frightened lightin' the gas.'

'Where's Lucy?' George asked.

'Where's Mummy?' the child demanded, tugging at Sara's dress.

'She's upstairs,' Sara told her. 'Don't pull me dress like that, Susan. It's naughty.'

George looked at his sister enquiringly.

'She's tidyin' the lodger's room up,' Sara puffed. 'I dunno why, it was done yesterday. She fusses too much.'

George lit the gas and put the kettle over the flame. 'Go an' sit yerself down, Sara,' he said, smiling. 'I'll make the tea. Come on, Sue, let me take yer coat off. Look, there's yer dolly. Now sit down at the table an' I'll find the dolly's clothes.'

When George put the biscuit tin of dolls' clothes down on the table Sue flipped open the lid and it dropped with a clatter on to the stone floor.

'Do be careful, child,' Sara scolded her. 'I've got a bad 'eadache as it is.'

The sharp tone of her voice brought tears to Sue's eyes and she jumped down from the table and ran out into the passage as her mother was coming down the stairs.

'What's the matter, luv?' Lucy asked with concern as the child buried her head in her skirt.

'Aunt Sara shouted at me,' she mumbled in a tiny voice.

'Whatever for?' Lucy said, directing her words at Sara.

'She banged that tin down on the floor an' I told 'er ter be careful,' Sara complained. 'I've got a splittin' 'eadache.'

'If you went out an' got some air in the mornin's instead of sittin' on yer arse all day yer wouldn't get those 'eadaches,' Lucy growled.

'I'm not well enough ter go gallivantin' about in this weavver,' Sara retorted indignantly.

'This weavver? It's a nice mild day, it'd do yer good.'

'Not the way I feel.'

Lucy gave her a stony look and took herself off to the parlour. The woman's getting worse, she thought, scowling. It's about time I had a word with George. Throwing childish tantrums and constant petty bitching are one thing, but upsetting the child like that for the slightest reason is another matter entirely. It's a pity she can't find a man to take her off our hands. George is feeling it too, but being her brother he suffers her in silence. Well, I won't, not for much longer. 'Is that tea ready yet, Sara?' she called out loudly.

33

'George is doin' it,' Sara replied as she walked into the parlour and sat down in her armchair with a heavy sigh. 'Is there any aspirin?'

Lucy reached for her handbag. ''Ere's two,' she said, imagining shoving the whole packet down her sister-in-law's throat.

'Can yer get me some water?' Sara asked in a small voice.

A few minutes later Charlie Foden knocked at the front door. 'I've got me case,' he announced, grinning at Lucy. 'Bought a pair o' shoes, too. Feelin' a bit more civilised now.'

Lucy smiled back as he stepped into the passageway. 'When yer've put yer case in the room I'd like yer ter meet our Sara,' she said, rolling her eyes in warning. 'An' you 'aven't met Sue yet.'

'Sue?'

'My daughter. She's four years old.'

Charlie nodded. 'Give me a minute,' he replied as he hurried up the stairs.

Susan came scurrying into the passage and followed him up to his room. 'Are you our lodger?' she asked, standing in the doorway.

'Well, as a matter o' fact I am,' he answered, kneeling down in front of her. 'An' who might you be?'

'I'm Susan an' I'm four.'

'An' do you live 'ere?'

'Yes. Wiv my mummy an' daddy.'

'An' Aunt Sara?'

'Yes, but she makes me cry sometimes. She's very grumpy.'

'Oh, an' why's that?'

'She shouts at me.'

'I wouldn't shout at you.'

'What's in that case?' Susan asked.

'All my clothes an' fings.'

'What fings?'

'All sorts o' fings.'

''Ave you got any dollies?'

'No. I'm too old ter play wiv dollies any more,' he chuckled.

Lucy had come up the stairs and was standing behind her daughter enjoying the chatter.

'I've got a dolly an' I've got lots o' dollies' clothes. Would yer like ter see 'em?'

Lucy bent down and scooped the child up. 'Now leave Mr Foden alone,' she said fondly. ''E's got some unpackin' ter do.'

'It's all right. I was really makin' some 'eadway there,' Charlie remarked with a smile and a wink in Sue's direction.

'I don't fink yer'll do as well wiv our Sara,' Lucy told him drily. 'She's got one of 'er bad 'eadaches. P'raps yer'd better come down an' say 'ello, though.'

Charlie followed his landlady down the stairs and entered the parlour behind her.

'Sara, I'd like yer ter meet our lodger, Mr Foden.'

'Charlie'll do, if yer've no objections,' he said pleasantly as he took a step towards her armchair.

Sara allowed him to take her limp hand. 'Pleased ter meet yer, Mr Foden, I'm sure,' she said without enthusiasm. 'Will yer be stayin' fer long?'

'I can't say,' he replied with a shrug. 'Maybe as long as you'll all 'ave me.'

Lucy gave him a smile and suddenly caught her sister-in-law's look of distaste. If Sara had her way Charlie Foden's stay would be very brief indeed, she realised.

CHAPTER 3

Lucy had made a meat pie for the Saturday evening meal and served it with boiled potatoes and mint peas. George sat at the head of the table with his daughter to his left, who seemed quite pleased to have Charlie on the other side of her. Lucy faced the lodger across tureens and was gratified to hear him say that the pie smelled delicious. Sara sat lackadaisically at the opposite end, and glanced at the cutlery before she began to eat. It was a habit that always irked Lucy, and she gave George a quick glance, but her husband was already tucking into the meal.

Sue seemed to manage quite comfortably with her knife and fork and she occasionally gave Charlie a coy look. His collusive wink made her smile and Lucy knew that one friendship at least was being forged. 'That's a good gel. Eat it all up now an' yer'll be as big as Mr Foden,' she said, smiling.

'Call me Charlie.'

'Can I call yer Charlie too, Charlie?'

'Yeah, course yer can.'

When everyone had finished the meal Lucy got up and gathered the plates. 'There's stewed apples an' custard fer afters,' she told them.

The tea was brewing under a cosy out in the scullery, and while Lucy served up their portions George carried the laden tea tray into the parlour. Outside the temperature had dropped and a river mist was creeping into the back-streets, but in the Parrys' parlour the fire was glowing and the licking flames reflected in the blue china cups intrigued the little girl, who sat at the table with her chin cupped in her hands as she drifted towards a wonderland of fairies and wizards, magic wands and shooting stars.

'She looks tired,' George observed.

Lucy nodded. 'There we are. Now eat it all up,' she said, putting the small portion in front of Susan.

When the plates were scraped clean and hunger was satisfied, the Parrys and their lodger leaned back in their chairs and began to get a little better acquainted.

'You work in the docks, then, Charlie?' George said.

'Yeah, I'm a plain docker. I work on the quay, the stevedores work the barges an' ships' 'olds,' Charlie explained. 'Mind you, there's very little work there at the moment, same as everywhere else. I'm lucky ter get two days' work a week. Usually it's only one day.'

'Yeah, it's bad all round,' George replied with a sigh. 'I'm sweatin' over my job foldin' up very shortly. I work fer a tobacco firm over the water, in the gift-wrappin' department, an' now the company are talkin' about stoppin' the gift coupons. If they do that it'll mean the dole queue fer all of us.'

Lucy wanted to steer the conversation away from unemployment and misery and she was pleased when Charlie quickly changed the subject. 'I noticed that photo on the mantelshelf,' he said. 'You was in the Navy.'

George's face brightened somewhat. 'Yeah. I went in the boys' service when I was sixteen an' I did twelve years' full service,' he replied. 'I came out ter get married, but I'm still on the reserve. They pay us a few bob every year an' it comes in very 'andy. I was an artificer.'

'You could be pulled back in if there was a national emergency?' Charlie queried.

George nodded a little self-importantly. 'Yeah. Knowin' all about marine engines means that I'd be straight in.'

'I read that the Germans are mobilisin' under that man 'Itler an' we're startin' ter build up our Navy,' Sara cut in.

Charlie glanced down the table. 'Yeah, that's right. There's bin quite a bit about it on the wireless lately. At least it'll put some more jobs people's way.'

Sara looked pleased with herself and wanted to impress a little more with her knowledge of current affairs. 'Of course, it doesn't 'elp when the Italians march into a poor, 'armless country like Ethiopia. Fascist bullyin', just like Franco in Spain.'

Lucy hid a smile. Sara was going to wind herself up if she wasn't careful and start one of her nasty headaches. 'More tea, anybody?' she asked, reaching for the teapot.

Sara passed her cup and saucer over. 'If it's not too stewed,' she said fastidiously.

Lucy got up and took the teapot into the scullery to add some hot water, and Sue turned

39

and tapped Charlie on the arm. 'I've got a tin box fer my dollies' clothes,' she announced.

'That's nice,' Charlie replied.

'Would yer like ter see 'em now?'

'Sue, let Charlie be,' George told her crossly. ''E doesn't wanna see dollies' clothes.'

Charlie saw the child's face drop abruptly and felt for her. 'Of course I would,' he enthused.

Sue jumped down from her chair and hurried out of the room as George grinned, raising his eyes to the ceiling. 'She spends hours dressin' an' undressin' that doll of 'ers,' he said.

'She's a little smasher,' Charlie remarked.

The child was soon back clutching the biscuit tin and she lifted the lid carefully, stealing a quick glance at Sara. 'Look, this is dolly's,' she said, holding up a tiny woollen vest.

'What a lovely jumper,' Charlie replied.

'That's not a jumper, it's a vest,' Sue corrected him quickly.

'Oh, I see. An' what's this?' Charlie asked, picking up a cardigan from the box. 'I know, it's a woolly coat.'

'No it's not, it's a cardigan,' she told him with a look of long-suffering superiority. 'Anyone knows that.'

'So do I now,' Charlie said, chuckling.

'Come on, leave Charlie alone, Sue. It's time fer your beddy-byes,' George reminded her.

'Night, Charlie.'

'Night night, luv. Sleep tight.'

Lucy placed the fresh tea down on the table and took Sue by the hand. 'I'll see to 'er. Pour the tea, Sara.'

George reached up to the mantelshelf for his cigarette makings. 'Care fer a roll-up?' he asked.

Charlie nodded. 'I smoke a pipe, but I'm confinin' it ter me room,' he said. 'The tobacco I use is a bit strong. I would like a roll-up, though.'

George pulled some tobacco strands and a strip of rice paper from the cigarette tin and passed the container over. 'We've bin lucky as a family so far,' he said, looking serious. 'Most o' the poor sods in the turnin' are out o' collar an' findin' it 'ard ter put a meal on the table. The Naylors' two boys were sittin' on the doorstep eatin' bread an' marge fer their tea yesterday an' they ain't got a decent pair o' shoes between 'em. Then there's the Whittles. Bill Whittle's bin out o' work fer almost three years now. 'Is wife's an invalid an' they've got five kids. They're existin' on the UAB money, such as it is. It's the same story at almost every 'ouse yer knock on in this turnin', an' it's the same everywhere else. Where's it all gonna end?'

Charlie had rolled his cigarette and was sliding it thoughtfully between his fingers. 'I dunno,' he replied with a sigh.

'It'll end when we're in our boxes,' Sara declared as she handed over the tea. 'It's the fate o' workin' people. Yer can get so far an' then somefing 'appens ter put yer back. There's too many people chasin' too few jobs, an' wiv mass unemployment there's always ovver fings that come wiv it, such as epidemics an' disorder. It'll take anuvver war ter sort fings out, I'm sorry ter say.'

Charlie lit his cigarette and blew a cloud of

41

smoke towards the ceiling. Maybe Sara was being melodramatic, he thought, but there was something in what she said. The influenza epidemic of 1918 had cost him dearly, as it had many thousands of others, and its virulent spread was linked to poor housing and living standards. Since then the old hovels had been pulled down and sewage now flowed through pipes instead of the gutters, but many people today were existing just above starvation level, and there was no easy way up.

'Are you married, Mr Foden?' Sara asked.

'Yeah, but we've lived apart fer quite a few years now,' he told her.

'I'm sorry. I shouldn't 'ave asked,' Sara replied with unaccustomed humility. 'I was just curious, the way you 'ad wiv Sue. I imagined you'd 'ad children of yer own.'

'It's OK, it doesn't upset me ter talk about it,' Charlie reassured her. 'It was a long time ago when we split up, an' ter be honest I fink we'd both realised early on that the 'ole fing was a mistake from the start. But there you are. None of us are perfect.'

George was surprised at his sister's rare show of interest, but felt encouraged by it. She could be trying at times, and was quite capable of driving a lodger away with her tantrums and attitudes. 'Sara keeps very busy at the church fellowship,' he said. 'She's always involvin' 'erself in somefing or ovver. What's the latest business, Sara?'

'Mr Foden doesn't want ter know about such fings,' Sara said quickly.

'On the contrary, I'd be very interested,'

Charlie replied with a smile.

'It's patchwork quiltin',' she informed him. 'We're makin' quilts fer those in need, an' there's a big demand as you'd imagine.'

'That's very commendable,' Charlie remarked.

Sara looked suddenly embarrassed. She stood up and gathered together the dessert dishes. 'I'd better make a start on the washin' up while Lucy's gettin' Sue settled,' she said.

George looked across at Charlie as soon as Sara had left the room. 'Me sister gets a bit morbid at times but she's very feelin',' he explained quietly. 'She spent a lot o' time lookin' after our mum, till the day the ole lady died as a matter o' fact, an' then she found she couldn't live in the empty 'ouse. Me an' Lucy told 'er she could stay wiv us fer a while an' she's bin 'ere ever since. We don't mind really, even though she's got 'er funny ways.'

''Aven't we all?' Charlie replied with a smile.

'Sara never 'ad a steady boyfriend,' George went on. 'Our mum was very critical o' the few lads who did come callin' earlier on. She seems to 'ave accepted the way fings are an' she's 'appy in 'er own way.'

Charlie took another drag on his cigarette and stared down for a few moments at the dying glow. How easy for George to make that assessment, he thought, and how wrong it probably was. Sara didn't strike him as a happy woman, though he had to admit that he hardly knew her. Who was it said everyone was an island unto themselves?

Lucy came back in and slumped down in the armchair. 'She's off ter sleep,' she announced.

'She got me readin' to 'er.' She smiled as she glanced at Charlie. 'She wanted ter know if you was gonna stay wiv us fer a while, 'cos she finks you're a nice man.'

Charlie grinned. 'Kids an' dogs, I never fail. It's adults I 'ave trouble wiv.'

'Sara's started the washin' up,' George told her.

Lucy gave him a hard look. 'All right, I'll take over in a minute or two,' she replied irritably. 'After all, it won't 'urt her ter do it once in a while.'

Charlie stood up. 'Well, I'll leave yer in peace,' he said. 'I've a couple o' letters ter write.'

'Look, you're welcome ter stay down 'ere as long as yer like,' Lucy said quickly. 'That's right, ain't it, George?'

'Yeah, course it is,' George agreed. 'We want yer ter treat this 'ouse as yer own. As far as we're concerned you can come an' go as yer please.'

'I appreciate that an' I'll bear it in mind.' Charlie smiled. 'I do 'ave a letter or two ter get off, though. By the way, the meal was excellent.'

'What d'yer fink of 'im?' Lucy asked as soon as she heard the bedroom door close.

'I fink 'e's a nice bloke,' George replied. ''E's certainly made strides wiv young Sue.'

'I've never 'eard Sue get so involved in the conversation neivver.'

''Ow 'old d'yer fink 'e is?' George asked.

'I dunno, about forty-five, forty-six. The grey 'air makes 'im look older.'

'Sara asked 'im if 'e was married an 'e said 'e was, but they'd bin livin' apart fer years.'

'I guessed 'e was married,' Lucy said. George

44

reached for his tobacco tin and she stood up. 'Well, I'd better see what our Sara's gettin' up to,' she sighed.

Along the narrow backstreet at number 20 Minnie Venners was preparing to make her own personal protest, if there was anyone out there who would take note or heed. People could not be expected to put up with things the way they were for ever, she told herself. Something would have to give. Perhaps soon the powers that be would scrutinise the whys and wherefores that had caused Minnie Venners to do away with herself. It shouldn't be too difficult for them to arrive at an answer. Her neighbours knew the score. They would tell of a woman whose husband was out of work for four years, during which time he changed from a lively Jack-the-lad into a man frightened of his own shadow, willing to take any nonsense from scum who weren't fit to lick his boots. They would tell of a woman widowed prematurely, losing her husband to a sudden heart attack. One or two of her closest friends would talk of a woman living on a pittance who had exhausted her supply of items for the pawnshop. They knew the score. Anyway, there was no sense in dwelling on it all. The decision had been made and that was that. First the gas. A tanner's worth would do nicely. Must put that down on the note as a PS, she thought. 'It was my last tanner.' It would add a bit of light relief to the proceedings.

Right then, where's that cushion, she wondered? The one with the hole in it. I should change by rights. This dress is a bit tatty. But the other one isn't much better. God, what am I worrying myself like this for? Talking of God, I hope he understands. I think it's the Catholics who say that suicide is a mortal sin which closes the door to heaven. Well, that's up to them, but I think that the good Lord'll understand. Albert will be there waiting, I'm sure. He'll be there to see me through.

The sharp knock on the front door made Minnie start and she screwed her face up in agitation. Who could it be at this hour? I won't answer it and they'll think I've gone to bed, she said to herself.

The knock was repeated, louder this time, and Minnie cursed as she hurriedly put the note in the dresser drawer and strode along the passage. Whoever it was had seen the parlour light and knew she was still up.

''Ello, gel. Sorry ter knock this late but it couldn't wait.'

Minnie stared at her best friend Elsie Farr. 'What couldn't wait?'

'Me Jenny's gone inter labour an' it's due any minute. Yer gotta come quick.'

'Me? Why me?'

''Cos Jenny wants yer there.'

'What about the midwife?'

'Jack's gone for 'er, but she might not get 'ere in time. The baby wasn't expected till next week, as yer know. Come on, Minnie, quick as yer can.'

Minnie grabbed her coat and keys from the peg and hurried out of the house, slamming the door behind her.

'Jenny knows yer used ter do the birthin' round 'ere, an' I fink she prefers you ter that 'orse-faced ole cow of a midwife,' Elsie went on as they hurried along the street.

'It's bin a long time since I 'elped a baby inter the world,' Minnie told her breathlessly.

A cold, lonely moon looked down on the Bermondsey backstreet as the first wail filled the stuffy bedroom.

'It's a boy an' it's got everyfing it should 'ave,' Minnie said, smiling at the hot face of the young mother.

Elsie boiled another kettle and made some tea while Minnie removed the bloodstained rubber sheet from the bed and tidied the room, and later, once Jenny had been settled with the newborn baby in her arms, the two older women sat facing each other across the table.

'I'm so glad you was still awake when I called ternight, Minnie,' Elsie remarked.

'A few minutes later an' I wouldn't 'ave bin.'

'I bet that midwife'll stink o' booze when she does get 'ere.'

'It's a lovely little mite.'

'They all are, ain't they?' Elsie grinned happily. 'Seeing 'em pullin' them funny faces makes yer ferget all yer trials an' tribulations. 'Ere, I almost fergot ter tell yer, what wiv all the excitement.'

'Tell me what?'

'Mrs Bolton's put 'er notice in. She's movin' down ter Kent ter be near 'er daughter, so I've spoke fer you, if yer still interested.'

'Interested? Elsie, I'm down ter me last tanner. Of course I'm interested.'

47

'I'll give yer a knock in the mornin' then, shall I?'

'I'll be ready. An' fanks, Elsie.'

'No, I should be fankin' you.'

'As it 'appens the fanks is due ter your Jenny,' Minnie replied, and seeing Elsie's puzzled frown she smiled. 'I'll tell yer why termorrer, but now I wanna take one more peek at the baby. I fink I'll give the little 'un me tanner ter start off its money box, an' a smackin' big kiss ter go wiv it.'

CHAPTER 4

The church bells of St Mark's rang out on a cold, gloomy November Sunday and as always Emmie Goodwright and her best friend Ada Black listened to them at Ada's front door. 'I always fink it's a lovely sound to 'ear on Sunday mornin's, them bells,' Emmie remarked.

Ada nodded as she leaned against the doorpost. 'Yeah. It makes yer feel sort o' charitable, like they're sayin' ferget yer worries an' troubles an' come ter church.'

Emmie could not always follow her friend's line of thinking and she frowned. 'Charitable? I'd like ter be in a position ter be charitable, Ada, but when you ain't got two pennies ter rub tergevver yer can't fink about charity.'

'Nah, yer don't get me meanin'. I'm talkin' about inside, bein' charitable in the way yer deal wiv ovvers.'

'Oh, I see.'

Ada doubted it but went on anyway. 'When I 'ear them church bells I wish I was a regular churchgoer, often as not. I fink about gettin' meself all spruced up an' goin' ter the mornin' service, an' singin' those lovely hymns like "Onward Christian Soldiers" an' ... an'...'

'"Jesus wants me fer a sunbeam",' Emmie offered.

'That's a Sunday school hymn fer kids,' Ada

retorted. 'No, seriously though, Emm, I really do get the urge ter try it one Sunday. Why don't me an' you go?'

'What, now? This mornin'?'

'Nah, soon. Next week maybe.'

'I dunno about that,' Emmie said, stroking her chin. 'I ain't bin inside a church since ole Mabel Stubble passed away.'

'Blimey, Emm, that was donkey's years ago. I remember that turn-out. Wasn't that when Mrs Branch from Lynton Road conked out durin' the service?'

'Nah, yer gettin' mixed up. Mrs Branch conked out at Mrs Turnbell's funeral, 'er who fell under the dray in the Ole Kent Road. Anyway, it was years ago, an' I'd feel ashamed goin' back inside there after so long.'

'Yeah, I s'pose so,' Ada conceded. 'As long as we try ter live a decent life an' don't go upsettin' anybody we're as good as all those who go ter church regular.'

The bells ceased to chime and a few minutes later the ice cream man pedalled his tricycle into the street and rang his own bell loudly. Children came running and formed a circle round the curious vehicle.

'Now line up prop'ly. I can't serve yer all at once,' the vendor growled.

Emmie shook her head slowly. 'Yer know, it amazes me,' she said thoughtfully. 'Those kids are wearin' cardboard in their shoes an' most o' their farvvers are out o' collar, but they still seem ter find the pennies.'

'I'm glad I ain't got little ones ter fend for,'

Ada remarked.

'Me too,' Emmie agreed. 'It must be a nightmare fer people wiv young families, the way fings are.'

'Mind you, though, the pubs are still full on Sunday mornin's, an' that's after five years o' chronic unemployment,' Ada pointed out.

'Yeah, but it's a different fing nowadays,' Emmie said, scratching the tip of her nose. 'My Bert was only sayin' the ovver week 'ow the blokes sit wiv the one pint where before it'd be gone like soapsuds down a drain'ole. 'E said there's none o' that "Wanna drink?" soon as someone walks in. Everyone buys their own now.'

Elsie Farr came hurrying along the turning. 'Mornin', ladies,' she said breezily. 'Our Jenny 'ad a little boy! Late last night it was born. Minnie Venners delivered it. We couldn't get the bloody midwife till it was all over. I'm gonna report 'er ter me doctor when I see 'im. I 'ate ter fink what might 'ave 'appened if Minnie 'adn't 'a' bin up, 'cos it was late.'

'She's a very nice woman,' Ada remarked. 'She used ter do a lot o' birthin' at one time, till those new-fangled midwives come on the scene.'

'Sorry I can't stop,' Elsie told them. 'I gotta get the *News of the World* before they sell out. There's a bit in there about that dirty ole git from Borough Road who's up fer bigamy. Apparently 'e's got four wives on the go. Would yer believe it?'

''Ow do they get away wiv it, that's what I'd like ter know,' Ada tutted.

'They do in the Arab countries,' Emmie cut in.

51

'Those sheiks 'ave a tentful.'

'Yeah, but they're only concubines.'

'Concubines, porcupines, it still ain't right. One woman should be enough, even fer the likes o' them.'

'It's the sun what does it,' Ada said knowingly. 'Makes 'em fruity.'

'If that's the case I'll get my ole feller ter sit in the sun when it comes out next,' Elsie chuckled as she hurried off.

Charlie Foden finished putting a polish on his best black boots out in the backyard and looked up to see George watching him from the doorway.

'I wondered if yer'd care fer a pint,' he suggested.

'I was gonna ask you the same,' Charlie told him.

'The Mason's Arms in Lynton Road's about the best pub round 'ere,' George said.

'Right then, let's go.'

The two men stepped out of the house into the overcast morning and walked along to the intersection with Lynton Road. As they turned left past the bootmender's on the corner Charlie noticed that the shop on the other corner was boarded up. George saw him looking at it. 'That was a florist's up until a few weeks ago,' he said. 'Before that it was an oil shop, an' if I remember rightly it was a greengrocer's fer a spell. Nobody seemed able ter make it pay.'

The Victorian houses with their steps leading up to the front doors stretched away into the distance and across the road a head-high red brick wall hid the railway track and freight yards.

'Nice places,' Charlie remarked. 'Bit noisy though, I should fink.'

George nodded. 'It used ter be worse at one time. We could 'ear the racket from our 'ouse. It went on right frew the night.'

They reached the pub and George led the way into the public bar. 'Wotcher, Mick,' he greeted the tubby landlord. Mick mumbled a reply and glanced quickly at Charlie. 'This is my new lodger, Charlie Foden,' George informed him.

'Mick Johnson,' the landlord said, holding out his hand. 'Are you from round 'ere?'

'Walworth, until recently,' Charlie replied.

George put a ten-shilling note down on the counter. 'I'll 'ave a pint o' bitter,' he said, and turned to Charlie.

'The same fer me, please.'

While the landlord poured the drinks Charlie took a quick look round. There were only a couple of elderly men propping up the counter on either side of him, and it struck him how few people there were in the place. A piano stood idle under a large figured window and in the far corner two young men were playing darts. The wrought-iron tables in the bar were mostly occupied by old men smoking pipes and one or two elderly women, all with blank, sad faces as they guarded their half-empty glasses. It was a sign of the times, the new lodger reflected. A far cry from the days when the ships came continually and the Tooley Street pubs were packed to overflowing.

'Wanna pint, Bill?'

'Nah, I'll get these.'

'Fancy a chaser?'

'Yeah, why not?'

'Give 'im a large 'un.'

Now the men stood quietly as they were called off, the few lucky dockers working the day and then going home sober. The rest made their way to sign on at the labour exchange, 'bomping on' as they termed it, and they all waited patiently for the ships to call again, the quays to ring out with expletives and the tall cranes to swing to and fro with their awkward sets, hauled up from the holds and expertly landed on the wet quays and waiting transport. Once there had been constant queues of traffic on the Tower Bridge approach as the centre span was raised repeatedly on the changing tides, but now the tide could change without a single lift.

The two men stayed at the counter after their drinks were served and when George had taken his first sip he pulled out his tobacco tin. 'This place used ter be packed out every Sunday lunchtime,' he remarked.

'Yeah, I was just finkin' about 'ow it is at the docks an' wharves nowadays,' Charlie replied. 'It's bin five years now an' no sign of any change fer the better.'

George brought the makings up to his mouth and licked the rice paper. 'I ain't told our Lucy, but it's cut an' dried at the factory,' he said quietly. 'We're all gonna be put off in two weeks' time. I know I should 'ave told 'er, but the time never seems right.'

'I'm very sorry to 'ear that,' Charlie replied sympathetically. ''Ave yer got any plans?'

George shook his head slowly. 'I've bin frew all the papers an' tried factories over the water but it's always the same answer. P'raps I'll get a part-time job be'ind the bar. 'Ow about it, Mick?'

The landlord was serving a nearby customer and he snorted. 'I've just 'ad ter lay our evenin' barmaid off,' he said. 'The pub trade's the worst I've known it in twenty years. What's even worse, they're closing the road off soon. They're diggin' it up fer new sewer pipes. That'll be 'alf me daily trade gone fer a burton. A lot o' the local firms' carmen call in 'ere at lunchtime. They won't be able ter get down 'ere now, will they?'

The old man who had just been served looked across the counter at Mick. 'Who's got the contract, any idea?' he asked.

'I dunno,' Mick answered. 'Does it matter?'

'Yeah it does, if yer lookin' fer a job diggin',' the customer replied quickly. 'If it's a main contract job the firm'll bring their own labour, but if it's subbed out there'll be some work fer the locals.'

'The Coleys 'ave bin recruitin' in Tooley Street,' Charlie informed him.

The old man looked disgusted. He held out his gnarled hands, palms upwards, and slowly turned them over. 'I used ter be in the game, an' these ole mitts o' mine 'ave bin wrapped round more shovels than I care ter remember,' he said in a measured voice. 'I've worked fer some decent firms in me time an' I've worked fer some real right bastards, but from what I've 'eard the Coley bruvvers take some beatin'. There's a couple o' young shavers who come in 'ere now an' then an' they was tellin' me they got a start wiv the Coleys down in Rovverhive. They said it was like bein' on a chain gang. Two weeks was all they could stick of it, an' then they 'ad a bloody 'ard job gettin' their wages.'

''Ow do they get away wiv it?' Charlie asked, already knowing the answer from talking to Fred at the hostel.

'Fer a start they're non-union,' the old man replied. 'Then there's a couple o' gangers in charge an' by all accounts they're nuffing more than animals. They'd fight King Kong if the money was right. They work the men flat out an' constantly bribe 'em wiv the promise of a big bonus at the end o' the contract. Course it's all pie in the sky an' yer don't find out till it's too late.'

George looked suddenly depressed. 'I'm game fer most fings but I couldn't work in a trench, diggin' away all day. It'd kill me.'

'Nah it wouldn't,' the old man said. 'Yer get used to it, an' if yer not too tall yer back'll stand up to it. Yer shoulders an' yer legs get stronger too. It's the tall blokes who suffer most wiv their backs, 'specially when yer get down ter the clay.'

George and Charlie began to feel more and more miserable as the old man elaborated on the hardships of trench digging, and as soon as they could they took their fresh drinks over to a far table. Only a few more customers came into the bar, but one of them caused a few heads to turn. The man was big, six foot three in his socks, with broad shoulders and lean hips. His neck was bull-like and he walked over to the counter with a confident swagger. Small dark eyes stared out of a wide flat face and his jawline was square, knotted with hard muscle. The landlord said something to him as he ordered a beer and he smiled, showing a set of large white teeth.

The old man Charlie had talked to at the bar got up and walked unsteadily to the toilet, and when he came back he stopped to lean over the table. 'Did yer notice that big geezer who just come in?' he asked. 'That's Sharkey Lockwood, the Coleys' right-'and man. 'E used ter wrestle at the Bermon'sey baths under the moniker o' The Vikin'. 'E's got an easier job now though, overseein' the poor sods who make the mistake o' signin' on wiv the bloody slave-drivers, an' considerin' 'e ain't bin in 'ere fer some time I'd say it's a pound to a pinch o' shit the Coleys 'ave got the contract. Sharkey's come in 'ere 'specially ter put the word out. Next week they'll be queuin' up outside, poor bleeders.'

George and Charlie finished their drinks and left the Mason's Arms to walk the short distance home. When they entered the house the smell of roast potatoes and beef cooking filled the passageway and George reached down for Sue as she came towards him. Charlie smiled at the little girl and hung his coat up on a hook by the front door. Even Sara was ready with a weak smile, and as Charlie walked into the scullery to wash his hands Lucy looked up from slicing the meat. 'What did yer fink o' the Mason's Arms?' she asked with a smile.

'It was pretty quiet,' Charlie replied.

57

'We go in there occasionally on a Saturday night,' she told him, 'but I prefer the Star in the Old Kent Road. It's much livelier.'

Charlie's eyes inadvertently strayed down to the tight-fitting blouse Lucy was wearing and he looked up quickly, but not quickly enough, and the young woman did not mistake what she had seen for a brief second in his frank hazel eyes.

Along the small turning there were houses where the money had not stretched to a joint of beef. The Marchants had mutton stew, and Ada and Joe Black sat down to corned beef and cabbage. Emmie and Bert Goodwright enjoyed a lamb chop apiece, while at number 16 Mrs Belton discovered that the chunk of corned beef she had kept for the Sunday meal was mouldy right through and she and her two boys had bread and jam instead. Sid Belton was not concerned. He was sitting in the Dun Cow, slowly slipping into a state of sublime intoxication which let him forget that regular meals on the table required money in his wife's purse. Annie Belton never forgot and she was feeling angry and bitter, as she often did these days, but Sid wore a stupid grin on his face as he pushed his empty glass across the counter and handed the barman the last of his dole money.

CHAPTER 5

November was ending the way it had begun, with yellow fogs and clammy mist, and on the last Friday of the month George Parry climbed down from the number 42 bus and walked the rest of the way home with his employment cards in his coat pocket. It was stupid of him not to have let Lucy know what had been going on at the factory during the past week, he realised now. He could have cushioned the blow, but he had been praying for the impossible, that the firm would have a last-minute change of heart and hold on to their workers. That sort of thing only happened in fairy stories. This was stark reality, and the truth of the matter was that from Monday morning he would be joining the rest of the human jetsam at the labour exchange.

Inside the house it was warm and cosy, and Charlie eased his position in his armchair as Lucy came into the parlour to lay the table. 'Can I do anyfing?' he asked.

She gave him a quick smile. 'No, it's all right, fanks. Everyfing's under control.'

Charlie watched as his landlady arranged the knives and forks around the table and brushed the spotless tablecloth with the palm of her hand. 'Are you OK?' he enquired in a quiet voice.

'Yeah, of course,' Lucy replied quickly. 'Does it look as though there's somefing wrong?'

'You just look a bit worried, that's all,' he said in embarrassment.

Lucy laid a large spoon in front of Sue's place and folded her arms over her clean apron as she turned towards him. 'I'm sorry if I jumped,' she said. 'Yeah, I am a bit worried. When George gets 'ome from work 'e's gonna tell me that 'e's got 'is cards.'

'P'raps not,' Charlie said supportively. ''E was only sayin' last night that nuffing definite 'ad bin decided as yet.'

Lucy smiled wryly. 'You ferget I'm married ter the man. I can read 'im like a book. I know 'e's only bin tryin' ter protect me, but I wish 'e 'adn't. Whatever 'appens we face it tergevver.'

Charlie looked up at the determined young woman and noticed how the tightly fitting apron accentuated her figure. Her fair hair looked nice too, the way she had of gathering it up carelessly and tying it at the back of her neck. He liked to see her uncovered small flat ears and the high forehead, the soft blue eyes and the movements of her expressive mouth. She was chewing on her lip nervously and Charlie stood up and glanced through the net curtains into the street. 'Do yer fink I should slip round ter the surgery an' escort Sara back?' he suggested. 'The fog's thickenin'.'

'No, she wouldn't fank yer for it,' Lucy told him. 'You know 'ow independent she is. Ter be honest I don't know why she bovvered ter go out on a night like this. She only wanted some more of 'er backache pills an' she's still got a few days' supply left.' Charlie pulled a face and rolled his dark eyes, which brought a smile to Lucy's face.

'You 'ave to admit she is tryin' at times.'

The front door opened and shut and George walked into the parlour, hardly casting the lodger a glance as he reached out to give Lucy a peck on her cheek. 'It's bin a bad day,' he said hesitantly.

'I know the worst, George,' she replied, 'so don't try to ease it out.'

He reached into his coat and pulled out the green and buff-coloured employment cards. 'I was 'opin' against 'ope, but–'

Lucy cut across him. 'Look, it's not your fault. We both knew it was comin'.'

'I'm very sorry, George,' Charlie added.

Lucy took control. 'Right then, you sit down an' I'll make us some tea, then I'll 'ave ter fetch our Sue. She's playin' next door wiv Gracie.'

'Where's Sara?' George asked as he slipped out of his coat.

'Gone ter the doctor's fer more backache pills,' Lucy told him, momentarily glancing towards Charlie.

At number 10 the two young children played happily together, untroubled by all that was happening around them, but for Roy and Mary Chubb it was a difficult day. Mary was still tormented by the fact that her husband had gone along to Lynton Road that morning. 'But yer've never done that sort o' work before,' she pointed out once again.

'I've done some buildin' labourin' in the past an' it's much about the same,' Roy replied. 'Anyway, I'm fit an' strong, an' if Danny Albury can do it so can I.'

'Yeah, but Danny Albury's used ter the work,' Mary reminded him. ''E was on the council road gangs fer a few years ter my knowledge.'

'Anyway, it's done now,' Roy said firmly. 'I start work on Monday in Lynton Road an' if I get on all right there's an option ter get a start at the next job in Southwark Park Road.'

When her husband had told her of his intentions that morning Mary had felt sick inside. Only the previous week Lucy Parry had been talking to her about the Coleys' impending recruitment in Lynton Road, and she had hoped that her husband wouldn't get any ideas about signing on. He was fit and strong, it was true, but he was a carpenter by trade, not a ditch digger, and there would be some building site jobs coming up soon, if he could just be a little more patient. After all, there were still a few shillings left in the jug, and with his dole money, a pittance though it was, they wouldn't exactly starve just yet. 'I'm just worried about yer,' she told him. 'I've 'eard so many stories about those slave-drivers.'

'An' who from?' Roy replied quickly. 'Lucy next door, an' where did she get 'em from? Yer can't afford ter take too much notice o' people. Remember it'll be December in a few days' time an' before yer know it Christmas'll be 'ere. The money's gonna come in very 'andy, an' if I 'ave ter sweat fer it, so be it. I tell yer this, Mary, I'd sooner sweat fer a few bob than 'ave ter stand in those dole queues waitin' fer an' 'and-out. It's soul-destroyin'. We're like the walkin' dead shufflin' along in line till we get ter the counter.

It feels like beggin', an' me wiv a trade.'

Mary got up and put her arm round his shoulders as he slumped back in the armchair. 'I understand, luv,' she said softly, 'an' I know 'ow yer feel. I just wanna keep yer in one piece.'

Roy chuckled. 'Don't you worry about me,' he told her. 'I can use a shovel as well as the next man.'

Mary leaned over and kissed him gently on the forehead. 'I know yer can,' she replied.

At number 2 Sammy Strickland leaned back in the armchair and puffed on his cigarette. 'I was surprised 'ow many was there,' he remarked to Peggy, his long-suffering wife. 'I got there early like yer told mc an' I thought ter meself, Sammy, yer got a chance 'ere, son. 'Alf the men in front o' me must 'a' bin in their late fifties an' most of 'em didn't look all that strong.'

'You're in yer late fifties,' Peggy reminded him.

'Yeah, but I got a bit o' meat on me. At least I looked the part,' he replied. 'Anyway, this geezer comes out o' the shed an' walks along the line starin' at us all, so I give 'im a wink, just ter let 'im know I was keen.'

'Yeah, I bet yer did,' Peggy said disbelievingly.

Sammy ignored the sarcasm. 'Then the geezer goes up ter the first man in line an' asks 'im a few questions an' suddenly 'e jerks 'is thumb an' ses, "Yer no use ter me, piss off." The next few in line get told ter go an' wait in the shed an' then 'e comes up ter me. "What's yer name?" 'e said. "Sammy Strickland, sir," I told 'im smart like. "Ever done any diggin' before?" 'e asked me.

63

"Plenty," I told 'im. "Who for?" "St Mary's," I said. "Are you takin' the piss?" 'e growled. "No, I done a spell o' grave diggin'," I explained. Wiv that 'e jerks 'is thumb an' tells me ter get lost.'

'Ignorant git,' Peggy exclaimed. 'And what did yer say to 'im? I 'ope yer did say somefing to 'im.'

'Do me a favour, gel,' Sammy puffed. 'The geezer was built like a brick shit'ouse. 'E even 'ad muscles on 'is muscles. I just left the line an' done me little trick.'

'What yer talkin' about, Sammy?'

'I slipped in the shed when 'is back was turned an' just waited.'

'Well, go on.'

Sammy flicked his cigarette stub into the hearth. 'It seemed like ages till the bloke come in, an' when 'e did 'e took all our names an' addresses. 'E told us ter be by the shed at seven firty sharp on Monday mornin' an' we'd be given wellin'ton boots an' a boiler suit each. 'E also said there was a certain amount o' work that 'ad ter be done every day, an' if we didn't reach our quota we wouldn't get our full pay fer that day.'

'An' what is the full pay?' Peggy asked impatiently.

'Fifteen bob a day.'

'So do yer start on Monday or not?' Peggy asked with irritation mounting in her voice.

''Ang on a minute, I'm comin' ter that,' Sammy told her with a frown. 'When the geezer finished takin' our names 'e told us we could go, an' as I walked out o' the shed 'e grabbed me by the scruff o' the neck an' pulled me back inside. "I thought I told yer ter piss off," he said. "I didn't 'ear yer," I told 'im. "Well yer do now, so scram," 'e shouted.'

'So yer didn't get the job after all,' Peggy said, puffing loudly.

'Nah. 'E said it was me 'ands.'

'What d'yer mean, yer 'ands?'

'The geezer took a gander at 'em an' said they 'adn't done an 'ard day's work fer years.'

'Well 'e was bloody well right,' Peggy growled.

Sammy reached down for the morning paper and sighed as he searched for the comic strip page. There wasn't much to laugh at these days, he thought, but that page did make him smile.

'So what's yer plans now, Sammy?' Peggy asked him after a while.

'I thought I might go an' see Ben Toland later on.'

'What for?'

'Ter see if 'e can fix me up wiv a couple o' days' work.'

'Paintin', yer mean?'

'What else?'

''E might not 'ave anyfing fer 'imself.'

'Buller Morris was tellin' me Ben's got the contract ter paint the Trocette cinema,' Sammy informed her.

'Well, what yer waitin' for?'

'Ben'll be in the Mason's by now an' I'm skint.'

Peggy sighed heavily as she fished into her purse. ''Ere, take it, an' fer Gawd's sake try an' get yerself fixed up. That's me last 'alf-crown.'

Lucy called next door and Mary Chubb led her

into the parlour. 'Sue, 'ere's Mummy. Now you an' Gracie gavver up those toys, there's good children.'

Lucy sat down and smiled bravely at her best friend. 'Well, it's 'appened at last,' she said with a sigh.

'George's job?'

'Yeah. 'E came in wiv 'is cards this evenin'.'

'I'm sorry, luv.'

Lucy shrugged her shoulders. 'We knew it was comin' but you always 'ope that there's a change of 'eart at the last minute. I know George was finkin' the same as me. Still, it's 'appened, an' we've just gotta get on wiv it like everyone else round 'ere.'

Mary pulled on her dark hair as she stood watching the children reluctantly putting the toys into a cardboard box. 'Look, they're all right fer a bit longer. Roy's gone out fer a pint. Let's me an' you 'ave a nice cuppa.'

Gracie immediately tipped the box of toys on to the floor and giggled at Sue.

'Now keep the noise down, you two,' Lucy warned them.

Mary was soon back with the laden tea tray. 'My Roy's found a job,' she said with little enthusiasm.

'Good fer 'im. Where?' Lucy asked.

Mary pulled a face. ''E starts wiv the Coleys on Monday.'

'Oh no,' Lucy said quickly. 'They're bloody slave-drivers. Remember George was tellin' me they work their men really 'ard.'

Mary nodded. 'What could I do, though? Roy's

just about at breakin' point. The way 'e is 'e'll take anyfing.'

'Yeah, I can understand,' Lucy replied. 'There's Christmas just round the corner an' 'ow d'yer tell kids there ain't no Farvver Christmas this year?'

'There won't be fer a lot o' kids, I'm afraid,' Mary said sadly.

Lucy watched her friend as she poured the tea. She had put on weight round the hips and her face too looked more full. Her dark eyes still sparkled and her skin was comparatively smooth and unlined. 'Mary, I dunno 'ow yer do it,' she said suddenly.

'Do what?'

'Keep yerself lookin' 'alf yer age.'

'Go on wiv yer.'

'No, I mean it. Yer do.'

'Well, it's not the good life nor the money, that's fer sure,' Mary said, grinning.

Lucy took her tea and leaned back in the armchair. ''Ow 'as all this affected you an' Roy?' she asked.

'What, 'im bein' out o' work fer so long, yer mean?'

Lucy nodded. ''Ow d'yer cope wiv it?'

'Well, at first it wasn't too bad,' Mary recalled. 'We 'ad a few bob saved up an' Roy expected ter get a start before long, but when it dragged on inter weeks an' then months an' the money we'd saved 'ad all gone we both got really shirty wiv each ovver. It got to a stage where I wouldn't let 'im near me an' then when I did want 'im 'e'd turn 'is back on me. It was as though we were punishin' each ovver fer what was 'appenin' to us, as though it was our fault. One night we came close ter blows an' suddenly we hugged each ovver an' cried on each ovver's shoulders. That night we emptied our grief, an' sat till the early mornin' talkin' everyfing over. We're closer now than ever, Lucy, though we still 'ave our little differences. I got on at Roy this evenin' about 'im takin' that job wiv the Coleys, but it's different now. We draw the line an' refuse ter step over it. It's what you'll 'ave ter do, luv. It'll get 'ard, believe me, an' when yer fink nuffing else can 'appen it will.'

Lucy looked sad. 'I wish I could 'ave 'elped yer more,' she said.

'You 'ave 'elped us, as much as yer could,' Mary replied. 'I've not forgotten the bits an' pieces you give us, but yer won't be in a position ter do it now, not any more. Yer'll be makin' friends wiv the pawnbroker, like most o' the people in this street. Where it was beef it'll be mutton stew, an' yer'll learn ter scrape an' scheme.'

Lucy's eyes filled with tears. 'I've bin wrong, Mary,' she said quietly. 'I've shut me eyes an' ears ter the rest o' the people in this street. George was workin' an' we 'ave decent meals. I've even taken in a lodger. I'm doin' all right, fank you very much. I didn't notice the neighbours wiv brown paper bundles under their arms, an' if I did I ignored it. That would never be me. Oh, no. I'd never resort ter takin' a pair o' best sheets over ter the pawnbroker's. I'd never 'ave ter put cardboard in me shoes or wear a patched-up dress. I've even got a winter coat.'

Mary put her empty teacup down. 'Now you

listen ter me,' she told her. 'We all do the best we can fer our loved ones. We all try ter be that little bit better, 'cos it's in our nature. But there comes a time when circumstances stop yer. Poverty don't pick its victims at random, it sweeps over all of us one way or anuvver. One man loses 'is job an' its put anuvver man out o' collar. Sooner or later we're all swimmin' fer our lives, our 'eads just above water, an' that's when yer sit down an' take stock, just like me an' Roy did. Yer decide ter fight it, swim fer it or go under. There's no middle ground, only the shore.'

'We'll be all right,' Lucy said. 'I'll see to it. George is inclined ter be a bit weak when decisions 'ave ter be taken, an' sometimes 'e lets fings get on top of 'im, but I'll be 'is crutch. I won't let 'im go under.'

'Good fer you, luv,' Mary said, smiling. 'Fancy anuvver cuppa?'

Lucy nodded. 'So what d'yer fink of our new lodger, then?' she asked casually.

''E looks very respectable,' Mary replied. 'Quite attractive, too. I spoke to 'im yesterday, just passed the time o' day, an' 'e introduced 'imself. 'E told me 'e's very 'appy wiv everyfing an' the food was excellent, which made me smile. Your lodger's a very shrewd man. 'E knew that livin' next door I'd most likely tell yer what 'e'd said.'

'Yeah, 'e's very nice,' Lucy remarked. ''E 'as a way wiv Sara an' I'm sure she fancies 'im. She asked me ter perm 'er 'air for 'er last week.'

'Well well, what d'yer know?' Mary said with a cheeky grin. 'An' what about you? Do you fancy 'im?'

'Mary!' Lucy said indignantly. 'I'm an 'appily married woman.'

'Which doesn't necessarily mean that yer can't fancy someone else,' Mary pointed out. 'You can look at the goods wivout buyin'.'

Lucy smiled dismissively, but deep inside she remembered how Charlie had occasionally given himself away with a lingering gaze or a surreptitious glance. The effect on her was increasingly exciting. She could not deny that she liked it whenever his eyes strayed, but refused to read anything into it. She was happily married and that was that. 'I don't see 'im that way,' she replied. 'Besides, 'e must be ten years older than me.'

'Which doesn't mean a fing,' Mary persisted. 'An older man can bring 'is own charm an' experience.'

Lucy felt that the conversation was getting a little dangerous and she might say something she could regret if pressed any more by her forthright friend. 'I expect you're right, but I like ter play it safe,' she said.

'Don't we all,' Mary replied, grinning.

Two tired young children slept soundly that night, but George Parry twisted and turned until the first streaks of dawn rose in the winter sky and he fell into fitful sleep.

CHAPTER 6

Monday morning dawned cold and dreary, and as Roy Chubb left the house he was feeling a little nervous. Stories were rife about the way the Coleys handled their workers, but he thought that if he could get through the first day without any mishaps then he had a chance. Mary had fixed him up with a packet of brawn sandwiches and had bought him a pair of thick angler's socks at the market to go over his own when he wore the wellington boots.

As he turned into Lynton Road he saw the men gathering up ahead. A wooden barrier had been placed across the turning and an arch-shaped shed of tarpaulin had been set up on the pavement. Next to it was the small wooden hut which the Coleys operated from. Roy could see Danny Albury from number 5 and a few other faces that were familiar.

'Right then, you lot, come an' get yer gear,' Sharkey Lockwood called out as he stepped from the shed.

For a few minutes there was chaos as men tried to sort out their boot sizes and grab boiler suits which would come somewhere near to fitting them.

'Oi, you. You can see they're too big,' Sharkey's voice rang out. 'The size is marked inside the top o' the boots. Surely yer know yer own size. An' what d'yer fink you're doin'? Put the poxy boiler suit on, don't try it up ter yer like some big nancy-boy. Oi, you. If yer fixed up get outside an' make room fer the ovvers. Come on, 'urry up, we start work in five minutes.'

Roy Chubb scrambled into his working gear and joined the rest of the men beside a marked area in the middle of the street, and after a few minutes Sharkey ambled over and took one of the men by the arm. 'Now, me an' 'im are gonna start off by loosenin' a few o' the cobblestones an' I want yer ter pick 'em up an' stack 'em all over there near the kerb,' he told them. 'Once we've got the first few out the rest'll lift easy.'

Willing hands soon cleared the prised-up stones and Roy found himself at work with a pickaxe. It took no time at all to remove all the cobbles inside the chalked area and when they were finished Sharkey called the men round him. 'Now, there's ten of yer an' I want yer ter work in pairs,' he explained. 'One'll use the pickaxe an' the ovver the shovel. Spell each ovver wiv the tools an' it'll be easier. Space yerselves out; I don't want anyone reportin' ter me wiv a pickaxe in 'is 'ead. Now as yer dig down move forward, like yer cuttin' steps.'

''Ow far down's the pipes?' one young man asked. 'We don't wanna pierce 'em, do we?'

'What's yer name, son?' Sharkey asked him.

'Watson. Gerry Watson,' he replied.

'Well, Mr Watson, it was good of yer ter point that out, but yer gotta realise that you an' the ovvers are employed ter dig, not fink. I'll do the finkin' round 'ere. If yer must know, the pipes are

72

over six feet down, so yer won't reach 'em just yet awhile. What I want from you is a nice straight trench an' no conversation. Just keep yer lip buttoned over that big mouth o' yours an' me an' you'll get on like an 'ouse on fire. Right then, get on wiv it.'

Once Sharkey had gone into the hut the young man looked up at Roy and gave him a sheepish grin. 'I'd 'ave put one on 'is chops, 'cept I need the work,' he remarked.

Roy returned the grin. Already he felt the heat building up inside his uncomfortable boiler suit as he brought the pickaxe down on the exposed hardcore. The secret was to pace himself, he thought. It was going to be a long day and his back was already beginning to feel the strain.

'Oi. Silly git,' Sharkey yelled. 'Why are yer chuckin' out on that side when everyone else is chuckin' out the ovver side?'

'Sorry, I wasn't finkin'.'

'Yer don't 'ave ter fink. Just copy the ovvers, or is that too much to ask?'

By ten o'clock the digging crew were at waist level in the trench and Sharkey took the boiling kettle from the coke brazier and turned back into the hut.

A heavily built man with a balding head and a flat wide face looked up from a blueprint spread out in front of him. ''Ow's it goin'?' he asked.

'Well, I've 'ad better crews, but they seem ter be gettin' stuck into it,' Sharkey told him.

Ben Coley smiled, displaying a gold tooth. ''Ow many yer keepin'?'

'Eight, same as last time. I got me eye on two.'

73

Coley leaned his arm on the sloping work surface while he waited for Sharkey to make the coffee. The system they used worked well. At first the men would set to work trying to show willing, but then as the toil wore on the obvious signs would be there. For some it became torture trying to lift a clay-filled shovel clear of the hole, and for others the wear and tear on the hands made it impossible to carry on.

'Oi, you, it ain't break time yet,' Sharkey called out from the hut.

'Just takin' a minute's breavver,' the man replied.

'Yer take a break when I tell yer, not before,' the ganger shouted at him. 'Piss off an' get changed.'

'But I'm only–'

'Are yer deaf as well as idle? Get changed an' quick about it.'

Gerry Watson mumbled something which Roy did not catch, and then he tried to look industrious as he saw Sharkey approaching.

'You seem to 'ave quite a bit o' trouble keepin' that trap shut,' the ganger growled. 'Would you like ter join 'im?'

Gerry looked up at the sorry figure making his way to the shed and shook his head vigorously. 'I'm dumb from now on,' he said, pushing his shovel into the soil with gusto.

At ten thirty Ben Coley stepped out of the hut and blew a whistle, and the digging crew scrambled out of the trench to a well-earned ten-minute break. At the kerbside there was a large metal container filled with steaming tea and an

74

array of chipped enamel mugs. Roy grabbed one and, having observed the man ahead of him, followed suit by dipping his into the tea.

'I don't fink I'm gonna last the day, let alone the week,' someone said nearby.

'Wait till we get down ter the clay,' Gerry groaned.

Roy studied his blistered hands and felt that he too would be very lucky to last the week. 'We'll just 'ave ter grit our teeth an' carry on,' he said with bravado.

A man sitting nearby leaned forward to catch Roy and Gerry's attention. 'I take it yer've met Ben Coley,' he said, and they answered with a shake of their heads. 'That was 'im wiv the whistle. Long as Frank stays away we'll be all right. 'E's the bastard. Sharkey's like a pussy cat next to 'im.'

The whistle sounded all too soon and the work got under way once more. Clods of clay were thrown up to the side of the trench and the men grew more and more fatigued as the morning wore on. Suddenly a shout rang out and Roy could see two men grappling at the front of the line. All work stopped as the two combatants fell in a heap, and when one man tried to separate them a cry went up. 'Leave 'em alone. Let 'em fight it out.'

Sharkey came running over and dropped down into the hole, tearing the two apart and holding them at arm's length. 'What's goin' on?' he growled.

'That stupid git nearly done me wiv the pickaxe,' one of the fighters said.

'It was nowhere near yer, yer bloody cry-baby.'

'Who you callin' a cry-baby?'

'What's goin' on 'ere?'

The men turned to see the huge figure of Frank Coley standing legs apart at the edge of the trench. He was inches taller than Ben and at least two stone heavier. His thick grey hair was swept back over his ears and his grey eyes glinted as he stared down coldly at the scene below. 'Fetch 'em both up 'ere,' he demanded.

Once they had scrambled out of the trench Sharkey prodded the men towards the workmen's shed.

'Who started it?' Frank asked as he sat down on the trestle table and rested his foot on a bench stool.

''E did,' the two said in unison.

'Do yer like fightin'?' Frank asked them. 'Well, do yer?'

'We just got a bit—'

'I asked you a question an' I expect a sensible answer. Do you like fightin'?'

The men shook their heads. Coley stood up and suddenly brought the back of his hand across the face of the taller one, drawing blood from a split lip. 'Would yer like ter fight me?'

The man shook his head as he licked his damaged lip.

'What about you? Would you like ter fight me?'

The other one stepped back a pace, fearing the same treatment. 'No, sir.'

Frank Coley grabbed him by his overalls and pulled him close. 'I don't allow fightin' on my jobs,' he said quietly. 'If anyone gets involved in fightin' they get put off right away, is that understood?'

The man nodded and was suddenly caught with a backhander.

'I said is that understood?'

Staggering back, the man mumbled a reply and turned to run from the shed, only to see Sharkey barring his way.

'Sit down, the pair of yer,' Coley snarled. 'You were on fifteen bob a day, right? A mornin's work makes it seven an' a tanner. We gotta knock off two bob fer the 'ire o' yer gear an' then there's a shillin' tea money ter do down. I make that four an' a tanner we owe yer.' The two men nodded, wanting to get away from what had to be a dangerous maniac. 'Yer'll 'ave ter call back fer yer money termorrer afternoon.'

As the two chastened workers hurried off in different directions Frank Coley stepped from the shed. 'Right, lads, stop what yer doin' an' listen ter me,' he ordered. Seven tired faces stared up at him as he stood above them. 'You lost one worker this mornin' fer takin' an unofficial break an' yer lost anuvver two fer fightin'. So there's just seven of yer left. We'll replace the ovvers termorrer, but in the meantime there's work ter do. I want them pipes cleared o' soil an' ready fer takin' out termorrer. Any complaints?'

The silence gratified Coley and he looked around at the blank expressions. 'Now I want yer ter listen carefully ter what I'm gonna say,' he went on. 'We pay fair wages an' we expect a fair day's graft. But it seems that recently some of yer 'ave taken umbrage fer certain reasons known

77

only ter yerselves. Complaints 'ave bin submitted at the employment exchange an' wiv the buildin' unions. We don't entertain unions an' we don't like you geezers spoutin' yer mouths off in the wrong direction, like wiv the local rags an' public busybodies. If yer do, be sure we'll get ter find out an' woe betide anyone we catch. We're talkin' about survival 'ere, yours as well as ours. We stay in business an' you don't starve. Do yer job an' yer'll be took on fer our ovver contracts in the area. Mess us about an' yer'll regret it, be sure. Right then, back ter work.'

Harold Wicks considered that he had been treated very unfairly. After all, it wasn't a crime to take a couple of minutes' rest. And to crown it all he had been sent packing without any wages – not that he'd earned that much. They could have paid him for the morning's work, though, but the gits seemed to do just what they liked. Well, it wasn't fair and a man had his rights. He'd make an official complaint at the labour exchange and see what they could do. Maybe it'd shake the Coleys up a bit if the union got involved as well. They should know what was going on at these non-union jobs.

Harold Wicks managed to scrape up enough coppers for a half-pint at the Mason's Arms that evening, and recognising one of the diggers from the site who was sitting alone he wandered over. ''Ere, Joe, did yer know I got chucked off the job wivout a penny?'

'No I didn't.'

'The way I see it I should 'ave bin paid fer the hour an' 'alf I worked,' Harold complained.

'I should go back termorrer an' ask fer it,' Joe Lambert advised him, knowing full well that the man wouldn't dare.

'I'm not gonna waste me time wiv those 'orrible bastards,' Harold sneered. 'I'm gonna make an official complaint at the labour exchange about the way I bin treated. I'm gonna see the union people as well.'

'I don't s'pose they'd be able to 'elp much, what wiv the Coleys bein' non-union,' Joe remarked.

'We'll see,' Harold said confidently.

Joe Lambert was a friendly soul who liked nothing more than a pint of beer and a cosy chat in a friendly pub, and after Harold Wicks had left he got into conversation with two men who were already discussing the digging works outside.

'I've done a bit o' diggin' in me time,' one was saying.

'Can't say as I 'ave,' his companion replied. 'That sort o' graft's too 'ard fer me, what wiv me dodgy back.'

'They're doin' the sewer pipes by all accounts,' the other man said. 'It's bloody 'ard work, especially when yer get down ter the clay. I done a spell wiv that firm once. Only lasted a week. They're poxy slave-drivers.'

Joe Lambert decided it was time to make his contribution. 'I started on there this mornin',' he put in. 'They certainly want their pound o' flesh. They chucked one bloke off the site fer takin' a breavver an' they ain't paid 'im a sausage. As a matter o' fact I was just talkin' ter the bloke. 'E

79

reckons 'e's gonna report 'em. Fat lot o' good that'll do.'

'In my opinion I fink 'e'll be better off keepin' 'is trap shut,' the first man remarked. 'If the Coleys get ter find out the bloke's bin makin' complaints about the firm they'll tune 'im up, that's fer sure.'

Amongst the few customers at the Mason's Arms that night was a gentleman by the name of Lennie Chivers, and most people who knew him were convinced that Lennie would sell his mother into slavery, if the price was right. Lennie came cheaply, and he knew where the Coleys' ganger did his drinking. For the cost of a pint he gave Sharkey Lockwood a full account of what he had overheard.

Harold Wicks never did put his complaint in at the labour exchange. Smouldering rags poked through his letterbox and then a verbal warning from a third party about the consequences of poking his nose into Coley affairs was enough to convince him that a few shillings' compensation was not good enough danger money.

CHAPTER 7

Lucy Parry and her best friend Mary Chubb sat chatting together in Mary's scullery on Monday evening. With the door pulled to they were safe in thinking they would not be overheard, and while Roy was snoring in the parlour they spoke openly of their worries.

'When I saw those 'ands I nearly cried,' Mary was saying. 'The blisters 'ad busted an' there was all congealed blood round 'em. I made 'im soak 'em in salt water an' then I smarmed 'em wiv Vaseline. God knows 'ow they'll be by termorrer.'

'Well, if 'is 'ands ain't any better 'e won't be able ter work,' Lucy told her. 'Yer gotta be careful they don't go septic.'

'You try tellin' 'im,' Mary groaned. ''E's so bloody obstinate at times.'

'I can understand it,' Lucy said, sighing. 'It's the manly fing. I'm tough, I can cope.'

'Yeah, but Roy's a carpenter not a bloody ditch-digger. 'E ain't used ter usin' a shovel all day.'

'Well, 'e 'ad the guts ter try it,' Lucy remarked. 'A lot wouldn't. 'E's only finkin' o' you an' little Gracie.'

'Yeah, I know that, but 'is 'ealth's gotta come first. I don't want 'im gettin' blood poisonin'.'

'Just see 'ow 'is 'ands are in the mornin',' Lucy advised. 'If they're no better tell 'im about Tom Creasey.'

'Tom Creasey?'

'You remember ole Tom, the feller in Lynton Road who 'ad to 'ave 'is leg off an' died o' blood poisonin'.'

'I thought it was an 'eart attack killed 'im.'

'It was, but I don't s'pose Roy'd know that.'

Mary forced a grin. 'What about you? You must be worried sick about George.'

Lucy nodded. ''E 'ad ter sign on this mornin'. 'E joined a long line o' people an' when 'e finally got ter the counter the bloke told 'im 'e was in the wrong queue. You 'ave ter give 'em all yer details when yer first sign on as unemployed.'

'Yeah, that's right. I know from what Roy told me. Apparently they 'ave a special queue fer tradesmen.'

Lucy smiled briefly. 'I know I shouldn't laugh, Mary, but George was tellin' me that when 'e finally got ter the counter this mornin' an' the clerk asked 'im what 'e'd done fer a livin' 'e told 'im 'e was a gift wrapper. 'E said when the clerk chuckled an' made some stupid remark 'e wanted the floor to open up. That's my George for yer.'

Mary got up from the table and filled the kettle at the chipped stone sink. 'I was finkin', Lucy. Me an' you might be able ter do a bit of office cleanin'.'

'An' what about the kids?'

Mary smiled as she lit the gas under the kettle. 'We could both look fer a job, an' then if we get lucky we can take turns.'

'I'm not wiv yer,' Lucy said, frowning.

Mary sat down again and folded her arms over

her ample bosom. 'Look, let's say one of us is lucky enough ter find somefing. The first week I'll go an' you can mind the kids, then the second week I'll 'ave the kids while you do the work. That way we can both earn a few bob. All right, it won't be much, but it'll be better than nuffing.'

'Assumin' we do find somefing, 'ow we gonna get away wiv it?' Lucy asked.

'No one's ter know,' Mary replied, smiling.

'What about the forelady, or the supervisor?'

'We don't go fer those sort o' jobs,' Mary told her. 'We only go after key jobs. You know the sort I mean, like small offices where yer let yerself in.'

Lucy nodded slowly. 'It might work, an' as yer say it'll mean a few bob fer both of us.'

Mary smiled. 'Even if we are found out we could say that you, or me, was standin' in frew illness. They wouldn't care, long as the place was gettin' cleaned.'

'Mary, you're a gem,' her friend said, grinning.

'It comes out o' desperation.'

'Yeah, an' I'll be gettin' as shrewd as you before long,' Lucy said pointedly.

'There's anuvver fing I got in mind,' Mary went on.

'An' I know you'll tell me.'

Mary stood up as the kettle began to sing and reached for the tea caddy. 'I 'eard that yer can get old tram sheets at the depot in New Cross.'

'Tram sheets? What's them?'

'They call 'em destination rolls,' Mary explained as she spooned tea into the china pot. 'You've seen the tram conductor windin' 'em round. They're made o' linen an' Mrs Venners

83

got one fer free at the depot the ovver day. She showed me. What yer do is soak them in salt water an' then peel off the black paint round the edges, cut 'em up an' fold 'em ter make 'em look like bedsheets.'

'Mary, are yer feelin' all right?'

'Fer uncle's benefit. Uncle, the pawnbroker.'

'Yer mean yer pawn 'em.'

'That's what Mrs Venners did,' Mary informed her. 'She cut the roll an' folded it flat an' then tied it up in a bundle. She tore the corner o' the brown paper parcel just enough ter make the pawnbroker fink she was pawnin' a pair o' good linen sheets. The best fing is, she's managed ter get four bundles out o' one roll. Mind you, she's gotta go ter four different pawnshops.'

'An' 'ope that one of 'em doesn't decide to open the parcel,' Lucy reminded her.

Mary shrugged. 'Well, in that case it'll just be a question o' blaggin' it out. What can they do? They can only chuck yer out o' the shop.'

'I s'pose it's all about survivin',' Lucy said, sighing.

The kettle boiled over and Mary grabbed the handle with an ironing pad. 'When we're desperate we revert ter desperate measures,' she declared.

'George might be lucky,' Lucy said with little enthusiasm. ''E may get somefing soon. I don't want 'im 'avin' ter stand in the dole queues day after day, week after week. It'll crucify 'im.'

Mary took two teacups and saucers down from the dresser and then gave the tea a stir. 'Look, luv, I don't wanna depress yer,' she said in a quiet voice, 'but yer gotta face up ter George possibly bein' out o' work fer some time. There's just nuffink doin' anywhere. There's no work in the factories, not while they're on short time, an' in Roy's case every buildin' site 'e's tried 'as bin fixed up wiv carpenters. People don't realise just 'ow bad it is out there, till their own ole man gets put off.'

'You're right,' Lucy replied. 'I've tended ter shut me eyes an' ears ter what's goin' on, but I'm beginnin' ter come ter terms wiv it.'

'Of course yer will,' Mary said with conviction. 'Me an' you are survivors, we're all survivors. We can cope, an' when fings do buck up we'll still be around ter pick up the pieces.'

Rain started to fall, drumming down on the tin bath hanging in the Chubbs' backyard. A distant roll of thunder crashed and Roy Chubb stirred in his chair. Sharkey Lockwood was coming towards him wielding a large shovel, his face contorted and a wild look in his dark eyes. Sharp pain ran up Roy's arm as he tried to fend off the madman and he woke up with a start, realising that he was clenching his fists hard.

'Are you all right, Roy?' Mary asked in concern as she came hurrying into the parlour. 'We 'eard yer shout out.'

'Yeah. I was dreamin',' he replied, wincing as he slowly opened his clenched hands. He looked up at Lucy and gave her a brief smile. ''Ow's George, luv?'

Lucy returned his smile. 'Bearin' up. 'E signed on this mornin'.'

Mary bent down over Roy. 'I fink I'll do those

85

'ands again before yer go ter bed,' she said.

Lucy touched her friend gently on the arm. 'I'd better get goin', luv. See yer termorrer.'

As she walked back into the house Lucy saw Charlie coming down the stairs clutching a soiled handkerchief.

'It's OK. Young Sue's just woke up cryin',' he said reassuringly. 'She's 'ad a bit of a nosebleed.'

'Where's George?' Lucy asked as she made for the stairs.

''E 'ad ter go out.'

'Go out? Where?'

Charlie shrugged his shoulders. ''E never said.'

Lucy hurried up the stairs and saw that her daughter was settled and breathing easily. Charlie had followed her back up and stood in the bedroom doorway behind her. 'I wet this and pressed it on the bridge of 'er nose,' he said. 'It seemed ter do the trick. I was a bit worried in case she was frightened of me but she was fine. She called me Charlie.'

'I'm very grateful. She does get the occasional nosebleed an' that's all I do, put a wet cloth on her nose.'

They went back down into the parlour and Lucy looked at the chimer in the centre of the mantelshelf. 'Sara's late again,' she remarked. 'Flirtin' wiv that new vicar, I expect. I'm worried about George, though. It wasn't fair of 'im expectin' you ter play nursemaid. Where could 'e 'ave gone, I wonder?'

''E might 'ave gone fer a drink,' Charlie suggested. ''E most likely needed it after terday. Those dole queues take some gettin' used to.'

86

'I can imagine,' Lucy said. 'Fancy a cuppa?'

'That'll be nice.'

The rain became heavier and thunder sounded loudly as Lucy stood in the scullery waiting for the kettle to boil. She saw flashes of lightning through the net curtains and counted the seconds till the thunder rolled.

'I make that almost over'ead,' Charlie said as he walked through.

Lucy turned quickly. 'Yeah, two seconds, two miles away.'

Charlie averted his eyes for a few moments then fixed her with a steady gaze. 'Look, I know it's none o' my business but George did ask me if I'd 'old the fort fer a few minutes till you got back. 'E also checked that Sue was sleepin' soundly before 'e left.'

'I'm not angry, just surprised,' Lucy replied with a frown. 'It's so unlike 'im ter go out durin' the week, an' on a night like this too.'

'I might be wrong, but I've a feelin' 'e just wanted ter sit quietly wiv a pint. Just ter get 'imself sorted out, come ter terms wiv what's 'appened.'

'You know, you're very perceptive, considerin',' Lucy said, and immediately wished she hadn't made the remark.

'Considerin' what?' Charlie asked with a smile.

'Now I'm gettin' embarrassed,' she said, turning her back on him while she spooned tea leaves into the china pot. 'What I meant was, p'raps people livin' alone don't often get in the 'abit o' noticin' what ovver people are goin' frew.'

'Ah, but I'm not alone,' Charlie replied.

'There's you an' George, an' young Sue, not fergettin' Sara, o' course. An' then fer all you know I might be 'avin' a passionate affair wiv some lady who lives nearby.'

'In that case it'd 'ave ter be durin' the day,' Lucy said, turning towards him and smiling. 'You're 'ere almost every night.'

Charlie sat down at the table. 'Well, I s'pose that's true. No, there's no one in my life an' there 'asn't been fer some time now.'

'Is there any chance you an' yer wife'll ever get back tergevver again?' Lucy asked.

'No chance at all,' he told her. 'The whole fing was a sham from the very beginnin'. I s'pose we were both tryin' ter make up fer the past ... past loves, past 'appiness. We were just substitutes fer each ovver. Can you understand what I mean?'

Lucy nodded slowly. 'Yeah, I believe I do. I take it there was someone once, someone who was very special to yer.'

Charlie did not answer. Instead he took out a folded black leather wallet from his back pocket and opened it. 'She was seventeen when this photograph was taken,' he said quietly as he handed it to her.

Lucy studied the sepia print of a young girl with deeply waved flaxen hair and a winsome smile. 'She's very beautiful,' she remarked.

'I first met 'er when she was eighteen,' Charlie said, his expression growing serious. 'I was in my late twenties at the time an' in the army. I'd bin wounded in France an' I was recuperatin' at a military 'ospital. She was a trainee nurse. She came from a very wealthy family.'

'What was 'er name?' Lucy enquired.

'Charlotte. Charlotte Farrington.'

Lucy looked down at the photograph once more then handed it back to Charlie. 'I'm sorry. I feel as though I've bin pryin',' she said respectfully.

'No, it's nice of yer ter be interested,' he replied. 'We were very much in love. It seemed to 'appen so quickly, an' then it was all taken away.'

'She died?'

'In the 1918 flu epidemic.'

'I'm so sorry,' Lucy said with genuine feeling.

Charlie's face relaxed slightly. 'It's a long time ago,' he said thoughtfully. 'Though sometimes it doesn't seem like it. Seventeen years. I was a long time comin' ter terms wiv Charlotte's death, an' then just when I felt I was startin' ter live again I met Claire. She'd lost 'er first love on the Somme in '16 an' we found ourselves bein' drawn tergevver, by our mutual loss really. Claire was a beautiful woman who reminded me of Charlotte an' she often said I favoured 'er first love in looks an' build. We were both hostages ter the past an' it couldn't work.'

Lucy looked at his dark eyes and sensed the pain and frustration he had struggled with. 'Do you see yerself ever marryin' again?' she asked hesitantly.

He shook his head. 'Claire's a staunch Catholic. She would never agree to a divorce.'

Lucy got up suddenly, the tea almost forgotten. 'I'm sorry. I bet yer fink I'm a nosy bitch.'

'No, not at all,' Charlie replied quickly. 'I was ready enough ter talk about it. Sometimes it's good fer a man to unburden 'imself.'

'That applies ter women too,' Lucy said, 'though we tend ter use our own sex as a floggin' post.'

They sat in the quiet scullery sipping their tea, and occasionally Lucy glanced up at the battered alarm clock on the dresser. 'What could 'ave 'appened ter Sara?' she wondered.

The answer was soon forthcoming when George's sister let herself into the house wearing a secretive smile. 'I'm sorry I'm late, Lucy. You weren't worried, were you? Yer knew where I was.'

'Yeah, but yer could 'ave met wiv an accident on the way 'ome.'

'I've bin voted on ter the committee,' she said smugly. She raised her voice. 'Did you 'ear, George?'

'George is out,' Lucy told her.

'Out? Out where?'

'I wish I knew.'

'Didn't you ask 'im where 'e was goin' when 'e went?'

'I was next door talkin' ter Mary.'

'I do 'ope 'e's all right,' Sara said nervously.

Then something banged against the front door and Sara put her hand up to her mouth. Lucy stood up but Charlie took her by the arm. 'Yer'd better let me go,' he warned her. 'It could be a drunk.'

When he opened the door Charlie found George leaning sideways, his outstretched arm supporting him against the doorpost. 'I'm 'fraid I'm … I'm…'

'Come on, pal, let's get yer out o' the rain,'
Charlie said kindly.

George leaned heavily on him as he walked
along the passage to the warm scullery, where he
collapsed into a chair at the table. 'I went fer a
drink,' he slurred.

Lucy forced a smile. 'I can see that,' she replied.

'I needed time ter fink. I ... I knew it was ...
was ... but yer see...'

'Look, I'd sooner wait till termorrer fer the
post-mortem,' she told him crossly. 'Now let's get
yer upstairs an' you can get those wet clothes off
yer before yer catch yer death.'

George tried to stand but slumped down again
in the chair. Charlie bent down and took his
weight. 'Come on, pal, let's do as she said, shall
we?'

George nodded and allowed himself to be
helped out of the scullery and up the stairs.

'Fanks, Charlie. I can manage all right now,'
Lucy said, giving him a grateful smile.

For a while Charlie sat on the edge of his bed,
deep in thought as he puffed on his pipe. The
rain had stopped and the quietness was
undisturbed but for an occasional clatter from
the freight yards. He could not deny it, the faint
stirring in his loins and the quickening of his
heartbeat as he thought about her. She was a very
attractive woman and she was getting under his
skin in a dangerous way. What of her, he
wondered? Had he stirred her feelings too?
Despite himself, he could not help hoping so.

CHAPTER 8

Coley's ditch diggers managed to stay together as a unit during a bitterly cold last week in November. Harold Wicks was replaced by a giant of a man who handled a shovel like a dinner fork, but there were no replacements for the two sacked for fighting and the work force was now down to eight. Gerry Watson realised that he had inadvertently upset Sharkey Lockwood on the first day and he made sure that he never slacked nor spoke a word while the ganger was anywhere around. Joe Lambert, the digger accosted by Harold Wicks, was another worker who seemed quite at home using a shovel, but Roy Chubb and Danny Albury were suffering.

'I can't understand why me 'ands are so bad,' Roy groaned to Danny during their midday break. 'I'm a bloody carpenter by trade an' I'm used ter workin' wiv 'em.'

Danny shook his head. 'It's those shovels an' picks we gotta use. They're all old an' rough, an' then yer gotta take inter consideration yer've bin out o' collar fer some time. Yer 'ands soon get soft. I soak mine in salt water every night. It 'elps 'arden 'em up a bit.'

Gerry Watson still looked in pretty good shape and after washing down the last of his cheese sandwich with cold tea he took out his tobacco tin. 'Well, there's anuvver week's work fer us, if

93

we can stick it,' he remarked. 'It's December next week an' the dosh'll certainly come in very 'andy.'

'Are yer married, Gerry?' Danny Albury asked.

The young man nodded. 'Yeah, an' I got two God ferbids, one of each. Me gel's four an' me little sproggo's just two.'

Danny jerked his thumb in the direction of the marked-out area further along the long turning. 'That'll give us a week at least,' he reckoned. 'Maybe even two. It's longer than this trench.'

'Don't you believe it,' Gerry said dismissively. 'Sharkey'll be on our backs the minute we start work there, you mark my words. 'E'll still want it finished by the weekend.'

As the crew left the hut to go back to work Joe Lambert sidled up to Roy and the others. 'See that big ugly git over there? Wally Coates? Watch what yer say in front of 'im,' he hissed. ''E's one o' the Coleys' men.'

The week dragged on and rain fell on Friday, making it harder to get the clay out from around the damaged pipes. When the job was finally finished an exhausted team of diggers expected to be paid early and sent home, but Sharkey had other ideas. 'Yer bein' paid till five so yer might as well get those cobbles up ready fer Monday,' he told them.

As the bedraggled men prised up the flintstones Sammy Strickland strolled past. He knew how close he had come to getting a job with the Coley brothers and he still had the occasional nightmare. His wife Peggy had been on to him to 'put himself about', as she termed it, since he would never find anything until he did, but Sammy wasn't all that worried. He had his unemployment money and Peggy had a regular job at the baker's shop in the Old Kent Road. They wouldn't starve, and if the worst came to the worst he could always get a few days' work helping on the stalls at the market, like in the past. Right now, though, he was quite happy to stand in the drizzling rain and watch other men toil.

'Bloody weavver's bad, ain't it?' he said out of genuine sympathy to the nearest worker.

'Poxy.'

'Don't they give yer no oilskins when it's pissin' down?'

'Nah.'

'Bloody disgustin'.'

'Yeah, it is.'

'You lot should go an' see the ganger. I would if it was me gettin' soaked ter the balls.'

Unknown to Sammy the man in question was eyeing him from the hut. 'Who's that geezer chattin' ter the men?' he asked.

Frank Coley strolled over to the doorway. 'Gawd knows,' he said. 'Go out an' send 'im on 'is way, Sharkey. 'E's 'oldin' up the works.'

As the big man stepped out of the hut he was immediately spotted by Gerry Watson. 'Yer better piss off, mate,' he said out of the corner of his mouth. 'Our ganger's in a bad mood.'

'People like that don't scare me,' Sammy told him with feigned grit. 'The bigger they are the 'arder they fall, that's my motto.'

'I 'ope you ain't disturbin' my boys,' Sharkey

growled at him.

'Nah, just watchin',' Sammy replied.

'Yer'd better be on yer way,' he was advised. 'There's nuffink ter see round 'ere.'

'I can watch, can't I?' Sammy said with spirit. 'It's a free country.'

'The rest o' the country might be, but not this bit,' Sharkey declared. 'I rule this bit an' I'm sayin' yer should piss off an' leave my men alone.'

'I ain't touched 'em,' Sammy replied.

'Now look, I'm a very reasonable man when yer get down to it,' Sharkey told him, 'but I don't take kindly to any little git like you givin' me lip so piss off while yer in front.'

Sammy saw the menace in the ganger's eyes and decided to take heed. 'You should fit 'em out wiv oilskins in weavver like this,' he remarked, sauntering off as calmly as he could.

Charlie Foden found time hanging heavy on him lately. There had only been one day's work at the docks in the past few weeks and he had spent his time keeping warm in the reading room of the local library, which prompted Lucy to chide him. 'Look, yer don't 'ave ter spend all yer time there,' she emphasised when he told her. 'This place is yours ter come an' go in, an' there's always a fire 'ere an' an armchair ter sit in.'

'Yeah, I know, Lucy, but yer don't want me under yer feet all day long.'

'Yer won't be under my feet,' she assured him. 'I'll be busy around the place, an' I might get a cleanin' job soon.'

'That'll be good.'

'Me an' Mary next door are gonna try an' get one between us,' she went on. 'It won't be much comin' in but at least it'll keep the wolves away from the door.'

'An' yer'll share the kids?'

''Ow did yer guess?'

'It didn't want much workin' out,' he said, smiling.

'I wish my George would crack 'is face wiv a smile now an' then,' she said sadly. 'I know 'e must be very worried but I've tried dozens o' times ter tell 'im that bein' out o' work's no crime. Trouble is 'e ain't come ter terms wiv it yet. Like the ovver night. I've never seen 'im drunk since our weddin' day, an' it came as a bit of a shock.'

'I fink it done 'im good ter let off a bit o' steam,' Charlie remarked.

Lucy merely nodded, recalling that night when George came home soaked to the skin and hardly able to walk, let alone talk. He had gone out with the intention of having a solitary pint while he thought things out, but unfortunately he had let himself get dragged into the company of a group of factory workers who had been paid off that evening. The beer was flowing and he drank more than he should have. There were other jobs available, the newly unemployed workers believed, so why not take heart? It was just a matter of time.

Late in the evening he left the friendly company and staggered home alone, stopping to rest awhile on a park bench in St Mark's churchyard, as far as he could remember. He had probably

97

not given a thought to the rain, nor to the fact that he had spent over ten shillings on a round of drinks. Lucy was supposed to understand.

She had tried, aware of how he must be feeling inside. He had always been able to provide for her and Sue and now he had lost the means. It was a question of pride and self-esteem, and she had got his wet clothes off and eased him into bed without a word of complaint, but she failed to understand how he could have been so careless as to lose his final pay packet. Surely he hadn't spent it all. It wasn't among his wet clothes and she could only guess that it had dropped out of his pocket either in the pub or when he sat in the church garden on his way home.

It had been hard the following week. The rent could not be found and the tallyman had to be persuaded to forgo his weekly payment. Mary Chubb had been a lifesaver, though, lending Lucy a pound out of the meagre savings she had been putting away for Christmas. George himself was distraught at having been so careless, but he had made matters worse by constantly carping about his run of bad luck. There was a bad atmosphere about the house for a few days and Sara had not helped with her miserable mood. The new vicar at St Mark's was apparently involved in a torrid affair with a pretty deaconess and it had come as a terrible shock to George's sister, who had felt that she herself was making headway in cultivating the cleric's affections.

Secretive to obsessiveness, Sara kept her feelings bottled up and told no one what was going on, but Lucy guessed that her sister-in-law's frame of mind had something to do with the church. It had to be; there was little else in her life which would have triggered off such sullenness.

'Don't serve me up anyfing,' Sara said. 'Me stomach's playin' me up.'

'Shall I get yer some tomato soup an' a slice o' bread?' Lucy offered.

'I just told yer me stomach was bad,' Sara puffed. 'Tomato soup'll only make me sick.'

'What about a couple o' slices o' bread an' marge?'

'I keep tellin' yer I don't want anyfing,' Sara growled.

'Well sod the lot o' yer then,' Lucy said with emphasis. 'I'm just about fed up wiv it.'

'That's right, take it out on everybody,' Sara replied in a raised voice. 'I 'ope yer don't leave 'im out.'

Lucy sighed. 'What yer talkin' about?'

'You know what I'm talkin' about.'

'If I did I wouldn't 'ave to ask yer, now would I?'

Charlie had just come in from the street and heard the sharp exchange. 'Evenin', folks,' he said, smiling sheepishly as he walked into the parlour. 'It looks like the fog's comin' in again.'

Sara stood up quickly, and without answering him she hurried out of the room with a haughty expression on her face.

'Take no notice,' Lucy told him. 'She's just bein' 'er usual charmin' self, bloody silly cow.'

Charlie stood for a moment, feeling in the way.

'Where's George?' he asked.

''E's gone after an advert in the *South London Press*,' she replied. 'It's fer a school caretaker.'

'Fingers crossed,' Charlie said, giving her a wide smile.

'What about you? What you bin doin' all day?'

He shrugged his wide shoulders and sat down facing her. 'There was no work this mornin', so I went ter the library an' then I killed time at the dockers' club. Played a few games o' darts, an' one ole chap insisted on a game o' shove-'a'penny. It turned into a marathon, actually.'

Lucy looked into his soft eyes and felt sorry for him. Charlie must be feeling the strains and stresses of being on short time just like everyone else, but he never showed it. His smile was never far away and she admired the inner strength of the man. He had so much self-control and seemed to ooze confidence. That wife of his must have been mad to let him go, she reflected, immediately cursing herself as she felt the hot flush rush into her cheeks. She was at it again, allowing herself to become far too inquisitive and intrigued. It was a dangerous game to play, even within the confines of her own mind. She was a married woman with a child and he was an older man carrying the baggage of a failed relationship. The barrier had to stay in place and he, like her, had to be aware of it.

''Ave you always bin a docker?' she asked as casually as she could.

He nodded. 'Me farvver worked in the docks an' I followed 'im in, but I've got no son ter pass me ticket on to, which makes me wonder if I should look around fer somefing else. After all, there's no work there ter speak of an' the future prospects don't seem all that good.'

As Lucy leaned forward to prod the fire with a brass-handled poker Charlie noticed how the heat from the coals flushed her face, and his eyes lingered on the black velvet strip at the nape of her neck where her fair hair was gathered together carelessly. She was a lovely woman, and in another time, another place, her portrait might well have graced the walls of an ancestral home. She would be in the company of giggling young women, of course, but her large blue eyes would constantly glance over in his direction. He would be in the dress uniform of the Light Horse, trying to seem relaxed on the eve of his regiment's departure for the Crimea. Her eyelashes fluttered as he boldly walked over and bowed stiffly. She stepped forward, her heart beating a little faster, and rested her hand on his proffered arm, allowing him to lead her on to the marble floor. The string quintet were warming to the occasion and he took her in his arms, tripping gaily among the couples to the delight of some and the envy of others.

'They make a fine couple, don't you think, Wheatcroft?'

'A marriage, surely, once the regiment gets back, Manvers.'

'Rather a premature assumption, I fear, Wheatcroft old chap. We'll be staring down the barrels of the Russian cannon to be sure.'

'Good lord, they've waltzed straight out on to the balcony,' Fairclough remarked.

'I'd cross her name off that dance card if I were you, Herbert old fruit,' his fellow officer suggested.

Charlie smiled to himself. The novel he was reading had taken him far away from the poverty and deprivation of thirties Bermondsey to a time of gallantry and honour, but now the beautiful Lucy Parry and he were back in the real world and the drama was left to run its full course on the tattered pages.

'I'm sorry the dinner's gonna be a bit late ternight,' Lucy said. 'I'll serve it up as soon as George gets in. 'E shouldn't be long now.'

'It's OK, Lucy, there's no rush on my part.'

She gave him a smile. 'You looked miles away just then.'

'If you only knew,' he said, smiling back at her.

They heard the front door and George walked in looking downcast. 'No luck,' he announced. 'It went yesterday.'

Sue ran into the room with her picture book and went over to her father. 'Daddy, will you read me my book?' she asked.

'In a while, luvvy,' he said as he took off his coat and hung it behind the door.

Sue was impatient and came over to Charlie. 'Can you read me my book, Charlie?' she asked him.

He lifted her on to his lap and opened the pages. 'Well, well,' he said in a shocked voice. 'There's no crunchy giant in this book.'

'Who's the crunchy giant, Charlie?'

'Well, 'e's really a nice crunchy giant an' 'e looks after the nice children.'

102

'Not the naughty ones?'

'No, not the naughty ones.'

'Will 'e look after me?'

'Yes. If you get lost in the forest the nice crunchy giant will be there ter show you the way 'ome.'

'Is there a bad crunchy giant?'

'Yes, but the nice crunchy giant doesn't allow 'im in the forest.'

'I like the nice crunchy giant,' Sue said in a tiny voice as she nestled her head against Charlie's chest.

He glanced up at Lucy with a bemused look on his face, and she smiled at him. 'Crunchy giant indeed.'

Sara joined the others at the table after a little coaxing from Lucy, and Charlie, feeling that somehow he might have been partly responsible for her upset earlier, was particularly attentive. 'More gravy, Sara?' he asked. ''Ow's the 'eadache?'

Lucy glanced at George with a brief collusive smile on her face and he looked across at Sara. His sister seemed to be enjoying the attention, judging by the way she rallied. 'I'm sorry the job 'ad gone, George,' she told him. 'Never mind, better luck next time.'

He put a brave face on and gave her a smile. 'Yer lookin' better, Sara.'

'I feel better this evenin',' she replied, glancing quickly at Charlie.

Lucy caught the look and the intonation of her sister-in-law's voice and then checked herself. No, surely not. She wouldn't be trying to let

Charlie know she was available. It was ridiculous even to consider such a thing. He was not her sort. He was rough, tough, the sort of man Sara would normally steer clear of.

For a few moments Lucy felt extremely irritated but then she pulled herself together. Who was she to be so judgmental, and why should the idea irk her so? She was being stupid. Opposites did attract, and why should it not work for Charlie and Sara?

'Do you read much, Charlie?' Sara asked.

'Quite a bit,' he replied. 'Do you?'

'Yes, I do. I like period romances.'

'I like the old classics.'

Lucy got up to gather the dirty crockery. Much as she disliked herself for thinking it, she preferred Sara when she was having one of her tantrums or sick headaches. That she could tolerate, but this was something again.

CHAPTER 9

Another week of hard toil, another pay packet to weaken the spectre of Christmas without the basic trappings, and for Gerry Watson it was one more stepping-stone towards the shore. His children would now be able to open a few presents on Christmas morning, and the money might even stretch to a bottle of port. Another week's work and the outstanding bills could be paid, which would ease the pressure and allow Amy to begin with a clean slate at the butcher's and the grocer's.

Ben and Frank Coley were feeling pleased with the team's progress, and once the next trench was excavated and the pipes replaced they would be able to get on with the last phase on the main sewer at the far end of Lynton Road.

'We'll 'ave ter go eight feet down before we reach the brickwork,' Ben reminded his brother as they stood together in the saloon bar of the Mason's Arms. 'It'll need ter be a shutterin' job, an' we can't afford any balls-ups. It 'as ter be ready fer the brickies right after Christmas. The twenty-seventh, as a matter o' fact.'

''Ave we got any carpenters on our books?' Frank asked.

'That geezer Chubb told me 'e was a carpenter by trade,' Ben said, taking a swig from his glass of whisky.

Officially the pub did not open till five thirty, but Mick Johnson made an exception in the Coleys' case. Their workers were to be paid out in the public bar and they would feel duty bound to buy at least one drink before going home. Keeping in with Ben and Frank was no bad thing, the landlord considered, though his wife Freda did not feel as enthusiastic as he.

'They're a couple o' no-good bastards, if yer want my opinion,' she said plainly, 'an' that ganger they've got is as bad as them. 'E's an 'orrible git. 'E treats the poor blokes like slaves.'

'Yeah, but yer gotta remember the Coleys are on a tight schedule,' Mick explained. 'They're subbers, an' if they fall be'ind they don't get any more contracts. Besides, most o' those workers need a kick up the arse now an' again.'

'Don't talk stupid,' Freda replied angrily. 'They're men who've bin out o' work an' desperate enough ter take any job they can get.'

'Well at least they get decent wages,' Mick said defensively.

'Don't make me laugh,' Freda snorted contemptuously. 'Would you like ter work in a waterlogged trench shovelling clay fer fifteen bob a day, an' then find out at the end o' the week yer've bin charged two bob fer overall cleanin' an' anuvver shillin' fer the tea?'

'Who told yer that?' Mick asked quickly.

'Sammy Strickland.'

'Yer can't believe what 'e ses.'

'Well I do,' Freda said firmly. 'Anyway, why should 'e lie?'

Mick shrugged his shoulders as he threw the

bolts back and opened for business.

As the men filed into the public bar and lined up by the far table Ben and Frank Coley came round from the saloon. 'There's anuvver week's work available on the pipes, if yer up to it,' Ben announced with a dark smile. 'Then, if all goes well, we've got work for yer right up till the end o' December on the main sewers at the end o' the turnin'. So it's up ter you.'

Sharkey Lockwood came into the pub carrying a blue money bag in his huge fist. 'Right then, let's get you lot o' lazy gits sorted out,' he said, sitting down at the table.

Gerry nodded as he was handed his pay packet and immediately opened it to take out some silver coins. One pint then straight home, he told himself.

Danny Albury and Joe Lambert paired off for a game of shove-'a'penny while Roy Chubb stood with Gerry at the counter.

'That main sewer job'll be a bloody 'ard graft,' he remarked.

Gerry nodded. 'I've done a bit o' main sewer work,' he said. 'Yer gotta go down deep ter reach the roof o' the tunnel, an' the trench 'as ter be shuttered.'

'Yeah. I've done a bit o' shutterin' work,' Roy told him.

'I'd let Coley know,' Gerry suggested. 'If yer get the job it'll be a sight better than 'umpin' bloody great shovel-loads o' clay all day long.'

'I dunno,' Roy replied, stroking his chin.

'I do. Tell 'em,' Gerry pressed him. 'It'll mean a few extra shillin's in yer pay packet.'

107

Roy drained his glass. 'I'll bear it in mind,' he said as he made ready to leave.

At that moment Ben Coley ambled over. 'Do I remember you tellin' me you're a carpenter by trade?' he asked.

Roy nodded. 'That's right.'

'Ever done any shutterin' work?'

'We've just bin talkin' about that,' Gerry told him.

Coley gave him a cold stare and then turned back to Roy. 'Well 'ave yer or not?'

'Yeah, I 'ave,' Roy replied.

Coley put a pound note down on the counter. 'Get these two a drink, an' the same again fer me,' he ordered Mick. 'Listen, Chubb, that main sewer job's gonna require shutterin'. We'll pay yer an extra shillin' a day ter take care of it, OK?'

Roy nodded. 'Yeah, I'll do it,' he said, trying not to look too enthusiastic.

Ben Coley picked up his change and left the counter with a parting shot at Gerry. 'Keep yer trap shut an' yer might be around ter see 'ow it's done,' he said with a cruel grin.

Lucy and Mary took their children along with them to the tram depot at New Cross on Friday afternoon.

'I 'ope we're gonna be able ter carry the bloody fing,' Mary remarked.

'We'll manage. We'll take turns,' Lucy replied with gusto. 'We could even get two if they're not too 'eavy.'

'Can yer tell us where the foreman is?' Mary asked a uniformed tram driver.

'You ain't come fer a job, 'ave yer?' the be-whiskered man queried with a wide grin. 'We ain't 'ad a woman tram driver 'ere since the strike.'

'Nah. We've come ter see the foreman on private business,' Lucy told him.

'Yer'll be wantin' the supervisor,' the driver replied. 'See that office over there? If 'e's not in there, 'e'll be in the workshop. Trouble is yer never can find ole Winkle when yer need 'im.'

Lucy and Mary crossed the wide terminus, holding on to Sue and Gracie who were giggling together about the driver's whiskers.

Mary looked into the office. 'Mr Winkle?'

There was a loud guffaw from two of the occupants and a growl from the other. 'I'm Mr Winkless, the supervisor,' he said. 'What can I do for yer?'

''Ave yer got any old destination sheets ter give away?' Mary asked.

'Nah, I'm afraid we don't, not any more.'

'We know a woman who was given one two weeks ago,' she pointed out.

'Yeah, but that was then. We're not allowed to give 'em away any more.'

'Why's that, then?'

'Don't ask me, luv. It's just company policy.'

'What d'yer do wiv 'em then?' Lucy asked quickly.

'I dunno. It's not my department.'

'But you're the supervisor.'

'Look, I ain't responsible fer everyfing that goes on in this depot,' the man said irritably. 'I s'pose the sheets get sent back ter where they come from.'

'Well, fanks fer yer co-operation,' Mary said sarcastically.

As they tramped across the covered concourse the driver with the whiskers stood watching them. 'Did yer see ole Winkle?' he asked, chuckling.

'Yeah, an' we didn't get much of a response from 'im,' Lucy said sharply. 'I reckon 'e took offence at us callin' 'im Winkle.'

''Ave yer come fer ole sheets?' the driver asked.

'As a matter o' fact we 'ave,' Mary told him.

'Some'ow I thought you 'ad.'

'That was observant of yer.'

The driver looked around quickly then leaned a little closer to them. 'I gotta tell yer it got a bit out of 'and, the number o' people callin' in fer those sheets, an' the guv'nor 'ad ter put a stop to it,' he explained. 'I could see 'is point. There's trams comin' in an' out of 'ere all day long an' yer can't 'ave members o' the public turnin' it into a market-place. I tell yer what yer can do, though. If yer go down the alleyway at the side o' the depot an' go round the back yer'll see the workshop. If there's any sheets about they'll be stacked up by the workshop dustbins. An' fer Chrissake keep 'old o' them kids. It's no place fer them, nor you fer that matter.'

Ten minutes later two happy women and their children stepped on to a number 38 tram. 'Can we put these under the stairs?' Mary asked the conductor.

He gave her a grin. 'I thought they stopped givin' those fings away,' he remarked.

'So they 'ave, but Mr Winkle took pity on us,' Mary replied with a straight face.

Come storm, hail, or fireballs from heaven, it would be safe to assume that Mrs Black and her next-door neighbour Mrs Goodwright would be out in it, if only to keep in touch with what was going on in the street. Even on that Friday evening with the fog thickening, the two hardy souls stood chatting with their coat collars turned up and their hands thrust deep into their pockets. Visibility was down to a few yards, but they persisted with their sentry duty and were suitably rewarded.

'What's Mary Chubb got there?' Emmie Goodwright asked.

'I dunno, but Lucy Parry's got one as well,' Ada Black commented.

''Ere, Bert,' Emmie called into the passage. 'Come out 'ere a minute.'

Bert did as he was bid. 'What's up?'

'What's those fings them two've got under their arms?'

''Ow the bloody 'ell am I s'posed ter know?' Bert growled.

Emmie watched the two women go into Lucy's house. 'I'd love ter know what they were,' she said.

'Yeah, so would I,' Ada replied.

'Why don't yer come inside out of it,' Bert grumbled. 'Yer lettin' all the fog in.'

Emmie reluctantly gave up the watch, but promised herself she'd get to the bottom of the mystery before long.

Sammy Strickland had had a hard week. Three

times he had been close to getting a job and it was becoming frightening. On each occasion he had left his long-suffering wife Peggy sitting with her fingers crossed, and on each occasion she had been both deflated and angry when he came back with that by now familiar hangdog look on his angular face. It was unbelievable, she sighed to herself. Most of the men in the street and in the immediate area were unable to find one position to go after, let alone three. Sammy seemed to pick chances out of a hat, but for some reason he was never successful. The digging job was a prime example, but there were other jobs he might have landed, with a little decorum and a sprinkling of luck.

'What was it this time?' she asked.

'I was too old.'

'Too old?' she queried. 'Ter be a nightwatch-man?'

'Yeah. It bloody well upset me, I can tell yer.'

'An' that ovver job yer went for, they said you was too young.'

'Yeah. That was a nightwatchman's job too,' he replied, making himself comfortable by the fire.

'An' the ovver job? More bloody excuses.'

Sammy shrugged his shoulders. 'It ain't my fault, luv,' he said, putting on his bad-luck face. 'It seems I'm never gonna get a start. It's makin' me ill.'

The only thing that would make Sammy ill was if someone actually gave him a job, she thought. 'So yer too old, too young an'...'

'An' too bloody nice, that's my trouble,' he groaned.

'You could 'ave looked a bit more mean an' nasty when yer walked in the place,' Peggy told him.

'I did,' Sammy replied. 'I put on me worst face ever. As a matter o' fact I looked at me reflection in a shop winder before I went in an' frightened meself. Anyway, I never fooled 'em. Still, when yer come ter fink of it, yer wouldn't like me bein' a debt collector, now would yer? Not you. You're the kindest person ever. You're the first to 'elp anyone out an' yer don't brag about it, that's what really pleases me. Some people never stop goin' on about what they do, but not you.'

Peggy could not help but enjoy such silver-tongued flattery, and she leaned back in her chair. 'I've never bin one ter blow me own trumpet,' she remarked.

'That's what I bin sayin',' Sammy agreed. 'An' yer'd be upset if yer knew I was chasin' people up fer money who didn't 'ave a pot ter piss in.'

Peggy had to agree. 'Never mind, luv, somefing'll turn up,' she said consolingly. 'Now, what d'yer want fer supper? I got a slice o' brawn left in the cupboard...'

CHAPTER 10

The folk of Cooper Street could not say with certainty just how long the bootmender's shop had been there on the corner of the turning. Ada Black said that as far as she could recall it was there when she moved into the street, and she'd lived there for twenty-five years. Emmie Goodwright was a little more specific. 'Nah, it was later than that,' she declared. 'It opened up the year o' the armistice.'

'Are yer sure?'

'Yeah, 'cos I moved in 'ere in '15 an' it was a tripe an' onion shop then.'

'Nah. The tripe an' onion shop was round the corner in Lynton Road.'

'I don't fink so.'

'Well I do,' Ada said firmly. 'I remember goin' round there on Friday nights fer me farvver's supper. They used ter sell 'alf sheep's 'eads an' skate's eyeballs. Me ole dad loved skate's eyeballs.'

Peggy Strickland was drawn into the controversy while she was on her way to the market. ''Ere, Peg, when did that bootmender's open?' Ada asked her.

'About nine o'clock, same as usual,' she replied.

'Nah, I mean when did ole Staples start 'is business up?'

'Gawd only knows,' Peggy said, stroking her chin. 'My Sammy'll know. There ain't much 'e don't know about round 'ere.'

The speculation had arisen after Ada saw the notice that Jimmy Staples had pinned up in his shop window.

'I can't believe it,' Emmie said when Ada told her.

'Neivver can I,' Ada replied. 'Fings must be bad fer ole Staples ter call it a day.'

'I bet 'e's made 'is pile, the time 'e's bin 'ere,' Emmie remarked. 'I expect 'im an' Marfa'll end up in some nice little cottage in the country.'

Her prediction was way off the mark, and if the truth were known Jimmy and Martha Staples were trying to close down as quickly as possible without fuss and bother, not wanting to attract too much attention.

'They're sendin' a van ter take the stitcher,' Martha reported.

Jimmy nodded. 'They'll take the sheets o' leavver as well, I expect.'

'What about the rest o' the stuff?'

'There's nuffink werf floggin', 'cept me knives,' Jimmy told her, 'an' I'm keepin' them. I can still repair our shoes if I got me knives an' the last.'

Martha was assailed by a deep sadness as she handed him a mug of tea. Jimmy was a craftsman and his repairs had always stood up to the crucial tests, the games of street football and a week's toil on the cobblestoned dock quays, but now people in the area were finding it impossible to scrimp together enough money for boot and shoe repairs and using cardboard and folded news-paper instead to line their worn-out soles. The sales of leather goods had trickled almost to a halt, and the belts and handbags which Jimmy Staples sold as a sideline had all been returned to the makers at a distinct loss.

'Where's it all gonna end?' Martha sighed.

'Gawd only knows,' Jimmy said heavily as he threw the bolts on the shop door for the last time.

The Staples' one-time customers Ada and Emmie were basically kind people, and though they were under the erroneous impression that the bootmender and his wife were retiring to the country in comfortable circumstances they still felt that a little going-away present would be nice. Nothing much, maybe a set of the jugs or glasses which could be bought cheaply enough at any of the Sunday markets.

'It's too late,' Minnie Venners told her friends the following morning when they sounded her out. 'They've gone.'

'Already?'

'They must 'ave left last night,' Minnie explained.

'They could 'ave waited till we 'ad a chance ter say goodbye,' Ada said stiffly.

'Well good riddance then, that's what I say,' Emmie growled.

In truth the Staples would dearly have loved to say their goodbyes before leaving the business Jimmy had run for over thirty years, but try as they might they had found it impossible to satisfy all their creditors. They left Bermondsey for good, moving into a small flat in Walworth, and the following Monday Jimmy started work as a factory clogmaker with an old-established company near London Bridge.

'I'd say it was a bloody disgrace if you was to ask me,' Sammy Strickland remarked to Peggy when he returned home with the evening paper.

'What is?'

''Avin' ter go right up ter the Old Kent Road ter get a newspaper an' fags,' he replied as he took off his wet coat. 'Did yer know it's pissin' down out there?'

'Yeah, I can see,' Peggy said as she skimmed a film of fat off the mutton stew.

'There's only two shops in this street an' they're both boarded up,' Sammy went on. 'Surely someone can see the sense in openin' up one of 'em as a tobacconist, or a grocer's shop.'

'It's understandable, the way fings are. There's no money about.'

'Banks lend money ter start businesses up,' Sammy pointed out.

'Tell me somefing I don't know.'

'I could get a loan,' Sammy suggested confidently as he kicked off his sodden boots.

'Who'd be stupid enough ter lend you money, pray?'

'Any bank manager wiv 'alf a brain in 'is 'ead.'

'Don't talk tripe.'

Sammy assumed a superior air as he warmed his hands over the open fire. 'I'm talkin' sense, an' you'd agree wiv me if yer'd just shut yer gob long enough to 'ear me out.'

'Go on then, Mr Clever, I'm all ears,' Peggy said sarcastically.

'Yeah, I can see,' Sammy remarked with a grin. 'No, let's be serious fer a minute. I got a policy on me life an' it was took out more than forty years ago.'

'This is the first time I've 'eard of it,' Peggy replied, frowning.

'I'd fergot all about it till this mornin', ter tell yer the truth,' Sammy confessed.

'An' what made yer fink about it this mornin'?'

'It was when I was gettin' the paper,' he explained. 'While I was waitin' ter get served I 'eard this geezer tellin' the bloke be'ind the counter that shopkeepers could get a business loan if they 'ad some sort o' security. I got ter finkin' about those two boarded-up shops in the turnin' so I 'ad a few words wiv the papershop bloke. 'E told me the geezer 'e was talkin' to worked next door at the insurance agency. 'E said 'e advises people who wanna start up in business. As I was walkin' back 'ome it struck me that I've got security wiv that old insurance policy. It must be werf a fortune, considerin' 'ow old it is. I remember when me dad retired from the slaughter'ouse. 'E said it was a little somefing if I ever fell on 'ard times.'

'So yer got the idea o' usin' it as security against a loan,' Peggy reiterated. 'Would yer mind just tellin' me an' puttin' me out o' me misery. Fer what?'

'To open up one o' those shops.'

'Yeah, I'm already wiv yer there, but what as?'

'An oil shop.'

'An oil shop?'

'An' why not?' Sammy said indignantly. 'Just fink about it. No matter 'ow poor people are, they still try ter keep their 'ouses clean an' warm. I could sell the usual fings, such as whitenin' fer steps, dusters, mops an' bug tapers. Then there's paraffin o' course, turps an' nails an' tin tacks. There's no end to it. I could sell canes, there's certainly a need for canes round this area. A lot of oil shops sell mugs an' enamel teapots an' kettles. Just fink of it, Peg. The shop would never be empty, what wiv one fing an' anuvver.'

Peggy was becoming impressed. 'An' you'd serve in the shop all day, every day?'

'Too bloody true,' he told her with enthusiasm. 'I'd be as 'appy as a pig in shit.'

'Well in that case, me little porker, you should go an' take that policy up ter the insurance agency an' see 'ow much you can raise on it,' Peggy concluded.

The second phase of the Coley workings had been completed on time, and now less than two weeks before Christmas the main sewer excavation was about to start. On the evening of Friday the thirteenth Ben Coley and his brother Frank were making final preparations with Sharkey Lockwood in the saloon bar of the Mason's Arms. 'We'll need ter take on a few more men,' Frank recommended.

Ben nodded. 'Yeah, five or six should do it. Maitland's 'ave confirmed that they want the brickies ter make a start on Friday the twenty-seventh.'

'We'd better make it six then,' Frank said. 'There's no margin for error on this job, not if we're out ter get the big one.'

Sharkey had caught his warning glance and knew just what was expected of him. All the diggers had been retained for the main sewer job and Roy Chubb had been assigned the job of shoring up the workings, but it was going to be a tricky operation. The thick clay level had to be removed from around the crumbling brick tunnel in two phases, considering the depth of the workings, and with only six extra hands involved it would be far from easy. 'Couldn't we stretch it to eight or nine?' he suggested.

Frank Coley leaned across the table. 'Up till now we've taken these jobs fer peanuts, just ter get our foot in the door, an' we've made it pay by keepin' the labour costs to a minimum,' he said pointedly. 'Maitland's know the score. This is a government contract they've got, an' if they can complete on time they stand ter get the big one, the job o' renovatin' the 'ole sewer system in Bermon'sey an' Rovverhive. Tests an' inspections 'ave shown that it's crumblin' everywhere, an' winnin' the contract would earn them a fortune. So yer see, we're puttin' ourselves in a good bar-gainin' position. I've bin assured by the Maitland people that they'll give us all the work we can 'andle if we complete this job on time, an' at an improved contract price, so if we get an 'undred per cent from every man on the team we'll be fine.'

Sharkey nodded compliantly, hiding his anger. He knew that the men would work till they were exhausted, and the hundred or so feet of old sewer tunnelling would be uncovered on time. If not he would be held responsible, rather than Frank Coley and his six extra hands. It made no sense. They could afford to break even on this contract, considering the work which would come their way if they did – and at an improved rate. It was sheer bloody-mindedness, he fumed.

On that Friday morning Charlie Foden drew the last of his savings out from the post office, a grand total of two pounds ten shillings, and bought a small Christmas tree at the East Lane market. The trader tied it up and Charlie walked home to Cooper Street with it tucked under his arm. The remaining money wouldn't go very far, he thought, but it would certainly help the family through a very hard time.

'You shouldn't 'ave,' Lucy reproved him mildly, grateful for his kindness.

Charlie smiled awkwardly. His gesture had been prompted the previous evening when Sue clambered on to her father's lap and asked him to read her a story. George had chosen a seasonal tale, and as he turned a page the child spotted the coloured picture. 'Where's that?' she asked.

'Fairyland,' George replied.

'I'd like ter live in Fairyland.'

'An' the children all looked out of the window an' saw that the snow was fallin' 'eavily,' George read on.

'Why is there a tree in that 'ouse?' Sue asked him.

''Cos it's Christmas. It's a Christmas tree.'

'Why can't we 'ave a Christmas tree in our 'ouse?'

'Because in Fairyland they can go an' pick a tree from the forest but where we live people 'ave ter buy them,' George told her with a kiss on

122

her forehead.

'Can we buy a tree fer Christmas?'

'Not this Christmas, darlin'. Maybe next Christmas.'

'My friend Gracie's got a Christmas tree in 'er 'ouse,' Sue said in a sleepy voice. 'Gracie said 'er daddy bought it ter put the presents under. Will we 'ave presents?'

'If you're a very good gel,' her father replied softly.

Charlie caught the look of desperation on George's face as he glanced at Lucy and he was filled with anger. He got up, took his pipe from his pocket and walked out to the backyard for a smoke. It was little enough to ask for, he thought. The right of a man to provide for his wife and children by earning a fair wage. His pride in a profession, a trade or simple muscle power which put bread on the table, clothes on the family's backs and shoes on their feet. Yes, and a few little extras, such as a Christmas tree with one or two presents laid out beneath it.

'Are you all right, Charlie?' Lucy asked as she looked out of the scullery door. 'It's cold out 'ere.'

He tapped his pipe against the heel of his boot and looked up. ''As Sue gone ter bed?' he asked.

Lucy nodded. 'She was dead tired.'

'Is George OK?'

'Yeah, I fink so. 'E's settlin' 'er.'

Charlie stood up from the rickety old chair. 'While you was gettin' the tea ready George told me 'e'd 'eard that the Coleys were recruitin' again,' he said in a serious voice. 'It was Danny

Albury who told 'im. Don't let 'im go after the job, Lucy, or at least try an' talk 'im out of it.'

''E's not mentioned anyfing ter me,' she replied. 'Obviously I'd try ter stop 'im, but 'e's gettin' really worried now. 'E'll take anyfing ter get a few bob fer Christmas.'

'Fings'll turn out all right,' Charlie said quietly.

'You're a big 'elp,' Lucy replied.

Charlie felt his face colour slightly. 'I'm sorry,' he said, misunderstanding her.

'No, I mean it, Charlie,' she emphasised with a warm smile. 'Whenever I get ter feelin' low or a bit down in the mouth, you're there wiv a few kind words.'

'It's nice ter be appreciated,' he said, returning her smile.

Lucy reached out and touched his arm. 'It was a good day when you came ter stay,' she said with feeling.

For a moment time stood still as he looked steadily into her blue eyes. He made no attempt to hide his feelings, concentrated calmly in his molten gaze. Her physical presence was working on him like magnetism and he felt himself slowly being drawn into its field of power, where the invisible, ineluctable forces of life would bring them together, just as night followed day, as the sun climbed in the morning sky. Was she mocking him now, her eyes laughing, her mouth trembling at the corners to hold a smile at bay, or was she merely amused by the intensity of his large dark eyes? Whatever the truth, it made him feel warm inside as the momentary spell passed and he followed her back into the house.

CHAPTER 11

George came down the stairs and smiled briefly at Lucy. 'She's gone off ter sleep but she seems a bit 'ot ter me. I 'ope she ain't goin' down wiv anyfing.'

'I'll go up an' take a look in a while,' Lucy told him. 'Look, there's a few bob in the jar. Why don't you an' Charlie go out fer a pint?'

He shook his head firmly. 'I wonder you could even suggest it. We're gonna need every penny, especially after...'

'Look, there's no good 'arpin' on it,' she said bluntly.

'But I feel terrible about it,' he went on. 'I just don't know 'ow it 'appened.'

'Take the money an' 'ave a pint,' Lucy said with a note of impatience in her voice. 'There's anuvver week not touched yet. Yer might be lucky at the labour exchange next time. Some blokes are. Mrs Farr's son-in-law got a start last week.'

George nodded reluctantly and took the jam jar down from the dresser. 'I'll take the 'alf-crown,' he told her. 'That's if Charlie fancies goin' out.'

'Yer'd better ask 'im. 'E's sittin' in the parlour.' George seemed hesitant and Lucy gave him a firm look. 'Well go on then,' she sighed.

Charlie needed no persuasion and he grabbed his coat from the back of the door. The two men walked through the misty evening streets, past the boarded-up shops, and when they reached the Mason's Arms in Lynton Road they found the public bar unusually full. Ben and Frank Coley were sitting alongside Sharkey behind two tables which had been hastily pulled together, facing a line of men.

'What's goin' on?' Charlie asked the landlord as he waited to be served.

'They're takin' on a few extra workers,' Mick Johnson told him. 'It's fer the main sewer job startin' next week at the far end o' the turnin'.'

''Ow many are they lookin' for?' George asked.

'Six, as I understand.'

Freda Johnson came over and leaned on the counter. 'They paid the diggers off soon as we opened this evenin',' she said, 'but they made those poor gits wait around till just now.'

'It's nuffink ter do wiv us,' Mick reminded her.

'It looks bad, though.'

'What d'yer mean?'

'What I say,' Freda retorted sharply. 'It makes it look like we've encouraged those two ugly gits ter keep the men waitin' so they'd spend a few bob in 'ere.'

'Well they didn't, did they?' Mick growled back at her.

'Of course not. What did you expect?'

Charlie saw that there were at least a dozen men in line and the one at the front seemed to be arguing with the older Coley. 'Sixty or not I can still pull me weight,' he said indignantly.

'Sorry, try anuvver time,' Frank Coley told him.

The man mumbled something as he walked away and the men at the end of the line looked a

126

little more hopeful as they shuffled forward.

Charlie turned to say something to George Parry and saw the pensive look on his face. 'You ain't finkin' what I fink you're finkin', are yer?' he asked.

'What 'ave I got ter lose?' George replied. 'I can stick it till Christmas.'

''Ave you ever done any ditch diggin'?' Charlie asked him. 'Yer'll be chuckin' clods o' wet clay up out o' the trench an' by the end o' the day yer 'ands'll look like raw meat. It's a killer of a job.'

''Ave you ever done any ditch diggin'?' George countered.

Charlie shook his head. 'No I 'aven't, but I know those that 'ave. I saw the state they got in.'

George suddenly put down his glass of beer. 'Like I just said, what 'ave I got ter lose?' He walked off to join the line.

Charlie shook his head sadly as he leaned on the counter. There was nothing he could say or do, short of physically restraining the man. George would have to learn the hard way.

The line moved forward and more men were turned away. Four had been accepted and the last six in line realised that the odds had shortened to three to one.

'What experience 'ave you 'ad?' Ben asked the man at the head of the line.

'I've worked for Langhams, Mowlems an' Williams, general labourin',' the man replied.

'What was yer last job?'

The man stifled a cough. 'It was wiv Williams. On the new quay they've built at the Surrey Docks.'

'Williams subbed out that contract,' Ben informed him. 'Slaters done the job.'

'Yeah, I know, but I–'

'Sorry. Next one.'

Charlie had been watching the exchange and he felt sorry for the man as he shuffled off. Sharkey Lockwood was grinning evilly as he mumbled something to Frank Coley and the two laughed loudly.

'I rue the day Mick allowed that pile o' shite inter this pub,' Freda said close to Charlie's ear.

'That ganger seems a charmin' sort, I must say,' he replied.

''E's nuffink but a big bully,' the landlady remarked with distaste. 'It only wants someone ter stand up to 'im an' 'e'd run a mile.'

Charlie felt she was probably being a little naive but he nodded nevertheless. 'I don't doubt it.'

The man in front of George was taken on and Frank Coley closed the large notebook at his elbow. 'Right then, that's sorted,' he said.

George leaned his hands on the table. 'Can't yer make room fer one more?' he asked.

'What d'yer fink this is, a workmen's charity or somefink?' Coley growled.

'I can work as 'ard as the next man,' George persisted.

'I ain't disputin' that,' Coley replied. 'The books are full an' that's the end of it.'

'Can't yer put me down as a standby?' George asked him.

'Standby fer what?'

'In case any o' the ovvers don't turn up.'

'If yer wanna be a standby feel free,' Lockwood

128

cut in. 'Be at the workin's at seven thirty sharp an' if someone don't turn up you can ask ter take their place. Mind you, yer won't be alone, so don't expect ter get a start.'

'Wouldn't it be better ter put a few standbys down in the book?' George asked.

Frank Coley's face darkened. 'Don't you start tellin' us 'ow ter run our business,' he grated. 'Now piss off out of it.'

George hesitated as he searched for a reply and he suddenly felt Charlie's hand on his shoulder.

'There was no need fer that,' Charlie remarked, his wide eyes fixed on Frank Coley. 'What my pal said made sense, ter me at least.'

The older Coley returned the stare. He prided himself on being a good judge of men and he felt sure that this character's confidence was not just a front. After all, it wasn't every day of the week that he and his team would be confronted in such a way. 'Look, it might make sense ter you, pal, but it's not the way we do fings, OK?'

'It's your prerogative,' Charlie said quietly, 'but it don't cost much ter let a man retain a bit o' dignity.'

'Oh, I see,' Frank Coley replied with a smirk. 'Would you prefer us ter say, "Sorry, sir, try again next week"?'

'Well, it would sound a bit better than tellin' a bloke ter piss off after waitin' in line,' Charlie said calmly.

Sharkey Lockwood leaned forward over the table. 'Are you 'is keeper?' he asked, nodding his head towards George.

'I don't believe I was talkin' ter you,' Charlie

said dismissively.

'Well I'm talkin' ter you,' Sharkey stormed.

'Save that big mouth o' yours fer the diggin's,' Charlie told him, menace in his widening eyes.

Frank Coley laid his hand on Sharkey's arm and then got up out of his chair, motioning Charlie towards the counter. 'Look, I'm sorry if yer pal's upset by the way I spoke,' he said in a civil tone of voice, 'but it don't always sink in when we turn 'em down. Some of 'em can get stroppy, yer know.'

'Yeah, I can understand that,' Charlie acknowledged, 'but it don't take no longer ter be polite to 'em.'

Coley did not reply immediately, beckoning instead to Mick Johnson. 'Give me a drink, will yer, Mick, an' one fer this feller an' 'is pal.' Then he turned to face Charlie. 'I didn't get yer name, by the way.'

Once the introductions had been made Frank Coley invited them over to a spare table in the far corner of the bar. 'Let's sit awhile,' he suggested.

They made themselves comfortable and the contractor took a large gulp from his whisky and soda. 'An' what d'you do fer a livin'?' he asked.

'I'm in the docks,' Charlie replied.

'I understand it's a bit iffy at the moment,' Coley remarked.

'That just about sums it up,' Charlie agreed.

George took a quick swig from his pint. 'It's only one day a week, ain't it, Charlie?' he said.

'You'd do better workin' fer me,' Coley let fall with a smile.

'No fanks,' Charlie replied quickly. 'I wouldn't

be much good on a shovel. Now give me a crane-set ter load on to a lorry or a cargo o' wine ter store an' there'd be no 'oldin' me.'

'I don't mean diggin',' Frank said. 'I was finkin' more along the lines o' ganger. That's if yer've considered surrenderin' yer docker's ticket.'

'Well, I've got no sons or nephews ter pass it on to,' Charlie told him. 'At the moment the job's a waste o' time an' I 'ave bin tempted ter chuck it in.'

Frank Coley put down his drink and straightened up. 'Look, I'm gonna put me cards on the table,' he said finally. 'I was impressed by the way yer took yer pal's part, an' no less by the way you 'andled my ganger. Yer didn't let 'im ride roughshod over yer, though I should say in passin' that 'e won't ferget it. I fink you'd make a decent ganger yerself, an' I need anuvver one fer the workin's after Christmas. There's a big contract in the offin', providin' we don't mess up on the job we start next week. We'll be workin' on two sites at once. You'd control one an' Sharkey the ovver.'

''Old on a second,' Charlie urged him. 'I don't know the first fing about ditch diggin'.'

'What d'yer need ter know? It's somefing yer'd pick up wiv no trouble. Bein' a ganger ain't about wieldin' a shovel, it's all about 'andlin' men. I'm considered ter be a good judge of a bloke an' I'd say wivout fear o' contradiction that you'd be able to 'andle the men every bit as good as Sharkey. Better, in fact. A good ganger gets the best out of 'is crew an' that's what I need, the best effort I can get. It's crucial if we're ter make a go o' this new contract.'

'If I agreed, when would yer expect me ter start?' Charlie asked.

'Next week,' Coley replied. 'Yer'd spend the week wiv Sharkey ter find yer feet an' then yer'd be on yer own. We've gotta clear over seventy feet o' main sewer so that the bricklayers can set ter work repairin' it, an' if we can manage it on time we'll get the length o' River Lane ter sort out by the end o' January. I'll pay yer six quid a week an' a decent rise when we win the new contract. What d'yer say?'

Charlie looked steadily at Frank Coley and saw the hardness in the man's deep-set eyes. There was no charity being offered here, only an opportunist deal that served Coley's purpose. From what he had said the firm stood to make a lot of money, providing they could hit their targets. 'I'll accept your offer on two conditions,' he answered in a measured tone.

'I don't usually settle fer conditions,' Coley told him, 'but go on.'

'Firstly I can't start till Tuesday. I need ter get a leave of absence from the Dock Labour Board. Secondly, yer give my pal George a start on Monday.'

Coley's eyes narrowed and his jaw muscles tightened. 'That's out,' he replied sharply. 'I've got me quota an' there's no changin' it now.'

Charlie smiled. 'Considerin' what's openin' up for yer, one extra man's wages pales to insignificance, in my opinion. Anyway, it's bin nice talkin' ter yer, Frank. Sorry it didn't work out.'

Coley drained his glass and pulled a face as the

fiery spirit burned his throat. 'You'd throw a good opportunity away fer that reason?'

'Yeah I would.'

'Fer a pal?'

'George ain't exactly a pal. I lodge wiv the family.'

Coley shook his head slowly and his face relaxed. 'I gotta say George should consider you as a pal, an' fink 'imself lucky. All right, it's agreed.'

Charlie finished his own drink. 'You'll get a fair day's work out o' both of us, you can be sure,' he replied.

Lucy glanced up at the clock again and it did not go unnoticed by Sara, who was busy casting off stitches around the neck of a cardigan she was knitting. 'They're late,' she remarked. 'I do 'ope Charlie's not plyin' 'im wiv drinks. George never could drink that much.'

'Charlie's got no money ter waste,' Lucy said quickly. 'I expect they're just 'avin' a good chat.'

A few minutes later the two men came in and the women were bemused by their humorous expressions. 'What's bin goin' on?' Lucy asked.

'Yer'd better ask Charlie,' George explained with a sly grin.

'Maybe you should explain,' Charlie retorted. 'You started it off.'

'An' you ended it,' George said, grinning.

Lucy raised her voice. 'Will one of yer please tell us what's bin 'appenin'.'

Charlie followed George's lead by sitting down at the table. 'Well, it was like this...'

Sammy Strickland had lost no time in making preparations to become a trader and to that end he got the name of the insurance man from the paper shop before calling into the insurance agency next door. 'I'd like ter see Mr Beecham, please,' he requested.

'What is it related to?' the receptionist asked.

'Business.'

'Business?'

'Yeah. My business,' Sammy emphasised, getting a little irked by the young woman's attitude.

'Just one moment, I'll see if 'e's available.'

Twenty minutes later a fidgety Sammy was shown into a large office.

'Sorry for keeping you, Mr Strickland,' Beecham said. 'Now what can I do for you?'

'Yer might as well call me Sammy, considerin' we're gonna be associates,' the prospective trader said, smiling broadly.

'We are?'

'Yes sir.'

'Can you be a little more specific?'

''Ow much more specific do I need ter be?' Sammy said triumphantly as he took out the policy from his coat pocket. 'Cast yer meat pies on this.'

Beecham studied the document for a few moments before looking up at his visitor. 'Am I right in supposing that you're thinking of submitting this policy as security against a loan?'

'Right on the button, pal.'

Beecham winced noticeably at the unwonted

familiarity and studied the policy again. 'It was issued in 1880, fifty-five years ago,' he remarked.

'Yeah. Me farvver gave it ter me before 'e snuffed it,' Sammy told him. ''E said it'd come in 'andy one day.'

'Can you remember what year that was?' Beecham asked.

'What, when 'e give us the policy, or when 'e snuffed it?'

'When he gave you the policy and when he died.'

'Now let me see.' Sammy pulled on his bottom lip. 'I remember it 'cos it was me twenty-first birfday.'

'When your father died?'

'No, when 'e gave me the policy. It was a birfday present, so me dad said.'

'And how old are you now, Mr Strickland?'

'Fifty-five.'

'That would be thirty-four years ago.'

'Yeah, that sounds about right,' Sammy said, frowning with confusion.

'Now what year was it when your father died?' the insurance man enquired.

'Er, 1914.'

'Twenty-one years ago.'

'Look, I'm gettin' all confused wiv these dates,' Sammy complained.

'I'm sorry, Mr Strickland, but I'm trying to ascertain who's been responsible for the premiums.'

'The payments, yer mean?'

'Exactly.'

'Well, it wasn't nuffink ter do wiv me,' Sammy

135

said quickly. 'I just took it ter be a present like me ole man said. I mean ter say, yer not expected ter pay fer yer own presents, now are yer?'

'Well, if your father kept up the payments until he died all well and good. It would be worth something,' the agent explained. 'But I have a nasty feeling that the premiums were not paid, which makes the policy not even worth the paper it's printed on.'

'Oh my good Gawd!' Sammy gasped. 'That connivin' ole bastard. That's why 'e gave it ter me, 'cos 'e couldn't afford ter pay it.'

'Look, I think it might be better if I keep this policy for the time being,' the agent said. 'I'll write you out a receipt for it. Give me a week and I should have some news, one way or the other. Just book another appointment for this time next week. The receptionist will arrange it.'

Sammy left the office feeling deflated, and when he got home he slumped in the armchair. 'When yer down, yer down,' he groaned. 'I've bin sittin' on that policy fer thirty-four years an' not a penny's bin paid on it all that time.'

'So it can't be used as security?' Peggy queried.

'The insurance man told me that if me farvver paid the premiums till 'e died then it would be werf a few bob,' Sammy explained, 'though it still wouldn't be enough ter stand as security against a business loan. But me an' you know very well that my ole farvver was as tight as a nun's arse. Me poor ole muvver struggled till the day she died. There was never any extras fer 'er, Gawd rest 'er soul. Nah, that stingy ole bastard gave the policy ter me so 'e wouldn't be responsible fer it.

I can just imagine 'im finkin', let 'im pay fer it, 'e's the one who'll benefit.'

'I wish the ole git 'ad reminded us ter keep up wiv the payments,' Peggy remarked.

''Ere, steady on. That's my dad yer talkin' about,' Sammy said with a big smile.

CHAPTER 12

Charlie Foden hadn't envisaged much trouble getting a leave of absence and he was right. 'As long as yer keep yer dues paid,' the union official reminded him. 'One less standin' on the line every mornin' gives anuvver poor bleeder a chance of a scratch.'

Charlie left the office in Tooley Street and immediately bumped into Fred Wilson, his friend from the men's hostel.

''Ow the bloody 'ell are yer, Charlie?' Fred asked. 'I ain't seen yer around.'

Charlie told him what had happened since their last meeting and Fred pulled a face. 'Yer gotta be orf yer 'ead workin' fer those no-good bastards,' he growled. 'After all I told yer. Some people never learn.'

Charlie put his arm round Fred's bony shoulders. 'Come on, pal, let's walk up ter the café,' he said, grinning.

The older man was quick with advice as they sat sipping huge mugs of sweet tea. 'Yer gotta let the men see yer no pushover,' he stressed. 'But yer gotta be fair wiv 'em too. They'll sum it all up. Sometimes, when yer back's fair breakin' an' yer arms are done in, a five-minute break comes as a godsend. Sometimes yer gotta be 'ard too, Charlie. Yer might spot a bloke who should never 'ave got the job in the first place. Yer better finishin' 'em up before they end up killin' themselves, or somebody else.'

'It's a shutterin' job, main sewers.'

Fred pulled a face. 'Sewer work can be dangerous, Chas, so watch out,' he warned. 'Make sure the feller doin' the shutterin' knows 'is onions, an' keep the timbers checked fer slippage. I've seen men buried under tons o' clay, 'ad ter dig 'em out, so don't take any chances. If I know the Coleys they'll go the cheapest way, an' that means no steel clamps, only timbers. It just means yer gotta be extra careful.'

Charlie smiled gratefully. 'Yer've bin a big 'elp, Fred,' he told him. 'I'm goin' in green.'

'You'll be OK. Just remember what I said,' Fred urged him. 'One fing more before yer shoot off, watch that ganger Sharkey Lockwood. I know quite a bit about 'im. 'E'd shop 'is own muvver fer a few bob. 'E's a bully, an' 'e'll pick on anyone 'e knows won't stand up to 'im. As a matter o' fact 'e used ter wrestle at the baths but 'e wasn't all that good. Before that 'e fancied 'imself as a boxer but I can tell yer now, 'e's got a glass chin. That's why 'e turned ter wrestlin'.'

Charlie smiled. 'That's somefing I'll keep in mind, Fred,' he said.

'I 'ope yer do, ole sport,' Fred replied.

That morning the main sewer diggings were being scratched over, with the top layer of soft soil soon removed. George Parry was expecting a very hard day, and after talking to Roy Chubb next door he had rubbed Vaseline into his hands, bandaged up the palms and then put on a pair of woollen gloves with the fingers cut away. He felt as prepared as he would ever be and prayed he would be able to last the first day out, remembering that Roy had said the first day was the killer.

Sharkey smiled at the sight of George wearing his mittens as he struggled into his boiler suit. 'I see we're lookin' after our 'ands, then,' he remarked sarcastically. 'Playin' the pianner ternight, are we?'

George bit back a suitable reply and merely smiled, but Sharkey was not finished. 'I want yer ter pair up wiv Wally Coates,' he said. ''E'll show yer the ropes.'

While they were coming out of the shed Roy Chubb managed to pass on Joe Lambert's warning that Coates was a stool-pigeon for the Coleys, and George resolved to be careful as he set to work. He was dwarfed beside the giant Wally, who handled a pickaxe like a child with a toy. 'Mind yerself,' were the only words he uttered all morning, along with a few mumbled orders for George to remove the soil he had loosened.

The new recruit worked as steadily as he could, knowing that he had to pace himself or be exhausted by lunchtime. He was pleased that his hands felt reasonably comfortable beneath their protection and he ignored the face-pulling of Coates, who seemed to find the mittens amusing.

''Ow yer doin'?' Roy asked as they scrambled out of the trench for the morning tea break.

'Apart from me back I'm fine,' George replied.

'Yer'll get used to it,' Roy said supportively.

'Swing the shovel from the shoulders – it'll ease yer back off.'

All too soon the men were back in the trench and by lunchtime they had made good progress.

''Ow's it goin'?' Ben Coley asked when Sharkey walked into the hut.

'No problems,' Sharkey replied as he picked up the mug of coffee Ben had made.

'Who yer gonna get rid of?' Ben enquired.

Sharkey shook his head. 'I know Frank wanted a space made fer that Parry geezer, but I ain't 'ad reason ter kick any o' the ovvers out, not yet anyway. They've all got their 'eads down.'

'Well, yer better get it sorted before Frank gets 'ere. 'E's due at two o'clock,' Ben reminded him.

'If it was left for me I'd out Parry,' Sharkey growled. 'The man's 'andlin' the shovel like some ole pouf. I can see Wally slowly gettin' the needle wiv 'im.'

'Parry stays,' Ben said firmly. 'An' tell that big gorilla ter keep off 'is back.'

Sharkey ambled out to the diggings and looked along the line of workers, all busy and now down to their waists in the trench. He spotted Gerry Watson, and with a sly grin he walked over to stand directly above him in the small gap between the workings and the growing pile of thrown soil. The young man swung a laden shovel and the earth landed on the ganger's feet. 'Sorry, boss. Didn't know yer was standin' there,' he said quickly.

'I'm big enough ter be seen,' Sharkey scowled.

'Yeah, but–'

'Don't start arguin',' the ganger sneered.

'That's the trouble wiv you, yer don't know when ter button that big trap o' yours.'

Gerry did not understand the reason for Sharkey's antagonism but he was aware that he had got off on the wrong foot from the start and knew that it was only a matter of time before things came to a head. This seemed like the moment, and with a show of pluck he drove the blade of the shovel into the loose soil and stood upright, his head tilted back to meet Sharkey's stare. 'I fink yer must 'ave got out the wrong side o' the bed this mornin',' he said. 'There's bin no damage done.'

The men near Gerry gritted their teeth and carried on working, knowing that he had over-stepped the mark.

Sharkey leaned forward over the young man. 'I 'ad you marked down fer a loud-mouthed git an' I wasn't wrong. You're paid ter work, not keep spoutin' yer bloody mouth off.'

Gerry knew that it was useless arguing with the big ganger. Any further remarks on his part could cost him physically, as well as in his pocket. He shrugged his shoulders and made to scramble out of the trench.

'Where d'yer fink you're goin'?' Sharkey growled.

'Yer want me out of 'ere, don't yer?'

'I'll tell yer when I want yer out o' there.'

Gerry reached for his shovel once more. 'I'll get back ter work, then.'

'Don't you ever listen?' Sharkey snarled hatefully. 'I'll tell yer when yer work, I'll tell yer when yer take a break, an' in your case I'll tell yer

143

when yer can take a piss.'

Gerry clenched his hands into two tight fists, dearly wanting to jump out and attack the man, but he knew that he would stand no chance. Better to keep cool and make a dignified exit, he decided. He quickly clambered out the other side of the trench and unbuttoned his boiler suit, glaring at Sharkey across the divide. 'OK, you win,' he said calmly.

'Put yer gear in the shed an' piss off, an' be quick about it,' the ganger shouted.

Gerry Watson rubbed his sore hands together and turned his back on the workings. There would be very few presents for the kids this Christmas, he thought regretfully as he made his way home, but at least Ellie had managed to get them a toy each from the market last Saturday.

On Monday morning Lucy went next door with Sue and sat chatting with Mary while the children played together.

'I've 'ad those sheets in soak fer a few days,' Mary told her. 'I've stuck a load o' salt in the water ter 'elp loosen the paint.'

'When we gonna start peelin' 'em?' Lucy asked.

'We could make a start ternight, if yer can manage it,' Mary replied.

'I'll be in soon as I can,' Lucy said. 'George'll get Sue off ter bed. 'E's better at it than me, anyway.'

''E might not be, not ternight,' Mary warned her. 'The first night my Roy got 'ome from the diggin's 'e just flopped in the armchair an' couldn't move. I 'ad ter give 'im 'is tea on a tray.'

'Yeah, I've not stopped finkin' about 'ow George is gettin' on,' Lucy said, sighing. 'Don't get me wrong, 'e's strong enough, but ditch diggin' ain't the same as wrappin' parcels, is it?'

'Don't worry, Roy'll keep an eye on 'im, I'm sure.'

'Charlie's startin' there tomorrow.'

'Yeah, so yer said.'

Mary had always considered herself to be fairly perceptive and recently she had noticed a slight change in Lucy's voice whenever she mentioned Charlie. It was hardly tangible, but there was a new enthusiasm there. She talked about him as if she was discussing a member of the family, Mary thought, but then a lodger who ate with them and shared their home would grow to seem like one of the family. 'The kids are all right fer a minute,' she said. 'Let's show yer those sheets.'

The two women went out into the tiny yard which was almost filled by the old tin bath and Mary lifted up the edge of one of the sheets. For a few moments she picked at the thick rubbery black paint and only succeeded in stripping off a small sliver. 'It's still not soaked enough,' she sighed.

'Did yer tell Mrs Venners we got the sheets?'

'Yeah. She said ter let 'em soak in salt water fer a few days, an' that's what I done.'

'Did she say 'ow long it took 'er ter strip the paint off?'

'Well, she did say it wasn't easy.'

''Ow long did it take 'er, Mary?' her friend coaxed her.

'She reckoned about a couple o' weeks.'

'Just ter get the paint off round the bloody edges?' Lucy said disbelievingly.

'As a matter o' fact, she ended up strippin' the 'ole lot off,' Mary told her reluctantly. 'Apparently she took one o' the bundles up ter that pawnbroker's in New Cross and 'e opened the parcel. Gave 'er a right mouthful, so she said. Anyway, once all the paint's off the linen'll iron up lovely. At least we'll 'ave a couple o' pairs o' new sheets.'

Lucy looked reluctant but she shrugged her shoulders. 'If we're ever gonna get them done we need ter start now,' she said.

'Well, come on then.'

'Shall we 'ave a cuppa first?'

'A good idea.'

While Mary was in the scullery making the tea Lucy sat by the fire, watching the two children playing in a corner with Gracie's cardboard box of toys. Sue was intrigued by a rag doll she had just found amongst them and Gracie was trying hard to put a vest on one of her small china babies. The toy's face was scratched and one eye and an arm were missing but Gracie spoke to it gently, transported to a world of make-believe where its kind caught cold, cavorted wide-eyed and talked back. The dolls were ancient, damaged and falling to pieces and Lucy smiled sadly. There would be very few replacements or additions to the cardboard box this Christmas, she thought. There was a small Christmas tree standing in her parlour, though, decorated with paper chains and a few sprigs of holly.

'There we are,' Mary said cheerfully as she

came into the room and set down a laden tea tray.

The children came over to the table and Mary gave them each a cup of milky tea with a chocolate biscuit. 'Now don't spill it,' she warned.

Outside the temperature was dropping and snow clouds were gathering, and as Lucy sat back in the armchair and sipped her tea she suddenly chuckled.

'What's tickled you?' Mary asked.

'I was just finkin'. 'Alf an hour out there in the yard pickin' at those sheets an' our fingers'll be droppin' off.'

'Yeah, we do time fings right, don't we,' Mary grinned.

'I reckon they'd be better laid out in the sun ter soften. Anyway, we won't get much time ter spend on 'em if we get that key job, will we?'

'Yeah. Ada Black was s'posed ter call this mornin' if she 'eard anyfing,' Mary reminded her.

The two children finished their tea and walked out of the parlour each carrying a doll, prompting Mary to ask them where they were going.

'We're takin' our dollies fer a walk,' Gracie told her.

'Ask a silly question,' Mary said to Lucy with a shake of her head.

Gracie led the way into the scullery and peeked through the net curtains at the filled bathtub. 'Shall we bath the dollies?' she suggested.

Sue's face lit up at the prospect and she hunched her shoulders excitedly as Gracie put a finger to her mouth and gently lifted the door

147

latch. Undeterred by the cold the two girls set about dipping the dolls into the icy water. Sue's doll became entangled in the sheeting and as she pulled on it the arm came off in her hand. Gracie reached further into the bath trying to pluck it up and only succeeded in soaking her dress.

'I'll get it,' Sue told her as she moved round the tub.

Gracie pulled the sheeting aside to help and Sue was immediately drenched. Suddenly the whole thing ceased to be an adventure, and with the two dolls back on dry land two very wet and by now very cold children hurried into the warmth of the house.

'Oh my good Gawd!' Mary gasped. 'Just look at yer both. Yer'll catch yer death o' cold. Get them clothes off.'

'You've bin very naughty,' Lucy said sharply.

It was not long before the two children were warm and dry, wrapped in bath towels in front of the fire.

'That's the trouble wiv leavin' it there full o' water,' Mary said, sighing.

'Yeah, well, it's only natural that kids would wanna play wiv the water,' Lucy replied supportively.

'I really dunno what we should do about it,' Mary said, stroking her chin.

'Nah. It's awkward, really.'

'I s'pose we could let Mrs Venners 'ave the sheets.'

'Yeah, I s'pose so,' Lucy replied, trying not to sound too enthusiastic.

'We won't 'ave much time, anyway.'

'Not really.'

'Is that settled, then?'

Lucy nodded casually, but she felt relieved inside. 'I don't fink I'd 'ave bin able ter bluff it out at the pawnbroker's,' she remarked.

Mary chuckled. 'Nah, me neivver.'

'Yer still OK about that key job, though, ain't yer?'

'Course I am,' Mary replied quickly as she reached for the teapot.

Lucy sipped her fresh tea and then looked up at Mary. 'I was just finkin',' she said. 'As far as I understand it, those key jobs are fer little offices where yer let yerself in an' out before they come ter work in the mornin's.'

'So?'

'Well, why can't the work be done in the evenin' instead?'

'There's no reason as far as I can see.'

'We could do a job each in the evenin's, providin' the fellers don't mind lookin' after the kids fer an hour or two.'

Mary nodded. 'If that scatty mare Ada does come over we could go after the job an' see if it'd work out doin' it that way. If it does we could look fer anuvver one.'

Lucy put down her teacup, hoping that Mary was not going to have any second thoughts about the original money-making idea. 'Want me ter give yer an' 'and takin' them sheets out of the bath?' she offered.

'Would yer?' Mary replied gratefully. 'I'm gonna be glad ter see the back o' the bloody fings, ter tell yer the trufe.'

CHAPTER 13

George Parry came home that evening from his first day at the diggings looking exhausted and hollow-eyed, and when Sue came running up to him as she always did he found it painful bending to lift her up into his arms.

Lucy let the child hug him for a few moments then took her from him. 'Daddy's very tired, so you be a good little gel an' let 'im 'ave a rest,' she told her.

As George washed his hands in the soapy water Lucy had made ready for him he winced painfully.

''Ow did it go, luv?' Lucy asked as she stood over the gas stove stirring the gravy.

He gave her a hard look. The cake of Sunlight soap was stinging his raw hands, his back was aching badly, and what with the sniggering he had had to endure from his work partner throughout the day, he had just about had enough. 'It's a job,' he answered flatly.

'Yer must be dead tired,' Lucy said kindly. 'You go in an' get warm by the fire an' I'll get yer a nice cuppa.'

Normally George would have been grateful for the thought, but tonight he felt irritable and utterly jaded and he walked out of the scullery without another word.

'Come an' sit 'ere by the fire, luv,' Sara told him

151

as she got out of her armchair. 'You must be dead tired.'

George gave her a weak smile and flopped down heavily.

'Look at yer poor 'ands,' Sara said, tutting. 'They look raw.'

He glanced down at them for a second or two and nodded. 'They'll 'arden up after a few days.'

Lucy came into the parlour with a mug of tea. 'There you are,' she said. 'Yer'll feel better after this.'

George sipped the tea, becoming aware of Sara staring into the mantelshelf mirror as she pulled on her mousy hair. In his current frame of mind he felt like telling the silly bitch to sit down, but he gritted his teeth instead and stared down at the glowing coals.

'George?'

'Yeah?'

'I've bin tempted ter get Lucy ter do me a perm,' she announced.

George looked up at her. 'Yer 'air's all right as it is,' he told her without enthusiasm.

'It's not. Just look at it.'

George was not going to let himself get dragged into a conversation about hairstyles and he shrugged his shoulders. 'Please yerself,' he replied abruptly.

'I will,' Sara said with spirit.

George gave his sister a quick glance. What was the matter with her, he wondered? It must be something to do with that church committee. 'Are yer goin' out ternight?' he asked.

Sara nodded. 'I've got a church outin' meetin','

she said importantly.

'Will the vicar be goin'?'

'No,' Sara replied quickly. 'Why d'yer ask?'

'No reason, 'cept you said 'e was a nice bloke who took an interest in all the church functions.'

'Well I've 'ad good reason ter change me mind,' Sara told him coldly. ''E's left the church – well, our church, that is. 'E ran off last week wiv one o' the deaconesses from St Jude's.'

'I'm sorry,' George replied, trying not to smile at the expression on his sister's face.

'There's nuffink ter be sorry about,' Sara said offhandedly. 'It's no skin off my nose, but I 'ave ter say it does reflect on the good name of the church.'

'Yeah, I s'pose so,' George sighed as he eased his aching back in the armchair.

Sara finally finished twiddling with her hair and sat down facing him. 'You look dead beat,' she remarked.

'Tea'll be in five minutes,' Lucy announced, putting her head round the door.

'Where's Charlie?' George asked.

'Up in 'is room,' Sara replied as she fingered her hair once more. Charlie would like her hair shortened, she felt sure. He was a man of few words, no doubt stemming from being alone so much. But he was responsive when drawn out and his opinions made good sense. He was a man she could suffer, given the chance, and she wanted to believe that he felt the same. She must get Lucy to fix her hair, and maybe she could wear the dress that her sister-in-law said made her look shapely. At the time Lucy only said that to turn her off the dress, but things had changed. She wanted to look shapely, wanted to be seen, and noticed. She wanted Charlie to notice her, make her feel a real woman, not a predictable fixture in her brother's home.

When the evening meal was over George sat chatting to Charlie while Sara helped Lucy with the washing up.

'It got to a stage when I wanted ter crown 'im wiv the shovel,' George growled. 'Apparently 'e's a Coley man. All the news goes back via 'im.'

'I know it's difficult, but yer gotta shut yer mind ter the piss-takin',' Charlie advised him. 'When that new contract starts, if it starts, there'll be better wages fer a kick-off. OK, it's not the sort o' job any of us would normally do, but fings are tight. There's millions out o' collar an' anybody wiv a job ter go to must consider themselves lucky.'

'Well I don't feel lucky,' George grumbled. 'At this moment I feel like I'm gonna break in 'alf.'

'Give it a few days an' yer'll feel a little more human,' Charlie said, smiling.

'Yeah, at least it's not fer ever.'

Sara came back into the parlour and gave Charlie a weak smile. 'I'm due at the church at eight o'clock,' she told him. 'I'm worried about the fog. It seems ter be comin' down thick.'

'Do you 'ave ter go out ternight?' George asked her.

'I do really,' she replied. 'It's a very important meetin'. Decisions 'ave ter be taken ternight. We can't just leave it.'

'Would yer like me ter walk along wiv yer ter

the church?' Charlie suggested.

Sara shook her head. 'I couldn't expect yer ter go out on a night like this, just fer me.'

Charlie smiled indulgently. Sara certainly knew how to twist her words. 'Gimme a shout when yer ready,' he told her.

At ten minutes to eight Charlie offered Sara his arm as they stepped out of the house on to the damp, greasy pavement. It was something she had not experienced since her youth. John Balcombe, it was. She was eighteen and he two years older. They were getting close, to the extent of walking out arm in arm, but her mother felt that she was too young to form a lasting attachment with any boy, however honourable his intentions. John Balcombe tried to overcome her mother's resentment and Sara's own problems of divided loyalty, but one evening the young man's anger exploded and he walked away, leaving the old lady smiling with satis-faction. She had known all the time that he wasn't the one for her vulnerable daughter, and nor were any of the other young men who dared to throw their hats into the ring.

'It's nice of yer ter see me ter the church,' Sara said now.

'It's OK,' he replied with a mischievous smile. 'After all, it can be a bit scary on a foggy night. The old imagination can play tricks, like seein' some dark character steppin' out o' the fog in front of yer brandishin' a carvin' knife.'

'Don't, Charlie. Yer scarin' me,' Sara said in a childish tone of voice as she took the opportunity to grip his arm more tightly.

They crossed the main road and walked through the church gardens to the huge oaken door, where Charlie took his leave.

'Enjoy the meetin',' he said.

'Fanks, Charlie.'

'Look, if yer've got any idea when yer gonna be finished I could call back for yer,' he suggested.

Sara shook her head. 'It's all right. One o' the men lives in Lynton Road an' 'e'll walk back wiv me. Fanks anyway, though.'

Charlie made his way back to Cooper Street deep in thought. For the past few days Sara had been extra pleasant to him. He had put her initial reserve down to natural mistrust, and the difference now had begun to concern him. He could recognise the signs and felt that she was making a play for him in her own individual way. The sly glances, the hanging on his words, little tokens that warned him to be careful. In retrospect it had been foolish of him to walk Sara to the church, but he knew that had he not offered George would have, and tonight he was in no fit state to leave his chair.

In the house, Lucy sat down by the fire and kicked off her shoes. 'Sara seems ter like Charlie, don't yer fink?' she said.

George nodded. 'I 'ope she don't go readin' anyfing into 'im takin' 'er ter the meetin',' he replied. 'Charlie's a loner, an' there was no ulterior motive, I'm sure.'

'No, of course not,' Lucy agreed. 'Though yer gotta understand Sara's position. She's on 'er own, same as Charlie, an' she must feel it at times. An' let's face it, Charlie's an attractive

156

man, an' 'e keeps 'imself respectable.'

'What about you?' George asked suddenly. 'Do you find 'im attractive?'

'I've never took that much notice, really,' she lied.

George looked at her closely. ''Ave I changed lately?' he asked.

'What d'yer mean, changed?'

'What I said, changed.'

'D'yer mean since yer've bin out o' work?'

'Yeah.'

'No, I don't fink so,' Lucy replied, ''cept for bein' a bit edgy at times, which is quite natural, what wiv the worry o' providin' fer the family an' everyfing.'

George shifted uncomfortably in his chair. 'Yer don't fink I've bin neglectin' yer lately, do yer?'

'Nah, of course not.'

'It 'as bin a few weeks now since we … you know.'

'George, I've bin too worried an' tired lately ter fink o' that,' Lucy said quickly.

He nodded towards the small Christmas tree standing in a china pot by the window. 'It's little fings that get to a man when 'e's on the floor. Yer feel like a failure fer not bein' able ter provide, an' then somefing like that 'appens.'

'Like the lodger bringin' 'ome a Christmas tree?' Lucy said with irritation. 'Fer God's sake, George, it was only a little gift, fer Sue mainly. You remember when she was sittin' on yer lap an' you was readin' to 'er. You 'ad ter tell 'er we wouldn't be 'avin' a tree this year an' it must 'ave got to 'im. 'E's a kind man, luv.'

'Yeah, an' I appreciate 'is thought, but–'

'Look, I've 'eard enough, so don't keep goin' on, George,' she said in exasperation. 'Yer feelin' sorry fer yerself an' it's showin'.'

'No I'm not,' he retorted.

'Look, let's stop right now, before we get into an argument,' Lucy suggested. 'I'm gonna make a pot o' tea.'

George rested his head back against the armchair and closed his eyes in an effort to think clearly. Lucy had always been rather demanding in bed and their love life up until recently had been very good, he thought. But it had cooled now and noticeably so. Neither of them had seemed very keen to initiate anything and it had reflected in their day-to-day lives. Gone were the little endearments, the sweet nothings, the looks that passed between them after a night of love, and in their place was an edginess, a reluctance to sit together chatting in the evenings, and now they had a way of turning their backs on each other when they climbed into bed.

Any further thoughts were quickly quashed when Sue came bounding into the parlour. 'Daddy read me a story,' she demanded.

George opened his eyes and straightened himself in the armchair before taking his daughter on to his lap. 'Right now, let's see,' he said with a large yawn.

She leaned back against him, her face turned up to his as he opened the nursery rhyme book and began with the misfortune of Humpty Dumpty.

'This one next,' the child urged, her hands on the pages.

'Don't be in such a rush,' George told her more forcefully than he intended, and it made her pull a face. 'Right then. Jack an' Jill…'

Sue took the book from him and closed it as she slid from his lap. The nursery rhyme she wanted to hear next was on another page. With the book under her arm she made for the door and turned briefly, giving him a look which was like a spear through his heart. He was failing them all: Lucy, Sue, and even Sara, whom he found difficult to talk to lately. The worry and degradation of being made redundant had got to him, and that day in the trench he had felt like an imbecile beside the giant Wally Coates and his silent sneering. He detested the man, the job and the exploitation of it all, but there was nothing he could do about it, except try to leave his frustrations and anger at the diggings.

Lucy stirred the tea slowly, her thoughts centred around Charlie and the effect he had had on her since his arrival. He was hardly out of her mind and it troubled her. Making his bed, even just being in his room, conjured up romantic fantasies, and she knew that if she was not careful things could very soon get out of hand. All Charlie needed was a little encouragement and he would respond, she felt sure. His eyes lingering covetously on her was proof enough, as were his efforts to please.

He had shown her without one word that he desired her and it made it all the more exciting.

Late that evening Ada Black knocked at Mary Chubb's front door. 'I know it's a poxy night ter be out but I 'ad ter come an' see yer, gel,' she began as she was shown into the cosy parlour. 'There's a key job goin' at Dolan's in Tooley Street an' I only found out this evenin'. It's a small office next door ter the post office. I found out from the man in the tobacco shop opposite when I 'anded my key in. 'E 'olds the keys fer a lot o' the jobs along there. Apparently the last cleaner wasn't suitable an' they gave 'er the push. Don't ask me why, I never enquired. Anyway it's yours, if yer want it.'

'Want it? Course I want it,' Mary replied with a grin. 'Who do I 'ave ter see about gettin' took on?'

Ada sat down by the fire and puffed as she loosened the top button of her thick coat. 'Go round ter Dolan's at ten o'clock termorrer mornin'. The bloke'll be expectin' yer.'

'I'm very grateful, Ada,' Mary said. 'Can I get yer a cuppa?'

'Yeah, why not? Where's Roy, by the way?'

''E's upstairs tryin' ter settle Gracie,' Mary told her. 'I expect 'e's fast asleep 'imself by now. 'E was absolutely bushed when 'e got in ternight.'

'George next door started work there terday, didn't 'e?' Ada queried.

'Yeah. I saw 'im comin' down the street this evenin'. 'E looked all in as well.'

'I don't doubt it,' Ada remarked with a down-turned mouth. 'Those Coley bruvvers are bloody slave-drivers. You earn yer corn workin' fer that pair of ugly bastards.'

'Yeah. I can tell by the state o' Roy when 'e gets in at night. Right then, let's get that kettle on.'

Ada stretched her legs out in front of the fire as Mary came back into the parlour. 'Once yer get yerself sorted out at Dolan's yer might be able ter wangle it like I do,' she said.

'Wangle it?'

'Yeah, go in ter please yerself, like me. Sometimes I do the cleanin' in the evenin's an' sometimes in the mornin's. It makes no difference ter them, as long as the offices are clean an' shipshape before they get in.'

'That sounds a good idea.'

The two sat sipping their tea by the roaring fire and suddenly Mary's face broke into a grin. ''Ere, yer don't know if Mrs Venners fancies any more tram sheets, do yer?' she asked.

'I'm sure she would,' Ada told her. 'She can pick those sheets faster than anyone in the turnin'. I saw a pair o' bedsheets she made out o' one of 'em. Really nice they were. She 'emmed all the edges an' embroidered a little pattern in the corners.'

'Well, I've got two an' she's welcome to 'em,' Mary said. 'Ter be honest I'll be glad ter see the back of 'em.'

'Couldn't yer get on wiv 'em?'

Mary laughed. 'Me an' Lucy Parry 'ad a go but we found it was takin' too long. We would 'ave still bin pickin' away next Christmas.'

CHAPTER 14

Charlie Foden felt apprehensive as he walked along to the Lynton Road diggings with George Parry. 'I'm wonderin' if I've done the right fing,' he said. 'Anyway, it's too late ter turn back now.'

'Not really,' George replied. 'I feel like doin' just that right now.'

'Yer'll be OK when yer get used to it,' Charlie said supportively. 'Yer'll be glad yer stuck it out when yer draw yer pay on Friday.'

George nodded. 'I can stand the shovellin' an' the diggin', an' I'll get used ter those poxy overalls an' rubber boots we 'ave ter wear, but I'm gonna blow apart if that ugly big git Coates winds me up again terday.'

Charlie looked at him with concern. There was a distinct note of desperation in George's voice and he was reminded of what Fred Wilson had told him. They were all going to be working in shuttered trenches and accidents were very prone to happen. If George lost his head in that situation it could spell disaster.

'So yer decided ter give it a try,' Sharkey said as the two men arrived at the site.

'That's what we arranged,' Charlie replied with a calm smile.

George went into the men's changing shed and Sharkey nodded his head towards the hut. 'Ben Coley wants a word wiv yer before yer

163

start,' he said.

Charlie stepped into the confined space of the hut and saw the big man crouched over an unrolled blueprint. 'Yer want ter see me, Mr Coley?'

Ben stretched out his hand. 'Welcome ter Coley Bruvvers. I don't stand on ceremony 'ere. I'm Ben an' I'll call yer Charlie. Yer know what I expect: a good day's work from the men. Watch the slacker an' the trouble-maker, keep a tight rein on 'em all an' don't stand no back-chat. It's one fing I won't abide. Sharkey's word is law ter them, an' so will yours be. Anyway, I've gotta go an' see the main contractors soon so I'll leave you in Sharkey's capable 'ands. Anyfing yer wanna know, just ask 'im an' 'e'll be only too glad to oblige.'

The December day was cold, a raw coldness that seemed to eat into the bones, and the sky above was patched with slate-grey snow clouds as the men filed out of the long tarpaulin shed wearing their ill-fitting, mud-caked overalls and cumbersome wellington boots. Soon they would be glad of them, once they were slithering and slipping in the slimy clay, but for now the diggers' faces were pinched with discomfort and awkwardness.

Sharkey walked up to the trench as the men clambered in. 'There's a bit of a way ter go yet so get to it,' he bawled out.

Charlie stood at his elbow, watching for any reaction, but all he saw were the blank expressions and bowed backs as the working day began. ''Ow far down 'ave they gotta go?' he asked Sharkey after a while.

164

'They'll strike the brick at about six feet,' he replied. 'Then it's a matter o' clearin' the soil an' clay round the outside o' the tunnel.'

'What about the shutterin'?'

'What about it?'

'When d'yer start proppin' up the sides?'

Sharkey swung his boot at a large pebble which skidded back into the trench. 'Soon as they reach the brick,' he answered as though he thought Charlie should have known.

'I can't see any wood lyin' around.'

'It's bein' delivered this mornin',' Sharkey replied as he turned on his heel and walked back towards the hut.

Charlie had purposely worn his heavy hip-length sea coat that he used on the quayside and he pulled its large collar up around his ears as he strolled along the length of the trench. George and Wally Coates were digging at the far end and as he approached he saw that the big man was wielding the shovel. Huge clods of earth were being thrown on to a rapidly rising mound at the side of the trench and Charlie quickly got the impression that Coates was working in competition with the rest. Occasionally he would look along the line and then put his head down again, grunting under the weight of the clay.

George looked up as Charlie stood over him and nodded briefly before taking another swing with his pickaxe at a section of hard soil.

Coates rammed the shovel into the earth and reached out his hand. ''Ere, give us that poxy pickaxe,' he growled.

George stepped back a pace while the big man

set about loosening the hard clog, and after a while Coates stood upright. 'That's ready ter shovel out now,' he declared, 'so get to it.'

'I was usin' the pickaxe, remember,' George said calmly, reassured by Charlie's presence.

'Yer was, yer mean,' Coates replied. 'Get it shifted.'

George did as he was bid, but Coates was not satisfied. 'Come on, or the ovvers'll beat us to it,' he growled.

'So what?' George said scornfully.

Wally Coates threw down the pickaxe at George's feet and grabbed him by the front of his overalls. 'I'm not gonna be seconded by that lot,' he snarled. 'There's not a decent digger amongst 'em.'

Charlie felt a sudden anger at being ignored. 'Oi, you,' he shouted at Coates. 'Take yer 'ands off 'im an' get back ter work. This ain't a competition.'

To his surprise the big man acquiesced and picked up the shovel. George smiled up at Charlie and retrieved the pickaxe. 'Don't worry, we'll be first,' he said to Coates as he set to work once more.

Charlie walked back into the hut to roll a cigarette and saw that Sharkey Lockwood was missing. It figured, he thought. He was being left to supervise without any firm knowledge of how things should be done, and he had half expected a trick like this. Sharkey was undoubtedly hoping that something would go wrong and it was a sure bet that he had sloped over to the Mason's Arms to sit in the warmth, waiting.

'We're down ter brick,' Coates shouted out.

Charlie came hurrying out of the hut and saw the big man freeing his boots from a pile of earth which had become dislodged from one side of the trench. 'Roy, come up 'ere,' he called out.

The carpenter fought his way along the slimy bed of clay and saw the concave wall of the trench. 'I'd better get started,' he said. 'That side looks very weak.'

'We've got no wood yet,' Charlie told him. 'It should be 'ere soon, though. Anyway, yer know where yer gotta start now.'

It was early afternoon when a lorry finally drew up, and the driver jumped down and went over to Sharkey, who had only just arrived back at the diggings with a smell of whisky on his breath. 'I've got on all we could find,' he said. 'Some of it ain't all that clever.'

'It'll do,' the ganger replied. 'Just back yer lorry over 'ere an' me an' Charlie'll 'elp yer unload it.'

'What's 'e mean, some of it ain't all that clever?' Charlie queried.

'Some of it's old wood,' Sharkey explained. 'It'll make no difference though, as long as it's wedged properly. By the way, yer'd better get inter some overalls. Some o' the wood's oily. There's a pair in that cupboard'll fit yer.'

Charlie slipped into the overalls and was glad he had. The wood was slimy, full of oil and grease, and there were lengths which were badly split. 'We'd better put these worst ones ter one side,' he suggested.

'Nah, put it all tergevver. It'll do,' Sharkey replied. 'We ain't after doin' a pretty job – it's

167

only shutterin', fer Gawd's sake.'

Charlie picked up a plank of wood which had a large wide split running almost from end to end. 'This piece is useless, fer shutterin' or anyfing else,' he insisted.

'Let the carpenter sort it out,' Sharkey said with finality.

Sleet started to fall later in the afternoon and by five o'clock it had turned to snow as the men clambered out of the diggings for the day. Roy Chubb had managed to shore up a long section but he looked concerned as he came up to Charlie. 'I don't like it,' he said anxiously.

'What d'yer mean?' Charlie asked.

Sharkey interrupted them. 'Get yer overalls off,' he growled. 'I wanna lock up.'

While the three men were walking the short distance home George turned to Charlie. 'You certainly shut Wally Coates up,' he said, grinning. 'I never got a bad word out of 'im after that. Mind you, 'e never spoke a word of any sort fer the rest o' the day.'

Charlie gave him a wry smile. 'Don't let it fool yer,' he replied. ''E won't ferget, so be on yer toes.'

Roy remained quiet until they were nearly home. 'A lot o' that wood I used was rotten right frew,' he said then. 'It might be an idea ter see if they can get some new timbers. I really need four by fours.'

'Tell me, Roy, 'ave you ever done any shutterin' work before this job?' Charlie asked.

'Yeah. Most carpenters workin' on buildin' sites get a fair amount o' shutterin' jobs. It's all part an' parcel o' the work. Why d'yer ask?'

Charlie turned to face him outside the house. 'I need ter be sure you know what yer talkin' about when I go an' see Coley termorrer,' he answered. 'If the request's comin' from someone who knows the business 'e'll be less likely ter refuse.'

Roy pulled on his front door string and pushed the door open. 'I tell yer this,' he said. 'While it's snowin' it'll be all right, but if there's a thaw an' the snow turns ter slush then we've got a problem. The walls are gonna be runnin' an' those rotten timbers might not 'old.'

'I'll see what I can do,' Charlie told him. 'In the meantime yer'll just 'ave ter use the best of what yer got.'

Roy smiled cynically. 'That's the trouble,' he said. 'All the poxy wood's the same.'

Will Jackson was in his late thirties, happily married with two young children. His wife Paula worked part time at the bagwash factory in Long Lane, but Will had never had a steady job for as long as he could remember. He earned a living as a handyman, gardener and stall helper, and by doing other jobs which sometimes he preferred not to talk about. Will was willing, and nothing was too small or too large for him to tackle, given the chance.

The Reverend Clarke acquired Will's services on a frequent basis, helping to tend the church gardens, and the market men used him to fetch from their sheds when their stocks were running low. Mrs Black paid him to unblock her guttering and he seemed to be unplugging the drain in Mrs

Venners' backyard on a regular basis. In fact on most days of the year Will found himself gainfully employed, until the depression began to bite. Now the market men hardly ever ran short of stock, and Mrs Venners managed to unblock the drain herself with a long stick. Mrs Black had not experienced any more trouble with her guttering, and if she did it would be a question of getting her husband to sort it out. As for the Reverend Clarke, he still got the handyman to do a little gardening, but on a very limited basis.

Will Jackson knew that he could hardly join the dole queues. He had no employment cards to present and no employer to blame for being out of work, so he decided he had to make some adjustments. He chopped firewood and tied it up in little bundles which he sold at front doors, and to supplement the meagre income he ran errands, fetching coke from the gasworks and people's clean washing from the bagwash factory in an old bassinet, and all the while he struggled to get by.

Always on hand with a cheery disposition, Will had endeared himself to local people, in particular those in Cooper Street where he lived himself. They felt mean not giving him the odd jobs as before, but money was very tight and they hoped he would understand.

Once in a while one of the neighbours did offer Will a bit of work, and on Tuesday morning Mary Chubb was glad to see Will coming into the turning with the morning paper under his arm. 'It's a raw mornin',' she remarked.

Will nodded. "Ow's the firewood?'

'I'll need two bundles termorrer,' she told him. 'By the way, I got a job needs doin' but I'm a bit wary of askin'.'

'I'm not likely ter bite yer 'ead off,' he replied with a smile, 'so tell me what yer want done.'

'I've got two big tram sheets out in my backyard,' Mary explained. 'They was soakin' in a bathtub but I've managed ter get 'em out. They're 'angin' over me line an' I gotta get rid of 'em – they're makin' the place feel like a bloody shit-tip. Mrs Venners picks the paint off 'em an' she told me she'd be glad of 'em. I'd take 'em to 'er meself but they're too 'eavy while they're still wet. I could wait till they're dry, I s'pose, but I'm scared our Gracie'll pull 'em over on top of 'er.'

'So yer want me ter deliver 'em for yer?'

'If yer'd be so kind.'

Will nodded. 'Give us a tanner an' consider it done,' he told her.

Mary gave him a shilling and Will was happy, though he had a bit of a struggle as the two weighty sheets were still soaked through. Mrs Venners was happy too, having them delivered to her backyard, and she took the opportunity to broach the subject of her old wringer. 'I gotta get rid of it,' she explained. 'It won't wring out. Just look at the rollers – they're all split. As a matter o' fact I've bin waitin' fer the totter ter call round the street but I ain't seen bugger all of 'im.'

Will stroked his chin and suddenly smiled to himself. 'Leave it wiv me,' he told her.

On Tuesday night Will Jackson broke into the premises which was formerly the bootmender's and was glad to see that he had remembered

171

correctly. There in the backyard was a rusting wringer with its rollers intact. He had first seen it on the evening he delivered some cardboard boxes Martha Staples had asked him to get for her, and that was when he had learned in confidence that she and her husband were moving out of the street within the next few days with only as much as they could carry in large suitcases and boxes, which meant leaving the wringer behind. Mrs Staples had told him it was a shame really. Only a few weeks previous she had got the rollers replaced.

It did not take long for the street handyman to remove the two heavy rollers, but as he stepped out into the street with one under each arm his heart missed a beat. Directly opposite, lit up by the streetlamp, was Ron Sloan the beat bobby, talking to Sammy Strickland.

'No, yer can't go rootin' in trenches fer bloody firewood,' the constable told him sternly.

'But it's not proppin' up anyfing,' Sammy tried to explain.

'What d'yer mean, not proppin' up anyfing?'

'It's just lyin' there amongst the dirt where the wall collapsed.'

'I'd better take a look meself,' Ron Sloan declared.

Just then Will Jackson hurried past, holding his breath. 'Evenin', constable.'

'Evenin', Will. 'Ere, where yer goin' wiv them?'

'I'm takin' 'em 'ome,' the handyman told him.

'Where d'yer get 'em?'

'Mrs Staples left 'em in 'er backyard for me.'

''Ow did yer get in?'

172

'Over the back wall.'

'That's breakin' an' enterin'.'

'I never broke anyfing,' Will said defensively.

Sammy Strickland was grinning widely. 'I was there when Mrs Staples told Will 'e could 'ave the rollers. Honest ter God I was.'

Ron Sloan chewed on his chinstrap for a few moments. 'I'll see yer termorrer about them,' he said. 'Right, Sammy, show me where this wood is.'

The not-to-be shopkeeper led the way to the diggings feeling angry with himself. He should have gone back there later and got the wood. He could have collected enough to keep the house warm right through the winter. Instead, he had to open his big mouth. 'Look, there's loads of it. Someone must 'ave just frew it in there,' he said, pointing into the hole.

'That's not bin thrown in,' the constable told him. 'That's collapsed shutterin', an' I'm tellin' yer now ter keep out o' that trench. It looks ter me like some more's likely ter go at any time.'

Sammy nodded, knowing full well what had really happened. After dark he had made his way to the diggings with the aid of a length of wood he had prised the main prop loose and levered on the side wood till the wall collapsed. As well as cocking a snook at the unsufferable Coleys, it had almost provided enough free fuel for him to open a stall, which he could have built out of more of the wood. Him and his big mouth!

Will Jackson breathed a sigh of relief as he stepped into his house, promising to buy Sammy a pint next time he bumped into him. Now he

173

had to negotiate a price for the renovation of Mrs Venners' old wringer.

The deal was done on Minnie Venners' doorstep half an hour later. 'I'll fix new rollers on it, clean off all the rust an' oil the cogs,' Will promised her. 'Oh, an' I'll also give it a coat o' brown gloss paint.'

'An' 'ow much is that little lot gonna set me back?' Minnie asked him.

'Call it a dollar,' Will told her.

Minnie shook her head. 'I can't afford a dollar.'

'Call it three an' a tanner, then.'

'Nah. I just ain't got it,' Minnie said.

'All right, seein' it's you. 'Alf a crown. 'Ow's that sound?'

'That sounds better,' Minnie told him.

Will smiled. 'Right then. I'll make a start termorrer.'

Constable Ron Sloan walked along Lynton Road listening to the noises from the freight yard. It had been a long spell, which thankfully was due to end at midnight, and all he had had to deal with throughout the shift was a devious character carrying a pair of wooden rollers on the King's highway, and another by the name of Sammy Strickland, who would no doubt stay warm even if hell froze over.

CHAPTER 15

On the cold December morning that Charlie started work as a ganger, Mary Chubb made her way to Tooley Street and was interviewed for the cleaning job at James Dolan, Dairy Products Ltd.

'I'm Mr Cuthbert, office manager. Do sit down, Mrs ... er...'

'Mrs Chubb,' Mary told him.

'Yes, of course.' Cuthbert took off his glasses and smiled out of a flat pallid face. 'The job entails the cleaning and polishing of all the offices, and the toilets, of which there are three. You will collect the key from the tobacconist opposite. He opens up at seven o'clock in the morning and if you pick the key up as soon as he opens it'll give you two hours to get the work done. By the way, you will also be expected to keep the insides of the windows clean. We'd expect them to be done once a week. The office opens up sharp on nine, but I'm a natural early riser and I often get into work before the morning rush. Obviously I don't mind you finishing off after I've arrived, but in any case I would like you to be finished by nine o'clock latest when we open for trading.'

Mary smiled in acknowledgement. 'I understand.'

Cuthbert pushed his desk chair back and got up. 'You'll be on trial, of course,' he said. 'We'll review the situation after two weeks. Is that all right with you?'

'Yes, that'll be fine,' Mary answered as she stood up.

Cuthbert seemed to linger at the door with a sickly smile playing around his lips and his eyes glancing over her body in a way that made her shiver. 'I'm sure we can work things out to our mutual satisfaction, Mrs Chubb,' he told her. 'And I want you to know that I'm always here should you need anything. Good luck.'

Mary walked to the tram stop with an image of the manager's pallid face in her mind and she began to wonder. Key jobs in cleaning were hard to come by and most women were glad to hold on to them. What had caused the last incumbent to give up this one? It could have been any of several reasons, but Mary had a feeling she was soon going to discover the right one.

Feelings were running high at the diggings on Wednesday morning, with Sharkey Lockwood bawling out the men as they struggled to clear the timbers from the trench. 'Come on, get 'em all out an' stack 'em by the side,' he shouted. 'No, not like that. Dig the poxy wood out, don't try an' tug it free. Oi, you, don't stand there gawkin'. Go an' fetch two more shovels.'

Charlie had changed into overalls and he grabbed one of the shovels the worker brought up and jumped down into the trench. Sharkey took the other one and together they prised the remaining timbers free.

'If I find out who's responsible for this I'll

crucify 'em,' he growled to Charlie.

'Someone wiv a grudge, that's fer sure,' Charlie replied.

'This delay is gonna put the Coleys in a right poxy mood,' Sharkey said, standing up to take a breather while the team removed the last of the wood.

Charlie glanced at the wall of earth where the shuttering had been and noticed two deep score marks. 'That's where it was levered off,' he pointed out.

Sharkey nodded. 'I knew it was no accident,' he scowled. 'The rest o' the wall's too firm an' dry. Shutterin' just don't fall down fer no reason.'

Roy Chubb was examining the timbers. ''Ere, there's 'alf the plankin' missin',' he remarked.

'Ben Coley'll go mad when I tell 'im we've gotta get some more,' Sharkey groaned.

'Well there's no ovver choice, is there?' Charlie said.

'We'll need a poxy nightwatchman now,' the ganger said as he stabbed the blade of his shovel into the clay bed. 'Right then, Chubb, yer'll 'ave ter do what yer can wiv what's left till we see the boss.'

Roy shook his head as he grabbed up a length of timber. 'This is gonna be like tryin' ter make a piece o' furniture out o' matches,' he said with a derisory laugh.

Ben Coley's face grew black when he saw what had happened. 'I'm not gonna buy new bloody timbers, that's fer sure,' he growled. 'Get that yard man to 'ave a good sort-out. Surely there's enough wood lyin' round the yard.'

'What about a nightwatchman?' Sharkey asked him.

'I s'pose we'll 'ave ter take one on now,' Coley replied. 'I'll get on ter the labour exchange soon as I get a minute.'

The digging got under way once more and Roy Chubb worked hard to shore up the sides where Wally Coates had first uncovered the brickwork of the crumbling main sewers. Sharkey had left the site to organise the yard man into finding fresh timbers and Charlie breathed a little easier. 'C'mon, lads, get yer backs into it,' he called out as he walked along above the excavation. 'Level that earth out beside the brickwork an' yer can take a ten-minute breavver.'

The men wondered if they were hearing things. Ten-minute breaks outside the specified times were unheard of, but it was a small treat to look forward to nevertheless and they worked with a will to uncover more of the dilapidated sewer, which had been damaged in no small way by a combination of natural earth movement and the constant vibration from the nearby freight yards.

At eleven thirty, in the absence of both Sharkey and Ben Coley, Charlie called a break, and as the men sat resting on the edge of the workings the novice ganger ambled up to Wally Coates. 'I don't expect ten minutes' pause is gonna put us be'ind in any way,' he remarked. 'In fact it'll give you lads more incentive ter push on even faster. Don't you agree, Wally?'

The big man nodded. 'It's a welcome break,' he answered, an unconvincing note in his voice.

'If the boss man does find out then we know

who's told 'im, don't we,' Charlie said with an edge to his words.

Wally Coates understood that he was being warned in no uncertain manner and he bit back on a smart reply. He had been lined up as a future ganger, but now it seemed his chance of promotion was further off than ever with the arrival of this cocky man who acted as though he had always been in the business. He felt his time would come soon, though, and when it did a few scores would be settled.

Sammy Strickland reached the front of the dole queue on Wednesday morning and made his usual dramatic plea for a job. 'I know fings are very tight but I'm desperate,' he said.

'If you'll just move to the next window I'll send someone along to see you,' the clerk told him.

Sammy was suddenly consumed with panic. This was very unusual. It looked like they were actually taking notice of him for once and it could be tricky.

'Ah, Mr Strickland,' the dole officer said as he appeared at the window. 'If you'll come along to the end I'll let you into the office.'

Sammy was shown into a comfortable seat facing the officer who sat upright at his desk. 'Is there anyfing wrong?' he asked fearfully.

'Wrong? Of course not. Why do you ask?'

'Well, as you know, I've bin comin' 'ere on an' off fer years now an' never got a start,' Sammy explained. 'So I said ter meself, Sammy I said, this can't be an offer of a job, it's gotta be somefing else.'

'Well I can assure you, Mr Strickland, there's nothing wrong,' the officer replied. 'Everyone who signs on here has a work record, and when we get employers phoning in with job offers we try to match them with suitable candidates. Now I remember clearly that you once called in with a request for a nightwatchman's job.'

'Twice,' Sammy corrected him.

The official continued regardless. 'I see here too that you are a trained shepherd. Rather a rare occupation in London, wouldn't you say?'

'Yeah, but it's true, strike me dead if it's not,' Sammy said, superstitiously crossing his fingers. 'When I was a young shaver I 'elped ter look after the royal cattle in Regent's Park. They wandered around on the grass an' they were my responsibility. If they 'ad too many little 'uns I 'ad ter cut their nuts off too.'

'Amazing,' the official remarked. 'Now to get back to the present. The nightwatchman's job. It's at the Coley Brothers' workings in Lynton Road. They require a man who is reliable and conscientious, and able to safely guard the workings through the night.'

'That's right up my street,' Sammy replied with a breezy grin. 'The workin's would be safe as 'ouses while I was on the job.'

'Well I'll make you out a green card and you can present it to Mr Coley,' the official said, smiling amicably.

The threat of being landed with a job had initially put the fear into Sammy, but he had bucked up immediately when he learned who it was with. He had about as much chance of getting the job with that rag-taggle outfit as becoming a shepherd once more. 'I'm very much obliged, sir,' Sammy said dutifully. 'I'll go there straight away.'

'Oh, you must,' the officer told him. 'We have more than forty applicants on our books who are unemployed nightwatchmen, and if it doesn't work out with you and Mr Coley we can always offer it to someone else.'

Sammy thanked the official profusely and set off with a satisfied grin on his face. Looking for work was becoming a hazardous profession, he realised. One day he was going to come unstuck, and he would have to be very careful in future.

Mary and Lucy were discussing the latest developments over their usual cup of tea and Mary was at pains to tell her best friend that their little scheme might prove to be a bit trickier than they thought.

'Ter be honest 'e seemed a dirty ole git, the way 'e leered at me,' she said. 'You know the sort, all eyes that undress yer. Actually 'e wasn't all that old, but it was 'is face. 'E looked sort o' dead from the neck up.'

Lucy giggled. 'You do 'ave a way o' describin' people.'

Mary smiled back. 'The fing I didn't like was when 'e told me 'e got in ter work early in the mornin's. I wouldn't wanna be cleanin' there while 'e was standin' over me, lecherous ole git.'

'So what d'yer reckon?' Lucy asked.

'I'll start termorrer as arranged an' see 'ow it goes,' Mary replied. 'Once I get ter know the tobacco shop bloke I might be able ter get the key off 'im in the evenin's. I'll bring Gracie in before I go, if that's all right.'

'Yeah, course, but it means draggin' 'er out o' bed early,' Lucy said.

'She's always awake early anyway.'

'If she's still tired you can put 'er in wiv our Sue.'

'Yeah, course I can.'

'Well that's settled then.'

'Yep.'

'Good luck wiv the letch.'

'Don't worry. I'll end up clonkin' 'im if 'e gets unnecessary.'

Sammy Strickland made his way to Lynton Road and paused near the diggings to catch his breath. This wasn't something a man could just rush into, he thought. Better to amble up and exchange a few pleasantries with the chaps before presenting himself to the management. Besides, him standing there over the hole might jog the loud-mouthed ganger's memory and the rest would be easy. 'Good afternoon, boys,' he said. 'Workin' 'ard, I see.'

The toil was torture for the back, arms and shoulders and generally exhausting, and no one in the trench had enough spare energy to feel pleasantly disposed towards the onlooker.

'I should piss off if I was you,' Danny Albury managed. 'Before Sharkey gets back.'

'As a matter o' fact I've come fer a job,' Sammy announced.

Danny's partner Joe Lambert quickly looked

him up and down. 'There's no vacancies fer diggers,' he told him.

'I ain't come ter dig. I'm the new watchman – if I'm lucky, that is,' Sammy answered.

Just then Ben Coley put his head out of the hut. ''Ere, is that the bloke who was 'ere before? The bloke you saw off?'

Sharkey followed Ben's gaze. 'Yeah, that looks like the same geezer. I wonder if 'e's come ter gloat.'

'Go an' fetch 'im over,' Ben growled.

Sharkey strode up to him. 'Oi you, ain't you the silly git I sent packin' last week?'

'Nah, yer made a mistake,' Sammy said pluckily. 'I've come ter see the guv'nor an' I was just passin' the time o' day wiv yer lads.'

'Get in there,' Sharkey scowled, motioning towards the hut and following him inside.

When Sammy saw the look on Ben Coley's face he swallowed hard. This was going to be difficult, he decided. 'Er ... er, Mr James sent me round,' he stammered.

'An' who might Mr James be?' Ben Coley asked him with a burning stare.

''E's the manager o' the labour exchange in Walworth Road.'

'Yer mean 'e sent you about the watchman's job?'

Sammy smiled bravely. 'Right first time.'

'An' I s'pose you fink you're very smart,' Ben snarled.

'What d'yer mean?'

'Last night someone tore all the shutterin' down in the trench an' now you appear askin' fer

183

the nightwatchman's job. Very convenient.'

''Ang on a minute, yer got me all wrong,' Sammy told him. 'Last night I come past the trench on me way 'ome from the pub an' I saw that all the sides were down. I wasn't ter know if there was someone trapped under there or not, so I did the best fing I could do, I went an' fetched Ron Sloan.'

'Who the bloody 'ell's Ron Sloan?'

''E's the beat bobby. Nice copper, actually, one o' the best.'

'An' what did 'e 'ave ter say?'

''E knew all about it. 'E'd already chased away some kids who were messin' about wiv the wood.'

'So it was kids?'

'Yeah.'

Ben Coley's dark eyes narrowed. 'If I thought you were lyin' ter me I'd–'

'I wouldn't lie ter yer, honest I wouldn't,' Sammy said quickly. 'If yer don't believe me speak ter Ron Sloan. 'E'll be along presently.'

Ben leaned back on his stool and glanced at Sharkey. 'What d'yer reckon?'

Sharkey leaned towards Sammy menacingly. 'If you was employed as our nightwatchman an' those kids came back what would yer do?'

'I gotta be straight wiv yer,' Sammy gulped. 'I'd run an' fetch the copper.'

'An' meanwhile the kids create merry 'ell in the trench.'

'I'd tell 'em ter piss orf first,' Sammy said weakly.

'An' what if they took no notice?'

'Then I'd go after 'em wiv this,' the little man

184

said with spirit, triumphantly pulling a wicked-looking scimitar out from underneath his coat. 'I'd chase 'em off wiv this an' I'd be swingin' it round in the air like this ter frighten the crap out of 'em.'

Ben Coley and Sharkey both staggered backwards as Sammy demonstrated. 'Take it easy, yer dopey git,' Ben shouted, 'or yer'll do us all an injury.'

Sammy carefully replaced the short sword inside his belt and took a deep breath. 'I 'ad to apply fer this job or I'd 'ave lost me dole money,' he explained, 'but ter tell yer the trufe I wouldn't be much good ter yer as a nightwatchman.'

'Why's that?' Ben asked.

'I can't stay awake after ten o'clock at night. Always bin in bed early, ever since I was a kid. I'm frightened o' the dark, yer see. I can't 'elp it, it's just one o' those fings.'

''Ere, give us that bloody form,' Ben growled. He scribbled 'NOT SUITABLE' in capitals in the appropriate box and handed it back. 'Take this back an' tell Mr What's-'is-name ter send someone 'alf sensible next time. Now piss orf.'

Sammy waited until he was out of sight before doing a little jump and clicking his heels together the way Buddy Ebsen did on the films. Peggy wasn't going to believe this, he thought, smiling victoriously.

CHAPTER 16

The last few days leading up to Christmas were bitterly cold, but the threatening snow held off and the Coley workmen were able to make good progress. They kept their heads down, not wanting to present the management with any reason to put them off, and both Sharkey and Charlie Foden found that they had little to do except prowl the workings and occasionally move the men about to keep the level of digging even. Roy Chubb was grateful for the few new timbers delivered but they were nowhere near enough and he prayed that the cold weather would continue. Any rise in the temperature could well cause movement in the soil around the trench as it softened, and heavy rain would put severe strain on the shuttering.

Charlie suggested getting some steel adjusting clamps to reinforce the shored-up walls but Ben Coley shook his head adamantly. 'They're not all that good an' a lot o' contractors prefer wood,' he replied. 'You just leave us ter decide. If we needed steel clamps we'd 'ave got some.'

Roy Chubb was dismissive of Coley's attitude as he walked home with George and Charlie. 'They used metal clamps on every site I ever worked on,' he said. ''E's just makin' excuses.'

George had been strangely quiet and Charlie guessed that Wally Coates was giving him a hard time. He had seen the tension on George's face and Wally's disdain for his partner as he patrolled the line. It was a strained coupling but in one sense it brought out the grim determination of the smaller man to pull his weight, despite the difference in their build and strength. Splitting them up would be the easy option, Charlie knew, but then Coates could be expected to antagonise his new partner and the progress of the diggings might well suffer as a consequence.

As the three men walked into the street the evening before Christmas Eve Charlie casually asked George if everything was all right, guessing what he might say.

'I want shot o' that no-good git on the next job,' George blurted out. 'I don't fink I could stand much more of 'im.'

'What's 'e bin saying?' Charlie asked.

'It's what 'e's not bin sayin',' George replied with a scowl. 'I'm gettin' the dumb treatment. All right, I know yer can't split us up on this dig, but I want a new partner on the next one. If I don't I'll end up clobberin' 'im wiv me shovel, so 'elp me I will.'

'Leave it ter me,' Charlie told him. 'If we get the job in Dock'ead that Ben Coley was talkin' about there's gonna be some changes made. It'll be a big job o' work, an' wiv a bit of luck it'll last through the year. There's literally miles of defective sewers in Bermondsey, so Coley was sayin'.'

George was not impressed. He was hoping to be long gone from ditch digging before the next year was out.

Lucy had an amused expression on her face as her husband and Charlie stepped into the house. 'Remember ter say 'ow much yer like Sara's 'air,' she whispered at the door. 'I finally got round ter doin' it this afternoon.'

George played along as he walked into the parlour. 'What've yer bin doin' wiv yerself, Sara? You look different,' he commented.

She patted the tight curls with her fingers. 'Well then, what does it look like?'

'Very nice,' George told her.

'Yes it does,' Charlie echoed. 'It makes yer look younger.'

'Not too young?'

'No, it's just right,' he assured her.

'I 'ad ter get it done,' Sara told them. 'I was getin' depressed wiv it the way it was.'

Sounds of childish merriment rang out from upstairs and Lucy went into the passageway. 'Now don't get too excited you two or there'll be an accident,' she called out.

George looked irritated as he sat down heavily by the fire. 'I fink Mary's got it easy, palmin' Gracie off on you all the time,' he said.

'She's no trouble,' Lucy responded quickly. 'An' she don't palm the gel off on me all the time. She looks after our Sue quite a lot.'

'All that screamin' an' shoutin',' George said. 'She'll be too excited ter get ter sleep early an' then she'll be in an' out of our bedroom all night.'

Lucy caught Charlie's eye but the lodger averted his gaze quickly, bending down to loosen the laces in his boots.

'It's Christmas, George, the kids are gonna be excited. It's only natural,' she told him.

'They do get more excited when they're ter-gevver, though,' Sara cut in.

'Well of course they do. So did you when you was their age,' Lucy replied sharply.

George could see an argument brewing and he looked up at Lucy. 'Is tea gonna be long?' he asked. 'I promised Danny Albury I'd go fer a game o' darts ternight at the Dun Cow.'

'It'll be ten minutes,' Lucy said, going out to check on the meat pie finishing off in the oven.

A loud bump sounded overhead and Sara touched her temple with the tips of her fingers. 'Mary Chubb's gone out ternight, that's why Lucy's bin mindin' Gracie,' she told her brother.

'I see,' George mumbled as he picked up the evening paper.

'Somefing about a job.'

'Oh yeah?'

'There's bin a bit o' whisperin' goin' on between Lucy an' 'er next door,' Sara went on. 'I 'eard 'em talkin' in the scullery about this cleanin' job.'

George felt in no mood to listen to his sister's bitching and he looked up at her with a frown. 'Mary Chubb's got a cleanin' job, that's all it is,' he said testily. 'Nuffing wrong in that.'

'I'm not sayin' there is,' Sara replied quickly. 'Long as Lucy don't get no ideas about me lookin' after Sue while she goes out ter work. I couldn't be up an' down those stairs, not the way I am.'

'Lucy wouldn't dream of leavin' Sue ter do a

cleanin' job,' George assured her.

'I would 'ope not,' Sara replied, keen to have the last word on the subject.

Charlie glanced over at George and saw that he had buried his head in the paper. Sara was staring moodily into the fire and suddenly he wanted to shout aloud, bang the table, stamp his feet, anything to break the charged atmosphere. He rolled his sleeves up and walked out to the scullery.

Lucy was bending over the oven and she straightened up quickly to let him pass her. 'There's some 'ot water in the kettle,' she told him.

Charlie filled the small enamel bowl in the sink and reached for the cake of Sunlight soap. 'It's gone a bit quiet in there,' he remarked with a grin.

Lucy smiled back at him and then quickly took the soap from him. 'Don't use that, it's only fer washin' clothes,' she said. ''Ere, use this.' She picked up a new bar of Lifebuoy from the dresser.

Charlie took the packet, the tips of his fingers closing over hers. 'You really look after me, don't yer?' he smiled.

'An' why not?' Lucy replied, withdrawing her hand slowly. 'You're part o' the family.'

Charlie soaped his hands and forearms. 'I'm a payin' lodger, Lucy, which brings me ter the question o' payment. I've bin givin' it a bit o' thought an' I reckon wiv all the food you supply an' the washin' you do fer me, fifteen shillin's don't seem enough. I'd like yer to accept a pound a week.'

'Well now,' Lucy said with a saucy grin

191

spreading across her face. 'That's a one-off. A lodger who feels 'e's not payin' enough.'

'I'm serious, Lucy. I'd like ter make it up to a quid.'

She picked up a clean cloth and pulled the meat pie from the oven, puffing with the sudden heat in her face, and she ran the back of her hand across her hot forehead. 'If you really insist,' she conceded. 'I'm quite 'appy wiv the arrangement as it stands, ter tell yer the trufe. Your comin' 'ere ter stay 'as bin like a breath o' fresh air.'

'It's also allowed me ter get ter know a very nice lady,' he replied.

'Yes, Sara's very sweet under that front she puts on,' Lucy joked.

Charlie grinned at her sly humour, then his face grew serious. 'I 'ave ter say yer do make me feel like part o' the family. In fact I find meself finkin' about you quite a lot durin' the day, an' sometimes when I'm in my room late at night.'

Lucy stared at the meat pie as she prodded it with a fork, an unreadable expression on her face.

'It's gettin' so I'm finkin' about you all the time,' he said in a low voice.

She turned towards him, her face flushed, her full breasts firm under the flowered apron she wore. 'I fink about you too, Charlie, an' I 'ave ter remind meself I'm a married woman.'

He glanced down at his feet momentarily, then when he raised his eyes again to meet hers the look in them was unmistakable. 'I can't 'elp the way I feel, Lucy,' he said. 'God knows I've tried. I know it's wrong. You're a married woman wiv a good carin' 'usband an' a crackin' little daughter, an' what's more I'm a guest in your 'ome. It makes it all the 'arder. Maybe I should consider movin' somewhere else.'

Lucy shook her head quickly. 'Don't, Charlie, don't even fink that way. I'd be miserable an' lonely if you left us. I've come ter lean on yer, see yer as a tower o' strength, an' it means so much ter me. It can never be more than that, but I can dream. We both can. Let fings stay the way they are. Let's not spoil it all.'

'Yeah, you're right,' he sighed. 'I was stupid to even mention the way I feel.'

'No yer not,' she said with a tremor in her voice. 'I've seen the way you look at me, the way you watch me, an' it's excitin'. I feel a warmth inside, an' I can take comfort from what yer've told me.'

They heard the telltale squeak as George got out of his armchair and Charlie grabbed the towel while Lucy turned to cut the pie into sections.

'I didn't suggest it before, Charlie, 'cos yer said yer was gettin' an early night,' George said as he walked into the scullery, 'but if yer change yer mind yer welcome ter join us at the Dun Cow.'

'That's good of yer, mate, but I really do feel tired,' Charlie told him. 'I don't seem to 'ave your energy.'

The younger man felt pleased with the compliment. He had started at the diggings wondering if he would last the day but sheer cussedness and determination had made him stick it out. Now his hands were callused and hard, his back was strong and his arms were more muscular than they had ever been. He had learned from the other more experienced diggers to shut off his mind and work at a steady pace and he survived. Now he felt able to hold his own with any of them, including the detestable Wally Coates, which made the situation between them all the more fraught with danger. George knew that one day it might well blow up into a violent confrontation and he suspected that Coates was feeling the same way. He tried to put it from his mind and hoped that the pairings would be changed when the new contract started after Christmas. 'Last day termorrer, then,' he said as he snapped off a small piece of pie crust.

'Yeah. It should be a bit easier,' Charlie replied. 'We've got the best part o' the brickwork uncovered. Who knows, we might get away a bit earlier.'

'I don't want no shop talk in my 'ouse,' Lucy declared with mock severity as she playfully tapped Charlie's arm. 'George, 'ave you washed yer 'ands?'

He winced as she waved him towards the sink. ''Urry up. I'm dishin' the food up now.'

Light snow started to fall later that evening as George left the house and Lucy propped the coconut mat up above the bottom of the scullery door against the draught. Sara had intended to go out to the fellowship but when George remarked that it was snowing as he went out she shivered and moved nearer the fire. Now she was reclining in her armchair, her face red with the heat as she dozed fitfully.

'What a picture,' Lucy said, grinning at Charlie.

Both knew that Sara was very devious. She could feign sleep and listen to other people's conversation, and for that reason they were a little careful what they said.

'Tell me, Charlie, are you intendin' ter stay wiv the Coleys next year?' Lucy asked as she sat down facing him at the table.

He shrugged his shoulders. 'I dunno. It all depends 'ow it goes. If they get the big contract fings should start to improve, conditions an' paywise. If not there'll be a few disgruntled diggers on their books.'

''Ow's George copin'?'

''E's doin' fine, considerin'.'

'Wally Coates?'

''E told yer about 'im then?'

'Yeah, 'e did.'

'Unfortunately there's always one on every site,' Charlie sighed, 'an' ter make matters worse the man's a grass. Everyone's gotta be very careful what they say an' do around 'im.'

'Keep yer eye on George, Charlie,' she said with concern. 'I know 'e's not a man ter make trouble but everyone's got a breakin' point, an' from what 'e told me last night 'e's very near it.'

'Yeah, I know,' Charlie replied quietly. 'Don't worry. Coates won't attempt anyfing while I'm around, but George must keep calm an' refuse ter rise ter the bait. I know it's 'ard but it's the only way.'

'I wish 'e could get somefing else, but there's no work anywhere, it seems.'

'I wouldn't worry yerself too much,' Charlie

195

told her kindly. 'Any work experience is valuable, an' at least George is lookin' very fit. 'E'll find somefing better in the new year, I'm sure.'

Lucy smiled impishly as she reached across the table and touched his arm, at the same time nodding towards the sleeping Sara. 'Well, I fink it's time I made a cup o' tea fer you an' me,' she said rather loudly.

Sara started to move in her chair and suddenly groaned as she straightened her neck. 'Deary me, I must 'ave dropped off,' she said.

Lucy narrowed her eyes. 'I don't s'pose yer fancy a cuppa yet, Sara?'

'I'd love one as a matter o' fact,' she replied. 'I feel parched.'

'I just wondered,' Lucy said, winking at Charlie as she got up from the table.

Next door the Chubbs were already sipping their tea by the fire and Mary was explaining her campaign plan to Roy. 'We decided ter wait till after Christmas,' she told him. 'It'll give me a chance ter get ter know the paper man a bit better. As a matter o' fact I fink 'e'll be OK, but yer never know. Best ter play it careful.' She paused to take another sip.

'Well, go on,' Roy urged her.

'So far the office manager's bin comin' in every mornin' about 'alf eight,' she said, 'just as I'm finishin' off the toilets. The first week after Christmas I'm gonna get in a bit earlier so I can get away before 'e arrives, an' if I don't get any comebacks Lucy's gonna do the followin' week. The ole goat won't be none the wiser.'

'Unless 'e comes in earlier still, just ter catch yer out.'

'Why should 'e do that?'

''E might guess yer doin' the job in the evenin's.'

'Why should 'e?'

'The shop bloke might tell 'im.'

'Nah, we'll prime 'im up. It'll be no skin off 'is nose. Anyway, I'll give it a try, an' if it works out me an' Lucy are gonna look out fer anuvver key job nearby an' we can do the two tergevver. It'll be better if there's two of us, especially round the Tooley Street area when it's dark.'

'Well I 'ope it works out fer yer,' Roy said, yawning wearily.

'It will, as long as yer don't mind lookin' after Gracie fer a couple of hours in the evenin',' Mary reminded him.

'I told yer I don't mind, but what about George?' he asked.

'Lucy seems ter fink 'e won't mind eivver,' she answered. 'The money'll certainly come in 'andy.'

Roy eased back in his chair. 'I just 'ad a thought. S'posin' yer can't get the key any earlier in the mornin's, what then?'

'The paper shop opens up at six o'clock fer the delivery boys,' Mary told him.

'Well, fingers crossed then.'

'I won't be really 'appy though till you get a better job,' she remarked with concern. 'I worry over yer workin' in that trench.'

'There's no need ter worry,' he replied dismissively. 'It'll do till I can get somefink decent.

I'm always on the look-out.'

'Yeah, I know you are.'

'At least I'm pretty well left alone doin' the shutterin', an' it's better than usin' a pick an' shovel all day,' he told her.

Mary shook her head sadly. 'I try ter keep cheerful, but it's 'ard, especially when fings seem like they're never gonna improve. I tell meself that fings can't get any worse, an' then they do. I wouldn't mind if we could put a few shillin's by.'

'But you 'ave,' Roy reminded her.

'Yeah, an' then I've 'ad ter dig into it.'

'That's what it was for, an emergency.'

'I know, Roy, but wouldn't it be nice ter get a few bob saved without 'avin' ter touch it? We could take a week somewhere like Margate, or Brighton. Gracie could go in the sea paddlin' an' we could walk along the promenade.'

'Fish an' chips at a seafront café,' Roy added.

'Lookin' out of our digs an' watchin' the sun go down over the water,' Mary fantasised.

'Me takin' you in me arms an' tellin' yer 'ow much I love yer,' Roy said in a deep voice for effect. 'We'd go ter bed an' I'd pull yer close...'

'Yeah?'

'I'd kiss yer neck an' yer ears, then I'd gently...'

'Yeah, go on,' Mary urged him.

'I can't. Gracie's just walked in the room.'

Mary giggled and went over to him, her arms encircling his neck as she kissed his cheek. 'Do you feel tired?' she asked.

Roy shook his head. 'Not really.'

'Let's go ter bed anyway,' she said, gently chewing his ear.

Maurice Oakfield folded the tatty, holed blanket and made it into a cushion of sorts to sit on in his sentry box, as he called it. The brazier was glowing nicely and Maurice felt at peace with the world as he set about boiling water for his midnight tea. The beat bobby would be along soon and he usually spent some time sharing the brew and chatting about this and that, which helped pass the long night away.

The deep trench stretched out from the sentry box to the end of the turning and Maurice made his usual patrol along its length at regular intervals, for the Coley nightwatchman was a creature of habit.

Up in the night sky the clouds were gathering and the falling sleet was changing to large white flakes. It was a pity, he thought to himself. Earlier it had seemed as though it would be a good night to study the heavens, which Maurice, being an enthusiastic amateur astronomer, did on a regular basis. He'd seen a glimpse of Orion that evening, with reddish Betelgeuse and bright Rigel in the hunter's leg, but any further stargazing was impossible now with the weather closing in. It mattered not, Maurice decided. If he could somehow shield the nightlight he carried in his pocket he might be able to read another chapter of *Nicholas Nickleby*. Charles Dickens was one of his favourite authors and the pupils he had once taught were left in no doubt as to which of the classics they should concern themselves with.

Maurice leaned back and reminisced while the

water was getting hot over the brazier. 'Come out here, Smythe, and bring me your notebook. Be quiet, Gates. And you too, Kelly. This is supposed to be an English lesson and it's degenerating into bedlam.'

Mr Chips would have been proud of him, he thought, or at least his creator James Hilton would have. His pupils had been proud of him too, he knew. Smythe came to visit the school just before he left for France and so did Gates. Kelly too paid a visit and was encouraged to speak to the class about the rigours and dangers of serving their country at sea. They were all long gone now, but he still heard their high-pitched voices in the playground and saw them file past in their uniforms of khaki and navy blue, as if in spectral tribute to their favourite master. The sound and fury of that terrible time was history now, but on his lonely vigils the former teacher often wondered how many of those young lives had been enfolded for ever into the quietness of the night.

The water was coming to the boil and Maurice prepared to make the tea. It was a far cry from the insipid tea and scones in the master's room at college, but it mattered not, he decided. A sentry is a sentry, whether in the palaces of Rome, on the ramparts in Elsinore, or in a backstreet in Bermondsey.

The snow was falling fast now and already the cobbles were disappearing under a carpet of white. Behind the wall that ran along the turning the sounds of freight being assembled split the stillness of the night and Maurice heard the steady footsteps of the approaching beat bobby.

Life as a nightwatchman was not all that bad, he reflected. It had its compensations: the occasional genial conversation, time for an uninterrupted reverie, stargazing and reading; time to refresh the mind, sharpen the wits and revisit the classics, though his enjoyment of things cerebral was undeniably poorer without the hungry minds of a young class to feed.

The water was boiling but first Maurice consulted his pocket-watch. It was one thirty. The tea would have to wait, he decided. After all, he was a creature of habit, and it was time to patrol.

CHAPTER 17

Charlie Foden walked the length of the trench at one o'clock on Christmas Eve, looking down at the uncovered Victorian brickwork that reminded him of a long reptile. Here and there the workmen were leaning against the crumbling tunnel waiting for orders and beginning to feel the cold penetrating them, now that the hard slog was over. One or two glanced up at him hopefully as he passed by but Charlie knew the decision to pull them out of the workings was up to Sharkey. He walked back to the hut where the ganger was drinking coffee and pulled up a stool. 'I don't see the sense in keepin' the men in the trench,' he remarked. 'The job's finished an' they'd be better off sittin' in the shed.'

'Ben Coley makes the decisions an' 'e ain't 'ere,' Sharkey answered.

'When's 'e due in?'

'I dunno. I ain't 'is keeper.'

Charlie fixed the ganger with his eyes. 'I'm gonna get the men out,' he said firmly.

'They stay there till Coley gets in,' Sharkey replied with a note of menace in his voice.

Charlie got up slowly and faced him. 'Surely 'e won't mind. There's nuffink for 'em ter do.'

'That's up ter Ben,' Sharkey said.

Charlie was suddenly filled with anger at the ganger's intransigence. 'I'm gonna pull the men out an' I'll take full responsibility,' he declared.

'I wouldn't if I were you,' Sharkey growled, his eyes flaring.

'Yer not gonna try an' stop me, are yer?'

'You're walkin' a thin line, Charlie. Don't overstep it.'

'Let me tell yer somefink,' Charlie said, leaning on the bench top. 'I fink you agree wiv me that those men should be out o' that trench but yer too worried what the Coleys might say. You wouldn't want them ter fink yer've gone weak all of a sudden. I've got you taped, Sharkey. Under that 'ard exterior you're just the same as me.'

'Piss off,' the ganger growled as he turned away.

Charlie stepped out of the hut into the bitter cold air. 'Right, men, out yer get,' he called down the line.

The enthusiastic scramble made him smile to himself and he jerked his thumb towards the shed. 'Yer can't get changed yet 'cos there might be some more tidyin' up ter do, so get in there an' keep the noise down.'

As he walked back to the hut he saw Ben and Frank Coley coming along the street. Both looked pleased with themselves and they nodded to Charlie.

'Are we finished?' Ben asked him.

'All done an' levelled off,' Charlie answered. 'I've pulled the men out o' the trench in case yer wanna check the brickwork. Yer can't do it wiv 'em all loungin' against it.'

Frank nodded. 'I'll take a look, then I wanna talk ter the men,' he announced.

There was an air of expectancy when Frank

Coley led the way into the long tarpaulin shed. 'Right, men,' he began. 'I'm pleased ter tell yer that from next Monday we'll be startin' diggin' at River Lane in Dock'ead. It's a main sewer contract an' part o' the 'ole sewage renovation scheme fer Bermondsey. It'll mean regular work fer at least a year an' you lot'll be retained. Anuvver fing. We're gonna operate a bonus scheme. If the target's reached each week there'll be an extra fifteen shillin's in yer pay packet, but if we fall be'ind I'll assume there's some slackin', an' that means two men'll get the push an' be replaced from names on the waitin' list. Fair enough?'

The men nodded, voicing their agreement, and as the noise level rose Frank Coley held up his hand. 'We're pleased wiv the effort you've put in, so we're lettin' yer go early. Yer can get changed now an' collect yer wages in the Mason's Arms before yer push off 'ome. Merry Christmas, men.'

Charlie felt a sadness welling inside him as he looked round at the men's happy faces. The few shillings in their pay packets were hardly recompense enough for the hard, back-breaking week's toil and the small perk of an early day was little enough appreciation for their efforts, which had enabled the Coleys to secure the lucrative main contract. A bonus in the men's pay this week would have been a far better gesture, but Frank and Ben Coley were shrewd, cold-hearted businessmen who were using the hard times to their advantage. While there were ten men waiting for one vacancy they could afford to operate with a rod of iron. The present workforce had been primed to suit and they worked like zombies, knowing full well that any misdemeanour, however slight, would mean a swift return to the dole queues.

Charlie turned and followed the Coleys out of the shed. 'I'd like a word, Frank,' he said.

Coley gave him an enquiring look. 'In the office,' he replied.

Ben turned to his brother. 'Me an' Sharkey'll start the payin' out. I'll see yer in the pub later.'

Frank led the way into the hut and sat down on the high stool. 'What is it?'

'I understand the new job's gonna start in two separate sections,' Charlie said.

'Yeah, that's right,' Coley replied. 'Ten men per section. The new men we're takin' on 'ave all worked fer us before so there'll be no novices ter worry about. You an' Sharkey'll each 'ave ten workers in yer team an' 'e'll get the new men.'

Charlie nodded. 'The reason I wanted ter see yer is, I've got a problem wiv Wally Coates. Nuffink I can't 'andle, but I want yer ter know that if it comes to it I won't 'ave no 'esitation in doin' what Sharkey does when someone don't shape up.'

'Who's Wally's partner?' Frank asked.

'George Parry.'

Frank Coley smiled. 'Still lookin' out fer that pal o' yours, I see.'

'George Parry's bin no trouble,' Charlie assured him. 'In fact 'e's turned out ter be one o' the best diggers on site, which I 'ave ter say 'as surprised me. Nevertheless 'e's got Wally Coates on 'is back all the time. The two don't get on an' Coates is upset that 'e can't wind Parry up.'

'So what am I s'posed ter do about it?' Frank asked testily.

'Let Sharkey 'ave Coates on 'is team.'

Frank shook his head. ''E stays wiv you. If I take 'im out it'll seem like you're callin' the tune. Anyway, Sharkey's gonna 'ave the new men ter deal wiv, so I don't wanna saddle 'im wiv someone like Coates. I will 'ave a word wiv the man, though.'

Charlie nodded. He knew it was useless to pursue the matter any further, but at least he had tried.

Bill and May Whittle were facing their trials and tribulations with a resolve that drew favourable comments from their neighbours, themselves struggling to get by this Christmas. Mrs Venners, the Whittles' next-door neighbour, was saddened by the fact that May Whittle was not getting any better, and she noted that the blue tinge in her face had become more prominent this last few weeks. May was finding it a great strain caring for her husband and five sons, all still at school, and the onus fell on Bill to take on more of the responsibilities of running the home and family. Things had not been made any easier early in November when Bill was thrown out of work. He took comfort in being around during the day to do more in the home, but he was desperately afraid that he would not be able to pay the bills or provide decent food for his growing boys.

''E's such a nice man too,' Minnie Venners

remarked to Elsie Farr's daughter as she held the new baby in her arms.

'So are the boys,' Jenny replied. 'They're very polite, good-natured little kids.'

'It must be a terrible worry fer poor ole Bill,' Minnie said. 'I'd like ter be able ter take 'em a bag o' shoppin' but we're all in the same boat as them really. I s'pose I could spare a cup o' sugar an' maybe a few spoons o' tea, but yer can't go knockin' at their door wiv little bits an' pieces like that, can yer?'

Jenny nodded. 'I've got a tin o' corned beef they could 'ave an' p'raps a few biscuits, but like yer say yer can't give 'em odds an' sods like that. It'd be like we were feedin' sparrers.'

Minnie suddenly brightened up. 'Yeah, that's right,' she said, 'but if we 'ad a whip-round in the street for 'em an' people put in what they could afford in the way o' food it'd mount up.'

'That's a good idea,' Jenny told her. ''Ere, you can start wiv this corned beef.'

'Got a carrier bag, Jenny?'

'Yeah, 'ere's one.'

'Right, let's get started.'

Ada Black donated a cup of sugar and a knob of cheese while her friend Emmie, not wanting to be outdone, gave a tin of condensed milk and a few Oxo cubes as well as a pat of margarine wrapped in greaseproof paper.

Mrs Naylor felt bad about not being able to add to the food collection but she had a new scarf and gloves which her sister had knitted for her. They were a shocking pink and they made her shudder every time she looked at them. 'What was the silly mare finkin' of?' she had ranted. 'I wouldn't be seen dead in these.'

The lurid scarf and gloves went into the hamper along with a pair of lisle stockings and Mrs Naylor felt quite relieved.

The cups of sugar donated gradually mounted up and by the time Mrs Venners reached the end of the street the carrier bag felt quite heavy. Homemade jam, tins of beans, a packet of salt and a few less practical items were accepted with profuse thanks and a tear or two by the ailing May Whittle, but she was at a loss for words when Will Jackson turned up with half a dozen bundles of firewood, and the promise to replace her cracked parlour window free of charge.

At number 16 Annie Belton threw another piece of wood on to the flames and sat back in her armchair to await the arrival of her husband Sid. There was time yet, she thought. He wouldn't dream of coming home until the Dun Cow turned out. Not that it mattered, though. He would be too drunk to assess the situation clearly and when he had fully recovered his senses the shock of what she had to show him would send him straight back to the pub.

'Why don't yer chuck 'im out, Muvver?' Annie's elder son Reggie said, scowling. 'The drunken ole bastard ain't never bin any good ter none of us.'

'Don't you talk like that about yer farvver,' Annie said sharply. 'Whatever 'e is 'e's still yer dad.'

'Reggie's right,' Mick Belton cut in. 'If it wasn't fer you goin' out cleanin' an' doin' that part-time job at the baker's we'd bloody well starve.'

'You two boys 'ave gotta remember that yer farvver wasn't always like 'e is now,' Annie told them. 'Once upon a time 'e was a smart man.'

'Yeah, once upon a time,' Reggie said mockingly. ''E's a bloody disgrace now.'

''E ain't werf a carrot now, Muvver,' Mick growled.

'Now don't you two start sayin' anyfing when 'e gets in,' Annie warned them fearfully. 'I don't want any trouble.'

'Last night 'e was in a bad mood when 'e got 'ome an' you took all the abuse wivout sayin' a word,' Reggie reminded her. 'At one point I thought 'e was gonna give yer a right-'ander. I tell yer now, Muvver, if 'e as much as lifts an 'and ter yer when 'e gets in I'm gonna do 'im good an' proper.'

'Yeah, an' I'll kick six buckets o' shit out of 'im too,' Mick added.

'Don't you worry, 'e wouldn't touch me,' Annie said, smiling at their concern. ''E never 'as done an' I don't s'pose 'e'd start now.'

''E might just, just when yer show 'im that,' Mick remarked, nodding towards the brown envelope propped up on the mantelshelf.

'No 'e won't.'

'Just let 'im try, that's all,' Reggie said with venom.

Lucy Parry relaxed in the armchair by the roaring fire and George sat opposite her, cuddling Sue whose eyes were drooping with sleep. Sara sat facing the fire next to Lucy and she hummed in time to the carols coming over the wireless. The table had been moved back to provide more room and Charlie was sitting at George's elbow in an easy chair with the evening paper resting on his lap.

'The pubs'll be packed ternight,' Lucy remarked.

'I'd sooner be by this fire,' George answered as he moved Sue into a more comfortable position.

'I used ter go dancin' on Christmas Eve,' Sara told them.

'Who wiv?' George asked, intrigued.

'Wiv a young man I knew.'

'I didn't know you could dance.'

'Well yer do now.'

'Talkin' of dancin', do you dance, Charlie?' Lucy asked.

'I did frequent the dance 'alls when I was a young buck,' he replied. 'but I wasn't all that clever at it.'

Sara seemed amused by something she had recalled. 'Shall we all 'ave anuvver glass o' port?' she suggested.

'It's yours ter decide,' Lucy reminded her.

Sara smiled. 'I was really surprised when they called out my number at the fellowship. It was the main prize: a bottle o' port, a bottle o' sherry an' a large Christmas puddin'.'

'Good fer you, Sara,' Lucy said as she held out her glass.

'More port, Charlie?' Sara asked, smiling sweetly at him.

'I'd be delighted to join you,' he replied, assuming a refined accent as he too held out his glass.

Lucy gave him a humorous smile. 'This is very cosy,' she remarked, and as Sara handed her back the replenished glass she raised a toast. 'May the good spirit of Christmas bless us all.'

'I'll drink ter that,' Charlie said.

'Yeah, 'ere's ter peace an' goodwill,' George added.

'I'm tired,' Sue said in a croaky voice.

'I'll take you up in a few minutes,' George told her.

'I wanna be asleep before Farvver Christmas comes,' the child said anxiously.

'You will, my love,' Lucy replied in a cooing voice.

Sara sighed deeply. 'There'll be many round 'ere who won't be gettin' a visit this year,' she remarked.

George got up with Sue holding tightly to his neck. 'I'll get 'er in bed,' he said.

Lucy stood up and planted a kiss on the child's forehead. 'Sleep well, darlin',' she whispered.

The fire was burning low and Lucy refuelled it with a large knob of coal. Outside an icy wind was blowing from the north, hiding the stars from view behind thick dark cloud. At the diggings in nearby Lynton Road Maurice Oakfield struggled with the nightlight in his sentry box and gave up as the wind increased. Constable Ron Sloan walked slowly along Cooper Street, chewing on his chinstrap and looking forward to a cup of hot sweet tea with Maurice, and at number 16 the Belton boys waited with their anxious mother for the homecoming of the prodigal father.

Lucy Parry poked at the large knob of coal that was starting to flare and listened to the wind rattling the windowframes. 'It'll snow in the night, I'm sure,' Sara remarked.

Suddenly a muffled noise sounded outside.

'What was that?' Sara said with a horrified look on her thin face.

'I dunno. It sounded like someone screamin',' Lucy replied.

'Don't open the door,' Sara warned her fearfully.

Lucy ignored her and hurried out to the passage, followed by Charlie. 'Better let me take a look,' he told her.

As he opened the door they saw him, a drunken figure reeling in the middle of the road. Blood was coming from his nose and he was struggling to stay on his feet.

'It's Mr Belton,' Lucy said in a shocked voice.

'An' don't come back, you drunken ole bastard,' a young voice yelled out.

Lucy and Charlie looked along the turning to see Annie Belton being comforted by her two sons.

''E punched our muvver,' Reggie called out.

'So we give 'im what for,' Mick added.

Sid Belton staggered towards the pavement. 'It's all 'er fault,' he slurred. 'We've bin given notice ter quit.'

'Piss off an' don't come back,' Reggie Belton shouted after him.

Charlie ushered Lucy back into the house and closed the front door just as George came down the stairs. 'I saw it from the bedroom,' he said.

213

'Looks like they've given their ole man a right pastin'.'

Lucy sighed sadly. 'Christmas, the season of goodwill to all men, unless yer name's Sid Belton. Mind you, 'e 'ad it comin' to 'im. C'mon, let's finish off Sara's port.'

CHAPTER 18

For most of the folk in Cooper Street the festive holiday had seemed little more than a normal weekend, and the prospect of a happy new year seemed especially remote for the Belton family. Annie was beside herself, wondering what she could do, if anything, about the official brown envelope sitting on her mantelshelf. For the Parrys and the Chubbs it had been a restful time. The small presents passed around had been accepted gratefully, everyone knowing just how hard it had been to raise the money for the luxuries.

'Go careful, both of yer,' Lucy called out as her husband and Charlie set off for the diggings in Dockhead through a carpet of fresh snow.

Roy answered their knock and caught them up halfway along the turning. 'It's a nice day ter go back ter work,' he remarked sarcastically.

'Summer's a long way off,' Charlie said, hunching his shoulders against the chill wind.

George remained quiet as they walked out of the street. Never very talkative in the mornings, he was feeling less inclined to say anything on this particular day. Having to work alongside Wally Coates again made him feel on edge, and he worried about what was in store at the new workings. Things couldn't go on the way they had been for much longer.

The men walked quickly past the Lynton Road

workings and turned right over the wide bridge that spanned the railway, crossing Southwark Park Road and finally coming out into Dockhead, the riverside district of tall warehouses, wharves and old tenement buildings. Smells of hops, spices and pepper greeted them and the sour tang of river mud rose in their nostrils as the receding tide laid it bare.

Frank and Ben Coley were already at the site talking in earnest with their ganger, and when the three men from Cooper Street arrived Frank beckoned to Charlie. 'I was just puttin' Sharkey in the picture,' he said. 'The soil round this area is very unsettled. The Electricity Board 'ad two cave-ins when they were layin' new power cables last summer an' they said there's water runnin' underground from the Thames. It'll mean we've gotta keep our eye on the shutterin'. I'm orderin' new plankin' fer a start an' I want every inch propped up securely. We're gonna be runnin' on a tight schedule an' there'll be no room fer delays. One o' Sharkey's new men is used ter shutterin' an' 'e's bin primed already. Make sure your man knows the score too. Get your team down the lane ter the ovver marked-out area, Charlie, an' you, Sharkey, you get movin' on this stretch. Right then, let's get ter work.'

River Lane ran parallel with the river, narrow in places but widening out to take traffic along a roughly cobbled surface. The lane afforded access to wharves and warehouses at its widest part, and where it narrowed into little more than an alley it served as a shortcut to the foot of Tower Bridge.

While the excavations were taking place River Lane would be closed at the narrow end and made accessible to light transport only, and Charlie thought about this as he led his men along towards the barrier. Of the two trenches to be dug, his would pose more problems in that it would have to be cut narrow, with less room to manoeuvre, while Sharkey's trench could be wider.

'At least we won't 'ave any lorries an' 'orse an' carts passin' back an' forwards while we're in the trench,' Mick Johnson remarked.

Charlie nodded, realising the added dangers passing traffic would pose on that unstable ground. 'Right, lads, let's make a start,' he said, then looked directly at Coates. 'An' remember we're not in a contest ter see if we can outdo Sharkey's team. Remember as well, we'll be workin' in a narrow trench, so be extra careful. Space out safely an' let's make sure we earn that bonus.'

At six thirty that morning Mary Chubb called into the paper shop in Tooley Street to collect the Dolan's key. Jack Crompton opened up at that time every day to sort out the morning newspapers he had started to sell a few months ago. He had a team of paper boys who delivered to the tenement blocks and flats in nearby backstreets and he felt that the extra profit coming in from the deliveries was worth the early rise.

'Mornin', gel,' he said cheerfully as Mary walked into his shop.

'Mornin', Jack. It's a cold 'un.'

'There we are.'

Mary took the key. 'Er, Jack. Would you mind if I collected the key in the evenin's from ter-morrer?' she asked gingerly.

He shook his head. 'I'd like to, gel, but ole Cuthbert's put the block on it. I did it fer the last cleaner till she got found out, an' Cuthbert told me the key can only be given out in the mornin's now.'

'What difference can it make to 'im?' Mary said. ''E's still gettin' the work done whichever way.'

'I shut at six thirty every night,' Jack explained, 'which means yer wouldn't be able ter give me the key back till the next mornin', an' Cuthbert don't like the idea of 'is cleaner 'avin' the key in 'er possession all night, not after the business in Long Lane.'

'What was that?' Mary asked.

Jack Crompton added several newspapers to a pile and put them all into a wide canvas bag. 'This woman used ter do cleanin' at an office in Long Lane,' he explained. 'One night while she was workin' 'er 'usband an' 'is mate were pickin' the lock of the safe in a director's office. They managed to open it an' they cleaned out over two thousand quid by all accounts. Of course she pleaded ignorant an' said 'er ole man must 'ave copied the key wivout 'er knowledge an' gone in the office after she'd left that evenin'. Trouble was, there was one o' them new-fangled time-locks on the safe an' the police knew exactly when the lock was picked. They stop goin' when the safe's opened, apparently, an' the time put 'er in the office while it was all 'appenin'.'

Mary smiled. 'If I was out ter rob the firm I could get the key copied anyway,' she pointed out.

'An' if there was no sign o' forced entry you'd be the prime suspect,' Jack reminded her. 'They'd wear yer down, gel, till yer confessed.'

'I s'pose yer right,' Mary replied. 'Never mind, it was werf a try.'

He smiled back at her. 'I'm sorry. If it was left ter me I'd let yer 'ave the key in the evenin's, but it's our Kate, yer see. She frets over the least little fing an' after that ovver business she'd worry 'erself sick if I let yer 'ave it.'

'I understand,' Mary said.

That morning Ernest Cuthbert arrived at twenty minutes past seven. 'Nice holiday, Mrs Chubb?' he enquired.

'Nice, but very quiet.'

'I thought I'd get in early this morning,' he said as he took off his grey mackintosh and trilby. 'I've got a backlog of work to catch up on. Nothing like an early start to get the blood flowing.'

Mary looked at his pallid face and thought it was going to take more than an early start to get his blood flowing. 'I expect you're right,' she replied.

'I stay pretty fit, you know,' he went on. 'Long walks and early to bed, that's the secret.'

Mary was standing with a duster in one hand and a handbrush in the other. 'I'm just about to—'

'Are you concerned about fitness, Mrs Chubb?'

'No, I can't say I am.'

'Actually it was my wife who introduced me to

body fitness,' he said. 'She's a naturist, you see. We both practise it whenever we can. Not this weather, of course – well, not outside. In the home, though. We find it very restful walking around with no clothes on.'

Mary struggled to keep a straight face. 'What about in the summer?'

'We go to a naturist club in Sussex,' Cuthbert revealed.

His eyes strayed over her body and Mary guessed what he was thinking. 'Well, I'd better finish off,' she said quickly.

'Have you ever thought about joining a naturist club?' he asked in a low voice.

'Good God no,' she replied, shocked at the question.

'I could give you the address of my club,' he continued regardless. 'I think that once you've tried it you'll be itching to take your clothes off at every opportunity.'

Mary nodded briefly and hurried out of the office with a hasty excuse. Cuthbert seemed to be working himself up into a lather, she thought, and she would have to be careful not to en-courage him in any way. She wondered about the last cleaner. Had he got to her with his views on nudism, or could it have been-

'Mrs Chubb,' he called out. 'Have you a minute to spare?'

When Mary walked back into the office Cuthbert was standing by his desk holding a magazine. 'Here we are,' he said, 'you can have this. It'll let you know a little more about naturism.'

Mary took the magazine and mumbled her thanks as she went back to her chores. Wait till I tell Lucy, she thought to herself.

Maurice Oakfield had been transferred to the new workings now that the main contractors were renovating the brickwork in Lynton Road, and being of an enquiring mind he was keen to inspect the site. Very close to the river, he thought. There'd be night mists sweeping in. Cold too, though the warehouses and wharves would help shield some of the wind. Might be a good place to put the sentry box, here by the gap between the two diggings. Must have a word with Mr Coley.

Satisfied, he made his way to the nearest pub and ordered a ginger ale. 'Thought I might introduce myself,' he said to the landlord. 'I'm the nightwatchman at the River Lane sewer job.'

'Sooner you than me, mate,' the landlord replied. 'I'd be a bit nervous o' that place at night.'

'Oh, an' why's that?'

'Well, it's steeped in 'istory round 'ere as yer might expcct, an' there's always stories.'

'You're perfectly right,' Maurice agreed. 'I'd imagine there are a few ghosts walking the lanes by the river on cold dark nights.'

'An' it doesn't worry yer?'

'Not in the slightest,' Maurice answered positively. 'Ghosts can't harm you.'

'Well I wouldn't like ter be chained to one,' the landlord said with a shudder.

Maurice finished his ginger ale and felt that his

finances might stretch to another. 'Fill my glass, stout yeoman,' he said cheerfully.

An elderly man walked into the quiet pub just as Maurice took up his refill and the landlord nodded to him. 'Mornin', Godfrey,' he said.

'Mornin', Stan,' the old man replied. 'I see they're startin' work at the River Lane.'

'Yeah, an' this is the nightwatchman who'll be on the site.'

The old man chuckled. 'Glad it ain't me. Sittin' there all night wouldn't be my cup o' tea. 'Ow d'yer pass the time sittin' in that little box?'

Maurice smiled indulgently. 'I read by the light of my nightlight if the wind's not too high, and then there are the stars to watch, if the sky remains clear. I take a regular stroll – well, it's a patrol really, just to make sure all's well – brew tea over the brazier and think about all sorts of things. It's quite pleasant on a friendly night, but I have to be honest, it's not much fun when the rain beats down and dowses the fire, or when an icy wind chills the bones.'

'What about the spirits?' the old man asked.

'Spirits? You mean ghosts?'

'Spirits, ghosts, phantoms, they're all the same,' Godfrey replied. 'River Lane was notorious at one time fer sightin's. People used ter come in this pub quakin', 's that right, Stan?'

'That was before my time,' the landlord answered. 'People don't use River Lane so much now.'

'Well I can assure yer that the spirits used ter congregate there at certain times,' the old man went on. 'Used ter be a prison back in the

Elizabethan days. It was mainly used fer naval prisoners: deserters, mutineers an' the like. The ole chronicles tell of the prisoners bein' starved an' tortured an' then they chucked the bodies in the river on the tide. Yeah, they say there's a regular assembly o' spirits at certain times down in River Lane. I don't mean ter frighten yer, but a man who's gonna do nightwatchin' in a place like that should be forewarned.'

'And for that I thank you, sir,' Maurice said elegantly. 'I will be on my guard.'

'Course, yer probably won't see anyfing unusual,' Godfrey continued, 'but it's the ground bein' disturbed. That won't 'elp. Last time they were workin' in River Lane the trench caved in an' two blokes were buried under a load o' soil. They were lucky ter be dug out alive.'

Maurice bade them goodbye and went home to his lodgings to get some sleep before his night on duty, and Godfrey Thomas took his place at the counter. 'I 'ope I didn't put the fear up 'im,' he said, chuckling.

'I don't fink yer did,' the landlord replied. ''E seemed a very cool customer.'

''E won't be if those ghosts start roamin',' the old man replied sagely.

At the diggings the work was getting under way and Roy Chubb was busy preparing the best of the planking for the job of propping up the slimy, muddy soil. 'We're gonna 'ave trouble if we're not careful,' he remarked to Charlie when the ganger walked up to him. 'The soil's like paste, even wiv this bitter weavver. If it gets milder it's gonna turn inter sludge an' then we'll know all about it.'

'I'm gonna go an' see Coley about that new plankin' 'e's promised us,' Charlie told him. 'I don't want Sharkey claimin' it all fer 'is team.'

Just then there was a shout from the far end of the trench and Charlie could see Danny Albury holding up his hand.

'It's Joe Lambert,' Danny said as Charlie came running. 'There's somefing wrong wiv 'im.'

The trench was barely knee-deep along its length and the distressed digger was hauled out and lowered on to the mounting pile of rubble to recover.

'It's me chest,' Joe rasped. 'I was shovellin' out an' suddenly this pain caught me. Christ! I thought I was gonna die fer a minute.'

Charlie saw how the colour had drained from the man's face. 'Get in the shed,' he told him, 'an' if the pain don't ease up soon yer'll 'ave ter go ter the 'ospital.'

'What d'yer fink it is?' Danny asked.

''E could 'ave pulled a muscle in 'is chest,' Charlie suggested. ''As 'e bin coughin'?'

'Yeah, 'e 'as,' Danny replied. 'It was a sort o' raspin' cough.'

Charlie walked over to the shed. 'Can yer manage ter get 'ome under yer own steam, Joe?' he asked.

'Yeah, course I can,' the digger answered.

'Right then, on yer way,' Charlie urged him. 'That could be a dose o' pleurisy yer got.'

'I've never bin troubled wiv anyfing like that before,' Joe declared.

'Anyway, yer better get it seen to right away,'

224

Charlie said as he helped him on to his feet.

Sharkey's trench was not free of incident either on that first morning, and it served to upset the local clergy.

'Well I'll be stuffed,' Ginger Gordon exclaimed as he uncovered a skull, complete with teeth. 'I wonder 'ow old this is?'

'Donkey's years I expect,' his partner replied. 'We could be diggin' over a plague pit fer all we know. They say there was a burial place round 'ere in the dark ages.'

'Better leave it fer Sharkey ter see,' Ginger said as he placed it carefully on the edge of the trench.

Lofty Williams the carpenter picked up a piece of splintered planking and hammered it into the soil before setting the skull on top of it. 'There we are,' he said. 'That 'ead's gonna jump down an' bite the ear off anyone who starts slackin'.'

The men set to work once more and the skull was forgotten until Father O'Riorden chanced to walk through River Lane. 'Holy Mary Mother of God!' he roared. 'Is this how you heathens treat our departed? Get it down, this instant!'

'Where can we put it?' Ginger asked him.

'Certainly not back in the soil,' the reverend father raved. 'Get something to put it in, and should you dig up any more human remains put them with it. They will all have been desecrated by you gaggle of pagans and need the holy blessing of reconsecration. Holy Mother! What next?'

'Silly ole git,' Ginger muttered as the irate father stormed off to seek out the Coleys. 'It was only a bit of a skeleton.'

'I can see you ain't a Catholic,' Lofty Williams remarked.

'No I ain't,' Ginger replied. 'Are you?'

Lofty shook his head slowly. 'We ain't 'eard the last o' this, not by a long chalk,' he said.

'Why's that?' Ginger enquired.

'That was Father O'Riorden,' Lofty told him. ''E's all fire an' brimstone.'

'Yeah, maybe, but 'e's still a silly ole git,' Ginger said as he buried his pickaxe in the cold damp soil.

CHAPTER 19

Though they drank toasts to the new year, 1936 began in much the same vein for the Coley diggers. The bitter weather continued and the unremitting, thankless toil seemed never-ending. As soon as the trenches were cleared for the bricklayers to start work a new section was to be opened up in nearby Morgan Street, and then once the contractors had finished renovating the two lengths of uncovered sewer in River Lane and the surface was made good the remaining fifty-yard length linking the two was to be dug up, on which score the two gangers were summoned to the hut.

'I want you two ter take a look at this blue-print,' Frank Coley said as he unrolled the large drawing on the benchtop. 'The reason we left a gap between the two trenches was the unstable soil conditions, marked 'ere in colour. One long trench would 'ave weakened the ground ter such an extent that there might well 'ave bin a large cave-in. Now you know we've got an arrangement wiv the contractors fer them ter fill in an' resurface the road wiv their mechanical equipment, but in this case there's a problem usin' the 'eavy machinery in the lane due ter the unstable soil conditions, so they've asked us ter do the job by 'and an' then they'll use a light road roller ter make good the surface.'

Coley paused to look at each of the gangers in turn. 'Now as yer know, the idea was ter tackle the Morgan Street section next week while they were brickin' up 'ere, but there's bin a change o' plan. We reckon the freezin' weavver'll prevent any natural slippage, so we're gonna press on wiv excavatin' the middle section which'll leave the 'ole lot ready fer the brickies next week. We've got the okay from the contractors, providin' the full length o' the trench is made safe fer their men ter work in. That means it's gotta be securely shuttered.'

'We'll need more new timbers,' Charlie told him. 'Some o' that wood we've got now is rotten.'

Coley nodded impatiently. 'We'll take care o' that. Now, I'm givin' you two o' Sharkey's team, Charlie, an' I want yer ter get that middle section dug out by the weekend. All right, I know it's cuttin' it fine, but that's the way it goes.' He turned to the other ganger. 'Sharkey, you can start right away in Morgan Street, then next week we can go back ter normal, everyone workin' in Morgan Street till we're called back ter fill in 'ere. It'll save us a few days by doin' it this way an' it'll make sure we don't 'ave the contractors breavvin' down our necks.'

Charlie was not happy about it. 'It's a tall order, expectin' the section ter be finished in two days, even wiv two extra men.'

'Tell 'em we're uppin' the bonus to a quid,' Coley replied. 'That'll fire 'em up.'

'What about Joe Lambert's replacement?' Charlie asked.

'You'll 'ave 'im termorrer fer sure,' Coley answered.

Lucy and Mary were holding a council of war. 'Trouble is, I can't get the key till 'alf six,' Mary explained, 'an' the lecherous ole goat's bin comin' in at 'alf eight every mornin'.'

'It makes yer wonder about the last woman,' Lucy remarked. 'Did 'e try it on wiv 'er?'

Mary shrugged her shoulders. 'I wouldn't be at all surprised. When I saw Ada Black down the market she asked me 'ow I was gettin' on there, but I didn't say anyfing to 'er about 'im. Yer know what a mouth an' trousers she can be at times.'

Lucy sipped her tea. 'P'raps it'll be better if you can carry on fer a bit longer,' she suggested, 'unless the ole goat gets too much to 'andle. Once 'e accepts yer won't play 'is little game 'e might start comin' in later.'

'I was 'opin' we could work the oracle there,' Mary said, pulling a face. 'I explained it ter Roy an' 'e could see what I was gettin' at. I told 'im that if we could manage ter do the job in the evenin's we could look out fer anuvver key job nearby an' do the two tergevver, as it wouldn't be very nice goin' up ter the likes o' Tooley Street at night an' those dingy offices'd be creepy places fer a woman ter work on 'er own. Anyway 'e said 'e wouldn't mind lookin' after Gracie while I was gone.'

Lucy stared into the fire for a few moments. 'I gotta tell yer, my George ain't too keen on me goin' out cleanin' at night. Course I 'ad ter go an' put me foot in it by sayin' it was really about 'im not bein' too keen on 'avin' ter look after Sue. 'E got really shirty. 'E's so irritable lately. 'E tends ter jump at the least little fing.'

'An' 'ow are you an' Charlie?' Mary asked with a sly grin.

'I don't know what yer mean,' Lucy answered with a wide smile.

Mary leaned back in her chair. 'I fink yer do,' she said.

Lucy waved her hand dismissively. ''Ere, let's 'ave anuvver look at that magazine the bloke gave yer.'

Mary giggled as she took it out from behind the cushion and reopened it. 'Just take a look at that feller,' she said. 'Don't it make yer feel sick?'

Lucy pulled a face. 'If I looked like 'er I'd wanna 'ide in a dark cupboard, not strip off fer everyone ter gawk at me.'

Mary flicked through the pages. 'Oh my good Gawd,' she exclaimed. 'She must be all o' twenty stone.'

Lucy pulled a face as she looked over her friend's shoulder. 'Get 'im,' she remarked. 'Look at the way 'e's eyein' that woman up. Dirty ole git.'

Mary quickly flipped through the remaining pages and then shut the magazine. 'D'yer fink we're bein' 'orrible?' she said. 'Those people must take it seriously.'

'Point is, does that Cuthbert bloke take it seriously, or is 'e just an ole letch?'

'I dunno,' Mary said, reaching for the teapot. 'By the way 'e talks about it I s'pose 'e does, but

230

it's the way 'e 'as o' lookin' at me what makes me fink different.'

Lucy handed over her empty cup. 'Like I said, maybe you should carry on by yerself fer the time bein'.'

'Coward,' Mary teased with a disarming smile.

Stan Mapson the landlord of the Bell was chatting to two of his regulars at the counter while Godfrey Thomas sat nearby listening to the conversation.

'Yeah, they've started diggin' up Morgan Street,' the landlord was saying. 'As a matter o' fact we 'ad the nightwatchman in 'ere earlier. Strange bloke if you ask me. 'E seemed educated an' pretty well turned out. Not yer usual night-watchman. What d'you reckon, Godfrey?'

''E's right,' the old man replied. 'I 'ad 'im down as a teacher ter tell yer the trufe.'

'Yer could be right,' Stan Mapson remarked. 'There's fousands o' people out o' collar who are glad ter do anyfing fer a few bob.'

The taller of the two customers nodded. 'I wouldn't be fussy. I ain't worked fer over two years now.'

'I'm the same as Bill,' his friend agreed. 'I'd even do a bit o' that diggin' if it wasn't fer me back. It wouldn't stand up to it, more's the pity.'

Bill Walters grinned. 'That's your excuse an' yer stickin' to it, ain't yer, Tom?'

Godfrey sidled up to the counter. 'Me an' Stan was sayin' 'ow the place 'as got a bad name, but the bloke didn't seem at all put out. I don't fink 'e believed us.'

'What d'yer mean, got a bad name?' Tom Smith asked.

'You know, ghosts walkin' in the dead o' night an' that,' the old man explained.

'Is that a fact?' Bill queried.

'Yeah. Apparently there used ter be a prison in Morgan Street many years ago,' Godfrey recounted, 'an' when one o' the poor bastards in there snuffed it they'd chuck 'im in the river, by all accounts, an' let 'im drift out ter sea on the tide. The gaol was fer navy men, yer see, an' I s'pose they saw it as a fittin' end.'

'Well from what yer've told me I wouldn't care ter be a nightwatchman on that job,' Bill remarked.

'Me neivver,' Tom added.

Stan Mapson grinned broadly. 'I can just imagine the watchman's reaction if one of us crept in the turnin' in the dead o' night clangin' a few stones in a tin can or somefink. I bet 'e'd be off like a shot.'

'Especially if we was wrapped up in an ole sheet an' groanin' like we was in agony,' Bill said, grinning back.

Time hung heavy for Bill Walters and Tom Smith, and in the warm public bar of the Bell there was time enough to dwell on the subject of ghosts walking abroad and unhappy spirits wailing. The time eventually came for serious negotiation with Stan Mapson about the possibility of adding another pint to their slates, and with a favourable result the two men were able to spend another hour by the fire.

''Ere, I was just finkin',' Tom said after a

232

lengthy silence. 'What if me an' you 'ad a bit of a laugh wiv that nightwatchman?'

Bill chuckled. 'Yeah, I'm game fer it.'

'We could find somefink ter put over us an' we could clang somefink ter make it more scary,' Tom went on.

The two sat plotting eagerly until even they felt that it was time to let someone else share the fire, and as they walked to the public library in the bitter weather the plot was fully hatched.

Charlie got his replacement on Thursday morning, a morose, heavily built man in his forties who introduced himself as Norman Gill and had little else to say, but he gave the impression of being able to cope with the heavy toil. In addition there were the two men from Sharkey's team who seemed happy at the change as they joined the rest in the shed, and Charlie took the opportunity to spell out the situation before they started work.

'We've only got terday an' termorrer ter get this job finished, so we've gotta put our backs into it,' he began. 'Now, the ovver two sections are well shuttered an' I don't want 'em weakened when we link up wiv 'em. Wally, I'm changin' yer partner. You can take Norman 'ere as George's replacement. I don't fink Joe Lambert'll be comin' back just yet awhile so George, you can work alongside Danny Albury.'

'Why not give the new man ter Danny?' Wally complained. 'Why should I 'ave 'im?'

'Because I said so,' Charlie growled at him, then he looked over at Norman Gill. 'It's all right. Wally likes a moan now an' then, it's nuffink personal. That right, Wally?'

The giant mumbled something under his breath and the two from Sharkey's team glanced quickly at each other and smiled.

'That's put 'im in 'is place,' Fergus remarked.

'Too bloody true,' Derek replied.

The work started with a vengeance. Wally Coates was eager to show the new man that he was under the wing of the best digger on site, while Fergus and Derek worked well as a pair, and with George happy to be away from the contemptible Coates it was a determined team that bent their backs, all eager to finish on time and earn the added bonus.

During the early part of the day Roy Chubb helped out on a shovel and Charlie joined him, preferring it to standing around on a bitterly cold morning. Wally Coates swung his pickaxe into the soil and levered it loose, matched all the way by Norman Gill, who quickly removed it with little effort.

'They make a good pair,' Charlie remarked to Roy as they took a breather.

'Yeah. I'm glad yer gave George a change. It was gettin' 'im down, an' ter be honest I thought once or twice 'e was gonna steam inter the big ugly git.'

Fergus took a quick breather and motioned towards Charlie. 'That's somefing yer never see wiv Sharkey.'

'Nah, yer right,' Derek replied. 'That miserable sod wouldn't dream o' gettin' 'is 'ands soiled.'

Charlie concentrated his efforts on getting the

diggers to work as hard as they could with encouraging comments and a ten-minute spell of rest for each pair in turn, and by the end of the morning they had made excellent progress.

Wally Coates and Norman Gill sat together on a pile of rubble while they took their break. 'No disrespect ter you, but I don't go a lot on the ganger piss-ballin' me about,' Wally remarked. 'Yer get used ter workin' wiv one bloke.'

'Yeah, I know what yer mean,' Norman replied. 'Soon as we started work I could tell that yer bin in this game a long while. You can always tell.'

Wally raised a rare smile. 'I bin doin' it since I was in me twenties,' he said. ''Alf o' these blokes are chancers. There's not one decent digger amongst the lot of 'em.'

Norman was not disposed to a prolonged chat and he took out his pipe and tapped it against the heel of his boot. 'Yeah, I can see that,' he agreed.

Wally fell silent and Norman puffed thankfully away on his briar until their break time was up, and late that afternoon after working flat out the duo scraped the last of the soil away to expose the roof of the sewer tunnel. The rest of the team were not far behind, and when Roy Chubb began to fix the shuttering Charlie breathed a huge sigh of relief. His method was paying off, he decided. The ten-minute break during the day had been a wise move and finishing the job by tomorrow evening now looked a lot more likely.

That evening Maurice arrived on the dot to begin his nightly vigil, and soon he had his brazier burning merrily with pieces of scrap wood and old newspapers he had brought with him. A few coals and then some dampened coke provided by the company finally had the brazier white hot and Maurice leaned back against the wooden sentry box to enjoy the warmth on a bitterly cold night.

As the midnight hour drew near something clandestine was happening at the far end of River Lane. 'Does this look all right?' Bill asked.

'Yeah, course it does,' Tom replied as he glanced at the tattered old bedsheet his friend was wearing round his flour-whitened face and over his shoulders. 'What about me?'

'It's enough ter frighten King Kong,' Bill told him as he put a handful of pebbles into a tin can. 'Right, let's go.'

Maurice was getting ready to make his periodical patrol when he heard a clanking noise and then the sound of wailing. He got up quickly and moved to his right, peering down the curve of the lane to see two shrouded figures coming along in his direction. Maurice swiftly crossed to the left of the narrow turning and hurried into a darkened warehouse doorway. His heart was beating fast and he fought to control his breathing. This was idiotic, he reasoned. Ghosts and spirits could not physically harm anyone, other than causing a heart attack by their very presence.

The two ghostly figures drew nearer and Maurice could clearly see them now and hear the metallic clanking which seemed to be coming from under their shrouds. He held his breath as they passed the doorway, making for the sentry box, and suddenly his face creased into a smile. The ghost to the rear was not floating, it was walking on two feet. The shroud had slipped slightly and a pair of dirty hobnailed boots were clearly visible.

Years ago at Whiteacres High School the sixth-form pupils had staged a ghostly gathering in the nearby woods, but their intention to march on the school dormitories to frighten the younger pupils had been scotched by the form masters, who joined in the spirit of the prank and turned the tables. Now would be a good time to re-enact the counterplot, he thought.

Bill and Tom had reached the sentry box, their wailing echoing in the narrow lane, and they exchanged grins when they realised that the nightwatchman had run away.

'What's that?' Bill exclaimed as he heard the scraping sound.

'I dunno,' Tom said in a low voice.

The scuffing noise got louder and suddenly a wailing filled the lane.

'I'm gettin' out of 'ere,' Bill said fearfully.

'Wait fer me,' Tom screamed out, struggling desperately to disentangle himself from his tattered shroud.

From his concealed position next to a pile of earth Maurice watched the men dash terror-stricken from the lane, and when he re-emerged with a smile on his face he saw the two tin cans lying by the sentry box. 'Oh well, time for my patrol,' he thought to himself with some satisfaction as he picked them up.

Throughout the rest of the night the ex-teacher

kept the fire banked up, did his patrols and managed a chapter of *The Hound of the Baskervilles* with the aid of his nightlight, untroubled by spirits, or jokers with brains addled by them.

CHAPTER 20

On Friday morning the diggers at the River Lane site set to work with a determination to finish on time and earn their bonus, and Roy Chubb passed down the fifty-yard stretch fixing pieces of planking against the sides as the soil was removed from around the tunnel. Wally Coates and his new partner were soon out in front of the others as the clay level was reached, and Charlie felt a little concerned as he went over to where Roy was cutting a length of timber on a makeshift saw bench. 'Make sure yer keep an eye on those two,' he warned. 'The way they're goin' they could cause us a problem if those walls ain't propped securely. They're two feet lower than the rest an' we can't ignore it. I should tell 'em to ease up a bit an' let the ovvers catch up, but it wouldn't go down well wiv Coates. The bloody idiot sees this as some sort o' contest an' it seems the new bloke's just as bad.'

Roy picked up a long length of thick timber and laid it down on the saw bench. 'Look at this,' he said. 'It's split in places an' there's a load o' wood rot in it. I thought we was gettin' some decent timbers.'

'I'll 'ave anuvver word wiv the Coleys soon as one or ovver of 'em shows up,' Charlie told him. 'They seem to 'ave left us ter get on wiv it.'

'Anyway, it looks like we'll be done on time,'

239

Roy remarked.

'I'll get Coates an' Gill out fer a ten-minute spell while you get some shutterin' up at their end,' Charlie said, sticking his hands deep into the pockets of his reefer jacket. He walked down the line beside the ever-growing piles of earth and clay.

Coates clambered out of the workings with a satisfied smile on his face and Gill followed him. 'Look at that lot,' he sneered. 'Didn't I tell yer?' He cupped his hand to his mouth. 'Oi, Parry, what's the 'old-up?'

George swung the pickaxe hard and levered it against the stubborn clay before looking up. 'Get knotted,' he growled back.

Danny Albury gripped him by the forearm. 'Don't take any notice. 'E's tryin' ter wind you up.'

George took another forceful swing with the pickaxe. 'I'm not standin' fer much more of it, whatever yer say, Danny,' he replied. 'I took enough piss-takin' while me an' 'im were workin' tergevver an' I ain't takin' it now.'

Danny threw a loosened lump of clay out of the trench and stabbed the blade of his shovel back into the protesting soil. 'Look, George, I'm a bit older than you an' I've got a lot more experience in this game,' he said as he pressed his foot down on the edge of the shovel. 'I've come across the likes o' Wally Coates on plenty o' diggin' sites in the past. They're bad news. Coates ain't got no family ter consider, an' as long as 'e earns enough ter pay 'is keep at the workin' men's 'ostel an' keep 'imself in beer 'e don't give a toss. 'E gets

240

pleasure out o' goadin' 'is workmates an' you 'appen ter be the one 'e's pickin' on at the moment. What you 'ave ter remember is, yer kept up wiv 'im when you two were teamed up an' it annoyed 'im, so now yer workin' wiv someone who's 'alf sensible you should ignore 'im.'

George took up his pickaxe once more. 'I'm more than 'appy ter be workin' wiv yer, Danny,' he remarked. 'We make a good team.'

'Oi, Parry! Is that pickaxe too 'eavy for yer?' Coates shouted.

'It's not too 'eavy ter bury in that fick 'ead o' yours,' George responded.

'Feelin' tough are we?' Coates growled as he scrambled on to his feet.

'Oi, you! Where the 'ell d'yer fink you're goin'?' Charlie yelled as he hurried along the line. 'Yer break's over. Get back in that trench the pair o' yer.'

'Don't worry, it'll keep,' Coates called out to George as he went back to work.

Maurice Oakfield was feeling pleased with himself as he strolled along to the Bell with a small brown paper parcel under his arm. 'Mornin', mine host,' he said breezily as he walked into the public bar.

'Well if it's not Mr Nightwatchman,' Stan Mapson replied. ''Ow's it goin'?'

'Mustn't complain,' Maurice declared, wanting to delay the presentation till the right moment.

The landlord had not been privy to the outcome of the River Lane spookery. In fact he had seen nothing of the two perpetrators, who were feeling too embarrassed to go into the Bell that morning. 'What'll it be?' he asked.

'A ginger wine if you will,' Maurice told him, looking round the bar as he placed his parcel down on the counter.

Just then the elderly Godfrey Thomas walked in, and when he saw Maurice he looked surprised. 'I didn't expect you ter be 'ere,' he remarked.

'Oh, and why's that?' Maurice enquired.

'I understand there was some strange goin's-on in River Lane last night.'

'You could say that,' the watchman said, smiling. 'It seems the place is prone to visitations. As a matter of fact I did see an apparition last night, but I'd be interested to learn how you know about it.'

Godfrey looked uncomfortable. 'Someone was tellin' me this mornin'. They said the local bobby was s'posed to 'ave seen somefing ghostly movin' about in the lane.'

'I could have done with that policeman's assistance last night,' Maurice told him. 'It was nearing midnight when I banked up the fire, and suddenly I heard a wailing and a clanging noise. I looked down the length of the trench and then I saw it.'

'Saw what?' the publican asked impatiently.

'It's hard to describe,' Maurice continued, milking the moment. 'I could see two white shrouded figures coming towards me. Strangely enough, they appeared to be floating along. It was really frightening, I can tell you.'

'So what did yer do, run?' Godfrey asked.

'Good Lord no,' Maurice said positively. 'That would have been the wrong thing to do. No, in these sorts of situations it's better to stay put, and let the spirits, ghosts, or whatever see that you mean them no harm. And let's face it, how do you harm a ghost?'

'What, then?' the publican asked.

'Well, I slipped into a doorway and watched points,' Maurice went on. 'The two spirits came right past me, and do you know what?'

'No.'

'I noticed that the ghost bringing up the rear was actually wearing boots. Remarkable, don't you think?'

'Yer mean they wasn't ghosts?' Godfrey queried.

'Just a couple of young men out for a bit of fun,' Maurice answered.

'Ah, but they could 'ave bin real ghosts wearin' ordinary boots just ter fool yer,' the landlord ventured.

Maurice unwrapped the parcel and held up the tin cans. 'These are what they used for the clanking noise,' he replied. 'Anyway, I thought it was time to do a spot of wailing myself, and when I did the two young men ran from the lane like bats out of hell.'

Stan Mapson shook his head slowly. 'I wanna shake yer 'and, pal,' he laughed. 'I really admire the way you 'andled that situation. What yer drinkin'? It's on the 'ouse.'

'In that case I'll have a whisky in the ginger wine, if you please,' Maurice told him.

Lucy sat by the fire helping Sue to identify the large coloured letters of the alphabet, and as the child responded in a sing-song voice Sara nodded to her sister-in-law. 'She's pretty good.'

'She'll be startin' school this year, won't yer, luv?' Lucy said encouragingly.

'Time certainly flies,' Sara sighed. 'Last year seemed ter flash by, which suited most. It was a year we'd all want ter put be'ind us.'

Lucy had long since fathomed her sister-in-law. She was never very talkative except when it suited her, and it was obvious now she would be seeking a favour. 'You asked me if I'd tong yer 'air terday. D'yer still want me ter do it?'

'I'd be very much obliged,' Sara replied.

Lucy smiled to herself. Of course it was Friday, and Sara usually made an effort to smarten herself up at weekends. Once her hair was done she would be certain to put on her fawn dress with the dark brown figured pattern over the bodice, and she'd use a light powder and a spot of rouge on her pale cheeks as a finishing touch before taking her place by the fire around the time the men got home. It had become painfully obvious that she was out to create a favourable impression on Charlie Foden, who had become rather embarrassed by it all, as had George, judging by his uncharitable comments the previous evening. 'The silly woman should get out more, an' I don't mean ter the church. She's involved wiv that fellowship business enough as it is, an' I'm sure it's not doin' 'er any good.'

'I know it's embarrassin' fer Charlie the way she carries on at times,' Lucy replied, 'but yer gotta feel a bit sorry for 'er. Let's face it, we know she fancies 'im but she just doesn't know 'ow ter go about it.'

'Maybe it's just as well,' George remarked. 'She'd only get a kick-back. If there's anyone 'ere Charlie fancies it certainly ain't our Sara.'

'An' what's that s'posed ter mean?'

'Come off it,' George replied curtly. 'Anyone can see 'e fancies you. I've seen the way 'e stares at yer at certain times.'

'Now you're bein' stupid,' Lucy told him. 'I've never bin aware of 'im starin' at me.'

'Yer would say that, wouldn't yer?' George retorted. ''E only wants 'alf a chance an' 'e'd be there.'

'That's ridiculous,' Lucy said with feeling. 'I'd never give 'im the chance an' I'm sure 'e'd never take advantage. As a matter o' fact I see 'im as a member o' the family now, an' if you was honest yer'd say the same.'

George leaned back in his chair. 'Don't get me wrong. I like Charlie, but I wouldn't trust 'im where you was concerned.'

Lucy realised that she should be angered by her husband's comments but instead a raw, fearful excitement had risen in her belly. Charlie did fancy her, and he had said as much. Only the agreement they had made kept him from making his move, but his eyes mirrored his true feelings and she relished his every glance.

Sue had had enough of the alphabet book and she slid down from her mother's lap. 'Can I go an' play wiv Gracie?' she asked.

'No you can't,' Lucy told her. 'I've gotta start

the tea soon, and in any case you're due fer an early night ternight, madam.'

'Will you 'ave time fer me 'air?' Sara asked.

Lucy nodded and stood up. 'Move away from that fire an' I'll get the tongs,' she said.

Sue climbed into Sara's vacant chair and watched while her mother set to work, testing the heated tongs by closing them over a piece of brown paper before using them on Sara's lank mousy hair.

'I've bin finkin',' Sara said after a while. 'Would Charlie feel it was a cheek if I invited 'im ter the fellowship next week?'

Lucy had to stifle a giggle. 'No, I shouldn't fink so,' she answered, 'but ter be honest, Sara, I don't fink 'e'd care ter go. It's not somefink Charlie'd take to.'

'I dunno,' Sara said. 'There's a few men at the meetin', widowers who go there fer company.'

'Charlie's not a widower,' Lucy said quickly, 'an' when 'e needs company 'e goes up the pub wiv George or down ter the dockers' club.'

'Do yer fink 'e likes me?' Sara asked.

Lucy was surprised at her sudden frankness. 'I'm sure 'e does, but I don't fink 'e's lookin' fer female company.'

''Ow d'yer know?'

'Charlie's lived on 'is own fer some time now,' Lucy pointed out, 'an' like most men 'is age, 'e's come to accept that way o' life.'

''E's not that old,' Sara replied quickly. ''E's only in 'is mid-forties. A man's s'posed ter be in 'is prime at that age, an' besides, 'e don't come over ter me as bein' celibate by choice. I fink 'e

246

just needs a little bit of encouragement an' 'e'd be all fired up.'

'Sara!' Lucy said in mock horror. 'You've got a naughty mind.'

Sara smiled smugly. 'I'm just makin' an observation.'

The younger woman knew that her sister-in-law had hit on the truth, but Charlie had no designs on Sara, and unless she was made to realise the fact there was only heartbreak and unhappiness ahead for her. 'There we are, all done,' she said. 'Just let me give it a quick brush out, then I'll 'ave ter be gettin' on wiv the tea.'

Danny Albury had decided to stay for a drink at the Mason's Arms but the other three diggers from Cooper Street walked home together through the gathering mist, and Charlie felt pleased with the way the day had gone. There had been no hold-ups, and even Frank Coley had raised a brief smile when he arrived to find that the work had been completed on time. George Parry was happy to be free at last from working alongside Wally Coates, but Roy Chubb was very thoughtful. He had been hard put to it shoring up the sides of the trench to his own satisfaction and he had fussed over the job, aware that he was working with sub-standard wood. Next week there would have to be some answers forthcoming, he told himself. Why hadn't Coley done what he promised and supplied new timbers? Any cave-in would doubtless be blamed on shoddy workmanship rather than the lack of proper materials, and it was vital that the request for more new timbers should be recorded and witnessed.

Across the small street Ada Black stood at her front door with her coat collar turned up against the chill as she chatted to her best friend Emmie. 'It's gonna be a foggy night by the look of it,' she remarked.

'Yeah, it looks like it,' Emmie replied. 'I've told our Bert ter bank the fire up. I won't be movin' far from it ternight, that's fer sure.'

Elsie Farr came hurrying into the turning with the evening paper. 'It's gonna be a foggy one ternight,' she said as she came up to her neighbours.

'I was just sayin' that to Emmie,' Ada replied. 'By the way, 'ow's the baby?'

''E's gettin' on lovely,' Elsie told her. 'Our Jenny's lookin' forward ter gettin' back ter work an' I'm lookin' forward ter mindin' 'im.'

'It's a shame she's gotta leave the little mite while 'e's so young,' Ada remarked, 'but if needs be.'

'She's got no option,' Elsie said a little sharply. ''Er Len's out o' work again.'

''Ere, 'ave you 'eard 'ow Sammy Strickland got on terday?' Emmie asked.

Elsie shook her head. 'Peggy told me this mornin' 'e was goin' after a job at the tannery, but I ain't seen anyfing of 'er since.'

'I dunno where 'e finds 'em,' Emmie went on. ''E's always goin' after jobs but 'e never ever gets one. I wish 'e'd let our Bert know. I'm gettin' sick an' tired of 'im under me feet all day. 'E's gettin' sick of it all too. It ain't right fer a man ter be mopin' about all day.'

'Well, I'd better get indoors an' start on the tea,' Ada said reluctantly, not wanting to leave the other women chatting together in case she missed any juicy gossip.

'Yeah, I gotta go,' Elsie told them.

Emmie Goodwright nodded. 'I s'pose I'd better be off too,' she said.

None of them was feeling confident enough to take the initiative, and it wasn't until Bert Goodwright came to the door to see what was keeping Emmie that the conference broke up.

CHAPTER 21

During the early hours of Saturday morning strong winds came in from the west, sweeping away the thick night fog and ushering in dark, threatening clouds. By dawn heavy rain was falling, with thunder rumbling in the distance, and as the Cooper Street womenfolk got ready to make their usual trip to the markets the storm broke in earnest. Torrential rain lashed the little houses, bouncing up from the pavements and cobblestones and running down into the gurgling drains.

At number 8 George and Charlie were both enjoying a lie-in and Sara had woken up with one of her headaches, which prompted her to go right back to sleep again, but downstairs it was less quiet. Sue and Gracie knelt together on a chair in the scullery watching the deluge and listening to the clanging sound as the rain pounded the tin bath hanging on the yard wall. Behind the children Lucy and Mary sat at the scullery table listening to their chattering.

'I get in that every Friday. Well, I fink it's when it's Friday,' Sue was going on.

'D'you remember when we got all wet?' Gracie said, giggling.

'Yeah, when we was barfin' our dollies.'

'My dolly's not very well, but I'm gonna give 'er some medicine an' she'll soon get better.'

'Shall I get my dolly's clothes?' Sue suggested.

Her little friend did not seem too enthusiastic and they continued to stare out at the driving rain. 'My daddy said we gotta 'ave rain ter make fings grow,' Sue remarked, 'but I don't like it. We can't go out ter play when it's rainin'.'

'We could play 'ospitals,' Gracie said, scratching her head. 'You could be the nurse an' I'll be the mummy.'

It was Sue's turn to show reluctance. 'Nah, we always play 'ospitals. I wanna go out an' play in the yard.'

'Well you can't,' Lucy told her. 'It's absolutely fallin' down.'

'When will it stop?'

''Ow do I know?'

'This afternoon,' Mary cut in. 'So you two 'ad better find somefing ter do in the meantime.'

'Let's go upstairs an' look at my books,' Sue said.

Gracie slid off the chair and went over to Mary. 'Mum, can I go an' get my books?'

'I'll get 'em later,' Mary said quickly. 'Now you two go upstairs an' play.'

'An' don't make too much noise. Aunt Sara's in bed. She's not very well,' Lucy added, with a meaningful glance at Mary.

The children wandered from the scullery and Lucy got up to put the kettle on. 'I've bin givin' it some thought about that job,' she said. 'Yer've got used ter the money now, an' I'm a bit worried in case it don't work out. You'd be the loser.'

'Well I say let's take a chance,' Mary answered. 'This last two days ole Cuthbert 'asn't bin comin' in early an' I've bin finishin' at twenty ter nine. Me wages are left on the desk in 'is office so I can't see 'ow it won't work out. If 'e does 'appen ter come in early an' catch yer out just say I'm not well an' I asked yer ter fill in fer me. Anyway, you could do wiv the few bob same as me.'

Lucy shook her head. 'Nah, it was an 'are-brained scheme, Mary. I'll wait till there's anuvver key job goin' up that way an' then we can do like we said, knock the two jobs out tergevver.'

'Are yer sure? Really sure, I mean?' Mary asked, looking a little concerned.

'Yeah, really.'

Her friend watched while Lucy took the boiling kettle off the gas and filled the china teapot. 'Is George all right?' she asked.

'Sort of.'

'That's no answer.'

Lucy shrugged her shoulders. 'Ter be honest, Mary, 'e's not bin the same man since 'e lost 'is job, but who is? Takin' that job diggin' wasn't a very good idea as far as I'm concerned, but you know George. 'Is pride wouldn't let 'im stand in those dole queues day after day, week after week. All right, I know fousands an' fousands are compelled ter do it, but it was drivin' 'im scatty. D'you know, 'e's 'ardly bin near me since 'e was put off, an' on the rare occasion it does 'appen it's over before I get goin'. I'm sure it's become a sort o' duty to 'im. Keep 'er 'appy an' let's get some sleep. Trouble is, it don't keep me 'appy, an' I can't seem ter talk to 'im about it wivout endin' up 'avin' a barney.'

'I'd say 'e's takin' a chance, especially wiv

anuvver man in the 'ouse,' Mary replied. 'What if yer turned ter Charlie fer comfort?'

Lucy shook her head quickly. 'I couldn't, much as I like the feller.'

'Yeah, yer say that, but yer never know,' Mary persisted. 'It could just be that one time when yer desperate fer arms round yer an' some lovin', an' George ain't there, but Charlie is. It 'appens.'

Lucy smiled indulgently. As well as being very observant Mary was never one to pull her punches, but her comments were welcome. She had always been there for Lucy and a good shoulder to cry on. Nothing Mary could say in good faith would be taken the wrong way and the woman knew it. 'Ter be honest it wouldn't be that 'ard fer it to 'appen,' she said quietly. 'Charlie ain't all that good at 'idin' 'is feelin's. I see the way 'e looks at me sometimes an' there's no mistakin' it. If I give 'im 'alf a chance 'e wouldn't need promptin'.'

'George is a fool,' Mary replied plainly. 'You an' 'im 'ave gotta get fings worked out or I can see big problems.'

Lucy sighed as she poured the tea. 'I'm all mixed up,' she confessed. 'On the one 'and I want George ter notice I'm there an' make the occasional fuss o' me, an' on the ovver 'and I don't want 'im near me. Does that make any sense ter you?'

Mary smiled. 'Yeah it does. I reckon you fancy Charlie strong enough ter go wiv 'im an' yer want a strong enough excuse. Bein' neglected as a red-blooded woman gives yer that excuse.'

Lucy added sugar to the tea and passed a cup

over to Mary. 'I tell yer somefink,' she said. 'Yesterday there was a letter came fer George, from the Royal Naval Reserve. They wanna know if 'e'd like to apply fer a promotion course ter petty officer. 'E was really bucked up about it an' although 'e wouldn't commit 'imself I'm certain 'e's gonna say yes. It'll mean 'im goin' ter Portsmouth fer a few weekends, an' when 'e showed me the letter I was pleased fer 'im, but I was also excited about the weekends at Portsmouth. D'yer know what I'm sayin'?'

'It's not 'ard ter guess,' Mary answered. 'It'd leave you an' Charlie alone in the 'ouse. Apart from Sara, of course, but she goes out occasionally.'

'Exactly, an' I was filled wiv guilt,' Lucy told her. 'Then I got ter finkin'. S'posin' I do let Charlie know I'm available an' me an' 'im do get at it while George is away, what 'arm could it do? It wouldn't be somefink wiv weddin' bells at the end of it. It'd just be a mad fling. 'E's bin on 'is own fer a long while an' I'm not exactly the contented wife. It could be very good fer both of us, an' it might even 'elp ter get me an' George closer.'

'A lot o' people say that a bit on the side sometimes 'elps ter strengthen a marriage,' Mary replied, 'an' I s'pose they always will, but it could be disastrous if fings don't go the way you want 'em to. What you an' Charlie get up to while George is away is your business, but as far as I can see, it 'as ter be spelt out from the start. No commitment from eivver of yer. Make sure it don't get serious ter the extent that yer can't stay

255

away from each ovver. In ovver words enjoy it fer what it is an' carry on bein' the dutiful wife, if you can bear it.'

Lucy sipped her tea, thinking about what Mary had just said. She was right, of course. Her marriage was solid, built on firm ground, and George was a good husband, despite his recent lack of feeling. She would rather die than let it flounder. 'I can bear it,' she said, smiling.

Since he had been confronted by Ron Sloan the beat bobby, Will Jackson had been very careful to keep his distance, for the time being at least. On that wet Saturday morning, however, he was keen to enlist the services of Sammy Strickland in a moving job, and he hadn't given the policeman a second thought. 'I can't do it on me own, Sammy, an' I thought you might like the chance to earn a few coppers,' he said as the two stood inside his front door.

'I'm always ready to earn a few shekels, but I gotta be careful o' me back,' Sammy told him. 'That's why I gotta know just what this job entails. I can't go movin' pianners, wringers' an' those sort o' fings.'

'I dunno exactly what Mrs Bright wants movin' but she ain't got no pianner, that's fer sure.'

''Ow d'yer know if yer don't know exactly what she 'as got?'

''Cos she said it'll all go on a barrer.'

'Well, that's different.'

'So yer gonna give us some 'elp?'

'If the price is right.'

'I'm chargin' 'er firty bob an' 'alf a crown fer

the barrer, 'cos that's what Tommy Dougan's chargin' me fer the loan of it,' Will explained. 'So we earn fifteen bob each.'

'Sounds reasonable.'

'I should say it is. It's only from Lynton Road ter Macklin Street, which is just round the corner. We could be done in 'alf an hour.'

'Right then, I'm wiv yer.'

'I told the ole gel I'd be there by twelve,' Will said, 'so if we get our skates on we could start now an' be finished by then.'

'Where's the barrer?' Sammy asked.

'In Tommy Dougan's yard.'

'Where's that?'

'In Briar Street.'

'That's a bit of a way.'

'It ain't far.'

'Far enough.'

'Now look, are you wiv me or not?' Will asked crossly.

'Yeah, course I am.'

'Well you go an' fetch the barrer while I go round ter see Mrs Bright.'

'Why me?'

''Cos it'll save time,' Will told him. 'By the time you get the barrer round ter Lynton Road I'll 'ave all 'er bits an' pieces packed away in the cardboard boxes she's scrounged. Now when yer go inter Briar Street from the Old Kent Road yer'll see a red door on yer right about 'alfway down the turnin'. That's Dougan's yard door. Just go in an' give 'im the 'alf-crown an' tell 'im Will Jackson sent yer. All right?'

'An' where's the woman live?'

'Number 10 Dennis 'Ouse, Lynton Road.'

'Right, I'm on me way.'

The street's handyman hurried through the driving rain to the block of council buildings in Lynton Road and when he arrived out of breath Mrs Bright had a cup of tea waiting. 'Them stairs 'ave bin killin' me,' she groaned. 'I really can't tell yer 'ow 'appy I am ter be movin' back into a little 'ouse. These buildin's are murder. You 'ardly ever see yer neighbour, an' when yer do yer can't stand gassin' at the front door like yer can when yer live in an 'ouse.'

''Ow come yer moved 'ere in the first place?' Will asked.

'I 'ad no option,' the woman told him. 'The place I lived in was condemned an' they stuck me in 'ere. Only fer a few months till we find an 'ouse, they said. Two bloody years ago that was an' I've kicked up merry 'ell ever since. Anyway, they finally found me a place in Macklin Street, fank Gawd.'

'Right then,' Will said, rubbing his hands together. 'Is this the lot?'

'Yeah, except the big stuff.'

'Big stuff? What big stuff?'

'The joanner an' me wringer.'

'Bloody 'ell, I didn't know yer wanted fings like that moved,' Will said, looking round the room. 'When I came round last time yer said it'll all go on a barrer.'

'Well it will, though not all at once, I grant yer.'

'I wish yer'd said that at the time,' Will puffed. 'Movin' pianners an' wringers is dearer than ordinary stuff.'

'Well I 'ave ter say I thought you was very reasonable wiv yer prices,' Mrs Bright said sweetly.

'It'll cost an extra 'alf a quid.'

'That's all right.'

'Anyway, where's the pianner?'

'Wiv the wringer.'

'An' where's the wringer?'

'In the pram sheds down the alley,' Mrs Bright told him. 'The council let me use two o' the sheds ter store 'em or I'd never 'ave agreed ter come 'ere in the first place.'

Will Jackson set about packing up Mrs Bright's bits and pieces and soon Sammy Strickland arrived looking hot and bothered. 'That bloody barrer's 'ard work empty,' he growled. 'The wheels need a good oilin'.'

Will knew that if he moved the small cartons first he would never get Sammy to come back for the wringer and piano. 'There's bin a change o' plan,' he said hesitantly.

Sammy looked suspicious. 'Go on then, tell me.'

Before he had finished explaining the helper shook his head sternly. 'Sorry, Will, but I just can't do it, not wiv my back.'

'It's only round the corner.'

'I don't care if it's next door.'

'I'll do the 'umpin'.'

'I don't care what yer do, I ain't movin' no pianner.'

Will scratched his head in consternation. 'Not fer an extra 'alf a quid?'

Sammy stroked his chin. 'All right then, but if

259

me back goes I'll 'ave ter leave it ter you.'

The two manhandled the piano from the pram shed and pushed it along the alley to the pavement, and then Will tipped the barrow on its end. 'We'll lean the joanner backwards an' then we'll be able ter pull the barrer back upright wiv it on it,' he said.

The job was not as hard as Sammy had feared and they were soon pushing the laden barrow along Lynton Road. Getting the instrument off the barrow in Macklin Street was no harder, but it took some considerable negotiation getting it into the house, and some tutting from Mrs Bright before they settled it in the parlour.

'Look at the bloody scratches on it,' she complained.

'They was there before we started,' Will replied irritably.

'Yer better bring the cardboard boxes next,' she told them. 'I got all me fings in the boxes an' I can't make a cuppa till they get 'ere.'

The barrow wheel was squeaking badly by the time the two removers got back to Lynton Road, and after they had finished loading up the six heavy cartons Sammy sat down on the kerbside to catch his breath. 'That wheel's gonna seize up before we've finished, mark my words,' he said.

Will was eager to get the job done and he leaned his weight against the shafts. 'C'mon, Sammy, give us a push,' he urged him.

As they reached Mrs Bright's house the wheel locked solid. 'There we are, what did I tell yer?' Sammy said self-righteously.

Will Jackson was not going to be beaten. 'We'll

let it cool a bit while we fetch the wringer,' he decided.

'Yer mean we're gonna push it round 'ere?' Sammy said, a look of horror on his pale face.

'Yeah, unless you got any better ideas.'

Mrs Bright came out of the house frowning. 'Yer fergot ter pack me teapot,' she told Will.

'Oh, no. I remember now. I left it on the drainin' board.'

'Fetch it wiv the wringer,' she ordered, 'an' don't ferget ter make sure yer shut the front door tight when yer leave.'

The two were feeling decidedly jaded by the time they had manoeuvred the rusting wringer into the street, and to make matters worse the rain had started to fall once more.

''Ang on while I go an' get that poxy teapot,' Will said testily.

Sammy leaned his weight against the wringer and it started to move. Encouraged, he continued, knowing that Will would not be far behind.

''Ello, 'ello,' a voice called out over his shoulder and Sammy turned quickly to see PC Ron Sloan strolling up to him. 'An' where yer goin' wiv that?'

'I'm 'elpin' me mate,' Sammy told him.

'It wouldn't be the 'andyman by any chance, would it?' the constable queried.

Sammy nodded. 'Yeah, Will Jackson.'

Just then the man himself came out of the block entrance carrying the teapot. 'Oh my Gawd!' he exclaimed.

'Stoppin' fer a tea break are we, Will?'

'Nah, we're movin' someone.'

Ron Sloan sucked on his chinstrap and rocked back and forth on his heels as he glared at the handyman. 'Why is it every time I bump inter you lately there seems ter be a wringer involved? You ain't collectin' 'em, are yer?'

'Nah, we're movin' it fer Mrs Bright,' Sammy cut in. 'It's only round the corner so we thought we'd push it instead o' puttin' it on the barrer.'

'So yer've got a barrer?'

'Yeah, but the wheel's seized up, so we left it in Macklin Street where Mrs Bright's movin' to.'

Ron Sloan looked suspicious. 'Let's take a look at this barrer,' he said.

The two removers accompanied him into Macklin Street and stood watching while the policeman walked round the old contraption. 'It ses "Tom Dougan" on the side,' he observed. 'Did you get this from Tom Dougan's yard?'

Sammy nodded. 'Yeah, I did.'

'Well I'm afraid yer in trouble, me ole beauty,' the policeman said in a grave voice. 'Tom Dougan called in at the station ter say someone walked off wiv 'is barrer.'

'That can't be right,' Will interjected. 'I sent Sammy ter get the bloody fing. I'd already made the arrangement wiv Tom Dougan ter loan it an' 'e said it'd be 'alf a crown. Sammy paid 'im, didn't yer, Sammy?'

The older man looked decidedly uncomfortable. 'Well, as a matter o' fact I didn't actually give 'im the money.'

'Why not?' the constable asked.

'Well it was like this, yer see. When I got there

Tom Dougan was walkin' off up the street wiv this ovver geezer an' I saw the barrer standin' in the kerb outside the shed, so I thought 'e'd put it out ready. I decided ter take it an' pay when I fetched it back.'

'Well you'd better bring that wringer round an' then get the barrer back ter Dougan quick as yer can,' the policeman told them. 'I'll be poppin' in ter see Tom later an' it better be back there, or else.'

The two men struggled to push the wringer into Macklin Street and finally set it in place in Mrs Bright's backyard.

'I 'ope you intended ter pay Dougan when yer took the barrer back,' Will remarked. 'Or was yer 'opin' you could put it back wivout bein' noticed an' pocket the 'alf-crown?'

'As if I'd pull a dirty trick like that,' Sammy said with a haughty look.

'I'm sorry I can't offer yer a cuppa,' Mrs Bright said as she settled her bill. 'I ain't got the cups unpacked yet.'

Sammy leaned on the barrow. 'The wheel don't seem so stiff now,' he remarked. 'I fink I can manage it OK.'

'You won't 'ave to,' Will told him sternly. 'I'm comin' wiv yer, just in case.'

CHAPTER 22

It had rained on and off all through the weekend and on Monday morning a drizzle was still falling. The temperature had risen too and Roy Chubb was feeling worried as he joined his two workmates and walked briskly out of Cooper Street. 'I'd like ter take a look at the River Lane site,' he said. 'It's on our way ter Morgan Street.'

Charlie nodded. 'You ain't worried about that shorin', are yer?' he asked. 'It looked a good safe job ter me.'

'Yeah, but there's been so much rain over the weekend it could 'ave moved,' Roy told him.

George Parry had his hands tucked into his coat pockets and his head held down against the rain, and as usual he had little to say. His thoughts were elsewhere on that particular morning and he had already made up his mind to go for the naval promotion course. Had he been able to predict what lay ahead that day he would have turned back home there and then.

The three made the slight detour into River Lane and Roy breathed a sigh of relief when he looked down into the muddy trench. 'Well, nuffing seems to 'ave shifted since we left it on Friday evening,' he remarked.

'I told yer it was a good job,' Charlie said, grinning. 'Just make sure yer do a good job in Morgan Street.'

'We ain't sure what the subsoil's like there,' Roy pointed out. 'Morgan Street runs directly down ter the river, remember.'

'What's the drill?' George asked unexpectedly. 'Is it gonna be one long trench, or are we doin' it in sections like River Lane?'

'One long section,' Charlie told him.

'Well I 'ope I can get the opposite end ter Wally Coates an' that ovver idiot 'e's workin' wiv,' George growled.

'I'll see what I can do,' Charlie answered.

Although Danny Albury lived in Cooper Street he always made his own way to work, and was already changed by the time his partner arrived. 'Stay clear o' Coates terday, George,' he warned. ''E's in a right ole mood.'

'That's nuffink unusual,' George replied.

'I ain't seen 'im as bad as this,' Danny said. 'Apparently somebody's nicked 'is pocket watch.'

'When was this?'

'Last night in the lodgin' 'ouse by all accounts.'

'I didn't know 'e could tell the time,' George remarked with a grin.

Wally Coates was sitting by the entrance of the shed, and as George and Danny walked past him he gave them both a hard stare.

'Shall I ask if anyone's got the time?' George joked.

Danny pulled a face. 'I wouldn't if I were you,' he muttered.

The two changed quickly into their overalls and wellington boots, and George pulled a woollen scarf out of his overall pocket and wrapped it loosely round his neck.

'Knit that yerself did yer?' Coates asked in a mocking voice.

'Yeah, plain an' purl,' George answered. 'You should try it sometime. It's quite easy really, but then again maybe not. Yer need at least 'alf a brain ter learn knittin'.'

Wally Coates stood up quickly, his eyes wide with anger, huge hands rolled into tight fists. 'You've bin askin' fer this, Parry,' he snarled as he moved forward.

George quickly put the long heavy table between him and the hulking digger. 'Calm down, Coates, or yer'll be doin' the walk,' he told him.

'If I do the walk it'll be over your mangled body,' the big man growled.

Roy Chubb was standing outside the shed talking to the other carpenter Lofty Williams when Coates made his lunge at George and he jumped back in, grabbing the giant round his middle. 'All right, calm down,' he said quickly.

Coates threw him off as though he were a child, and using the bench seat to clamber up on to the table he dived at the smaller man with a roar.

''Old tight, Sharkey's comin',' someone called out.

George had gone down under the bully's weight and he fought like a wildcat to get free, suddenly feeling as if his head would burst as Coates grabbed him round the throat.

'What's goin' on 'ere?' Sharkey called out as he hurried into the long shed.

'Get 'im off George!' Danny implored the ganger.

Sharkey stood back a pace and turned away

267

from the flailing arms and legs. 'Right, you lot, let's get ter work,' he shouted. 'C'mon, not in a minute, now!'

'Stop 'im, fer Gawd's sake!' Danny screamed at Sharkey.

Alerted by Roy, Charlie rushed into the shed, leaned over and grabbed Coates's hair at the back, yanking hard until the man's head was arched enough for him to slip his other hand round his neck. 'It's over, big man, now let's get ter work,' he said breathlessly as he shoved Coates away, then he turned to George. 'You too, George, there's work ter do, at the opposite end.'

Sharkey stood next to Charlie, watching the men take their digging tools from a pile and set to work on the trench. 'Coates ain't no slouch,' he remarked. 'I wonder why 'e didn't turn on you?'

'I should 'ave thought that was obvious,' Charlie replied. ''E gets a few privileges as the Coleys' eyes an' ears, but even they wouldn't sanction 'im settin' about a ganger an' 'e knows it.'

'Yeah, I can see that, but that's if the man's finkin' straight, which I don't fink 'e was.'

'Well let's assume 'e prefers ter mark time,' Charlie said with a sardonic smile. ''E'll get round ter sortin' me out, if 'e can, I've no doubt.'

'I expect yer wonderin' why I didn't pull 'em apart,' Sharkey said as he slid his hands into his jacket pockets.

'It did cross me mind.'

'I was quite 'appy ter pick up the pieces,' Sharkey explained. 'I've got no time fer eivver of 'em, but if I tried ter sack 'em I'd be overruled by Frank Coley, so why should I risk gettin' 'urt?'

Charlie looked along the line. ''Ow d'yer wanna work this one?' he asked.

'It's a twenty-man workforce an' we're talkin' about an eighty yard stretch,' Sharkey replied. 'Let's share it. We'll walk the line tergevver an' then spell each ovver.'

'Sounds OK,' Charlie said. 'One fing, though. If we do well terday we'll be startin' ter shore up the sides termorrer an' we'll need more decent timbers, not that woodworm-ridden rubbish we've bin usin'.'

'What d'yer expect me ter do?' Sharkey asked.

'Back me up when I see the Coleys.'

'Yeah, OK.'

As the mounds of shifted earth started to grow at the side of the workings heavy rain and driving winds made working conditions very difficult, and before long sludge ran back into the trench and the men gritted their teeth and grunted with exertion as they heaved out shovelfuls of mud that seemed to weigh a ton.

Mary Chubb hurried along Tooley Street and went into the papershop a few minutes after Jack Crompton had opened up.

'You're sharp this mornin',' he remarked.

'Yeah. I got someone comin' ter see me later an' I wanna get done early,' Mary told him.

'Don't owe 'em any money, do yer?'

'I shouldn't fink so,' she replied, smiling.

As she crossed the wide thoroughfare and stepped out of the gloomy winter's morning into an equally gloomy set of offices Mary felt flat. She knew she should have been glad to get a key job, which was considered far better than working for a cleaning company. She knew also that Gracie was being well cared for in her absence and Lucy had refused to accept any money for the chore, but she could not shake off the depression. She and Lucy had planned to share the job but since her friend had changed her mind the initial enthusiasm had vanished. Maybe another key job would come up soon, she hoped, and then they could share the jobs as planned.

Lorries and horse carts were arriving to load and unload at the Tooley Street wharves and warehouses, and purposeful footsteps sounded outside as the early workers turned up to begin another day. In the Dolan offices Mary worked with a will, and after cleaning the toilets she glanced up at the clock in Cuthbert's office. It was eight thirty and she set about her final chore, polishing Cuthbert's large desk.

Suddenly he was there, standing by the open door, still holding his briefcase and rolled umbrella, his watery grey eyes staring out of a pale face. 'Good morning, Mrs Chubb,' he said in his reedy voice.

Mary was taken aback. 'You scared me,' she gulped. 'I never 'eard yer come in.'

'I'm very sorry,' he replied as he slipped his umbrella into the stand and struggled out of his light mackintosh. 'I seem to have missed you in the mornings. As a matter of fact the trains have been a little erratic this past week or so, but I'm pleased to say that the Southern Railway appear to have overcome their problems and I hope to see more of you now.'

Mary smiled and set to work polishing the desktop. Not if I can help it you won't, she thought. 'There we are, I'm just about finished,' she told him.

He looked disappointed. 'Wouldn't you like to stay for a coffee?' he asked. 'I have the facilities to make some.'

'No, really,' she said, smiling. 'I need ter get back 'ome. I 'ave somebody lookin' after my daughter an' I don't like ter take liberties.'

'I'm sure they wouldn't mind if you were a few minutes late,' Cuthbert pressed.

'No, really.'

He walked over and eased himself into his large padded desk chair. 'Tell me, Mrs Chubb, would you have any objection to me addressing you by your Christian name?'

'It's Mary,' she said.

'That could be the oldest Christian name of all,' he said with a stab at humour. 'Tell me, Mary, did you have a chance to view the magazine I gave to you?'

'Well I ... I sort of...'

'It's quite all right,' he assured her. 'I understand your reluctance to admit to perusing a rather forward periodical, a publication that some people would find rather objectionable.'

'I didn't find anyfing bad in it,' Mary replied. Cuthbert's eyes were moving again and she felt uncomfortable. 'Well, I'd better be off,' she said quickly.

'Mary, can I ask you something?'

'Yes?'

'After studying that magazine does the thought

of communing with nature excite you? Can you imagine the sense of freedom when a naked body is offered to the elements, the wind cooling the hot brow, stinging rain chastising the flesh, and the warm spring sunshine gently caressing and stimulating the sensuous regions? It's something to live for, believe me.'

'I must admit I didn't look at it like that,' Mary replied, trying not to laugh aloud at the way his voice sounded as he delivered his flowery speech.

Cuthbert raised a finger as a gesture for her to wait and he reached down into a bottom drawer and brought out a key. 'This is not just an ordinary key,' he said with conviction. 'This key represents freedom and exquisite pleasure. On any given day, at any time, I can climb the stairs to the top floor and use this key to let myself out on to a flat section of the roof. The design of the building makes that part completely private. It is there that I take off all my clothes and experience a freedom of expression, and the exquisite sensation of the elements assailing my nude body. Can you understand? Could you envisage joining me there at some time? If you can, and do so, you will feel as I do, experience pleasures heretofore denied you. Think on it, Mary, and reread the magazine with a more enlightened outlook. You may surprise yourself.'

Mary nodded as she moved backwards from the room. 'Good day, Mr Cuthbert,' she faltered.

Jack Crompton gave her a cheery nod as she walked into his shop and handed him back the key. 'See yer termorrer,' he said.

'I doubt it very much,' she answered.

CHAPTER 23

The morning rain had never let up and by lunch-time when the bedraggled workmen climbed out of the deepening trench they were feeling decidedly miserable. They had cut down at an angle to hold the sides in place but already sludge was oozing into the workings.

'I can't start shorin' it up yet,' Roy said to Charlie as the two stood watching the men slouch into the shed.

Charlie was determined that there would not be a repeat of the morning's rumpus and he was pleased to see that George and his partner Danny Albury had moved down to the far end of the shed, away from Wally Coates and Norman Gill who always sat by the entrance. 'It's like a bloody powder keg,' he sighed. 'It only wants one word out o' place, one bad look, an' it could all be off.'

'I don't fink George is gonna provoke 'im again,' Roy answered, 'but as far as Coates is concerned I dunno.'

He turned his back on the shed and walked over to where the timbers were stacked. 'There's not much good stuff 'ere,' he said as Charlie joined him. 'See fer yerself, most of it's sodden.'

'As I said, I'll 'ave a word wiv Ben Coley soon as 'e gets back,' Charlie told him.

Roy was not impressed. 'It's like talkin' ter that

bloody shovel. We're gonna need more plankin', good or bad, ter shore up over eighty yards o' trench.'

It was late afternoon before Ben Coley made an appearance and he nodded impatiently when Charlie mentioned the need for some more timber. 'Leave it ter me,' he grumbled. 'I'll get some out 'ere first fing termorrer.'

Charlie walked along the line and noticed that George and Danny had stationed themselves far enough away from Wally Coates and his partner to avoid any backchat, but had he heard their conversation he would have been concerned.

'I ain't finished wiv 'im yet,' George growled. 'Next time 'e 'as a go at me I'm gonna crown 'im, mark my words.'

'It ain't werf it,' Danny replied. 'Just ignore 'im.'

The muddy state of the trench slowed the work, and by five o'clock when the men scrambled out of the workings the tunnel roof had still not been uncovered.

In Cooper Street the rain trickled off Ada Black's umbrella as she stood at her front door chatting to Emmie. 'I was talkin' ter Paula Jackson at the market this mornin',' she announced. 'Apparently 'er Will was complainin' about Sammy Strickland.'

'Oh?'

'Yeah. It seems Will got Sammy ter give 'im a bit of 'elp wiv this movin' job 'e 'ad an' 'e sent 'im ter fetch this barrer from Tom Dougan,' Ada explained. 'It'd all bin arranged, yer see. Anyway, the dopey git saw a barrer outside Dougan's shed an' 'e just took it wivout askin' first. As it 'appened the barrer was due to 'ave the wheel sorted out an' by the time they'd finished it was ruined. Somefink ter do wiv it seizin' up an' causin' the axle ter twist.'

'Well it would do,' Emmie said, without understanding what Ada was talking about.

'The outcome was, Dougan told the pair of 'em ter bugger off an' not expect ter borrer any more barrers,' Ada went on. 'Paula told me 'er Will was gutted. 'E always gets barrers from Tom Dougan.'

'I dunno 'ow Peggy Strickland stands that bloke of 'ers,' Emmie remarked, 'an' I dunno why Will Jackson asked 'im ter lend an 'and. 'E'd 'ave bin better askin' Charlie Pease.'

'Well I reckon she's got the patience of a saint meself,' Ada replied. 'She was tellin' me that Sammy went fer anuvver job in the week. It was at the tannery in Long Lane apparently. She said 'e come back grinnin' all over 'is face an' she thought 'e'd finally clicked, but then 'e showed 'er what the bloke 'ad put on 'is green card. It was somefing about 'im bein' allergic ter leavver dyes. O' course Peggy went on at 'im about not wantin' ter get a job an' comin' in grinnin' like a Cheshire cat, an' Sammy told 'er 'e was only grinnin' 'cos 'e was still alive. Can you imagine? The story was, they was takin' 'im round the tannery an' showin' 'im the pits where they soak the skins when the silly git chucked a dummy, an' it was only the quick finkin' of the foreman who stopped 'im tumblin' 'eadfirst inter the chemicals. The foreman told 'im later that one mouthful o' that stuff in the pit would 'ave killed 'im stone dead.'

'Not Sammy,' Emmie chuckled. ''E'd 'ave just sprouted a pair of 'orns.'

''Ere, I saw Sara Parry walkin' up the street yesterday,' Ada said. 'I thought she looked quite nice for a change. She'd obviously 'ad 'er 'air done an' she was wearin' a decent coat.'

'She was probably off ter the fellowship,' Emmie replied. 'P'raps she's got a bloke there.'

'I doubt it,' Ada remarked. 'She's a typical spinster. Flat shoes, long clothes, old-fashioned 'airstyle an' a silly 'at. Yer don't attract the blokes lookin' like that, do yer?'

On the contrary, a certain Randolph Cadman had thrown his cap into the ring in pursuit of Sara Parry's favours, only to realise that no one else had bothered, which the enlightened suitor, who introduced himself with the suffix Civil Service, retired, found very encouraging.

Currently he was a member of St Mark's fellowship, recruited for the choir and recently voted on to the committee alongside Sara, which pleased him even more. It pleased Sara too, who felt that he was a very good tenor as well as a very knowledgeable and thoroughly nice man. Now perhaps the committee could get back to normal functioning after the trauma of the young reverend's recent elopement.

Randolph Cadman hoped so too, for his own reasons.

When darkness fell the rain finally ceased, and as

Maurice Oakfield settled down at the new site in Morgan Street he felt the damp air seeping in from the river. It was the sort of night that chilled the bones, and he paid particular attention to making sure his fire burned bright. He was also very keen to catch a glimpse of a few constellations that night, such as Pegasus to the west, Leo in the east and maybe even Cygnus, but for the moment very few stars showed through the banks of cloud that still crowded the dark sky.

Morgan Street was yet another commercial byway in the Dockhead area, much the same as River Lane. Alongside the grimy warehouses fed from the nearby Thames were a couple of allied manufacturing concerns, a harness maker serving the many horse transport firms in Bermondsey, and a rope-yard, whose high-quality ropes and cables spanned a thousand of the barges and freighters using the Pool of London and the local wharves. The end of the turning farthest from the river led into Tooley Street with its large tenement blocks, built by trusts to replace the workers' slums of the late nineteenth century. Gloomy and badly lit, Morgan Street was a place the local people neither cared nor needed to use, and after dark only reckless lovers sought its solitude.

Maurice was quite prepared for a lonely vigil. He had not made the acquaintance yet of the local bobby, but he was content to pass the night away reading and viewing the changing night sky, weather permitting. What Maurice was not prepared for was the old man who shuffled along the turning after midnight and stopped to admire the glow of the brazier. 'It's a cold damp night for sure,' he said through his long scraggy beard.

Maurice smiled. 'Come closer, sir, and feel the warmth,' he replied, saddened to see the rags that passed for clothing on the man's bony frame.

'It's very decent of you,' the stranger said in a cultured voice. 'I was on my way to Barstow's.'

'Barstow's?'

'It's a derelict warehouse on the river's edge,' the old man explained. 'It's a place a man can get his head down and there are sacks galore to wrap up in. I've had many a cosy night at Barstow's, even at the height of winter.'

Maurice lifted his iron teapot from a grid which he had fixed to the side of the brazier. 'Would you care for some tea?' he asked.

'That's very civilised of you, sir,' the old man replied.

Maurice filled his own mug and the one he had kept for Ron Sloan when he paid him a visit. 'Sugar?'

'Two, if you please.'

Maurice passed the tea over and pulled up the makeshift saw bench which Roy Chubb used. 'There we are, sit yourself down for a few minutes,' he said.

The stranger did as he was bid, and as he gratefully sipped his tea Maurice studied him. His hands were smooth, with long thin fingers that might once have elicited music from keys or strings, but his frame was narrow and bowed, as though deprived of regular nourishment and creaking under his own private burden. The

278

collar of his long brown tattered overcoat was pulled up round his ears and he wore a grease-stained trilby cock-eyed on his head. His feet were shod in down-at-heel boots tied up with string, and most noticeable of all was the drooping blue wild flower that was pinned to the front of his coat.

'I'm William Darcy, a man of the open road,' he said, smiling through his beard.

'Maurice Oakfield, nightwatchman for Coley Brothers, civil engineers,' Maurice replied. The two shook hands and he was surprised at the visitor's strong grip. 'This is what you might call a temporary job,' he added. 'I hope to go back to my vocation very soon. I'm a teacher.'

'That's very good,' the old man said. 'I hope you do. Anything less would be a waste.'

'More tea?' Maurice asked.

'You're most kind,' William said, holding out his empty mug.

The two sat in silence for a while, then the old man said something which made Maurice frown. 'Are the nights quiet?'

'Very much so,' Maurice replied. 'Few people need to venture here at night.'

'No, I was referring to the noises. I hear them while I'm waiting for sleep to come at the warehouse.'

'What sort of noises?'

'Dull booming,' William told him. 'Like a distant drum. A whistling noise, like wind gusting through trees, and a deep, almost inaudible groan that rises and falls at certain times.'

Maurice forced a smile. 'I'm afraid this is my

first night in this area, so I wouldn't know of any undue noises.'

'Yes, I'm aware of that,' the tramp replied. 'I walk through this turning every night. Be circumspect, but take heart. You're not in any danger. I believe the sounds are from another time, when Morgan Street was a riverside meadow crowned with a gallows and gibbet, and people came with their children to witness the executions while they drank beer and ate their bread and cheese. I've been able to study the history of this place and it's no wonder the sounds remain. It has a violent past, you can be sure.'

Maurice looked skyward for a few moments, catching a glimpse of a bright star he imagined to be Sirius before the moving cloud hid it from view, then he fixed his eyes on the old man. 'Do you think the digging in this street would have upset the balance of things?'

'It would have disturbed things, undreamt-of things that we know little about,' William answered in a quiet voice.

Maurice felt a shiver run down his back and he rolled his shoulders. 'I'll be careful not to add to the noise,' he said with a smile. 'I'm paid to guard this site, and that's what I intend to do, come hell or high water.'

'And I will outstay my welcome if I'm not careful,' the old man replied, 'so I'll say goodnight to you, and fear not. Remember, the darkest part of the night is just before the dawn.'

Maurice watched him leave. 'Goodnight, William,' he called out.

280

The tramp answered with a wave of his bony arm, and then he was gone, swallowed up in the dark night.

Maurice banked up the fire, made his regular rounds and sat reading with the aid of his nightlight. Occasionally the night sky opened out between the clouds, like a window into eternity, and he was able to pinpoint the stars and constellations he was familiar with. It stayed quiet, apart from the earthly sounds of a fussing tugboat's whistle, the late tram rattling through nearby Tooley Street, and the crackle of the burning log on the brazier.

When the men arrived at the diggings Maurice took his leave, and on impulse he decided to take a look at Barstow's warehouse. He found nothing but a large open space next to the Shad Thames wharves. 'Was this where Barstow's warehouse stood, constable?' he asked the passing policeman.

'Yes, sir. It was pulled down back in the twenties, I believe.'

Maurice was not ready for his bed, so he made his way to the local library. 'Have you any local newspapers from the twenties in your archives?' he enquired.

'Come this way,' the librarian replied.

Maurice was led down to a basement room, complete with a very large polished table and shelves full of heavy binders along the four walls. He spent more than two hours searching the old papers and then he found what he was looking for in a June 1924 edition of the *South London Press*.

'Bermondsey Says Goodbye'

The people of Bermondsey lined the streets today for the funeral of William Darcy the well-known local character who called himself a man of the open road. William tramped the streets and slept rough, and he was never seen without a wilted flower pinned to his coat. He always had a kind word and a cheerful smile for everyone he encountered.

He was said to have been educated at Eton and then went on to serve as a First Lieutenant with the Royal Fusiliers in France during the Great War. Disenchanted by his war experiences, William Darcy gave up a promising career in banking and chose to live his life walking the streets and relying on the goodwill of the people of Bermondsey for sustenance.

He seemed an uncomplicated man, but his death will remain a mystery. What made him end his life by jumping into the River Thames?

Maurice Oakfield hardly noticed the people passing by as he walked home lost in thought. Had he dreamed it all? What other possible explanation was there? One thing was for sure, though. His self-imposed period of rehabilitation was now over, and he would apply to be reinstated at the college as soon as possible.

CHAPTER 24

When the diggers started work on the dull Tuesday morning early in January they did not imagine that the day was going to be any different from the rest, and as they set about clearing the earth around the buried sewer tunnel there was the usual friendly banter between them, with the exception of Wally Coates and his partner. They were left to their own devices and totally ignored during the short breaks which had now become the norm. Any attempt at good-natured persiflage would incur a frosty reply at the least, and more likely a stream of abuse from the giant of a man who seemed devoid of humour and tended to treat everyone with utter contempt.

As expected, Coates and Gill were making fast progress, and as they dug deeper around the tunnel that afternoon Roy Chubb began the shoring-up process beside them. Lofty Williams the other carpenter began his task at the other end of the trench and as Charlie made his way along the ridge he felt pleased that everything was going as planned. By this evening the twenty-man team would be almost finished. One more day would see the job out, and then the men would learn from Frank Coley that the main sewer excavation was to get underway, along the whole of the eastern side of Tooley Street down as far as Jamaica Road.

At four o'clock the rain started again and soon it was lashing down. Sludge from the piles of earth at the side of the trench ran back into the diggings and the trench walls became soggy and unstable. Charlie worked under Roy's guidance helping to fix the shuttering and Sharkey joined Lofty Williams at the opposite end.

'I don't see any sense in tryin' ter go deeper ternight,' Charlie told his fellow ganger. 'What d'you reckon?'

Sharkey nodded. 'We'd better get the men out of our way while we finish off. They can sit in the shed till it's time ter knock off.'

The diggers needed no coaxing and they scrambled out of the trench by way of the raised platforms used to make the removal of soil easier, but Danny Albury hesitated, bending down with his hand pressed to the side of his stomach.

'What's wrong?' George asked him with concern.

'It's OK. I get the cramp now an' then an' it's just caught me,' he said through clenched teeth.

'It ain't an 'ernia, is it?' George asked.

Danny shook his head, gingerly straightening himself up. 'Nah, it's just the cramp. It ain't troubled me fer some time.'

'Give us yer pickaxe,' George said.

Danny passed it to him and George threw it out of the trench, then as he picked up his shovel he saw Wally Coates coming towards him.

'I fink me an' you 'ave got some unfinished business ter see to,' the big man growled.

'Give it a break, Wally,' Danny cut in. 'What

'appened yesterday is all over an' done wiv.'

'You keep out o' this,' Coates snarled. 'This is between Parry an' me.'

''As someone been windin' you up?' Danny asked him.

'Leave it, Danny,' George said quickly, turning to face Coates. 'I'm surprised you ain't got yer dummy wiv yer. Is 'e fed up wiv you pullin' 'is strings?'

Coates's eyes widened and he suddenly lunged forward but Danny stepped in front of him. 'Look, I ain't aimin' ter get the bullet fer scrappin', an' nor should you,' he growled. 'Why don't yer piss off out the trench an' let us do the same.'

'Get outta me way, you little rat,' the giant roared.

'Make me.'

Coates grabbed at him and slammed him roughly against the side of the trench, drawing back his fist to hit him, and George quickly swung the shovel with all his force. It smashed into the side of Coates's head and he staggered backwards a pace then fell heavily against a shoring prop, dislodging it as he collapsed into the bottom of the trench. Suddenly soil and sludge was pouring into the diggings and in seconds Wally Coates was completely buried under earth and fallen timbers. Danny had been lucky and he managed to struggle out of the morass as his partner frantically scooped the muddy earth from around his waist and legs.

Charlie had seen what happened as he stood by the side of the workings and he shouted out for the others to help the buried man before jumping into the trench himself and trying desperately to free him before he suffocated.

'What's 'appened?' Sharkey yelled down.

'Wally Coates is under that lot,' Charlie shouted back at him. ''E's gonna need an ambulance, an' a doctor as well.'

'I'll use the phone box in Tooley Street then I'll chase up the doctor,' Sharkey turned on his heel and dashed along the turning.

There was no shortage of volunteers to get the big man out. Charlie scraped the sludge away with his bare hands as the other rescuers dug frantically, and the ambulance bell was sounding as they reached him. Sharkey had managed to summon a doctor from his practice in Tooley Street and willing hands helped him down into the trench.

'Get this prop off 'is 'ead,' one of the rescuers shouted as the doctor bent down over the still figure.

A stretcher was lowered and within minutes Wally Coates was being rushed to Guy's Hospital.

During the rescue operation George and Danny had stood to one side, and now as Charlie came towards them they could see the worried look on his face.

'Is 'e dead?' George asked fearfully.

Charlie nodded his head slowly. 'It looks that way.'

George dropped down on to the wet earth. ''E was comin' for me an' 'e was gonna 'ammer Danny,' he groaned. 'Jesus God, what 'ave I done?'

'Now you listen ter me,' Charlie hissed. 'When anybody asks yer what 'appened this is what yer say. Coates was 'avin' a dig at yer about you bein' slow but you an' Danny ignored 'im, then as 'e started ter climb out the trench 'e suddenly slipped an' fell backwards, dislodgin' the prop as 'e fell. Just remember, that's what 'appened an' there was nuffink you could do ter prevent it.'

'What about the mark on 'is 'ead from the shovel?' George said in panic.

'It must 'ave bin caused by the 'eavy prop that was layin' across 'is face when we got to 'im,' Charlie answered. 'Clean the mud off that shovel right away an' there'll be nuffink ter show.'

Frank and Ben Coley looked anxious as they came out of the hut after speaking briefly with Charlie.

'Send the men 'ome, Sharkey,' Frank told him, 'but make sure Parry an' Albury stay in the shed. I wanna see 'em. You two come inside right away.'

When they crowded into the hut Ben Coley pulled two stools out from under the bench and motioned Sharkey and Charlie to sit beside him. Frank pulled his chair over to the closed door and sat with his back resting against it. 'The doctor told me that Wally Coates is dead,' he began. 'It'll mean an inquest. Now I know you saw what 'appened, Charlie, but I want George Parry an' Danny Albury ter tell me their version. You told me they saw it 'appen.'

'Yeah, that's right, an' they're both shocked rigid,' Charlie answered.

'This could balls everyfing up,' Coley growled. 'I was duty bound ter report the accident ter the police an' they'll be sendin' someone round later. In the meantime there's questions need answerin'. What was Coates doin' up that end o' the trench? What caused 'im ter slip? After all, 'e knows 'is way round a trench. Was the shorin' secure? The answers we get are gonna be crucial. If it points ter malpractice or skylarkin' then the individuals concerned can be dealt wiv an' no blame'd be attached ter the management, but if the accident was caused by bad workmanship, insecure shorin' or weakened timbers then we're gonna be 'eld responsible, an' I don't need ter spell it out. We'd lose the contract an' any furvver work fer Maitland's.'

'Some o' those timbers that come away 'ad split in 'alf,' Charlie told him.

Frank Coley looked worried. 'Is there any new plankin' lyin' around 'ere?' he asked.

Ben Coley shook his head. 'The delivery's due termorrer.'

Frank glared at him. 'You'd better get it delivered right away, before the police arrive,' he said quickly.

Ben grabbed his coat. 'I'll take care of it.'

Frank turned to Charlie. 'Will yer go an' fetch George Parry?'

Charlie was soon back with the ashen-faced workman, having quietly reminded him to stick to his story, and Frank Coley waved him towards Ben's empty stool.

'Look, I know this must 'ave bin a terrible shock, but we 'ave ter know just what 'appened,' he impressed on him. 'Take yer time an' tell us exactly what yer saw.'

George drew a deep breath and explained as calmly as he could how he and Danny were being taunted, and how when they did not respond Wally Coates turned to leave and slipped backwards as he tried to get out of the trench, dislodging the main cross prop as he fell.

'You never pushed 'im, or caused 'im ter slip?' Frank asked, staring hard at him.

'Certainly not.'

'Why should Wally Coates 'ave it in fer yer?'

'I dunno. I never slacked or left the bulk o' the work to 'im when we were teamed up,' George said with spirit, 'but fer some reason best known to 'imself 'e was always gettin' on ter me.'

'All right, you can go. I'll speak ter yer again termorrer,' Frank told him. 'Let's 'ave Danny Albury in.'

Danny's version of the incident matched that of his partner and Frank Coley gave him a dark look. 'Now listen ter me,' he said. 'If Parry caused the accident in any way an' you don't come clean you'll be just as guilty as 'im, so yer better fink about it.'

The little digger stood up to his full height and looked Coley square in the eye. 'I know it's common knowledge that Parry an' Coates never got on, but when the big man come along the trench an' started goadin' 'im an' me we took no notice. 'E called us a few choice names an' went ter get out o' the trench. That's when 'e slipped. Like I already told yer, it was a pure accident.'

'Tell me,' Coley continued. 'Did Coates go off fer 'is lunch break or did 'e stay in the shed?'

''E stayed in the shed an' ate 'is grub like the

289

rest of us,' Danny answered.

'Right, you can get off 'ome,' Coley told him. 'I expect the police are gonna be askin' you an' Parry some more questions termorrer.'

After the digger had left Frank Coley turned to Charlie. 'I got a feelin' those two were lyin',' he remarked pointedly.

Charlie turned on him angrily. 'I've already told yer I saw Coates slip. If they're lyin' so am I, an' I assure yer I'm not a liar.'

Coley raised his hand in a conciliatory gesture. 'I'm not callin' you a liar,' he said quickly. 'I'm suggestin' yer might 'ave missed somefink, bin distracted fer a moment.'

Charlie shook his head slowly. 'I was standin' right above Parry an' Albury when Wally Coates fell. They were nowhere near 'im.'

Frank Coley nodded. 'OK. Sharkey, you'd better wait around till Ben gets back wiv those timbers. You too, Charlie. The police'll need a statement from somebody who saw what 'appened.'

It was after eight o'clock when Charlie walked into the house and Lucy met him in the scullery with a look of concern in her eyes. 'You must be worn out,' she said. 'George told me what 'appened. It's just terrible.'

As Charlie rolled up his shirtsleeves Lucy filled the bowl with hot water. 'I've kept yer meal in the oven. I 'ope it ain't too baked up,' she remarked.

'I 'ad ter stay be'ind ter give the police a statement,' he replied as he dipped his hands into the bowl.

'I'll take this in fer yer,' Lucy said as she took the plate from the oven.

'Don't bovver. I'll eat out 'ere,' he told her. 'It'll save you layin' the parlour table again.'

Lucy moved behind him as he sat down, placing her hand lightly on his shoulder as she reached across him to get a knife and fork from the dresser drawer. 'George came in lookin' as white as a ghost,' she said. ''E's left 'alf 'is tea. Mary popped in an' said Roy came in lookin' all shook up even though 'e never saw what 'appened.'

'It's natural,' Charlie replied. 'I've seen it on the quayside. A man gets killed or badly 'urt an' it brings it all 'ome ter yer. It could 'ave bin you.'

'What's gonna 'appen now?' Lucy asked.

'There'll be a post-mortem,' Charlie explained, 'an' then there'll be an inquest, so the police said.'

Lucy placed her hand on his shoulder once more and he felt the slight pressure of her fingers. 'Get on wiv yer tea. We can talk later,' she said.

The hour was late and the fire burned low when Charlie sat facing Lucy in the parlour. 'I was glad when Sara decided ter go ter bed,' Lucy remarked. 'I'm sure she made George feel worse the way she was goin' on about it before you came in. She wants ter know the ins an' outs of a nag's arse.'

Charlie had had no chance to talk with George alone that evening before the troubled man went off to bed, but he had seen the fear in his eyes when he told him how he had been questioned by the police and asked to give a statement about all he had seen. He hoped George would continue to keep the truth from Lucy, but he was less than optimistic. He knew that it was playing on George's mind and before very long he would confess to her. He would have to speak to him as soon as possible and try to make him see that it wouldn't help anyone to dwell on what had really happened. Better to let it rest where it was, however hard. ''E'll be all right in a few days,' he said reassuringly, 'once the initial shock wears off.'

'Well at least 'e's got this weekend at the naval reserve,' Lucy replied. 'It'll 'elp take 'is mind off it.'

Charlie stared into the fire for a few moments, then his eyes met hers. 'Are you all right?' he asked quietly.

'Why d'you ask? Do I look tired or somefing?'

'No. You look very nice, as a matter o' fact, but I can see the worried look in yer eyes,' he said with a brief smile.

'I am worried about George,' she answered. 'When 'e told me about the man bein' buried alive I went all cold. I suddenly realised just 'ow dangerous that job can be. It could 'ave bin George, or you.'

'I'd try not ter worry too much,' he said softly. 'These sorts of accidents aren't very common where all the necessary precautions are taken. Roy put that shorin' up an' 'e did a good job. It wasn't 'is fault it collapsed. The man who was killed was a big feller. I'd say 'e weighed all of eighteen, nineteen stone.'

Lucy felt her cheeks grow hot and raw excitement course through her body as she watched him speaking. At that very moment she wanted him to take her in his arms, hold her tightly and kiss her breathless, but she fought the need, as she had to, averting her eyes and breathing in deeply in an effort to calm herself. This was crazy. Every time she allowed her emotions to run rampant would only strengthen her desire for him, but she wanted him to know just how she felt, wanted him to need her every bit as much as she desired him. Yes, it was crazy, but deep down inside she knew that there would come a time when their mutual feelings would inevitably overwhelm them both. 'Are you 'appy 'ere, Charlie?' she asked suddenly.

The question took him by surprise. 'I've felt at 'ome in this 'ouse from the very first night I arrived,' he answered.

'You wouldn't leave us, would you?' she said. 'I couldn't imagine one day wivout you bein' 'ere.'

'I won't leave you, Lucy,' he told her softly. 'I wouldn't want ter go frew a day wivout seein' yer, talkin' to yer, watchin' the way you move about, the way you 'ave of dealin' wiv fings.'

'Like our Sara?' she said, smiling, trying to bring some sanity into their dangerous game.

'Yeah, like Sara fer instance.'

Lucy looked up at the clock on the mantelshelf. 'I'd better get off ter bed,' she said almost reluctantly. 'George might be lyin' awake.'

'Yeah, me too,' he replied. 'Lucy?'

'Yeah?'

'I'd like very much ter kiss you goodnight,' he said huskily, rising from his chair.

She took his outstretched hands in hers as she got up and allowed him to pull her to him. His kiss on her trembling lips was soft and warm and very brief as he held her close, and when she moved back, still held in his strong arms, she knew that there was no going back. His kiss had told her all she wanted to know and she shivered with pleasure. 'Goodnight, Charlie,' she said quietly.

'Goodnight, Lucy.'

CHAPTER 25

All work had stopped at the Morgan Street diggings, and when the men reported for work on Wednesday morning they were told to wait in the shed. Charlie pulled George Parry and Danny Albury to one side and warned them that the police would want to speak to them first. Then he looked around at the anxious faces of the men. 'Now listen ter me,' he began. 'We're all sorry this tragedy 'appened, even though none of us liked the man, so least said the better about any confrontations wiv 'im. I'm referrin' ter the little set-to in 'ere the ovver mornin'. It could be seen by the police as a reason fer a revenge attack, so I don't want any of yer ter mention what 'appened. Is that understood? As far as you lot are concerned you've never witnessed any confrontations.'

The men chatted amongst themselves, but Danny and George both sat quietly while they waited to be interviewed by the police.

Charlie stepped outside and immediately saw the police car drive into the turning. He looked back into the shed and motioned for George and Danny to join him. 'They've just arrived,' he told them. 'Just try ter stay calm when they ask yer what 'appened. Remember, apart from you two I was the only one who saw the accident.'

'Yeah, but it wasn't an accident,' George mumbled.

'You'd better pull yerself tergevver, George,' Charlie retorted angrily. 'Yer didn't mean ter kill the man.'

''E's right, mate,' Danny said, putting his arm round George's bowed shoulders. 'You was only lookin' out fer me. If we just stick ter the same story we'll be OK.'

'Right, I've gotta see Frank Coley,' Charlie announced. 'Now just remember what yer gotta say, 'cos if yer don't get it right I'm gonna be dragged right into it as well.'

Frank Coley's face was dark with anger as he faced his two gangers in the work hut. 'I've just 'ad words wiv Pat Lawrence from the contractors,' he told them. ''E threatened ter tear up the contract if we don't get this business sorted out quickly.'

'There's only 'alf a day's work left on the site,' Sharkey cut in. 'Can't we get it finished?'

'Nah, we 'ave ter wait till the coroner's man inspects the cave-in spot,' Frank replied. 'At least we've bin able ter replace some o' those old timbers, so they can't put the accident down ter bad wood. As fer the shorin', they'll see that the rest of it's safe an' solid, so there's no reason fer 'em ter say it was bad workmanship.'

'As we've already said, we gotta make sure they 'ave no reason ter suggest it was management negligence,' Ben Coley reminded them, 'an' ter be honest I'm a bit worried about this goadin' business concernin' Coates.'

'What d'yer mean?' Charlie asked quickly.

'Granted yer split Coates an' Parry up when yer found out about it,' Ben went on, 'but why was

296

Coates allowed ter come along almost the 'ole length o' the trench ter sort Parry out after bein' told like the rest ter get out?'

Sharkey and Charlie exchanged quick glances. 'I was standin' above the middle o' the trench when I saw Coates comin' along an' I asked if 'e was deaf or somefing,' Charlie told him. ''E just ignored me, an' the accident 'appened too quick fer me to do anyfing ter stop it. That was what 'appened an' that's in me statement.'

'There'll be an inquest, an' let's 'ope the coroner ends up satisfied,' Frank said with emphasis. 'If 'e ain't then we're effectively out o' business. That much was spelled out by Pat Lawrence.'

The policemen stepped out of their car and the coroner's man in civilian clothing introduced himself to the Coley brothers. 'If you'll show me where the accident happened,' he requested.

While the official began his inspection the uniformed sergeant took both men's statements in the hut and then went to the workmen's shed to speak with the rest of the diggers.

'I'll be sending a photographer along some time today,' the coroner's man told the Coleys, 'and once he's finished there'll be no reason to hold you up any further.'

'You two might as well get off 'ome,' Frank said to his gangers. 'I want you in bright an' breezy termorrer, so we can 'ave that trench ready to 'and over by lunchtime at the latest. We've gotta keep the contractors sweet now.'

Charlie joined George and Danny outside the shed and as they set off home he noticed how relieved the two looked.

'The sergeant was a real nice bloke,' Danny remarked. ''E didn't rush us or anyfing, an' 'e said that we did the right fing not lettin' Coates wind us up.'

''E asked me about all the goadin,' George added. 'I just told 'im that me an' Coates didn't get on an' when I asked yer fer a change o' partner yer got me one. There was one fing, though. The copper wanted ter know if I'd ever lost me temper when me an' Coates worked tergevver an' I told 'im it never bovvered me that much. I said I put it down ter the man's ignorance. I also told 'im that none o' the men got on wiv 'im an' we all tended ter stay away from 'im as much as we could.'

'Yer did well, both of yer,' Charlie said with a smile. 'Now yer gotta put it ter the back o' yer minds. Nuffink good's gonna come if yer dwell too much on it.'

'I blame meself fer what 'appened,' Danny frowned. 'I got Coates's back up an' George did what 'e did ter save me gettin' a pastin'.'

'An' you stood up ter the bully ter save George gettin' a pastin', so it's neivver one nor the ovver,' Charlie told him forcefully. 'Do like I say an' put it where it belongs, an' don't start losin' any sleep over it. After all, nuffink can be changed. It's 'appened an' that's that.'

The tragic incident was very soon on everyone's lips in Cooper Street and Peggy Strickland was prompted to tell Ada and Emmie that it came as no surprise to her. 'If you'd seen my Sammy that day 'e went fer the nightwatchman's job,' she said with a sour look. "E came 'ome really upset. Coley told 'im 'e wasn't suitable an' Sammy 'ad a right ole go at 'im. After all, it don't take much sense ter look after a bleedin' 'ole in the road, does it? I mean ter say, it ain't goin' anywhere. Then there was the time Sammy took a stroll when they was diggin' up River Lane an' 'e stopped ter chat wiv the blokes, like yer would. Coley sent this great big bloke out the office after 'im an' 'e threatened 'im.'

'Who, Sammy did?' Emmie asked.

'Nah, the bloke threatened Sammy.'

'Sounds a right nasty firm ter work for,' Ada remarked.

'They certainly want their pound o' flesh,' Peggy said disgustedly.

'Lucy Parry's lodger works fer the Coleys as well,' Ada told her.

'So I 'eard,' she answered. "E's a ganger, by all accounts.'

Emmie nodded. 'Mary Chubb's ole man works there too.'

'Mind you, there's not much ovver work fer 'em ter do, is there?' Ada went on. 'My ole man would 'ave gone there fer a job if 'e was a few years younger, but they don't take anyone on who's over fifty.'

'My Sammy's over fifty,' Peggy said.

'Yeah, but 'e was applyin' fer a night-watchman's job, not as a ditch digger,' Emmie reminded her.

Ada slid her hands deeper into the sleeves of her coat. 'While I fink of it,' she said. 'Did you know that Sara Parry's gone an' got 'erself a bloke?'

'Never.'

''S true. Quite a presentable bloke too.'

'Where'd yer 'ear this?'

Ada quite liked being able to pass on snippets of information and she took her time in replying. 'Well as it 'appens,' she began with suitably conspiratorial glances, 'I was standin' by Tommy Atwood's fruit stall when Mrs Penfold came up an' said 'ello. I 'adn't seen 'er fer Gawd knows 'ow long, so I asks 'ow she was an' she was tellin' me about 'er nervous breakdown. She put it down ter the worry she's 'ad wiv 'er ole man. Anyway, the doctor told 'er she should get out a bit more so she joined the muvvers' union at St Mark's. Then she got to 'ear about this fellowship they've got there an' she went along one evenin'. Apparently they do all sorts o' fings there, like sewin' an' embroidery, an' they make fings fer Christmas bazaars.'

'Go on,' Emmie said impatiently.

Ada looked up and down the turning. 'Mrs Penfold got chattin' ter Sara Parry an' they struck up a friendship, like yer do, an' after a few meetin's Sara confided in Mrs Penfold that she quite liked this bloke who'd recently joined the fellowship.'

'I thought it was only women who went ter the fellowship?' Emmie queried. 'Surely men wouldn't be interested in sewin' an' embroidery?'

'Nah, they 'ave discussion groups,' Ada told her, 'an' they do oil paintin' an' fings like that, accordin' ter Mrs Penfold.'

'Did she say what the bloke looked like?' Emmie wanted to know.

'Mrs Penfold reckons 'e's quite smart,' Ada went on. 'She said 'e's fifty or thereabouts, a bit podgy an' a bit shorter than Sara but 'e talks nice an' 'e seems ter like 'er.'

'Well I 'ope 'e can put up wiv 'er moody ways,' Emmie remarked uncharitably. 'That woman never seems two minutes alike. One day she'll be all friendly an' anuvver time she'll walk right past yer.'

'Yeah, she's done it ter me,' Ada replied, 'but I don't fink she means ter be off'and. She's just a bundle o' nerves.'

Emmie nodded. 'It could be the makin' of 'er, I s'pose.'

With the Morgan Street diggings made ready for the bricklayers and the River Lane site filled in there was no more work available and the men were paid off.

'Well, it's back ter the bloody dole queue,' Danny sighed.

''Ow long d'yer fink it'll be before the next job starts?' one of the diggers asked.

'Gawd knows,' his partner replied. 'Nuffink's gonna 'appen till this inquest takes place.'

'I 'eard the contractors are blamin' the Coleys fer the cave-in,' another chipped in.

''Ow we gonna know when we can come back ter work?' the first man asked.

'By word o' mouth, the way it always goes.'

'Mind you, I'd like ter be in a position where I could tell the Coleys ter stick the poxy job right up their arse,' Danny remarked, 'but the way fings are at the moment I don't fink there'll be much chance o' that.'

The men left the site with their few hard-earned shillings in their pockets and the nagging worry that it might be some time before they could earn any more.

On Thursday night at the fellowship Sara helped to serve the tea and biscuits, and then with a feigned look of surprise found that she was sitting next to Randolph Cadman. 'I never saw you there,' she said sweetly.

'I'm honoured,' he replied with a smile. 'This is a very nice cup of tea, but then that's not surprising with you making it.'

Sara smiled coyly. Randolph could be so charming, she thought, and it made it much easier for her to converse with him. How different from Charlie Foden, who never seemed to respond to her when she tried getting to know him better. Maybe it was just as well. He was a rough diamond with little finesse, and much as she would have liked him to take notice of her there would always be that between them. Perhaps if she'd had Lucy's cheek and brashness she would have made better progress, but that sort of demeanour was alien to her. Besides, she had had very little experience where men were concerned, and she was not the sort of person who could flaunt herself. It would have been necessary with Charlie to make him realise that she was interested in him, but it wasn't with Randolph. She could be herself and not have to put on an act for his benefit.

'How's the choir comin' along?' she asked him.

'Very well, Sara,' he replied. 'I'm rather rusty but a few practice sessions will soon bring back the volume. It all stems from the diaphragm, you know. Down here,' he said, tapping his midriff.

Sara smiled. 'Would you care fer some more biscuits?' she asked.

Randolph shook his head. 'I'm afraid I'm off my food at the moment,' he told her.

'Oh dear. Nuffink serious, I 'ope?'

'No, it's nothing really, but when certain pressures build up they do tend to affect me that way. I suppose I'm a born worrier.'

'You say certain pressures,' Sara probed. 'Are they ter do wiv your work?'

He nodded. 'I work in the City, you see. Actually I'm employed by a City broker and you'll appreciate what a bad time we're having. Shares everywhere have fallen to a disastrous low and some, or I should say most, of our clients have lost considerable sums of money. It will improve, of course, but not in the short term. Trying to safeguard their investments in such a financial climate has become a terrible responsibility and a very hard burden to endure.'

'It must be awful for yer.'

He sighed deeply. 'The worst thing of all is knowing that there is a solution, and not being able to be part of it.'

Sara found that the conversation was beginning to go over her head but she persevered. 'Isn't it possible?' she asked.

He smiled indulgently. 'There is one essential

condition,' he told her. 'A few of my colleagues have decided to break away from the company and go into the stocks and shares business on their own. They want me to join them, but it comes down to an old chestnut. Ready cash. With collateral we could buy certain shares at a ridiculously low figure and sell them for a large profit. It's a foolproof scheme with these particular shares because we have inside information that a bid is going to be made very soon by an old-established company, which would send them climbing to a record level. The fact of the matter is that we have to buy the shares before the knowledge becomes public. That's the problem.'

'It sounds very excitin'. I only wish I was in a position to 'elp yer,' Sara said sincerely.

'You're very kind,' Randolph replied, 'but even if you were in a position to help financially I couldn't possibly expect you to take the gamble on my word alone. Good lord, I could be a confidence trickster for all you know.'

'Never,' Sara said with a passion which surprised her. 'I'm a good judge of a person an' I know you'd never trick anyone.'

Randolph felt the time was ripe and he reached out and gently squeezed her hands in his. 'What a lovely thing to say,' he said softly.

Sara felt her cheeks getting hot. This was very intimate, and it sent all the right messages through her body. Here was a man she could feel perfectly at home with, a man who treated her as though she were Dresden china. 'It's a pity, really,' she said. 'I do 'ave one or two valuable possessions in the way o' jewellery, but they couldn't be put up as security, could they?'

He stroked his chin for a moment or two. 'That would depend on the value,' he replied. 'The newly formed company could get a substantial bank loan, providing we have the necessary collateral. Rings, bracelets, necklaces and paid-up insurance policies and endowments are acceptable.'

Sara held out her hand palm down and he saw the large ruby flash in the uncertain light. 'That's a remarkable ring,' he said, nodding. 'It must be very valuable.'

'I've got a five-stone diamond ring at 'ome that was left ter me by my poor muvver, God rest 'er soul,' she told him. 'There's bin times when I've bin tempted ter pawn 'em, but I couldn't bring meself ter do it, desperate as I was.'

Randolph's eyes lingered on the ruby ring for a few seconds, then he looked up at her and smiled. 'Do you know,' he said, 'I don't think I've ever met such a nice, trusting person before, but rest assured, I wouldn't even consider accepting personal items of jewellery from my friends as security, and especially not from you. It wouldn't be right. It would be asking too much from someone who's only known me for a very short time.'

'It seems as if I've known yer for ages,' Sara replied, flushing slightly.

'I too feel as though you and I are old friends,' he declared. 'Sara, I want you to know that I came to this fellowship out of loneliness, and I know that meeting you was meant to be. It was fate. You and I are two kindred souls and I want to get to know you much better. Come to Brighton with me this weekend.'

Sara looked shocked. 'I couldn't. It wouldn't be right,' she said quickly.

Randolph laughed aloud. 'Good lord, you don't think my intentions are anything but honourable, do you? We'll have single rooms at a little seafront guesthouse I know, and the sea air will do wonders for you, even in winter.'

'I don't know. It's all so sudden,' Sara said hesitantly.

'Say you will and make me a very happy man,' he entreated her with a disarming smile.

'All right, I will.'

CHAPTER 26

Frank Coley's face was a dark mask as he prodded the tabletop with his forefinger. 'Charlie Foden was lyin' as far as I'm concerned,' he growled. 'I'd bet any money George Parry was the cause o' Wally Coates's death, 'im an' that idiot Danny Albury.'

Ben Coley quickly looked round the saloon bar of the Mason's Arms to make sure his irate brother was not being overheard. 'I go along wiv that,' he said. 'Coates never slipped. 'E was clubbed.'

Sharkey sat moodily contemplating his pint. He knew the Coleys well and suspected that something nasty was brewing in Frank Coley's head.

'There's no way we're gonna find out, though,' Ben added. 'They'll stick ter their story an' leave us sweatin'.'

'Yeah, an' we could effectively be put out o' business,' Frank replied. 'That coroner's man was payin' a lot of attention ter the timbers by the cave-in an' I 'ad this feelin' 'e's suspected they'd bin changed.'

'Nah, I don't fink so,' Ben said dismissively.

'I didn't like the way 'e walked the length o' the trench to inspect the rest o' the shutterin',' Frank went on. 'There was a lot of old wood used. It's gonna feel like a long time before that inquest gets under way. If the outcome's down ter misadventure an' we get criticised fer bad workmanship we can say goodbye ter the rest o' the contract. Maitland's won't look at us, not wiv that government-sponsored deal they've got.'

'Well there's no sense in worryin' about it now,' Ben answered. 'There's nuffink we can do ter change fings.'

'That's a matter of opinion,' Frank said, smiling evilly.

Ben looked at him and grinned. 'What's in that schemin' brain of yours?' he asked.

'It'd be a different fing entirely if eivver Albury or Parry owned up ter bein' the cause o' Coates's death,' Frank remarked. 'It'd put us in the clear, wouldn't it?'

Sharkey sat up straight in his seat as the brothers looked at him. 'Now wait a minute,' he said quickly. 'I ain't gonna go beltin' it out of 'em. I don't fancy going down fer GBH.'

'I wouldn't want you ter get involved, Sharkey,' Frank told him with a grin, 'but wiv your influence an' knowledge, I'm sure you could get a couple o' reliable lads ter give Parry an' Albury a good goin'-over. I don't fink they'd 'ave too much trouble knockin' the truth out of eivver of 'em. Just tell 'em ter make sure they don't go over the top. We don't want any killin's on our 'ands, after all. We've gotta be kept out of it. See what yer can do, will yer?'

Sharkey nodded. 'I'd better be makin' some enquiries, then,' he said, getting up from his chair. 'What's the figure?'

'They get a tenner each now an' anuvver tenner

when the job's done,' Frank replied. 'But make sure they're reliable. They can say they're friends o' Wally Coates, but under no circumstances do I want our names mentioned.'

Sharkey left the Mason's Arms with mixed feelings. He knew a few of his old pals down on their luck who would jump at the chance of earning twenty pounds for a short job of work, but there was also a sense of misgiving nagging at his insides. If the Coleys were put in a corner they'd act like rats and go for the throat – his throat if it suited them.

The troubled ganger made his way to Dockhead and walked into the Crown public house, ordering a pint of beer and a large whisky chaser as he looked around for familiar faces. The germ of an idea was growing in his mind and he had to think it through thoroughly. Any slip and he would end up like a slice of meat between two rounds of bread.

On Thursday morning George Parry and Danny Albury joined the long winding dole queue at the labour exchange in Mollings Street off the Old Kent Road. They had decided enough was enough as far as working for the Coleys was concerned, and they would wait on the chance of getting offered some other work, however remote.

The queue seemed to go on for ever and it was over an hour before the two were anywhere near the front entrance. Men stood with shoulders slumped, blank looks on their gaunt faces and hands stuffed deep in their coat pockets against the chill day.

'I dunno if we've done the right fing,' George said despondently. 'What chance 'ave we got wiv this lot in front of us.'

'Well, at least we'll be able ter register fer unemployment money,' Danny told him.

'Yeah, I s'pose yer right,' George agreed.

''Ere, look at that geezer,' Danny said quickly.

George glanced down the line and saw a tall thin man walk up carrying a screwed-up newspaper in his hands and say something to one of the men.

'Go on, piss off,' the man scowled. 'Don't come that one wiv me. D'yer fink I'm stupid or somefink?'

'I'm not lyin' ter yer, pal,' the newcomer told him. ''E said 'e'd mind me place while I went fer some chips.'

'Who did?'

'The bloke who was standin' next ter yer.'

'Yer never said anyfing ter me,' the man in front spoke up.

'Nah, not you, the ovver bloke what was 'ere.'

'No one's moved away since I was 'ere,' the first man said sharply.

'Well I assure yer I'm not tellin' porkies,' the newcomer replied.

'Look, piss off while yer still able,' the first man growled.

Suddenly the line was broken as men started pushing and shoving, then fighting erupted, and the chancer found himself on the ground with blood dripping down his chin on to his chips. Around him there seemed to be a general fracas.

310

Men who one minute before had been standing peaceably in line were now like a pack of rampant animals as hits were thrown at random and blows received were given back with interest.

Two elderly women who were passing by suddenly spotted one man throw a cowardly punch to the back of someone's neck and they waded in with relish, raining blows on his head.

'Stop it! Stop it, d'you hear!' a loud voice yelled out, and slowly the fighting began to calm down. 'This behaviour is disgraceful. I'm inclined to close this exchange down for the day.'

'Give us a chance, guv,' one of the men called out through bruised lips. 'It was some dodgy 'Erbert who started it all. We've queued up 'ere fer hours all peaceful like.'

'Very well then,' the official replied, 'but if there's any repeat of this disgusting behaviour I'll make sure you don't get seen to today.'

Danny shook his head. 'I've never seen grown men act like this before,' he remarked. 'It's like they were waitin' fer the chance ter steam in.'

George raised his eyebrows and shrugged. 'It's bottled-up anger,' he answered. 'There's gotta be anuvver way o' dealin' wiv this, surely. 'Avin' ter stand fer hours on end in a dole queue is soul-destroyin'. It makes yer feel useless. Well, it does me.'

'It does that to all of us,' Danny said quietly.

The man who had started the rumpus came walking down the line still clutching soggy chips in a grubby piece of newspaper. 'I'm pushin' orf 'ome,' he told a man standing in front of Danny. 'They're all bloody mad 'ere.'

'Well go on then, piss orf, don't tell me,' the man retorted.

'Fancy a chip?'

'No I don't want one o' yer poxy chips.'

'No need ter be nasty about it.'

'Piss orf.'

'All right, I'm goin'.'

George looked at Danny and smiled. 'That's 'ow we'll end up if we 'ave much more o' this,' he muttered.

The man in front turned round and nodded towards the departing chancer. 'That's Manny Corrigan,' he told them. 'Daft as a brush 'e is. Last week 'e came 'ere wiv an ole tom on 'is arm. Pissed out o' their brains the pair of 'em. Gawd knows where 'e gets 'is money from.'

'I saw 'im singin' in the streets round the Elephant an' Castle,' another man remarked. ''E sells oddments out of a suitcase down East Lane as well.'

Danny glanced at his friend. 'P'raps we should try that,' he said, grinning.

They eventually filed through the door into the relative warmth, and after another lengthy delay they finally reached the counter and signed on as unemployed.

Mary and Lucy were having their regular get-together and Gracie stood obediently by the armchair while her mother pinned two pieces of linen together round her middle. 'There'll be enough 'ere fer you ter make one as well,' Mary told her neighbour. 'Minnie Venners said she'd given me enough fer two dresses. I thought it was nice of 'er. I told 'er she shouldn't feel obligated. Those tram sheets would 'ave still bin in the bathtub if I 'adn't given 'em to 'er.'

'Too bloody true,' Lucy replied.

Mary brushed the creases out of the material and looked up at her friend. 'I showed Roy that magazine,' she said. ''E was really shocked. Until then I'm sure 'e thought I was exaggeratin' about that lecherous ole git.'

'Anyway, you're well out of it,' Lucy told her. 'You just fink what might 'ave 'appened on that roof wiv 'im.'

'It don't bear finkin' about,' Mary said, shivering.

Gracie started fidgeting and Mary held her by the shoulders. 'Just a tiny bit more an' you can go an' play wiv Sue,' she coaxed.

'What yer gonna do when yer've sewed it up?' Lucy asked her.

'I'm gonna dye it green an' put some fancy lace round the collar an' sleeves, an' at the bottom,' Mary said, smiling confidently.

Lucy waited till the child had gone to find her friend, then she leaned forward in the armchair. 'Sara's started courtin',' she said quietly.

Mary looked surprised. 'That's one fer the book. Who is it? D'yer know 'im?'

Lucy shrugged her shoulders. 'She came 'ome last night full of it. It's bin goin' on fer a few weeks by all accounts, an' this feller wants 'er ter go ter Brighton wiv 'im this weekend.'

'Bloody 'ell, 'e ain't wasted any time.'

'Sara was quick ter point out that it was all above board. They're gonna 'ave separate rooms.'

'Is this someone from the church?'

'Yeah, the fellowship.'

'Did she tell yer what 'e's like?'

'She said 'e's good-lookin' an' very charmin', an' 'e sings in the choir.'

'An' 'ow old is 'e?'

'About Charlie's age.'

'Good fer 'er,' Mary remarked. ''Ere, d'yer reckon 'e'll creep in 'er room in the middle o' the night an' take 'er by surprise?'

'Not by surprise, if I know Sara. She'll be expectin' 'im.'

'P'raps it'll be the makin' of 'er,' Mary chuckled.

'I was gettin' worried about 'er, ter be honest,' Lucy confided. 'She started playin' up ter Charlie fer a while but she was makin' it look so obvious it was embarrassin' 'im. Poor Sara, she didn't 'ave a clue 'ow ter go about it.'

'Which is just as well, I should fink,' Mary replied. 'Especially if Charlie wasn't interested.' She gathered up the offcuts of linen and caught Lucy's eye. 'George's off an' all this weekend, yer said.'

'Yeah. It's gonna seem strange.'

Mary gave her a sly grin. 'I don't s'pose Charlie's goin' anywhere, is 'e?'

Lucy averted her eyes. 'I dunno really.'

Mary sat back in her chair and picked some strands of cotton from her flowered apron. ''Ow long 'ave we known each ovver, Lucy?' she asked suddenly.

'Ages. Ever since I moved inter the street.'

'Well, as an old friend I feel I can say this.

Whatever you an' Charlie get up to, don't let it ruin yer marriage.'

'We're not gonna get up to anyfing,' Lucy said quickly.

'Don't try ter kid a kidder,' Mary told her with a cheeky grin. 'You're crazy about this bloke. I see the look in yer eyes every time yer mention 'is name. It's OK, yer don't 'ave ter fight it. Just remember ter keep it on a sensible level.'

Lucy knew that it was useless to pretend any longer. Mary knew the truth but she was right about another thing too. Nothing was more important than her marriage, and if any lapse did occur it would have to remain just that, a fleeting pleasure. Something to be enjoyed in passing, like a moment out of time. 'You're sayin' all this about me an' Charlie,' she smiled, 'but I don't really know if Charlie's interested in me.'

'Now I know yer gotta be jokin',' Mary snorted. 'Anyone wiv 'alf a brain can see it. Sara can, an' so can George, an' I bet yer George only tolerates 'im as a lodger 'cos 'e finks you're not interested yourself.'

'Well, I 'aven't given 'im any reason ter fink ovverwise.'

'Don't. An' be careful,' Mary warned her. 'George might seem preoccupied wiv all that's 'appened lately, but 'e ain't stupid.'

Lucy sighed sadly. 'Do you know, Mary, I fink if me an' Charlie cuddled in front of 'im 'e wouldn't notice? We seem to 'ave become like strangers to each ovver. I can't remember the last time 'e showed any interest in me. The times I've wanted ter reach out fer 'im in bed but 'e's bin

315

snorin' 'is 'ead off.'

'It 'appens in the best o' marriages at times,' Mary said reassuringly, 'an' the times we're livin' frew at the moment ain't exactly conducive ter bein' 'appy in bed. We take our burdens up those stairs wiv us at night instead o' leavin' 'em be'ind. I reckon everyone must lie in bed wonderin' where the next penny's comin' from, an' 'ow they're gonna pay the bills. I'm no different from you in that respect. You an' George are gonna come frew it. Just make sure yer don't pull the rug from under the pair of yer.'

'Mary, you're a gem,' Lucy told her warmly. 'But yer do go on at times. Over an hour I've bin sittin' 'ere an' not one cup o' tea's passed me lips. Shall I put the kettle on?'

Mary got up. 'Leave it ter me,' she said with a crooked smile. 'Just sit back an' get yer rest while yer can.'

Although the diggers had been paid off Sharkey and Charlie had been told to report for work the following morning, and Frank Coley was feeling confident as he spoke to them. 'All bein' well we'll be gettin' back ter normal soon an' we'll need ter let the men know,' he said. Then he turned to Ben. ''Ave we got all their addresses?'

His brother nodded. 'Most of 'em are 'ere, in the notebook. There's also the name of a pub against some of 'em so we could contact 'em quickly when the work gets underway again.'

Frank took the notebook from Ben and flipped through the pages. There were blanks beside Danny and George's names and he looked up at

Charlie. 'What about your two pals?' he asked. 'Do they still use the Mason's?'

Charlie nodded. 'Occasionally.'

Sharkey made a mental note. He would be expected to pass on the information to the two ruffians he had recruited, who were ready and waiting to earn their wages.

Frank Coley reached for his coat. 'Yer'd better come wiv me, Ben,' he said. 'We've got some talkin' ter do.' Then he looked back at the gangers. 'Mind the fort, will yer? We'll be back soon as we can.'

Once they were alone Sharkey pulled out a stool from under the bench and sat down heavily. 'Yer know they won't rest until they nail Parry an' Albury,' he remarked tentatively.

'Yeah, I know, but they won't,' Charlie replied. 'It wasn't 'ow it 'appened an' they can't prove ovverwise.'

Sharkey clasped his large hands together on his lap and leaned back against the bench. 'Ter be honest I don't care if Parry did clobber Coates,' he went on. 'The man was a troublemaker, an' 'e wouldn't 'ave bin tolerated in ovver firms. 'E suited the Coleys, though. They could trust 'im ter keep 'em informed.'

'Yeah, then they got you ter do the business for 'em,' Charlie replied coldly.

'It's what I'm paid for, an' if I showed any weakness it'd be taken advantage of by the men,' Sharkey said, shrugging his shoulders. 'You know I'm right. Fortunately fer you, though, you 'aven't needed ter get rid of anyone yet.'

'If it crops up I 'ope I do it in a more civilised

317

way than you,' Charlie answered.

Sharkey narrowed his eyes and smiled mirthlessly. 'We all 'ave our methods.'

Charlie gave him a hard look as he stood up. 'I'm goin' outside for some fresh air,' he said offhandedly.

'Wait a minute,' Sharkey urged him. 'There's somefing yer need ter know, but first, I want your word you'll keep what I tell yer strictly between us two.'

'Can yer trust my word?'

'I believe I can.'

Charlie sat down once more. 'Go on then, Sharkey.'

'The Coleys told me that the inquest's set fer next Friday, an' they asked me ter line up a couple of 'eavy geezers ter sort Parry an' Albury out before 'and. The idea's ter knock the trufe out of 'em, then make sure they admit as much at the inquest.'

Charlie looked shocked. 'They've told the trufe already,' he said quickly. 'An' s'posin' they do agree ter change their story ter save a beatin', what's ter stop 'em stickin' ter the trufe at the inquest? They could even tell the coroner they've bin threatened. 'E'd be obliged ter bring in the police.'

Sharkey smiled scornfully. 'You don't know these geezers. They're not gonna stand arguin' the toss first. They'll just say they're Wally Coates's pals an' steam in. Once Parry an' Albury 'ave bin well seen to they'll be told what ter say at the inquest, an' if they don't do as they're told they can expect more o' the same. An' I gotta tell yer it won't stop at that. They'll be made aware that their families'll be included next time. That's 'ow this sort work.'

'You've got some right nice friends,' Charlie said sarcastically.

'They're no friends o' mine,' Sharkey replied quickly. 'I was just asked ter recruit someone who could do a good job. What you gotta understand is, the Coleys could go under if the inquest verdict goes boss-eyed. They're desperate, an' they'll do what they 'ave ter do.'

'Which means that Parry an' Albury are gonna be obliged ter go into 'idin' till the inquest.'

'That's about the strength of it.'

'If they do get waylaid an' forced ter change their story it'll fly in the face of what I'll be sayin', or 'ave the Coleys lined me up too?' Charlie asked with a searching stare.

'No, they'll just sort Parry an' Albury out. It'll be their word against yours, an' the coroner's gonna realise that you've got good reason ter lie,' Sharkey reminded him. 'You were the ganger in charge. As far as 'e's concerned you couldn't be 'eld responsible fer a man slippin' over an' causin' 'is own death, but yer could be if there was a confrontation an' you failed ter nip it in the bud.'

'Parry an' Albury were tellin' the trufe,' Charlie said firmly.

'You try tellin' the Coleys as much,' Sharkey growled. 'Like I said, I ain't bovvered eivver way about what 'appened, but I ain't intendin' ter be the patsy if it all goes wrong. They'll stick me in the frame if they 'ave to.'

''Ow they gonna play it?' Charlie asked.

'They know where Parry an' Albury live an' they'll pick their time.'

'When will it 'appen?'

'Soon as possible,' Sharkey said, 'bearin' in mind the inquest is only a week away.'

Charlie felt relieved that George would be out of the area that weekend, but he was worried about Danny Albury. The man was too brave for his own good at times. Standing up to Wally Coates had taken some nerve and he would do the same with the heavies, which would only make matters worse. 'Why don't you give those scum bruvvers the elbow an' go back ter wrestlin'?' he remarked.

'I might even do that,' Sharkey replied with a brief smile.

Charlie stood up to leave. 'I don't s'pose you're worried about what I might fink of yer,' he said quietly, 'but I want yer ter know I appreciate you takin' a chance in tellin' me. I'll tell yer somefing else too. I'm glad we never needed ter come on 'ead to 'ead.'

'Yeah. It could 'ave bin a right ole set-to,' the ex-wrestler replied. 'Let's go get a drink. They won't be back yet.'

CHAPTER 27

On Friday evening Charlie Foden held a council of war at the Mason's Arms. Sharing a table with him at the far end of the public bar were George Parry, Danny Albury and Roy Chubb.

'Are you sure she's all right?' Charlie asked Danny.

'Look, you can take my word fer it,' the dapper man replied. 'Freda Johnson's as good as gold. I knew fer a fact she's bawled Mick out plenty o' times fer gettin' too cosy wiv the Coleys. She told me 'e's servin' in the saloon ternight so 'e won't even know we're 'ere. Not that it matters. We're allowed ter come in fer a drink, surely ter Gawd.'

Charlie nodded. 'Now this is straight from the 'orse's mouth, so listen carefully an' don't make light of it,' he began, staring at Danny and George in turn. 'You two 'ave 'ad yer cards marked. The Coleys 'ave got a couple o' bruisers ter sort you out. The idea is to 'ammer the truth out o' the pair of yer, an' make yer confess that you caused Wally Coates's death.'

Both looked shocked. 'They can't do that,' Danny said quickly.

'S'posin' we went ter the police an' said we've bin threatened?' George added.

Charlie shook his head. 'Let me try ter put yer in the picture,' he went on. 'In the first place the Coleys 'ave got someone ter recruit the two

321

geezers, an' as far as they know it's prob'ly one o' Coates's mates who's puttin' 'em up to it. The Coleys 'ands are clean. What's more, the person who warned me 'as got my word I won't drop 'im in it, so if yer go ter the police they won't be able ter do anyfing. They'd need proof.'

'What's this all about?' George asked.

'The inquest is set fer next Friday,' Charlie explained, 'an' if they can get a confession out of eivver one of yer before then, they can use it as evidence that the management weren't ter blame fer Coates's death. That leaves 'em in a position ter talk terms wiv the main contractors fer the rest o' the trenchin' contract.'

Danny Albury seemed puzzled. ''Ow do they know who we are?'

'They've bin given yer addresses an' they know the pubs you use,' Charlie told him. 'They only need ter make a few enquiries anyway. They could say they're ole friends or somefing, an' someone could point you out.'

'If they threaten us we could promise ter say anyfing an' do the opposite at the inquest,' Danny said.

'They won't threaten yer, they'll come at yer,' Charlie stressed, 'an' by the time they'd finished wiv the two of yer you'd say anyfing an' stick wiv it. If yer didn't, they'd come back at yer families as well as you. That's the dangerous sort they are, believe me.'

'What can we do about it?' George asked.

'Well in your case you'll be away fer the weekend,' Charlie reminded him, 'an' we can sort somefing out when yer get back on Sunday night.

As fer you, Danny, yer gotta stay off the street. Make sure yer know who's at the door if there's a knock, an' if yer don't then don't answer.'

'I usually go out fer a pint on Saturday nights,' Danny groaned.

Roy Chubb had been silent so far, but now he smiled. 'I like a drink on Saturday nights too,' he said. 'I'll come an' collect yer.'

'Not on yer own yer won't,' Charlie said bluntly. 'Yer'd need ter be mob-'anded.'

'You know Benny an' Fatty Wallace, an' Les Green?' Roy asked, looking at Danny. 'We'll call round tergevver. We all use the Swan on Saturday nights.'

'I don't go out on Sundays,' Danny said, 'but what about when me an' George go down the labour exchange on Monday mornin'?'

'We'll work somefing out later,' Charlie answered. 'In the meantime be extra careful. I'll be 'avin' a discreet word wiv Ron Sloan soon as I can. I'll put 'im in the picture an' 'e'll be able ter keep a look-out fer any strange faces lurkin' about in the vicinity.'

'I'll warn a few o' the lads ter be on the look-out as well,' Danny added.

Charlie drained his glass. 'I might be wrong, but I got an idea they won't try anyfing this weekend,' he said thoughtfully. 'They'll wait till early next week.'

The group left the pub together and walked briskly into Cooper Street. 'Remember what's bin said, Danny, an' take care,' Charlie told him as they reached the little man's front door.

Sammy Strickland left his house on Friday evening and strode off towards the Dun Cow in the Old Kent Road. That week he had earned a wage helping out with some house painting, and when he had laid out the money on the scullery table Peggy felt quite faint. 'I dunno what ter say,' she gasped.

'There's nuffink to say,' he replied. 'I done it fer you. I was just about sick an' tired o' seein' you struggle, an' when ole Fuller offered me the work I jumped at it. Actually there might be some more o' the same comin' up but I'll wait till next week ter see 'im. I ain't gonna go wastin' money lookin' fer 'im at the Dun Cow.'

'Is this every penny yer've earned?' Peggy asked.

'Every penny, love.'

'Well you take a coupla bob back an' go an' get yerself a drink. You've earned it,' Peggy told him with a smile.

Sammy was not aware of the large man who had watched him come out of the turning and had now fallen into step a few yards behind him. Nor did he see the other bulky figure who came up and joined the first man. Sammy's mind was on that pint of frothing beer, and as he stepped into the public bar he licked his lips in anticipation.

'It looks like it's gonna be a nasty old night,' the stranger remarked casually to Sammy as he and his colleague stood next to him at the counter.

'Yeah, it does,' Sammy replied as he gratefully pulled the brimming glass towards himself.

The man ordered two pints of bitter and turned

to face Sammy. 'I take it you're a local round these parts, pal,' he said amiably.

'All of firty years,' Sammy told him with a smile.

'You'd most likely know Danny Albury an' George Parry, then.'

'Know 'em? I live in the same street as them.'

The big man smiled. 'Me an' my mate Frank 'ere used ter work wiv 'em, yer see, an' we was 'opin' we'd bump into 'em in 'ere. They told us once they used the Dun Cow.'

'Not very often,' Sammy replied. 'They use the Mason's Arms or the Star on the corner o' Kingsley Street.'

'Fanks, pal,' the big man said. 'We'll pop in there later. It'd be nice ter see 'em again.'

Sammy drank his beer with relish and decided that one more pint was in order, and as he reached into his trouser pocket Will Jackson walked in.

'Wotcher, Sammy, 'ow yer doin'?' he asked.

'Not so bad. What about you?'

'Fings are a bit quiet lately, which is ter be expected,' Will replied, taking out a handful of copper from his pocket.

'Leave it ter me,' Sammy told him. 'I 'ad a good week by way of a change.'

The two carried their pints over to a vacant table and Will took out his tobacco tin, a serious look on his wide face. 'I just come from Alice Albury's,' he said. 'I'd put a new pane o' glass in 'er scullery winder an' as I was clearin' up the mess Danny walked in. 'E looked worried out of 'is life an' 'im an' Alice went inter the parlour. I could 'ear Danny talkin' quickly but I wasn't earwiggin'. Anyway, they called me in a few minutes later an' Danny told me 'e's 'ad 'is card marked. ''Im an' Alice are in a right ole state. Worried out o' their lives they are.'

'What's it all about?' Sammy enquired.

Will Jackson sipped his pint. 'Apparently there's a couple o' nasty geezers after givin' 'im and George Parry a goin'-over.'

'George Parry as well?'

'Yeah. It's over that accident at the diggin's in Morgan Street, so Danny told me. These two geezers are out ter make 'im an' George change their story of 'ow it 'appened.'

'What for?'

'I dunno. Danny was sayin' it's so that the Coleys don't take the blame,' Will replied. 'It was all a bit over me 'ead, but I can tell yer Danny looked really worried. So did Alice. I bin asked ter watch points an' let 'em know if anyone strange comes askin' questions.'

Sammy's face had slowly lost its colour as Will was talking and he now looked as white as a freshly laundered bedsheet. 'Don't look round, just keep yer eyes fixed on me,' he hissed.

'What's the matter?'

'I'll tell yer what's the matter,' Sammy gulped. 'I just bin approached by two big geezers at the counter askin' about Danny an' George.'

'Oh my good Gawd!' Will gasped. 'What did yer tell 'em?'

'They said they was ole workmates an' they wanted ter meet up wiv 'em again, so I told 'em they usually go in the Star or the Mason's Arms.'

'Yer never.'

'I did.'

'Bloody 'ell.'

'What we gonna do, Will?'

'What you gonna do, yer mean,' Will said sharply.

'I'll 'ave ter go an' warn 'em ter keep away from those pubs,' Sammy decided.

'Yer'd better tell 'em what those two geezers look like as well, so they'll 'ave 'alf a chance o' dodgin' 'em,' Will advised him.

Sammy studied his glass of beer for a few moments and then a smile started to play around the corner of his mouth. 'I've got an idea,' he said.

'It better be a good one,' Will growled.

'Look, you finish yer pint an' then walk out the pub,' Sammy told him. 'I'll see yer in the Samson in about ten minutes.'

As soon as Will Jackson had left Sammy sidled up to the counter and stood next to the two bruisers. 'Did yer see me talkin' ter that bloke just now?' he asked them. ''E lives in the turnin'. 'E told me they've just took Danny Albury ter the Rovverhive Infirmary in an ambulance. Suspected appendicitis by all accounts.'

'That's bad news,' the man nearest to him answered.

'Anyway, yer'll be able ter visit 'im in there,' Sammy went on. 'Maybe take a few grapes in. I'm sure Danny'll appreciate it. Well, must be off. I'm 'avin' a drink wiv me bruvver-in-law later when 'e comes off duty. 'E's the local beat bobby. Nice feller. A bit 'ard wiv the Jack-the-lads at times, but 'is 'eart's in the right place.'

As Sammy left the Dun Cow the bigger of the two thugs drained his glass. 'C'mon,' he said quickly.

'Where we goin'?' the other asked.

'I can smell somefing fishy 'ere,' the first man replied. 'We're gonna pay a trip ter the Rovver-hive Infirmary an' find out if a Mr Albury was admitted this evenin'.'

When Will Jackson left the Dun Cow and made his way along to the Samson he almost bumped into the local bobby. 'What, no wringers?' the policeman remarked, looking down at the smaller man with a sarcastic smile. 'You must be slippin', Will.'

'I'm strickly kosher these days,' he replied. 'I gotta fink o' Paula an' the two kids.'

'Nice to 'ear yer say it,' Ron Sloan said, rocking back on his heels.

Will Jackson looked up at the policeman with an earnest expression on his face. 'Does your beat go as far as the Old Kent Road?' he enquired.

'Just about. Why d'yer ask?'

'As far as the Dun Cow?'

Ron Sloan shook his head. 'What's this all about, Will?'

The handyman cast a quick glance along the street. 'I just bin 'avin' a drink in there wiv Sammy Strickland an' 'e pointed out these two ugly great geezers who are after sortin' out Danny Albury an' George Parry.'

'What for?'

'Yer'd need ter talk ter Sammy about the whys

328

an' wherefores,' Will answered. 'All I know is those two geezers are out ter make George an' Danny change their statements at the inquest on that bloke who got killed in Morgan Street.'

'If that's the case they're duty bound ter report it ter the police,' Ron said emphatically. 'What's more, if you can identify these two men you should go wiv 'em too.'

'It ain't as simple as that.'

'No, it never is,' the policeman growled.

'If you could see Danny Albury or George Parry they'd be able ter put yer in the picture,' Will suggested.

'I might just do that,' the policeman told him. 'Now can yer give me a description o' these two villains?'

Will shook his head. 'I only got a quick flash of 'em, but Sammy was talkin' to 'em before I arrived at the pub an' 'e'd remember what they looked like.'

Ron Sloan nodded. 'Is Sammy likely ter be in before the pubs turn out ternight?' he asked.

'Yeah. I'm on me way ter see 'im at the Samson now,' Will replied, 'but Peggy wouldn't allow 'im ter stay out that late.'

PC Sloan knocked at the Alburys' front door and saw the curtains move in the parlour before his knock was answered. Later he called at the Parrys' house and faced Lucy's wrath. 'My George would never 'arm a fly,' she insisted. 'An' who in their right mind's gonna admit ter somefing that never 'appened, especially when it could get 'em inter trouble, even get 'em sent ter prison?'

'People do some strange fings when they're frightened, Mrs Parry,' the policeman remarked, then turned his attention to Charlie. 'You say you were warned about what's bin planned on the premise that yer'll keep yer contact's name secret. Well let me tell you somefing. If this ever gets ter court you'll be summoned as a witness an' you'll be on oath. You might well find yerself in contempt, which, as I'm sure yer know, could land you in prison.'

'Yeah, I realise that,' Charlie replied quietly.

Ron Sloan got up to leave. 'I'm obliged ter put what's bin said in my report, so if I were you I'd get round the station first fing termorrer an' see the Super.'

Lucy showed the policeman out and then walked back into the parlour with a dark look on her pretty face. 'I've got a nasty feelin' I'm bein' kept in the dark,' she complained.

George leaned back in his chair. 'There's no way they can make me lie about what 'appened in that trench,' he said firmly. 'Wally Coates slipped an' fell back on the shorin' prop. 'E was a big man an' 'is weight dislodged it. That's what me an' Danny saw, that's what we put in our statements an' that's what the coroner'll be told. It's the trufe.'

Charlie hated lying to Lucy, but it was for the best, he thought. 'Yer can't go wrong wiv the trufe.'

'I wonder if we should do as Ron Sloan suggested?' George said.

'If we do I gotta keep my contact's name out of it,' Charlie told him, 'come what may.'

330

'I'm sure they'll understand,' George replied.

Lucy got up and collected the tray of used crockery from the table. 'I was 'opin' Sara wouldn't walk in while that copper was 'ere,' she remarked. 'Those sewin' evenin's don't run all that late as a rule.'

That particular sewing evening had in fact finished early, due to the heating boiler having broken down, and as the women filed out of the church Sara was thrilled to see Randolph standing in the porch. 'I thought I'd look in to see if you'd like me to walk you home,' he said, smiling. 'It's a nasty night.'

'That's very nice of yer.'

'I managed to see Mr Saward this morning,' he told her. 'Things are looking good.'

'You mean you'll be able ter get the business started?'

'Well, it all depends on my being able to raise the necessary funds,' Randolph said as they walked along Lynton Road. 'I'm hopeful, and if it works out the company could be in full flow by the summer. We'd be financially established and in a position to challenge the big fish. Believe me, Sara, the prospects are almost frightening in their intensity.'

'I'm so thrilled fer you, Randolph,' Sara said sweetly. 'I want you ter remember what I said. You're more than welcome ter use my jewellery as security. I've got every confidence in you.'

'I must admit it would solve a problem or two, but I stop short of asking you. It's just too much to expect.'

'Don't be so silly,' Sara told him in her childish

voice. 'If all else fails yer must ask me, do you promise?'

'I promise.'

They had reached the corner of Cooper Street. 'Goodnight, Sara,' he said, taking her hand in his and giving it a little squeeze.

'Goodnight, Randolph.'

He quickly kissed her cheek and walked away, leaving her with a satisfied smile on her pale face which was suddenly wiped away as she saw PC Ron Sloan leave the house.

'Whatever's 'appened?' she gasped as she hurried into the parlour.

'It's all right, calm down, Sara,' George told her. 'Ron Sloan was only tellin' us that the inquest's fixed fer next Friday.'

'But you already knew that.'

'Yeah, but the copper never knew I knew,' George said, smiling.

'I was worried out o' me life when I saw 'im come out the 'ouse,' Sara went on. 'There's always somefing comes up ter spoil a nice evenin'.'

'So you 'ad a nice evenin'?' Lucy said.

'I did, and when I came out o' the church there was Randolph waitin' to escort me 'ome.'

'That must 'ave bin nice,' Lucy replied, trying to look serious.

'I 'ope yer'll be careful this weekend,' George remarked.

'George, Sara's not a child, she's a mature woman,' Lucy said quickly, giving Charlie a brief glance. 'She's goin' ter Brighton, not Timbuctoo.'

'Yeah, but she 'ardly knows this Randolph

feller,' he replied. 'Yer read so many bad stories in the papers an' I'm just warnin' 'er ter be careful.'

'Randolph's a real gentleman an' I'm goin' ter be well looked after this weekend,' Sara said indignantly.

Yeah I bet you will, Lucy thought, and she smiled amiably at her sister-in-law. 'You just 'ave a nice time,' she said.

CHAPTER 28

Police Constable Ron Sloan had been the beat bobby around the Cooper Street area for a number of years and he was known to everyone. Many a young buck had been turned aside from the road to incarceration by a judicious clip round the ear at a most impressionable age, and many a usually law-abiding citizen had been let off when apprehended in suspicious circum-stances by the discerning bobby, who knew only too well that desperate men took to desperate measures. Ron Sloan was no soft touch, however, as many a local publican would testify after seeing him break up a fight or calm down an enraged customer.

The constable took his job seriously enough to have turned down the chance of becoming a sergeant, which would have effectively taken him from his beat, and he was at his best in difficult situations.

'Yer'd better 'ave a word wiv the Super,' the station sergeant told him after reading his report.

Ron Sloan was able to convince his superior that it could all be sorted out satisfactorily if he was allowed to deal with it informally, and to that end he was given permission to change to early shift beginning on Saturday morning.

'Any chance of a cuppa, Sammy?' he asked the very surprised chancer who answered the rat-tat in his nightshirt.

'Bloody 'ell, don't you ever sleep?' Sammy growled as he showed Ron in.

'Sammy, I wanna use your parlour fer a while this mornin'. Is that all right?'

''Ere, you ain't bringin' a dodgy woman in 'ere, are yer?' Sammy asked, wide-eyed.

'Don't be silly. I've got a nice little woman at 'ome,' Ron Sloan told him. 'I'm after watchin' points.'

'Is it ter do wiv what I told yer last night?'

The policeman nodded. 'I got a gut feelin' they'll be turnin' their attention towards George Parry an' they may even call on 'im. I 'ope they do, then you can make a formal identification.'

''Ere, I ain't goin' ter court ter pick 'em out, so you can get that right out o' yer 'ead,' Sammy said with passion.

'They won't be goin' ter court if they don't do anyfing,' the PC told him. 'That's what I'm after, sortin' this before it gets nasty.'

'Right, I'm wiv yer,' Sammy said, grinning. 'Now you do what you 'ave ter do while I make the tea. Peggy's 'avin' a lie-in this mornin'.'

Ron nodded. 'I'll 'ave a quick cuppa, then I'm gonna pop over ter see the Parrys before George leaves.'

Bonny Watson and Snatcher Bayliss sat by the window in a steamy café off Lynton Road and slurped tea from large mugs.

'I don't like it. I don't like it one little bit,' Snatcher was saying. 'It's as though we're bein' watched.'

336

'Look, d'you still wanna earn that score, or 'ave yer gone bottly all of a sudden?' Bonny asked.

'Course I wanna earn it, an' I ain't gone bottly,' he replied. 'It's just that we've bin took on, an' I'm askin' meself fer why? Danny Albury wasn't admitted ter the 'ospital last night. Why should that ole boy tell us ovverwise?'

''E could 'ave got the 'ospitals mixed up.'

'Cobblers. 'E sussed what we were up to an' wanted ter put us off the scent.'

Bonny grinned. 'If I was asked fer someone's whereabouts I'd be cagey, 'specially if the blokes looked like we do.'

'What's the matter wiv us?' Snatcher said indignantly.

'Well, we're not exactly yer average person's idea of good ole pals, are we?'

'Nah, I s'pose not,' Snatcher conceded, rubbing at his cauliflower ear.

'Now come on, drink up. We're gonna join the street corner mob,' Bonny told him.

'Street corner mob?' Snatcher frowned.

'Yeah. There's always blokes standin' round on street corners on Saturdays. We're gonna make a few discreet enquiries. Well, I am. You just keep stumm.'

Bonny was right, and as they strolled casually up to the three men lounging on the corner of Cooper Street by the boarded-up cobbler's shop they were given suspicious looks.

'Me an' my pal just got moved on from the corner o' Mason Grove,' Bonny growled. 'I dunno what the bloody copper thought we was after. We was only watchin' the draymen puttin' the beer in the pub. Can't stand round anywhere these days.'

'Our bobby don't mind us 'angin' around on this street corner,' Mike Stiles told him. 'Long's we don't start shy-'ikin' people.'

''E must be a decent copper, that's all I can say,' Bonny replied. 'That bastard Priestly ain't 'appy unless 'e's 'avin' a go at somebody.'

Women were passing to and fro carrying shopping bags and the rag-and-bone man came trundling his barrow into the turning as the young men lounged against the shop hoarding. Bonny took the opportunity of checking the door numbers and pinpointed George Parry's house.

'Where d'you come from?' Dennis Grainger asked.

'Down the Blue,' Bonny told him.

'D'you know the Ashley bruvvers?' Ted Wicks enquired.

'Yeah. They're a bit 'ard,' Bonny remarked.

'Yer don't mess wiv them,' Snatcher cut in.

Ted Wicks looked at Snatcher's mutilated ear and decided that the Ashleys must really be a hard crowd if someone looking like him was wary of them. 'You look like you can take care o' yerselves,' he ventured.

'We do our scrappin' in the ring,' Bonny informed him. 'We do a bit o' wrestlin'.'

The three loungers were full of questions but Bonny suddenly cut them dead, nudging his friend as he spotted three men coming out of number 8. 'C'mon, Snatch, we've got some business ter take care of,' he said quietly.

As agreed, Charlie Foden and Roy Chubb

escorted George towards the bus stop in the Old Kent Road, and as they disappeared out of the turning the curtains at number 2 moved very slightly. 'I bloody well knew it,' Ron Sloan growled. 'Quick, Sammy, take a gander.'

'Yeah, that's 'em,' the chancer replied. 'Yer couldn't mistake those two. They look like they've done fifteen rounds wiv Pedlar Palmer.'

Ron Sloan waited until the two wrestlers left the turning, then he slipped out of the house and trailed in their wake at a reasonable distance. As planned the three friends walked along Croft Street, ignoring Bell Alley, a quiet shortcut which would take them into the Old Kent Road directly opposite the bus stop. Bonny and Snatcher kept back a little and stood looking in a shop window as the three joined the bus queue.

'What now?' Snatcher asked.

'I don't bloody well know,' Bonny scowled.

A number 21 bus pulled up at the stop and the lurkers noticed that only one of the three men boarded the bus.

'This is a waste o' time,' Snatcher groaned.

'No it ain't,' Bonny said sharply. 'That was Parry who got on that bus. I know 'im by sight now. The ovver two are 'is minders.'

Snatcher was not convinced. It could be a ploy to mislead them, he thought. The man could get off at the next stop and wait for his escort to arrive. 'What we gonna do, foller the ovver two?' he asked as the minders set off back to Cooper Street.

'Nah. We'll 'ang around on the corner an' see if the ovver geezer makes a show.'

'Yer mean this Albury bloke?'

'Who else,' Bonny said with contempt.

Snatcher ignored it. Bonny considered himself to be the brains of the partnership but there were times when Snatcher had to question it, though silently. This little job of work was going wrong before it got underway and the twenty pounds he would receive for his trouble was going to be well earned, Snatcher knew that much. As they turned back from the bus stop they were immediately confronted by Ron Sloan, who had stepped out of the alley.

'Don't I know you two,' he asked, hooking his thumbs in his polished belt.

'I don't fink so,' Bonny replied quickly.

'Someone pointed you out ter me an' told me you've bin askin' 'im questions.'

'We ain't bin askin' questions, 'ave we, Snatch?'

'Nah, course not.'

'Well, I must 'ave bin mistaken then,' the constable said with a sly smile. 'But just so you an' me know where we stand, let me put yer in the picture. My name is Ron Sloan an' I'm the beat bobby fer Cooper Street an' the surroundin' manor. Everyone knows me an' I know everyone back, which makes it nice an' cosy. When I'm off duty I've got eyes an' ears looking out fer fings, know what I mean? Then when I come on duty I can get on wiv keepin' the peace, fer my people's benefit, if yer get my drift. Well, do yer?' he asked in a slightly raised voice, and the two men nodded dutifully. 'Now it's come ter my attention that you two are after sortin' out a couple o' my people, an' it grieves me, so let me make it all nice an' clear. If I see eivver o' you 'angin' around the neighbour'ood again I'm gonna come down on yer so 'ard yer'll fink a bloody great wall's fell on yer, an' before yer've got over the shock I'll 'ave yer down that station an' charge the pair o' yer wiv everyfing I can make stick – loiterin' wiv intent, threatenin' conduct, conspiracy ter commit a felony, conspiracy ter pervert the course o' justice, abusive language, resistin' arrest, treason an' mutiny on the 'igh seas. Want me ter go on?'

The two villains merely shook their heads in shock and the constable tapped his breast pocket. 'Yer'll notice that I ain't got me little book out an' wrote yer names down,' he reminded them. 'I don't need to. I never, ever ferget a face. That'll do fer me. Now on yer way, an' if yer know what's good for yer remember everyfing I've said. By the way, you can 'ave my name an' number. 143, Constable R Sloan.'

'Big-'eaded git,' Bonny growled as the two slouched off.

'That's it as far as I'm concerned,' Snatcher declared. 'Sharkey can keep 'is poxy score.'

'I'm gonna 'ave words wiv 'im,' Bonny replied. 'It's as if everyone round 'ere knows what we was up to an' was waitin' fer us ter make our move.'

'Come on then, let's see if we can find 'im,' Snatcher said. 'I reckon 'e'll be in the Crown by the time we get there.'

Sara Parry felt her heart flutter a little as she took her seat in the morning train to Brighton. Randolph was sitting close and she could feel his shoulder touching hers. It made her feel quite young again and she sighed.

'Are you all right, my dear?' he asked.

'I'm feelin' very well,' she replied, smiling at him.

Randolph leaned his head back against the white linen square. 'First class is the only way to travel,' he remarked. 'It gives one a feeling of importance. Not in a pompous sense, you understand, more by way of being catered for, as opposed to all that confounded finger-snapping and doffing of caps in the presence of the mine owner or the works manager. Sitting here in this carriage we could be a double act on the music halls, a lord and his lady, or even runaway lovers being pursued by the lady's wicked stepfather who has designs on her.'

'Oh, Randolph, you make it all sound so romantic.'

'It's my aim to please, to make you feel gay.'

'You do, you do.'

At the Redhill stop another passenger entered the compartment and sat in the seat facing them. He was elderly and wearing the collar of holy office. 'A miserable day,' he said politely.

'Yes it is,' Randolph replied.

'Going to Brighton?'

'Yes. Are you?'

'No, I'm getting off at Haywards Heath. Visiting an old friend.'

'That's nice,' Sara said with a smile.

'Are you taking the baths?' the cleric asked.

'No, just the air and the rest,' Randolph told him.

'Good place for that is Brighton,' the cleric went on. 'I served in London for many years, in Hoxton and Shoreditch to name but two parishes. Now in my autumn years I'm serving the parishioners at Plough-Deeping, little more than a hamlet near Redhill. Still plenty of work to do there, though. There are souls to be saved everywhere.' He drew out a wallet from inside his coat, opened it up and took out a crumpled photograph. 'There it is, Plough-Deeping. Rather quaint, wouldn't you say?'

Randolph looked at the photograph and passed it to Sara. 'I see they have a village pump,' he remarked.

'Yes, all the water in the village is drawn from that pump,' the cleric replied. 'There are plans to lay water pipes but it's still some way off, I'm afraid. Question of funds, you understand. I did ask the Redhill council to help finance the project and I got a rather tart reply. They suggested I should contact my own governor for help.' He raised his eyes towards the ceiling of the compartment.

Sara tutted and Randolph shook his head. 'Disgusting,' he declared.

At Haywards Heath the cleric stood up and held out his outstretched hand over Sara's head, then Randolph's. 'May the good Lord go with you,' he said reverently.

They watched as he climbed down from the carriage and disappeared into the crowd. It was then, as the train pulled out of the station, that Randolph noticed the small card lying at his feet. The vicar must have dropped it, he thought as he leaned down to pick it up while Sara was still looking out of the window.

Bernard Goggings
Entertainer extraordinaire. West End trained. Theatre and music hall. Home and holiday bookings accepted at short notice. Children's party specialist. Puppets, magic and party games. Your satisfaction guaranteed. Contact Bernard on ROD 1769.

'What a nice man,' Sara remarked.

'Very talented too, I should say,' Randolph replied with a smile.

'I could sense the piousness o' the man,' Sara said. ''E seemed very open an' honest.'

'I agree,' Randolph answered, secretly pocketing the card.

Bernard Goggings had walked along the platform and then re-entered the train further down just as the porter waved his green flag. That couple were too wrapped up in themselves to be of assistance, he thought. Better to concentrate on the elderly ladies. Water pipes for Plough-Deeping would be an expensive project and every penny helped. Of course the rare five-pound note instead of the customary one-pound bills would contribute handsomely to the endeavour, or rather the well-being of Bernard Goggings on his working trips to the south coast.

In the privacy of their compartment Randolph took Sara's hand in his. 'I do hope you enjoy the brief respite from London, dear,' he said quietly.

'I'm sure I will,' Sara told him. 'I 'ope you do too.'

'I'm sure I will,' he said, crossing his fingers by his side.

'Randolph?'

'Yes?'

'What was that place the vicar mentioned?'

'Plough-Deeping.'

'I bet I'd 'ave a job tryin' ter find it on the map,' she remarked.

'I'm sure you would,' he said, hiding a smile.

CHAPTER 29

When Charlie arrived back at the house Lucy met him with an anxious look on her face. 'I've bin so worried,' she said. 'I was imaginin' all sorts o' fings.'

Charlie squeezed her arm gently as he stepped into the dark passageway. 'There was no need to,' he told her. 'They wouldn't try anyfing wiv three of us. Anyway, George got the bus an' 'e seemed quite cheerful.'

'Yeah, I expect 'e was,' Lucy said grudgingly. ''E's out of it, but Danny Albury's not, an' nor are we.'

Charlie followed her into the parlour and sat down in the armchair by the warm fire. 'Where's Sue?' he asked.

Lucy eased herself into the armchair facing him. 'She's playin' next door. I'm gonna collect 'er in a few minutes.' She sat forward in the chair. 'I'll put the kettle on.'

Charlie leaned forward and placed his hands over hers. 'Look, there's no need ter get all agitated 'cos we're on our own,' he said with a smile. 'Sit fer a while. Talk ter me.'

Lucy smiled back at him. 'Do you realise this is the first time you an' I 'ave bin alone in the 'ouse?'

'The thought did occur ter me,' he replied.

Lucy slowly withdrew her hands from beneath

his. 'I thought George might 'ave made some comment about it before 'e left but 'e was more concerned about not missin' 'is train,' she said, raising her eyes expressively.

''E was worried about leavin' yer in case those blokes called,' Charlie replied, 'but I assured 'im I wouldn't leave yer on yer own fer a minute while 'e was away.'

'That should 'ave made 'im fink,' Lucy said with a brief smile. 'Just put yerself in 'is place. Would you be all that 'appy ter leave yer wife alone in the 'ouse wiv the lodger?'

'Well, that all depends on the lodger,' Charlie answered. 'I mean, 'e could be a lecherous ole goat, or a bookworm, or 'e could be genuinely attracted ter the lady o' the 'ouse.'

'Where d'yer put yerself amongst that lot?' she asked.

'Don't you know yet?' he replied quietly.

She nodded. 'I've known fer some time, an' I knew fer sure the night you kissed me.'

'I'd bin wantin' ter do that fer a long time,' Charlie confessed. 'I just looked at yer an' wanted desperately ter feel yer against me, take yer in me arms an' kiss yer, an' I tried ter resist it, but I couldn't. When I asked yer I truly expected yer ter say no, but yer never did. Yer let me kiss yer, an' 'old yer close fer a few seconds, an' it was wonderful.'

'It was fer me too,' Lucy said quietly. 'That night I went up ter bed still feelin' yer lips on mine an' I sat on the edge o' the bed fer ages, just finkin'. I needed time ter calm down, an' as I sat there I became more an' more irritated by

George's snorin'. I became angry, Charlie. I started ter blame 'im fer what I'd done, an' then I hated meself fer bein' so selfish. I can't 'elp it, though. George doesn't seem ter know I exist lately. I sometimes fink if I confessed ter lettin' you kiss me 'e'd merely nod an' bury 'is 'ead in the paper.'

'It'd be easy fer me ter come on ter yer if that was the case,' Charlie said, 'but we both know it's not like that. George loves yer, but it's bin 'ard fer 'im lately.'

'It's bin 'ard fer ovver men too,' she replied. 'Do they all ignore their wives as well?' She looked fixedly at him and he shrugged his shoulders. 'You're a good man, Charlie, an' I respect yer fer sayin' what yer did, but I need love an' attention just like any ovver red-blooded woman. Sometimes I feel my life is merely tickin' away like a clock, an' each day I'm gettin' a little bit older. I feel I'm missin' out on so much.'

Charlie looked down at his feet for a few moments and then his dark eyes came up to meet hers. 'If somefing 'appened between us, 'ere an' now, would yer stop feelin' like you were missin' out, or would you end up 'urtin' more inside? There'd be no future in it fer eivver of us. We're both married an' you wouldn't leave George, nor would I be able ter get a divorce.'

Lucy reached out and rested her hand on his. 'What are yer tryin' ter tell me, Charlie?' she asked quietly. 'Are yer excusin' yerself fer not makin' any more passes at me?'

'No, Lucy, I'm tryin' ter be honest an' up front,' he replied in a husky tone that made her feel sick with excitement. 'I'm lettin' you know that I understand what the situation is. I'm not a young man any more, and you're a wife an' muvver. We can't make each ovver promises, we can't make plans tergevver. Stolen hours, that's all we can 'ave, an' all we can ever 'ope for. I wish it could be so much more but it can't, an' I'd 'ave ter live wiv that an' make it enough fer me, but it might not be fer you.'

'I could live wiv that, Charlie,' she said in a voice she hardly recognised. 'I know I can't expect the world or turn back the clock, but I'd enjoy every second we 'ad tergevver an' live fer the next encounter.'

'Wiv you an' me livin' under the same roof?'

'It'd 'ave ter be that way. It's the only way. Every day I'd see yer, an' I'd take comfort in 'earin' your voice, watchin' yer smile an' shiverin' wiv pleasure every time yer looked at me in that certain way.'

Charlie rose slowly from his chair and reached out to her. She came to him and their bodies melted together as he found her eager lips. Time seemed to stand still as she held on to the kiss, her sweetness arousing him, stroking and rubbing her lips against his to excite him still further. Then, his strong hands clasping her to him, she moved her head back to look deep into his burning eyes. 'You know I want yer, Charlie,' she gasped.

He smiled in the way she had come to adore. 'I've never needed anyone more than I need you right this minute,' he told her. 'I feel like a youngster, achin' fer the chance ter love yer fully an' completely.'

'Don't, Charlie,' she breathed. 'I'm shakin' all over.'

He moved back half a pace, still holding her by the shoulders. 'You are beautiful, an' just lookin' at yer takes me breath away.'

She rose up on tiptoe and kissed him quickly on the lips. 'Let me calm down a bit, Charlie,' she said. 'Sit down while I make the tea, an' then I've gotta fetch Sue from next door.'

The wintry sun peeped fitfully from gathering clouds and a chill wind came off the sea as Randolph and Sara walked along the Brighton promenade. She held his arm lightly and occasionally he glanced at her as they made for the Cadogan Hotel.

'I'm still not sure I should be doing this,' he told her.

'Don't be so silly,' she chided him. 'It's only an appraisal, after all's said an' done.'

'Yes, but it's the principle of the thing.'

'Principle my eye,' Sara said with a passion that surprised her. 'If the jeweller gives us a good evaluation then you can feel more confident in yer future negotiations. You've explained it all an' I'm 'appy ter be in a position to 'elp yer. Let's just see what 'e 'as ter say first.'

The doorman in his olive-green uniform gave them a polite nod as they stepped into the warmth of the Victorian hotel, and Sara was immediately taken by its splendour. The ornate ceiling seemed as high as a cathedral's and huge gilt and crystal chandeliers hung down along its length. The black and white marble floor and oak furniture were complemented by rose-flowered tapestry and covers, while on a discreet dais to one side of the large reception area a pianist tinkled away on a beautifully polished Steinway. Ahead, a wide flight of stairs led up to a balcony which encircled the lower area like a halo, and it was there that Samuel Horowitz was waiting, his bulky frame reclining in a plush lounger.

'Ah, Randolph. How good to see you again,' he declared, getting up and smiling to show his small, tobacco-stained teeth.

They shook hands and then Randolph encouraged Sara forward with his hand on her back. 'This is the young lady I was telling you about, Samuel,' he said.

Sara held out her gloved hand and the Russian Jew took it gently in his much larger one, debonairly inclining his head. 'A pleasure I'm sure,' he told her.

Randolph looked around the balcony. 'Can you do the appraisal here?' he asked.

'I think we should go over by the window,' the jeweller replied. 'It's the lighting, you see. A jewel is like a living thing – it reacts to natural light.'

Sara found herself sitting at a wrought-iron table by a large window and she watched intrigued as the jeweller polished the ruby ring with a piece of blue velvet. He then took out a jeweller's eye-glass and studied the ring for a few moments. 'Yes, it's undoubtedly Burmese,' he remarked. 'Mined in the Mandalay area. It's identifiable by its depth of colour. Rubies from Ceylon are more pink and the Siamese type are darker in colour. This particular ruby is exquisitely cut and quite valuable. The mounting was most probably done in South Africa. I would hazard a guess at three-quarter carat. Yes, this is a very valuable ring. Is it insured?'

Sara shook her head. 'It was left ter me by my muvver,' she told him. 'My farvver gave it to 'er when 'e returned from the Boer War.'

'Well, I can assure you this ring would gladly be accepted as security for a considerable sum,' Horowitz said, looking at Randolph. 'If sold it would fetch over two hundred pounds, I should say.'

Sara had been waiting for this moment and she quickly delved into her handbag. 'What about this one?'

Randolph looked taken aback. 'Sara, no,' he said quickly.

She brushed away his objections. 'I was keepin' this as a surprise.'

Horowitz studied the diamond ring carefully, grunting once or twice. 'Yes, once again it is very good quality. The diamonds are South African white, brilliant cut and very well matched, and the setting is very ornate. Early Victorian I would say. Very good workmanship indeed.'

Randolph shook his head slowly. 'Sara, you shouldn't.'

'An' why not, pray? These two tergevver would allow yer ter go fer a large loan.'

The two men exchanged satisfied smiles and Horowitz stood up to go. 'I look forward to seeing you at the next session, Randolph,' he said, extending his hand.

'What session did 'e mean?' Sara asked as soon as they were alone.

'Oh, it's nothing of importance,' Randolph told her. 'We belong to the same club. It's a City thing, merely boring men talking about boring subjects over insipid coffee. C'mon, my dear, let's you and I go back to our rooms and we'll see about arranging a meal.'

Sara felt happy and quite light-headed as they walked back along the promenade in the failing light. What an adventure this was.

Sue hurried into the house and stood poised in the parlour doorway with a picture book tucked under her arm. 'Uncle Charlie, will you read fer me?' she asked.

'Of course, my little love,' he said, grinning.

'Not the first one 'cos it makes me 'ave bad dreams,' the child told him as she clambered up on to his lap. 'Read me that one.'

'But I always read yer that one,' Charlie complained with a pouting bottom lip.

'This one then,' Sue replied, flipping the pages over quickly.

'Could I tell yer the story about the nice crunchy giant?' he asked.

'If yer like, but it won't make me 'ave bad dreams, will it?' the tot queried with a serious look on her pretty face.

'Now sit still on Uncle Charlie's lap,' Lucy told her. 'I'll 'ave yer tea ready very soon, an' then it's an early night fer you, missy.'

Charlie gave Lucy a reassuring smile and leaned back comfortably in his armchair, letting

Sue nestle against his chest.

'Once upon a time there was a crunchy giant who was very nice really,' he began. ''E lived all alone in the forest but 'e was becomin' very lonely. All 'is friends 'ad left an' there was no one 'e could talk to or play wiv, so the crunchy giant decided ter leave the forest an' go an' live wiv a nice family who would take care of 'im. 'E walked all day an' was becomin' very tired an' 'ungry when 'e arrived at Coopertown. It 'ad rained all day an' the giant was not only 'ungry an' tired, 'e was wet all the way frew to 'is skin.'

'Was that like when me an' Gracie got wet washin' our dollies in 'er mummy's barf?' Sue enquired.

'Yes,' Charlie replied, his eyes straying to Lucy, who had seated herself at the table. 'Anyway, the crunchy giant knocked at one o' the 'ouses which looked very warm an' cosy, an' 'e said, "Is there any room 'ere fer a lonely giant who loves children?" an' the man sent a lady out ter see the giant, an' when 'e saw 'er 'e gave a very big sigh. She was the most beautiful lady 'e 'ad ever seen. "Come in out o' the rain," the lady said, an' the crunchy giant stepped inter the warm parlour. 'E was given a lovely meal, 'is clothes were dried an' 'e went ter bed in a cosy bedroom that 'ad a nice fire, an' before 'e went ter sleep the crunchy giant said 'is prayers. 'E fanked Jesus fer givin' 'im a lovely 'ouse to live in an' a lovely lady who could care fer 'im, an' fer makin' sure that 'e would never need ter feel lonely again. I don't know if the giant lived 'appily ever after, 'cos there was a page missin' in the story book about the crunchy

355

giant, but I would fink 'e did live 'appily ever after, an' when I find that page I'll find out fer sure.'

Lucy came over and took the sleepy child up into her arms. 'I won't be long,' she told him in a soft voice. 'Put the kettle on, Charlie.'

CHAPTER 30

The cold, damp night had closed in and the thickening fog glowed eerily in the light of the Victorian streetlamps that lined the Bermondsey backstreets. It was a night for sitting round a warm fire, listening to soft music on the wireless and letting the cares of the day fall away as eyelids grew heavy and heads drooped.

There would be no Saturday night reverie for Margaret Lindsey, however, and her lonely footsteps echoed along Lynton Road as she walked quickly by the large patch of light issuing from the Mason's Arms. This must be it, she told herself as she reached the boarded-up corner shops. She saw the street sign and went down the small turning, glancing up at the door numbers until she came to number 8. It was going to take some explaining, but it had to be done while there was still time.

Lucy's face grew frightened as she heard the heavy knock and Charlie got up quickly. 'Stay 'ere,' he told her firmly.

'Be careful, Charlie. It's late fer people ter come knockin'.'

When he opened the front door Charlie was surprised to see the middle-aged woman standing on the doorstep with a worried look on her pale face.

'I'm very sorry ter trouble yer, but does Sara

Parry live 'ere?' she asked hesitantly.

Charlie nodded. 'Is there anyfing wrong? 'As anyfing 'appened to 'er?'

The woman shook her head. 'No, but it's important I speak ter someone close to 'er.'

'Yer'd better come in out o' the fog,' Charlie told her.

Lucy had come out to the passage and she led the way back into the parlour. 'I'm Lucy Parry, Sara's sister-in-law,' she said. 'Won't yer take a seat, 'ere by the fire?'

'I'm Margaret Lindsey. It's OK, I'll sit at the table if yer don't mind. I don't wanna get too warm.'

'Is Sara all right?' Lucy asked with a puzzled frown.

'I 'aven't seen 'er, but I'm sure she is,' the visitor replied. 'I understand she's gone ter Brighton fer the weekend.'

'Yeah, that's right.'

'An' the man she's wiv is Randolph Cadman?'

'Yeah.'

Margaret smiled wryly. 'In actual fact 'is real name's John Lindsey an' 'e 'appens ter be my 'usband.'

'Oh my God!' Lucy exclaimed. 'Poor Sara. She's besotted by 'im. She finks 'e's wonderful.'

Margaret nodded slowly. 'Yes, I can understand that,' she replied. 'John 'as that effect on women. A proper charmer at times, but 'e can be nasty an' cruel. I've seen that side of 'im as well durin' the past few years.'

''Ow did yer find out our Sara was seein' 'im?' Lucy asked.

Charlie had been hovering by the door, and he coughed to get Lucy's attention. 'Shall I put the kettle on?' he said.

'Would yer, Charlie?' she replied with a smile.

The visitor rested her hands on her large handbag and sighed deeply. 'I fink I'd better start from the beginning. I married John Lindsey seven years ago an' two years after we were married I discovered that 'e was involved wiv anovver woman. I don't know 'ow long it'd bin goin' on, 'e wouldn't tell me, but I found out later that 'e'd talked 'er inter partin' wiv a large sum o' money as well as valuable jewellery an' bonds. Apparently 'e'd conned this woman inter believin' that 'e was involved in startin' up a company in the City an' stood ter make large sums of money by buyin' an' sellin' short term. A year later 'e was at it again, an' when I found out I left 'im. Soon after that 'e was arrested an' sent ter prison fer three years fer embezzlement. When 'e finally came out we got back tergevver again. 'E promised me faithfully 'e was a changed man, an' I believed 'im. Fings seemed ter be goin' very well fer us, until...'

Lucy watched as the woman delved into her handbag and pulled out an envelope. 'This letter addressed ter me arrived last week,' she went on. 'I'll spare yer the details but it said that John was busy wormin' his way into a lonely woman's affections at the fellowship of St Mark's Church in Bermondsey, and 'e was operatin' under the name o' Randolph Cadman. The writer o' the letter said that she 'erself 'ad bin taken in by 'is charm while she was there, but when 'e

359

suggested that she might like ter get involved in makin' a lot o' money by puttin' up 'er jewellery as security she got suspicious. She got a man friend ter make enquiries before partin' wiv any of 'er valuables an' 'e was able ter find out about the embezzlement charge, an' 'e also got 'old of a photo o' John taken at the time 'e was sent ter prison. The woman went on ter say that she left the fellowship as soon as she discovered the truth, but recently she bumped inter one of 'er friends who was still there an' found out that Randolph Cadman was becomin' very friendly wiv a Sara Parry, anovver o' the lonely women who seem ter frequent the meetin's.'

'Didn't yer know yer 'usband was a member o' the fellowship?' Lucy asked.

Margaret shook her head. 'I thought John was playin' in a darts team at our local pub on Wednesday nights. That was what 'e told me 'e was doin'.'

Charlie came into the parlour with a laden tray and Lucy filled the cups with strong hot tea. 'Did yer approach 'im about it?' she asked.

The visitor nodded. 'We 'ad a big row an' I walked out. That was the day after I got the letter an' I 'aven't seen 'im since, nor do I want to.'

''Ow did the woman get your address?'

'It was easy, though it grieves me ter say it,' Margaret replied. 'She knew where I lived. She'd bin in my 'ouse wiv John while I was workin'. While we were rowin' 'e actually told me as much, bold as brass. Anyway the woman said in the letter that she felt it was 'er duty ter prevent some ovver poor woman from bein' duped as she nearly was, an' the best way ter nip it in the bud was by letting Cadman's wife know what was goin' on. She was right. I can't stand by an' see someone bein' conned out o' their valuables by that snake of a man. I 'ad ter let 'er know what was goin' on. I 'ad ter find out where Sara lived, so I decided ter pay a visit ter the church. I spoke ter the vicar an' told 'im everyfing. I'm sure 'e thought I was makin' it all up at first, but I managed ter convince 'im that it was true an' I asked fer Sara Parry's address so I could warn 'er.'

Lucy handed the woman a cup of tea. 'I'm very grateful to yer fer the warnin',' she said, 'but 'ow did yer find out about 'em goin' ter Brighton fer the weekend?'

Margaret sipped her tea. 'As a matter o' fact the vicar didn't 'ave Sara's address, but luckily there were two members o' the fellowship in the church at the time. They were doin' some flower arrangin' or somefing, an' they produced a notebook wiv all the members' addresses in. One o' the women knew that Sara was plannin' ter spend this weekend in Brighton wiv a friend. She said Sara 'ad bin unusually bubbly when she told 'er, an' seein' the attention Randolph Cadman, as 'e calls 'imself, was payin' 'er it wasn't 'ard ter guess who the mysterious friend was.'

Lucy shook her head slowly. 'I can't believe it of Sara,' she sighed. 'Usually she's so suspicious o' strangers, especially men.'

Margaret smiled coldly. 'My 'usband's a charmer, as I've already said, an' it seems that lonely women are easily taken in by 'im. A lot came out at 'is trial, an' if you'd 'ave bin there you'd understand better.'

'Our Sara's not a wealthy woman,' Lucy said, frowning. 'She 'as a couple o' nice rings that were left to 'er, one she 'ardly ever wears. She keeps it in a drawer by 'er bed.'

'Are they valuable, would yer know?'

'They could well be, but I've never asked 'er. The ruby ring she wears all the time. It's a large stone.'

'Would yer know if she's got any insurance on 'er life, or an endowment?' Margaret asked.

'Only a small life policy. Just enough ter bury 'er.'

'No bonds?'

'No, I'm pretty certain she 'asn't got anyfing like that stashed away.'

Margaret finished her tea and put the empty cup down on the table. 'I 'ope I'm wrong, but I'd bet Sara's bin encouraged ter get 'er rings valued.'

Lucy stood up. 'I won't be a moment,' she said, hurrying out of the room. Less than a minute later she was back. 'The diamond ring's not in the drawer,' she announced. 'She must 'ave took it wiv 'er.'

'It figures,' Margaret replied. 'You must try ter warn 'er as soon as she gets 'ome. I just 'ope it's not too late.'

Sara Parry sat on the edge of her bed in the small guesthouse near the seafront and smiled happily. She and Randolph had had a fish supper at a nearby restaurant and they had gone back to their rooms so that he could make one or two urgent business calls. Poor Randolph, she thought, he never seemed to stop working. He was wonderful. All her life she had wanted to be loved and cherished by the man of her dreams, but it had never transpired, until now. As a young woman she had cared for her ailing mother and stayed loyal to her while the rest of her siblings were making a life for themselves. She had tried to form one or two friendships but her mother was terrified of being abandoned and had usually managed to put a stop to it, one way or another. She was dead now, and there was no hardness in her daughter's heart towards her memory, only sadness and frustration at being totally unprepared and too lacking in confidence to forge a friendship and romance with a man. Her attempts to make Charlie Foden aware of her had been pathetic, she knew only too well, and they hadn't been helped by the obvious attraction between him and Lucy. The casual glances they shared and their ready smiles were quite obvious to her and she hoped George hadn't noticed anything. He was her brother and she loved him, and it had hurt her to think that Charlie Foden was trying to make up to Lucy under his very nose. George was quiet and not very demonstrative whereas Lucy was inclined to flightiness at times, and Sara realised that she would have to keep an eye on the potentially dangerous situation.

As she sat ruminating Sara studied her fingertips and vowed to let her nails grow. She would have to do something about her hair, too. She wanted to look her best for Randolph, wanted to please him, and she suddenly experienced a little shiver. He had always been the perfect gentleman, had assured her that his intentions were honourable, and she had to trust him. He would be knocking soon to take her down to the bar for a nightcap and she did not want to disappoint him by declining. Alcohol went to her head very quickly and she could not remember the last time she had set foot in a public house, but a small sherry in pleasant surroundings would do her no harm, and it might even help her to sleep.

Lucy came into the parlour and giggled as she saw Charlie hunched in the steaming tin bath in front of the fire. 'This is the largest towel I've got an' I've warmed it over the gas,' she told him.

Charlie strove to hide his embarrassment by pretending to hunt for the soap. 'Fanks, Lucy. I won't be long,' he replied.

She made no attempt to leave the room. 'Would yer like me ter scrub yer back?'

He smiled sheepishly. 'If yer want.'

Lucy came over and hoisted her long dressing gown above her knees before bending down beside the tub. ''Ave yer got the soap?'

Charlie was roused by her show of shapely thigh and he quickly handed her the bar of Lifebuoy. 'It must be nice to 'ave a place wiv a built-in bath,' he remarked.

'Those new council buildin's 'ave got bathrooms,' she replied as she dipped the soap in the water beside his leg.

Charlie leaned further forward to hide his

nakedness and Lucy smiled. 'It's the first time I've seen yer wivout yer shirt on,' she said saucily. 'I always imagined yer to 'ave an 'airy chest.'

Charlie felt the soap gliding over his back and he chuckled. 'I 'ope yer not disappointed.'

She shook her head as she squeezed water from the flannel over his lathered shoulders. 'I wouldn't mind if yer was bald all over, Charlie,' she told him.

He looked at her and liked the way she had pulled her hair up on top of her head and fixed it with a black velvet band. He could see her small flat ears and her slim neck and he shook his head slowly. 'Lucy, you're a very attractive woman,' he said with quiet sincerity.

She giggled again as she rinsed his back with the flannel. 'It's a good job you never saw me in the bath, or yer might 'ave changed yer mind.'

'As a matter o' fact I was tempted ter see if yer wanted me ter scrub your back, but I thought it might give yer the wrong impression.'

'No, I'd 'ave liked that, Charlie.'

He splashed water into his face and rubbed his fingers through his thick greying hair. 'I'd better get out,' he said, taking the towel from her.

She stood up but made no attempt to leave the room. 'OK, go on then.'

His look of surprise brought another giggle from her and she turned and walked to the door. 'I'll put the kettle on,' she told him with a saucy wink.

Charlie dried quickly and slipped on a heavy dressing gown, knotting the belt tightly. The bath had to be emptied and the fire was burning low.

Outside the temperature had dropped and the fog had disappeared. In its place a thin film of frost covered the cobblestones and pavements and shrouded the roofs of the small houses, tiny crystals of ice glistening in the wan light of a crescent moon. Inside the house Sue slept peacefully in her warm bed and downstairs Lucy and Charlie sat facing each other by the glowing fire, sipping tea and trying to look innocent and unaffected, but Lucy felt excitement growing steadily in her belly. Charlie knew that the gods had conspired that evening to provide the opportunity, and he had read the signs. He knew he must not fail. It had been a long time, and he had resigned himself to leading a celibate life, until that fateful night when he knocked on the door soaked to the skin. Seeing Lucy for the first time had jolted him from his complacency and over the past two months he had come to desire her with an intensity which made it harder than ever to disguise.

She put her empty cup down on the table and stretched leisurely. The time for pretence was over. Tonight she was going to seduce him if she had to. She stood over him, almost tormented by the thrilling inside her. 'Charlie.'

'Yeah?'

'That night you asked me fer a kiss. Did yer fink about it afterwards? I mean, did it make yer feel good?'

He stood up slowly. 'I went ter sleep still feelin' yer lips on mine,' he said huskily.

'It's my turn now, Charlie,' she replied. 'Kiss me.'

He reached out and pulled her gently to him. He could feel her firm, rounded breasts against his chest and her thighs touching his. He smelt the scent of her body and the aroma of her freshly washed hair, and he closed his eyes as he found her eager lips. It was a kiss that transformed them. Her mouth was open hungrily and her tongue tantalised his as she threw her arms round his neck. All her passion, all her repressed feelings seemed to be released in one wild moment and she pressed her need against him, rubbing her sex against his stiff manhood. There was no going back now, no memory of guilt or betrayal, only the desperate need to be fulfilled in an explosion of love.

He stepped back a pace and swept her up in his strong arms, and as he climbed the flight of stairs she let her head rest against his chest. His room was lit by a solitary gas lamp and warmed with a small fire, and the curtains had been pulled against the cold night. She sighed with pleasure, closing her eyes as he eased her down on to his bed and lay beside her, gently moving her dressing gown away from her heaving breasts. Her nipples were hard and she shivered as his lips savoured them. More, she thought, more, and reaching up to him she slid his dressing gown off his broad shoulders and arms and cupped his head in her hands, urging him down towards her smooth flat belly. There was no time to be coy and she arched herself as he explored lower and lower. He tasted her sweetness, felt her swollen cherry, caressed it vigorously with his tongue. In an intensity of forbidden delight she moaned,

367

throwing her head back as she felt an ecstasy rising through her body. Charlie's sensitive probing and licking had found her most intimate spots and suddenly she could hold out no longer. She gave a deep groan and clenched her fists tightly as her love juice flowed.

Charlie gently stroked her belly, waiting for her throes of passion to subside, then he rose up and slid his arm under her waist, easing her over on top of him. Her legs locked against his flanks and she lowered herself down for him to enter her with a groan of unadulterated pleasure, riding him like a stallion, driven into delicious abandonment as he raised himself up on his elbows and clasped her hips, moving with her sensuously. She could feel her passion overwhelming her once more and knew that he was struggling to contain himself too. 'Charlie!' she cried. 'Oh, Charlie!'

CHAPTER 31

Sara Parry wiped her eyes and looked with disgust at her puffed image in the bathroom mirror. 'Whatever did 'e see in you in the first place?' she muttered to herself tearfully. 'You're nuffing but a stupid, frustrated old maid an' yer can't seem ter do anyfing about it.'

Sara went back into the bedroom and sat down despondently on the edge of the bed. It had all started so well, too. He had escorted her down to the bar on Saturday evening and she had enjoyed the convivial chat, fortified with two glasses of sherry, one more than she intended, and she had felt quite daring. When they finally returned to their rooms she had taken Randolph's arm at the door and kissed him on the lips, making some silly remark about nice girls wouldn't do that sort of thing, and naturally enough he had taken it as a come-on. Unfortunately, she had been unprepared for what had happened next.

His knock was soft and his eyes reflected a gentleness as he came into her room a few minutes later. He sat holding her hand as he confessed to wanting to make love to her, but she had laughed him off. Mistake number one, she sighed.

His eyes seemed to burn with desire and he pressed her down on to the bed to kiss her protesting lips. He was not to know, how could he know, that she had never experienced the love of a man in her whole life and was still as pure as the driven snow. He should have been gentle, arousing her slowly with patience and panache, and he would have done so, she felt sure, had she confessed to him her ignorance of carnal matters. Her silent protestations only served to make him feel that she was toying with him and he became angry. For one terrifying moment she was convinced he was going to rape her, but he brought himself under control and turned away, sitting with his back to her. 'Do you find me repulsive?' he asked suddenly.

'Of course not,' she replied fearfully. 'You took me by surprise. I wasn't prepared.'

He sighed deeply, not knowing quite what she meant. 'You and I have got on so well, Sara, I really thought you wanted our relationship to progress. You must forgive me.'

At that moment, she now realised, she could have made it all right, but still she could not bring herself to explain to him her lack of experience. 'We'll both feel better after a good night's sleep,' she told him weakly.

Back in his room Randolph Cadman, alias John Lindsey, poured himself a stiff drink. The stupid woman was playing games with him, he fumed. Who the hell did she think she was? Certainly no raving beauty. He would have to employ a different tactic if he was to make the weekend a success after all, financially speaking.

On Sunday morning Randolph was all charm as he escorted Sara along the quiet seafront. Gulls dipped and dived, driven ashore by the choppy conditions in the Channel, and the sky was full of rain-laden cloud. Ahead they could see the pier half shrouded in mist, and apart from an old man exercising his dog they had the promenade to themselves.

They took lunch at a little pub tucked away in a narrow cobbled street and spent the afternoon sitting in the comfortable lounge at the guest-house reading the Sunday papers. Randolph went out at five o'clock, saying he had to get a printed valuation from Horowitz, and Sara was left to her own devices. She had at first decided to take a short nap, but resisted the urge when she noticed the couple sitting nearby being served with coffee. She folded her newspaper and attracted the attention of the elderly waiter. A few minutes later she was served with China tea and she took out a ten-shilling note from her hand-bag.

'Wouldn't you like me to put it on your bill, Mrs Devenish?' the man enquired.

'No, I'd sooner pay, thank you.'

The waiter was soon back with a few coins in a small silver salver and Sara deliberately left a shilling as a tip.

'That's very kind of you, Mrs Devenish,' the man said, smiling.

'I fink yer've got me mixed up wiv someone else,' Sara told him.

The waiter looked perplexed. 'I saw you at breakfast with Mr Devenish and I assumed ... I'm terribly sorry.'

'The name of the man you saw me wiv is Randolph Cadman.'

The waiter was quite obviously embarrassed. 'I'm sorry. My eyes aren't what they used to be. I'm afraid I mistook Mr Cadman for Mr Devenish who was here a few weeks ago.'

Sara smiled and thought no more about it. Her mind was too full of how she would handle the coming evening. Maybe Randolph would not try anything on again, and in that case it wouldn't matter too much if she cried off from a night at the bar or at a pub by saying she had a bad head-ache. If, however, he made his intentions clear, she would have to make him understand that she needed encouragement and guidance in the art of love-making.

As she sipped her tea on the soft cushioned divan Sara began to romanticise, and she decided to place last night's little episode in the bin of ex-perience gained. If anyone could steal her heart and make her a fulfilled woman it was Randolph.

On Sunday morning PC Ron Sloan knocked at number 8 with the news that he had frightened the two ruffians off. He looked pleased with him-self as he sipped his tea in the parlour, flanked by Lucy in her dressing gown and Charlie with his shirt buttoned carelessly. 'I 'ope I didn't call too early,' he said, trying not to smile as he stared at Charlie's crooked collar.

Lucy shook her head and pulled her dressing gown closer around her shapely figure. 'I was up, an' so was Charlie,' she told him.

'Sara's still in the land o' nod, I take it,' he remarked with a grin.

'No, as a matter o' fact she's gone ter Brighton

372

fer the weekend,' Lucy replied.

Ron Sloan raised his eyebrows slightly. 'Good fer 'er. An' when's George due back 'ome?'

'Ternight,' Lucy answered. 'I'm dyin' ter find out 'ow 'e got on.'

The constable looked enquiringly from one to the other for a moment and then eased back in the armchair. 'I got 'em dead ter rights watchin' you an' George an' Roy Chubb at the bus stop,' he said, addressing Charlie. 'I don't fink they'll bovver ter show their faces round 'ere again, unless the ante's upped an' they fink it's werf it fer the extra money, so yer still gotta be careful. Keep yer eye out an' let me know if yer see any dodgy characters lurkin' about. By the way, yer might 'ave a word wiv the geezer who warned yer in the first place. 'E might know the score.'

Charlie nodded. 'Yeah, I will, soon as possible.'

The policeman took another sip of his tea. ''Ow's Sara takin' all this?' he asked suddenly. 'Or are yer keepin' it from 'er?'

'She doesn't know anyfing about it,' Lucy told him. 'It's better she don't know, the way she is. In any case, she doesn't answer the door if I'm shoppin' an' she's 'ere on 'er own.'

Ron Sloan nodded. 'Well, I'd better pop over an' 'ave a word wiv Danny Albury.'

As soon as the constable had left Charlie took Lucy by the arm. 'C'mon, darlin',' he said, 'before that bed gets cold.'

She took his hand and followed him up the stairs and into his room.

'I love you, Lucy Parry,' he said, pulling her to him.

373

'I love you too, Charlie,' she sighed.

Charlie undressed again quickly and Lucy took off her dressing gown before they slipped under the covers. He sought her lips and she turned and snuggled up close, feeling his strong body pressing against her. 'Charlie?'

'Yeah?'

'Do yer believe me when I say I love yer?'

'Of course I do.'

'But is it possible ter love two men at the same time?'

'I fink so, though I can't say as I've never loved two blokes at once.'

Lucy kissed his neck and ran her fingers through his matted hair. 'Do you realise we've only known each ovver fer less than three months?'

Charlie brushed a strand of hair from her face. 'It seems I've known yer fer ever.'

'Charlie?'

'Yeah?'

'Charlie, yer not just treatin' this as a bit o' fun, are yer?'

He propped himself up on one elbow and looked down into her troubled eyes. 'It is fun, 'owever intense it is,' he said softly. 'Neivver of us are available, marriage-wise I mean. I'm mad about yer an' I want us to enjoy the pleasures we're sharin', not feel guilty about it.'

'I try not to, Charlie. But some'ow I can't 'elp feelin' a little scared.'

He kissed her quickly on her open lips and laid his head on the pillow beside her, slipping his arm across her and cuddling her to him. 'Look,

George'll be 'ome this evenin', an' Sara termorrer,' he said quietly, 'an' we'll 'ave very little chance to be alone tergevver. I'll look at yer an' I'll want yer desperately. You'll look at me an' remember this weekend, an' we'll need all the patience we possess ter see us frew. We'll 'ave ter grab our chances when we can, an' in between we'll carry on in the way we always 'ave. You'll be the dutiful wife an' mum, an' I'll be the respectable lodger. The secret we share'll see us frew the lonely times an' the desire'll be tenfold when we do get the chance to make love.'

'I can wait, Charlie,' she answered with a deep sigh, 'as long as you're there, as long as I can see yer an' 'ear yer voice.'

'An' I'll watch yer movin' about the 'ouse, I'll savour the sway of yer body an' the way yer smile an' pout at times, an' I'll save all me lovin' fer that special time we'll share.'

Lucy rolled on top of him and moved her hips sensuously against his, bringing him to a full erection, and she licked her tongue around her dry lips as she felt him enter her. His slow erotic rhythm sent shivers of pleasure coursing along her spine and she could feel his hot breath on her face as the loving became intense. She drew her knees up, raised herself and arched her body backwards to take all the pleasure she could as his hands cupped her full breasts, and he gasped to feel her eager thrusting. He fought to hold back his explosion till she was ready and then as she groaned and shuddered he jerked involuntarily and felt his love flow free.

They were lying close, wrapped up in each

other's arms, when they heard a movement on the stairs. The door creaked open and then Sue looked in. 'Mummy, I couldn't find yer, I'm firsty.'

'All right, darlin',' Lucy said. 'Go back ter yer room an' I'll get yer a drink.'

Charlie had lain perfectly still beneath the bedclothes and when the child went out again he jumped out of bed and grabbed his trousers. 'I 'ope she didn't see me,' he said with a worried look.

Lucy was more calm. 'She's still 'alf asleep. She won't remember any o' this.'

Charlie looked at the clock on the chair by his bed. 'Christ, it's turned eleven.'

Lucy grinned as she slipped on her dressing gown. 'Don't time fly when yer enjoyin' yerself?'

'It's a good job Sue didn't come in a few minutes earlier,' he said, smiling sheepishly.

'I didn't expect 'er ter wake up too early, after the time she went ter bed last night,' Lucy remarked. 'It must 'ave bin all of ten o'clock.'

Charlie took a clean pair of socks from the tallboy drawer. 'I need ter see Sharkey Lockwood at lunchtime,' he said, grunting as he bent over to put them on.

'You be careful, Charlie,' she told him. 'You mind they don't take it out on you.'

He grinned lopsidedly. 'No chance.'

'Mummy.'

'All right, darlin', just comin',' Lucy called back.

Ada Black and Emmie Goodwright braved the

cold Sunday morning to have their usual con-
fabulation and Ada looked a little irritated. 'I
dunno what's goin' on in this street lately,' she
remarked. 'I saw Ron Sloan come out o' the
Stricklands' early yesterday mornin' an' then 'e
knocked on the Parrys' front door.'

'Did 'e go in?' Emmie asked her.

'Yeah. 'E was in there fer a good 'alf hour.'

'I wonder what that was all about?'

'Gawd knows.'

'It makes yer fink,' Emmie said, shaking her
head slowly.

'Did yer know George Parry's away this
weekend?'

'No. Where's 'e gone?'

''E's doin' a weekend at the naval barracks in
Chatham by all accounts,' Ada said. ''E's still in
the reserves, yer see, an' Mary Chubb was tellin'
me 'e's doin' some trainin' fer promotion. She
said if 'e passes 'e'll be a petty officer.'

'That's nice.'

Ada looked quickly up and down the turning
before leaning closer to her friend. 'Lucy an'
Charlie Foden are on their own this weekend.
Sara's gone ter Brighton wiv that chap she's met.'

'The one at the fellowship?'

'Yeah.'

'I bet George is all on edge, leavin' them two in
the 'ouse on their own.'

'It's only natural, ain't it?'

Emmie slid her hands further into her coat
sleeves. 'I don't fink there's anyfing goin' on between 'em, or George would 'ave known. Even if
'e just suspected somefing 'e wouldn't go an'

leave 'em tergevver, surely ter Gawd?'

'Yer never know, do yer?'

'Nah, yer right.'

'Mrs Albury told me the inquest's this Friday.'

'It'll be in all the papers, I should fink.'

'Well, I'd better get in an' start the dinner.'

'Yeah, me too. What yer got?'

'Lean ribs.'

'I got some sausage-meat. My ole man likes that wiv some taters an' gravy.'

Frost still clung to the cobblestones as Charlie made his way along to the Crown in Dockhead, where with a bit of luck he hoped to find Sharkey. A chill wind met him on the corner of Lynton Road and he pulled the collar of his coat up round his ears, but inside he was glowing.

CHAPTER 32

Sharkey Lockwood sat slumped on a bar stool in the saloon as Charlie pushed open the door and walked in. He looked enquiringly along the polished counter at the newcomer and forced a brief smile. 'I expect yer've come ter tell me the game's up wiv those two prats,' he said.

Charlie laid a half-crown on the counter and jerked his head towards Sharkey's glass. 'Same again?'

The bigger man nodded. 'Yeah, why not?'

Charlie leaned sideways on the counter facing the ganger. 'Yeah, they are a couple o' prats,' he remarked with slightly narrowed eyes. 'All they achieved was ter get everyone in the street watchin' out fer 'em, an' the local copper marked their cards too.'

Sharkey smiled cynically. 'You only get what yer pay for an' the Coleys weren't prepared ter dig deep inter their pockets,' he replied. 'Physically they were more than capable, but they ain't got a brain between 'em.'

Charlie took a sip of his beer. 'You was aware o' that when yer picked 'em, wasn't yer?'

Sharkey looked noncommittally at his co-ganger. 'I 'ad my reasons.'

Charlie nodded his head slowly. 'Parry an' Albury are gonna stick ter their story at the inquest on Friday,' he said matter-of-factly, 'an' in the meantime they'll be escorted everywhere they go. They won't even use the bog unless there's someone standin' guard.'

'That's nice,' Sharkey said sarcastically.

'The thought occurs ter me,' Charlie went on. 'You're gonna be obliged ter face the Coleys, an' I can't see them bein' too 'appy about the way fings 'ave turned out.'

'That's my problem,' Sharkey replied. 'I've talked wiv those two idiots I recruited an' they're sure someone's bin doin' some talkin'.'

Charlie smiled. 'They could be right.'

Sharkey drained his glass and pulled the fresh one towards him. 'I'm goin' back ter wrestlin' again,' he announced. 'As far as I can see the Coleys are on their way out an' I'm not 'angin' around fer the end. It won't be very nice, that's fer sure.'

'I'll come an' see yer first bout,' Charlie told him with a grin. 'I 'ope it'll be werf the entrance fee.' He drained his glass and held out his hand. 'Well, I'll see yer at the inquest, pal,' he said warmly.

'Take care, pal,' the big man replied.

Sara Parry joined Randolph for a late evening meal at the guesthouse on Sunday evening and she was very surprised by what her escort had to say.

'There it is in black and white,' he told her, passing the slip of paper across the spotless tablecloth. 'The ruby's a large stone of high quality and the setting is perfect. It'll serve to raise a very considerable sum if we can use it

380

along with the diamond ring as security. Of course it would have to be deposited at the bank, and you have to be certain in your own mind that the decision is a sensible one. If you have any doubts I want you to tell me now, right this minute.'

'I trust you, Randolph,' Sara replied. 'I'd trust you wiv my life.'

He smiled gratefully. 'If there was any chance, however remote, of you losing your valuable assets I would cancel the whole project, but I know that very soon we'll be up and running. Neither of us will ever need to look back.'

Sara returned his smile, suddenly feeling elated. 'Randolph,' she almost whispered. 'You won't leave me alone tonight, will you? Promise.'

He reached across the table and closed his hand over hers. 'I promise,' he replied.

Sara lowered her head, feeling quite emotional. It would be all right tonight, she swore to herself. It had to be. This chance would never present itself again and she must grab at it with both hands.

Thomas Walburton was now approaching sixty-seven, and he had been in the hotel business since leaving school. At first he had worked as a bell-boy at some of the best hotels on the south coast, going on to become porter and receptionist during the heady days of yore, when music hall stars and politicians of note came there to relax and pursue their own private pastimes. Thomas had a pleasant personality and a smart appearance, which earmarked him for a job waiting on tables at the very exclusive Ambassador Hotel in Brighton. He learned fast and enjoyed many years attending upon some of the most famous and most notorious in the land. His mind was sharp and he prided himself on never forgetting a face.

Mrs Charlotte Blake had managed the Westland guesthouse for the past five years and she had been saddened to see the rapid deterioration in her neighbour after his retirement from the hotel business at the age of sixty-five. She spoke to her employer in glowing terms of Thomas Walburton's capabilities and was able to get him a part-time job there as a waiter. Thomas now had a new lease of life and was eternally grateful to Charlotte for her kindness.

They often shared their breaks and chatted amiably over cups of tea in the staff room behind the reception desk, and on this particular Sunday evening Thomas was feeling somewhat upset.

'I must be getting past it,' he sighed. 'I felt awful when I was corrected by Mrs Devenish ... I mean Miss Parry.'

'I shouldn't place too much importance on it, Thomas,' Charlotte told him. 'None of us are perfect.'

'But I was so sure,' he went on. 'In fact I'd have bet everything I had on being right. It's very upsetting.'

Charlotte could see that her old friend was indeed quite distressed and she had an idea. 'Thomas, will you do me a favour?' she asked. 'I can't leave the reception area, but could you fetch me the guest book from my office? You'll find it on the shelf by my desk.'

While he was off on the errand Charlotte quickly scanned through the guest signatures in the reception book and found the signature of Harold Devenish beneath that of Benjamin Rosamin. She then compared it with Randolph Cadman's and smiled smugly.

'Here it is,' Thomas said as he marched back into the staff room.

Charlotte opened the book and scanned the pages of photographs, signatures of notables on letter headings, and messages from appreciative guests. 'I thought I was right,' she said, grinning widely.

Thomas looked bemused. 'What's that?' he queried.

Charlotte stabbed her forefinger at a photograph. 'Remember when the Rosamins got wed?' she asked him. 'This is a group photo. It was taken in the dining room. Look in the background at the other guests. Do you recognise anyone in particular?'

Thomas took out his glasses and sniffed loudly as he put them on. For a while he studied the photograph and then a large smile creased his face. 'I was right,' he said triumphantly. 'There he is, Mr Harold Devenish, alias Mr Randolph Cadman. What's going on, Charlotte?'

She shook her head slowly, a serious look appearing on her wide, open face. 'I don't know, but I don't like it,' she replied thoughtfully.

Thomas stroked his chin. 'I've seen them at work over the years, believe me,' he remarked. 'Con men, preying on gullible, lonely women, and if you were to ask me I'd say that Miss Parry falls into that category.'

'Really it's none of our business,' Charlotte reminded him. 'There's not a lot we can do.'

Thomas shook his head. 'I'd hate for us to stand aside while that poor woman gets fleeced for every penny she owns. We could show her the photograph.'

'I don't know,' Charlotte said hesitantly.

Thomas was adamant. 'You must let me approach the poor lady,' he urged her. 'You know I'd do it very discreetly.'

She thought for a few moments. 'Do it, Thomas.'

Sara waited. It was getting late and she had had time alone to compose herself. There had been the opportunity too for a hard think, and she now knew the way ahead.

'Darling, are you sure?' he asked quietly as she welcomed him into her room.

'You've no need to ask, Randolph,' she replied. 'Last night I was all at sixes an' sevens. I was overcome an' I made it seem so wrong. Will you forgive me? Please.'

He took her in his arms and kissed her gently on her trembling lips before leading her by the hand towards her bed.

'Please be gentle wiv me, Randolph,' she gulped nervously.

He hid his distaste as he took her by the shoulders and eased her down on the counterpane. The silly woman must be all of fifty, he thought, and she was acting like a young virgin.

'I'll love you most gently, and you'll be fulfilled as a woman, even beyond your wildest dreams,' he told her grandiloquently.

She lay down under his prompting and felt him lowering his body on to her, and she shivered in expectation. He rubbed up and down like a terrier for a few moments then lifted himself off to slide her nightdress up from her milky white thighs. His hands were warm and sweaty and she closed her eyes and felt her face grow hot as he explored her most secret parts. He used his fingers in a practised way designed to relax her taut muscles and then he exposed himself to her. She gasped at his size and feared she would never be able to accommodate him, but there was no going back now and she let him close in on top of her. Suddenly he was going inside her and she felt the stretching and the sharp pain as her maidenhead was torn. She gasped at his ferocious movement and her fingernails drew blood from his back as he slid her legs further apart. He was dripping with perspiration in the short time he needed to climax and then with a deep shudder that she felt inside her he ejaculated.

Sara was teetering on the edge of an unknown abyss when he exploded and she clung to him, wrapping her legs round his waist as she used his still hard member to bring herself to completion. He pulled away from her quickly as though suddenly shamed, and she lay back and looked up at him. Gone was the confident look, the warm light in his eyes. Instead she saw a naked expression of disgust. It was hard to bear, but his mute regard, crucifying as it was, told her all she needed to know.

On Monday, a damp, dreary January morning, Charlie Foden took his leave of the Coleys, telling the brothers that he was going back to his job in the docks. They took the news with little more than sullen looks, but Frank Coley had a parting shot. 'I just 'ope the inquest turns up the right verdict, fer all our sakes,' he said meaningfully.

'There's no need ter fuss over us,' George remarked when Charlie arrived back at the house and told him he would accompany him to sign on. 'They wouldn't try anyfing at the labour exchange, not wiv everyone millin' about.'

'Yer most likely right, but it's better ter be on the safe side,' Charlie replied. 'Anyway, it's only till Friday. Once the inquest's over it'll be too late fer 'em.'

Lucy watched as the two men walked across the street to knock at the Albury house and her heart fluttered as she thought of that weekend of love. Her memory of those wonderful hours was tempered by a sickly feeling of guilt, the endlessly nagging awareness that she had been unfaithful to George, but she dared not dwell on it. She knew she would end up putting all the blame on her devoted husband, using his lack of passion, his surly ways of late, to justify what had happened, and it wouldn't be fair. She was about to go back indoors when she spotted Sara coming along the turning.

'You look frozen,' she said by way of greeting as

her sister-in-law reached the house. ''Ow did it go?'

Sara shrugged her shoulders as she stepped inside. 'No better than I expected,' she replied.

Lucy took her coat from her and went into the scullery to put the kettle over the gas, and by the time she went back into the parlour Sara was sitting in her usual place and warming her hands as though nothing had happened. Lucy felt suddenly angry but she fought to control herself as she sat down facing her. 'Look, I dunno 'ow ter tell yer this, but yer gotta know sooner or later.'

'Tell me what?' Sara said quickly.

'Saturday night there was a woman called,' Lucy explained. 'She told us she was Randolph Cadman's wife. In fact Cadman's not 'is real name. It's John Lindsey. The woman 'eard from a friend who goes ter the fellowship that you an' 'er 'usband were gettin' very close an' she was worried yer'd get taken on like all the ovvers.'

'Taken on?'

'Yeah, get relieved of yer valuables.'

Sara raised a smile. 'Randolph wants me ter put up me rings as security against a big bank loan,' she said. ''E told me there's no risk attached an' in a few months I'll make a large profit as a share'older.'

Lucy stared at her sister-in-law with anger boiling up inside her. 'Ain't you bin listenin' to anyfing I've said?' she exclaimed. 'Randolph Cadman's a con artist. 'E's out ter fleece yer fer every penny 'e can get.'

Sara's smile grew. ''E won't fleece me.'

'Yer've still got yer rings?'

'Too bloody true.'

'We thought the worst,' Lucy told her.

'I was lucky. I was warned off,' Sara answered. 'The rings are safe in me 'andbag an' Mr Randolph Cadman'll be waitin' in the tearooms at London Bridge Station fer me this afternoon. I'm s'posed to 'and 'em over to 'im there. Actually 'e wanted me ter pass 'em over last night but I told 'im I wanted ter do it right by puttin' 'em in their boxes first.'

'Sara, you amaze me,' Lucy said with new-found respect.

Sara smiled again briefly, then her face changed. 'I've never trusted men, an' ter be honest I've never felt relaxed in their company,' she said quietly. 'This episode makes me realise once an' fer all that I could never ever take up wiv a man, sad as it sounds. I missed the boat years ago, when I was too young ter worry about their intentions. Now I 'ave ter be content wiv livin' the life I live an' enjoyin' ovver pleasures. What little I 'ave got out o' this affair, if you could call it that, will be enough fer me. We all 'ave our memories, Lucy.'

The younger woman wanted to throw her arms around her and comfort her with soft words, until Sara spoiled it all by saying, 'One man can breed trouble, but two men under the same roof spells disaster, so be told.'

Lucy went into the scullery to make the tea feeling uneasy. Sara's words had troubled her, but it was what she hadn't said that really frightened the young woman.

CHAPTER 33

The women of Cooper Street were out early on Friday morning, wrapped up against the cold as they stood at their front doors waiting and talking together in low voices. For some the verdict would mean little if anything, but for others it would be the final chapter in the Coley saga which had been the major talking point around meal tables and by the fireside on the long dark wintry nights.

George Parry was uneasy as he put a quick polish on his best boots. His stomach was knotting with a sickly feeling and his wife Lucy picked up on it that morning.

'You can't go wivout 'avin' any breakfast,' she told him. 'I 'ad it all wiv Sara this mornin'. I'll do yer some toast – it'll settle yer.'

George looked at her with a puzzled frown. 'Did Sara say where she was goin'?' he asked.

Lucy shook her head. 'I asked 'er an' she just said it was unfinished business. I've never known 'er ter go out so early. Now what about some toast?'

He nodded compliantly. Lucy was right. 'Just one slice,' he sighed.

Charlie Foden had been up for hours, it seemed. He had fetched the morning paper and was now seated at the scullery table flipping through the pages, a mug of tea by his hand. How could he stay so calm and collected, George thought with irritation as he cast a critical glance at him? He had as much to lose as anyone, more maybe. He had been the ganger in charge on that terrible day and it would be noted by the coroner.

'Mornin', folks,' Mary Chubb said cheerily as she walked into the scullery. 'Lucy, can Roy come in an' wait? 'E's bin ready fer hours an' 'e's gettin' under me feet.'

'Of course. There's no need to ask,' Lucy chided her.

Mary smiled. 'Roy said 'e feels like 'e's goin' to a funeral.'

'I'll be glad when it's all over meself,' George sighed.

Lucy gave Charlie a quick glance and smiled to herself. He was reading something in the paper that appeared to interest him and was oblivious of what was going on around him.

'Mornin', Charlie,' Mary said pointedly after getting no initial response from him.

'Sorry, luv, I was jus' readin' this bit about the docks,' he replied. ''Ow's Roy?'

'You might well ask,' Mary answered with a sigh. ''E's like a cat on 'ot bricks.'

George was standing by the yard door looking a little anxious. 'Shouldn't we make a move?' he suggested.

Charlie folded the paper and stood up. 'Yeah, we might as well. We'll give Roy a knock,' he said to Mary as he reached for his coat.

Danny Albury sat waiting. 'What's the time, Alice?' he called out.

'It's ten past nine, five minutes on from the last time you asked me,' she said sarcastically as she popped her head into the parlour.

'I'll 'ave ter get this bloody clock fixed,' he told her as he rocked the chimer standing on the mantelshelf.

'That's 'ow the bloody clock got broke in the first place,' Alice scolded him. 'Yer s'posed ter wind the poxy fing, not shake the works out of it.'

'I'd better get goin',' he declared. 'I fink I'll go an' give George an' Charlie a knock.'

Alice waited while he put his coat on and then gave him a quick peck on the cheek. 'Good luck, luv,' she said. 'Yer'll be all right.'

The Coley brothers were at the courthouse early and they took their seats at the back of the large room. Frank looked along the row and nudged his brother. 'I guessed they'd be 'ere,' he remarked.

Ben followed his brother's gaze and saw the two Maitland men sitting impassively in the far corner. 'I thought they'd send their messenger boys,' he growled.

The room started to fill up, and when Charlie and Roy walked in closely followed by Danny and George an usher led them to the front row.

Not too far from the Bermondsey courthouse, in the tearooms opposite London Bridge Station, another drama was about to unfold.

'You should have insisted it didn't matter about the boxes,' Horowitz remarked irritably. 'You could have got the rings last Sunday and we'd have been long gone. Instead, we've lost a full week. This is just a sheer waste of time.'

'You don't understand,' Cadman replied quickly. 'She was a difficult woman to handle, believe me. I had to treat her with kid gloves. She's been too long without a man and it was far from easy getting her interested in the first place. She'll be along as promised.'

'What time's your train?' Horowitz asked.

'Eleven thirty from Paddington,' Cadman told him.

The fence nodded. 'We'll meet up at the Royal Hotel in Exeter tomorrow afternoon, providing I can dispose of the rings by this evening.'

Cadman sipped his coffee. 'It'll certainly be a change plying our trade in the west country,' he remarked.

'Yes, I'm looking forward to it,' Horowitz replied. 'It's getting a bit hot here in south London.'

Sara had surprised herself with her ingenuity. On Monday afternoon she had gone to the tearooms with a note one hour before she was due to turn up. She described the two men to the manageress and asked her if she would be so kind as to hand them the message when they arrived around four o'clock.

Cadman had cursed at the delay, but her being incapacitated with a very heavy cold could not have been foreseen, he had to admit, and he hoped, as the note said, that she would shake off the chill in a few days if she stayed indoors and would definitely be there to hand over the jewellery at eleven o'clock on Friday morning.

The respite gave Sara all the time she needed. A visit to the fellowship and a frank discussion with all the members was followed by an extraordinary meeting to plan the way ahead, which Margaret Lindsey attended with another victim of her husband's deception she had managed to encourage along. Then there was one thing left to do.

Sara looked pale and nervous as she entered the tearooms on Friday morning and Cadman was very attentive, greeting her with a kiss on the cheek and helping her into a chair. 'I hope you feel better, Sara,' he said. 'I take it you've got the rings?'

She nodded, reaching into her handbag. ''Ere they are,' she told him.

Suddenly the tearooms seemed to be full with milling people and Margaret Lindsey looked down on her cheating husband with contempt. 'It's all over,' she declared quietly. 'You're finished.'

'I believe you 'ave somefing o' mine,' her companion said to him scornfully.

Cadman looked aghast at the women and Horowitz got up from his chair. 'I think I'd better leave you to it,' he said with a nervous smile.

A detective barred his way. 'I don't think you're going anywhere just now, Stymie,' he said firmly.

'What is this, Randolph?' the fence appealed to him.

'I think you'd better accompany us to the station and get this sorted out,' the policeman suggested.

Sara was still grasping the two rings and she smiled with satisfaction as she dropped them into her handbag. 'You won't be needin' these where you're goin',' she said with venom.

The coroner looked over his thick-rimmed glasses as George Parry took the stand. 'Your statement here mentions that the deceased was constantly goading you,' he said in a hoarse voice. 'Can you be a little more precise?'

George clasped the rail in front of him. 'We worked as a team fer a few weeks an' durin' that time Wally Coates kept on about me bein' too weak ter do the job properly.'

'How did you respond?'

'I ignored 'im.'

'You never argued wiv him?'

'No, I never did.'

'Did you ask to be put with another worker?'

'Yes.'

'And were you?'

'Charlie – I mean Mr Foden – put me wiv Danny Albury.'

'And did you get on with Mr Albury?'

'Yes, very well.'

'I want you to describe in your own words the events which led up to the death of Mr Coates,' the coroner said.

'Mr Foden ordered us inter the shed, an' as me an' Danny were gettin' ready ter leave the trench Wally Coates came towards us. 'E started goin' off about us bein' a liability ter the rest o' the workers but we ignored 'im.'

'Go on, Mr Parry.'

''E turned an' spat down by our feet an' started ter climb out o' the trench,' George explained. 'Suddenly 'e slipped on the mud an' fell backwards on to a cross pole that was supportin' the walls. It collapsed under 'im, an' before we could do anyfing about it the walls on both sides caved in. 'E was buried completely.'

'Mr Parry, are you sure you never touched the deceased at any time while he was there with you?'

'Yes, I'm certain.'

'What did you do to help?'

George hesitated for a few moments. 'Mr Albury was partly covered by the cave-in an' once I was sure 'e could get out OK I joined in wiv the ovver men tryin' ter free Mr Coates.'

'That'll be all, Mr Parry.'

Danny Albury was next on to the stand and he was asked the same questions, which he answered in a loud voice. As he was about to step down the coroner held up his hand. 'Just one more question, Mr Albury,' he said. 'Was your ganger, Mr Foden, aware of what had happened?'

'Yes. 'E was organisin' the rescue,' Danny told him.

'Thank you. That'll be all.'

Roy Chubb was the next worker to be called and he stood with his shoulders thrown back like a sentinel while the coroner scanned the sheaf of papers in front of him.

'Mr Chubb, you were employed by Coley Brothers as a shuttering carpenter.'

Roy looked a little hesitant. 'No, I was

395

employed as a digger, but they knew I was a carpenter by trade so they gave me the job o' shutterin'.'

'As a carpenter would you be expected to perform the shuttering operation?'

'At most building firms, if it was needed,' Roy told him.

'Now I want you to think about my next question and answer truthfully,' the coroner said in a consequential voice. 'In your opinion was the wood you were using sub-standard?'

'Some of it.'

There was a low murmur around the room and the coroner held up his hand for silence. 'Was the wood holding up the walls where the deceased was buried sub-standard in your opinion?'

'No.'

'Oh?'

'I'd complained about the condition of it an' the ganger ordered some new planks,' Roy explained.

'But the rest contained some sub-standard timbers, you say.'

'Yes.'

The coroner turned a page and looked over his glasses. 'Mr Chubb, are you familiar with the adjustable metal props which are used by some building firms in similar conditions?'

'Yes.'

'Do you prefer them?'

'It depends.'

'Will you elucidate for us?'

Roy took a deep breath. 'Wooden wedgin' props are 'ammered inter place while the metal sort 'ave arms that are extended by a screw thread. Too much pressure can cause the timbers ter split, an' sometimes cold weavver causes the metal ter shrink while they're in place just enough ter loosen the grip. It's a matter o' choice, an' the conditions on the job at the time.'

'Would you have preferred to use the metal type on the diggings in Morgan Street?'

'No, I was 'appy wiv the wood props.'

'That'll be all, Mr Chubb, and thank you for your clear and concise explanation,' the coroner said with a brief smile.

Frank Coley leaned towards Ben. 'That wasn't too bad,' he hissed into his ear.

'Will Charles Foden take the stand.'

The mumble of voices was stilled once more by the coroner raising his hand. 'Mr Foden, you were employed as a ganger by Coley Brothers, is that correct?'

'Yes.'

'And were you in charge of the men in the trench when the fatal accident occurred?'

'Yes I was. I was sharin' the responsibilities wiv Mr Lockwood.'

'And it was you who gave the order for the men to leave the trench?'

'Yes.'

'Did you see the deceased walking along the trench at that time?'

'Yes, an' I asked 'im if 'e was deaf,' Charlie replied.

'Mr Coates took no notice of your instruction?'

'I fink 'e was goin' to, but 'e wanted to 'ave a few words wiv Mr Parry an' Mr Albury first.'

'Go on, Mr Foden.'

'A few words were said by Wally Coates an' then 'e turned 'is back on Parry and Albury an' started ter climb out o' the trench. I saw 'im slip an' fall back on the cross-prop. 'E was a big man, about sixteen, seventeen stone, an' the prop was dislodged.'

'It didn't snap?'

'No, it got dislodged.'

'Mr Foden, I understand that Mr Parry came to you with a request to be paired with another partner during the diggings. Did he say why?'

''E was bein' got at by Mr Coates.'

'Got at?'

'Mr Coates treated Mr Parry wiv contempt,' Charlie explained. 'Anyone who worked wiv Coates would 'ave bin liable ter the same bullyin'. The man was a loner an' very unsociable.'

'In your opinion.'

'In the opinion of all the ovver workers,' Charlie said plainly.

'As a ganger shouldn't you be responsible for stopping this bullying and harassing?' the coroner asked.

'I did as much as I could,' Charlie replied. 'I warned Coates on a number of occasions, but apart from standin' beside 'im all day I couldn't totally stop 'im.'

'Not even by threatening him with dismissal?'

'It wouldn't 'ave worked. Coates was a company man.'

'A company man?'

'Yeah. 'E was a long-time employee who could

only be dismissed by the guv'nors themselves,' Charlie told him.

'One last question, Mr Foden. Are you satisfied, in your own mind, that you did enough to get better quality timbers supplied for the shuttering?'

'Every time I asked the company fer stronger timbers they sent a few new planks, but it was never gonna be enough.'

'Thank you, Mr Foden,' the coroner said, taking off his glasses to stroke his brow.

The policeman attached to the coroner's court then made his appearance on the stand and his statement was devastating. 'I inspected the timbers which the rescuers said had been thrown to one side during their attempts to free the deceased and I found them to be mainly dry. In my opinion they would have been sodden if they had supported wet and muddy walls for a few days. I mentioned this fact to Mr Frank Coley but he was noncommittal.'

'Are you saying that the original timbers had been replaced?'

'It's a distinct possibility in my opinion,' the officer replied.

The last witness to go on to the stand was Frank Coley and he stood upright and expressionless as the first question was put to him. 'Mr Coley, did you authorise the timbers to be changed at the scene of the accident?'

'Certainly not.'

'Did you comply with your ganger's requests to supply new timbers for the shuttering?'

'Only one request was made an' I ordered new

timbers myself straight away.'

'Enough for all the shuttering?'

'Yes.'

'Then can you explain why a section of the trench was supported with sub-standard timbers?'

Coley took a deep breath. 'I employ gangers ter take care o' the operation an' it's usual fer them ter make sure the shutterin' work carried out is safe. If the timbers are not up ter scratch then the carpenter informs the ganger who sees me. As I said, only once was I asked ter replace bad timbers an' I did so, immediately.'

The coroner glanced up at the clock. 'We'll break off for lunch now and reconvene at two o'clock,' he announced.

The two Maitland observers telephoned an initial report and Sir Isaac Maitland nodded his head as his works director offered his advice.

Charlie and George went out with Roy and Danny to slake their thirst at a nearby pub, and very little was said as they sat around a table with their pints in front of them. It had been a draining couple of hours, and Danny summed it up for them all as he leaned forward in his chair and rubbed the back of his neck with a gnarled hand. 'I feel like I've done a day's work in the trench,' he groaned.

At two o'clock the coroner began his deliberations. 'It is clear from the evidence I've heard this morning that the deceased brought the accident upon himself by his insistence on going to an unfamiliar part of the trench to berate Mr Parry and Mr Albury. His bulk was a contributing factor in the dislodgment of the supporting prop which he fell on top of, and with no involvement or interference from Mr Parry and Mr Albury which might well have precipitated a misadventure I can only bring in one verdict. Accidental death.'

He held up his hand as the murmuring grew louder. 'I wish to add a rider, however,' he went on. 'Although it would be impossible to declare whether or not stronger supervision could have prevented the tragedy in this particular case, it poses the question. I would also say that until legislation comes into force to compel con-structors to obtain safety certificates from building inspectors, the building industry should seriously consider implementing a voluntary scheme.'

The coroner's words of wisdom were heard and digested by the two company observers and they hurried back to the Maitland offices at Waterloo.

'Shall I inform them, sir?' the works director asked.

'No, get Pat Lawrence to do it,' Sir Isaac Maitland replied. 'After all, he has been in regular contact with the Coleys, and I'm sure he'll let them down gently.'

Hard on the heels of the Maitland observers were the local newspaper reporters, and the tenor of their dispatches would serve to supply the people of Cooper Street and the surrounding area with much food for thought, and rumour.

CHAPTER 34

The Maitland executive waited a few days before delivering the communiqué to their sub-contractors, just long enough for the local newspapers to report on the Morgan Street inquest. It made their decision seem all the more appropriate in the circumstances, and in taking the decision they had the old-established company would appear to be retaining their impeccable record in the building industry.

Frank and Ben Coley were expecting the worst. The coroner's rider had been picked up on by the press, and in particular by the *Weekly Journal* which included it in their editor's comments, and the brothers fumed as they read it. It seemed that too many accidents were taking place in the building trade and the implementation of proper safeguards was long overdue. The editor was scathing about lack of proper supervision, untrained personnel and the cost-cutting methods of sub-contractors which must be stamped out. It was all very commendable, the Maitland executive agreed, and they promised in a statement to the *Journal* that in future they would thoroughly vet any further sub-contractors they used.

'We've bin done over,' Frank growled to Ben as they sat in the saloon bar of the Mason's Arms. 'It'll be back ter scratchin' fer a livin' now, an' I put it down ter that parcel o' shite we took on.'

'You took on,' Ben reminded him as he twirled his glass of whisky.

'I took on, you took on, what does it matter?' Frank scowled. 'We could 'ave avoided this if that idiot Sharkey 'ad picked a couple o' geezers wiv a bit o' sense.'

'I dunno so much,' Ben disagreed. 'The writin' was on the wall. We should 'ave watched points more, instead o' leavin' those two gangers ter sort everyfing out.'

'Yeah, but I still say Parry an' Albury caused Coates ter slip an' Foden saw what went on,' Frank insisted. 'Wiv a bit o' persuadin' they'd 'ave told the truth at the inquest an' the verdict would most likely 'ave bin one o' misadventure, which we could 'ave used to our advantage. The onus then would 'ave bin on skylarkin' instead o' bad workmanship, 'cos that's what that poxy paper's alludin' to.'

Ben shook his head slowly. 'You won't face it, Frank,' he said plainly. 'Whatever the verdict Maitland's would've wanted out. It's all bad publicity an' they've got too much ter lose wiv their main sewer contract.'

Frank drained his glass and his eyes narrowed as he stared at his brother. 'I've realised we should 'ave paid fer a couple o' professionals ter sort Parry an' Albury out an' next time I won't penny-pinch.'

'What d'yer mean, next time?' Ben asked with a frown.

'I ain't finished wiv them, nor Foden, not by a long chalk,' Frank answered.

The women of Cooper Street had read the local newspapers and Ada mentioned the *Journal*'s editorial comment to Emmie as they stood at their usual spot by Emmie's front door. 'Charlie Foden was the ganger an' 'e was partly ter blame fer the accident,' she told her. 'It said in the paper that the supervision left a lot ter be desired.'

Emmie nodded. 'It must be pretty awful 'avin' that on yer conscience.'

'Too true,' Ada agreed. 'It said in the papers that the bloke who got killed was at logger'eads wiv George Parry an' Danny Albury. Yer'd fink the firm would 'ave bin able ter sort it out before it got out of 'and.'

'They should 'ave sacked the bloke, or all of 'em, come ter that,' Emmie said firmly.

'Well, it's too late now,' Ada concluded in a voice that told Emmie that that particular topic of conversation had been exhausted.

There was an angry mood in the Parry household and Lucy was adamant as she faced Charlie across the parlour table at teatime. 'I fink that reporter wants shootin',' she fumed.

'It was the editor,' Charlie corrected her.

'I don't care who it was,' Lucy told him, 'they shouldn't try ter put the blame on you an' that ovver ganger, what's-'is-name.'

'Sharkey Lockwood.'

'The way that editor went on anybody'd fink you killed the poor sod yerself. It was a pure accident, fer Chrissake.'

'It's all down ter sellin' papers,' George cut in.

'They never consider people's feelin's.'

Sara refrained from comment as she worked away on a piece of embroidery, her thoughts focused on that Sunday night when Randolph Cadman came to her room at the guesthouse.

Lucy looked at Charlie and saw the pain in his face. He was trying to make light of the whole thing but he hadn't fooled her. How she would have liked to go to his bed once more and hold him in her arms, let him love her and take away his anguish. It would have been nice just to sit on his lap by the fire and run her fingers through his thick hair. He liked that and said it relaxed him. Anything, just to tell him how much she wanted him, but it was nigh on impossible. George was going to the naval centre again next weekend but Sara would be housebound, she was willing to bet.

It was as though Charlie had read her mind. He looked over at her with a desire that Lucy had come to recognise only too well and it made her shiver. Was he feeling as frustrated as she was?

George stood up and stretched, tired of watching Sara working away at the piece of cloth. 'I'm gonna go fer a stroll,' he announced.

'At this time o' night,' Lucy queried.

'It's only 'alf nine,' he told her. 'I need some air.'

'Why don't yer go fer a pint?' she suggested.

In reply he patted his pocket and smiled. 'I'm boracic.'

Lucy stood and reached up to the mantelshelf for her purse. 'Take this,' she said, handing him a half-crown. 'It's all right, I've got enough ter last till yer dole money.'

George took the coin with a brief smile. 'Don't worry, I won't be out o' collar fer very long,' he assured her. 'I'm gonna do the rounds termorrer.'

'Look, I'm not worried, George,' she replied quickly. 'I know you're doin' yer best ter get work, but yer can't get any if it's not there ter be 'ad.'

He looked serious-faced as he went out and Sara looked up momentarily. 'Where's George gone?' she asked.

''E's gone ter get pissed,' Lucy said unkindly.

'I beg yer pardon?'

''E's gone ter stretch 'is legs,' Lucy told her impatiently.

Sara poked at the fire and pointed to the coal scuttle. 'You wouldn't like ter fill it, would yer, Charlie?' she asked him.

'Yeah, sure,' he replied, getting up quickly.

Lucy was trying to control her irritation towards Sara but finding it increasingly difficult. Most nights she would have gone to bed earlier than this but tonight it seemed she was intent on staying up late. Was it because George was out of the house? 'Would you like a cuppa, Sara?' she asked.

'I'd love one.'

'I'll put the kettle on, then.'

Charlie came back into the scullery clutching the coal scuttle and saw Lucy standing by the gas stove. 'Sara must be feelin' the cold,' he said, smiling.

'Put that down an' 'old me,' she whispered.

He looked at his messy hands but Lucy came to him. 'I want a kiss,' she sighed.

He held her, careful not to let his hands touch her dress, and she reached up to him, her lips hungrily closing over his. 'I love yer an' I want yer, Charlie,' she said huskily.

'I love you too,' he told her, his eyes straying to the door, half expecting Sara to walk in on them.

'When, Charlie? When are yer gonna love me?'

'I need to, I want to, but it's so difficult.'

They heard the chair squeak in the parlour and Charlie quickly picked up the scuttle.

'I fink I'll kill Sara,' Lucy said, grinning. 'I'll poison 'er.'

Charlie turned back in the doorway. 'Do it quick,' he muttered.

It was getting late when Sara decided that her eyes were not up to any more sewing and she eased herself out of her armchair. 'I fink I'll take a drink up ter bed wiv me,' she announced.

Lucy gave Charlie a quick glance then got up. 'All right, Sara. I'll do it.'

'No, it's all right, I'll make it,' Sara insisted. 'The last one wasn't sweet enough. I can't stand cocoa wivout enough sugar.'

'Please yerself,' Lucy replied.

They heard her footsteps on the stairs a few minutes later and Lucy saw that it was ten thirty by the clock. She glanced at Charlie. 'George'll be in soon,' she said.

Charlie reached his hand across the parlour table and laid it on hers. 'Yeah. There'll be times, darlin',' he replied in a low voice.

She sighed deeply. 'That first time we made

love. I felt guilty then, but I don't now, Charlie. I can't wait fer us ter get tergevver again. Say you feel it too.'

'I do,' he answered. 'We agreed we'd 'ave ter be patient, but sometimes I get desperate. I feel I wanna carry yer off, like a desert sheik. I dream about sweepin' you up on ter my white stallion an' gallopin' off inter the moonlight.'

'Yeah, go on,' she told him with her chin propped on her hands.

'Well, I'd take yer ter my tent at the oasis an' we'd be alone beneath the stars. I'd lay yer down on exotic silks an' I'd make love to yer all night. We'd love as never before an' when we'd finally become exhausted you'd sleep the sleep o' love there in my arms.'

Lucy sighed, realising that her cheeks had grown hot. 'Charlie, you amaze me,' she said.

'When I'm wiv you I amaze meself,' he said quietly.

'What are we gonna do, darlin'?' she asked with anxiety in her voice.

'The way I see it, we've got no choice but ter wait till the opportunity arises,' he answered. 'We've got somefing special, Lucy, a magic that won't disappear just because we can't make love whenever we feel like it. In fact I try ter use it ter my advantage. I watch yer, watch the way yer move, catch the look in yer eyes an' the love inside me grows. I pray fer the chance ter make love ter yer, Lucy, an' I wait.'

'But you're so calm an' collected,' Lucy said. 'You can 'andle it. I'm findin' it almost impossible.'

'I didn't say it was easy, but we've gotta play it the only way we can. There's no ovver way. We take each day as it comes, an' let the love flourish inside us.'

'I wish I could put inter words what I feel, Charlie,' she said, her eyes filling. 'I 'aven't got your way wiv words, but you must know.'

'I know,' he replied softly.

They heard the front door open and Charlie quickly grabbed up the newspaper while Lucy slipped into the armchair and closed her eyes.

George looked pleased with himself as he walked into the room. 'I was at the Mason's,' he said. 'I 'eard that the Coleys were in there earlier. Apparently they've lost the Maitland contract. Freda told me. She was well pleased. She can't stand those Coleys.'

Lucy stretched and yawned. 'I didn't know it was so late,' she said, yawning again. 'Did you 'ave a nice drink, George?'

'Yeah. I played a few games o' darts wiv Danny.'

'Can I get yer some supper?'

'No I fink I'll get ter bed. I'm feelin' bushed.'

Charlie folded the paper and rubbed his hands over his eyes. 'Yeah, it must be catchin',' he said, smiling.

'You should come out wiv me next time,' George told him. 'Anyfing's better than watchin' Sara sewin'.'

'Or fetchin' the coal,' Charlie joked.

Lucy was the last to go upstairs to bed, after sliding the bolts and raking the ash from the fire. George was already slipping off to sleep and she lay next to him, listening to his irregular breathing. She reached out and touched his arm gently. 'G'night, George.'

He grunted something unintelligible and turned on to his side. Lucy sighed deeply and stared up at the cracked ceiling, partly illuminated by the glow from the streetlamp. How easy it would be to wait until George was snoring his head off then creep into Charlie's room, but she would have to run the gauntlet. Sara was unpredictable and she was a light sleeper. No, she mustn't even think about it. Our time will come soon, Charlie, she thought to herself as she turned over and buried her head in the cool pillow.

CHAPTER 35

The poorly dressed menfolk standing in the winter dole queues shivered against the winds from the east and prayed for the snow which hadn't come. The temperature would rise a few degrees, and there would be some casual snow-clearing work available at the council yard.

Charlie had managed to talk his way back into work at the docks but there was little trade and only one day's labour a week most of the time. As for George Parry and Danny Albury, they stood in line at the labour exchange and dreamed of a job offer, anything that would bring a few shillings into the home.

The winter days wore on and the cold weather persisted till the end of February, when a fitful sun began to show its face a little more often. During that time the relentless ritual continued and Charlie joined his friends in the queue most days, now feeling a little less conspicuous as he walked through the turning. At first the tongues were wagging constantly and the sudden silence as he passed by his women neighbours told him what the topic of conversation was. He began to feel like a murderer and wanted to scream out his innocence to the whole street, but his good sense prevailed. Better to ride it out and let the women tire of it all, he decided. They would soon have something else to gossip about.

Throughout the depressing days of forced idleness Charlie found his salvation in the few stolen moments he spent with Lucy. George was now going to the naval barracks every weekend until he took his exams in March, and it was left to Sara to determine whether or not they could be alone.

'I might go ter the church ternight,' Sara declared, 'but then again I might not. It all depends on 'ow I feel, an' the weavver.'

Lucy gritted her teeth and drew a deep breath before using a little guile. 'I wouldn't,' she said. 'Yer know 'ow you suffer wiv yer back.'

As far as Sara was concerned it was all right for her to announce a backache or a chill coming on but she objected to anyone else pre-empting her health bulletins. 'There's nuffing wrong wiv my back at the moment,' she scoffed.

'You could stay in an' listen ter band music wiv me an' Charlie,' Lucy went on with her fingers crossed behind her back. 'We love that brass band music.'

Sara always felt that brass band music brought on her headaches and she gave Lucy a hard look. 'I don't fancy listenin' ter that noise all evenin',' she said firmly.

'If yer do go out try ter get back a bit early,' Lucy told her. 'I worry if yer out too late.'

'I can look after meself, thank you very much,' Sara retorted. 'Us on the committee 'ave ter wait till last – there's always someone wiv a problem.'

'Well, just see 'ow yer feel later,' Lucy conceded.

Charlie tried to appear disinterested behind the

evening paper. He thought that Lucy was playing a very tricky game, but he felt reassured when he saw the look of defiance on Sara's face. She would go out tonight in a blizzard just to be awkward, he felt sure.

As the days grew longer and the winds changed to the west it became obvious that there would be no snow-clearing this year. A warm summer would certainly create a few jobs, though. The breweries often took on casuals during good weather, and the many bottle-washing firms operating under the Bermondsey arches took on extra female workers.

'Mary's goin' ter get 'er name down at Bentley's,' Lucy told George one evening. 'I fink I'll go wiv 'er. Susan an' Gracie'll be startin' school at Easter.'

George shook his head. 'Mary can do what she likes but I don't want you bottle washin',' he said firmly.

'Why ever not?' Lucy replied sharply. 'The pay ain't bad an' it's an eight-hour day.'

George looked angrily at her. ''Ave you ever seen those bottle washers?' he asked. 'They 'ave ter wear clogs an' great big rubber aprons an' caps, they've got their 'ands in water all day an' the bloody place reeks of ammonia. I know 'cos Danny's wife used ter do that work an' she told me all about it. All those bottle washers are the same.'

Lucy ignored George's objections and went with Mary anyway. Sara continued to hold the lovers to ransom, and Charlie marvelled at

Lucy's new-found deviousness.

'Sara?'

'Yeah?'

'I was finkin'.'

'What about?'

'Well, you're on the committee an' you must 'ave some input.'

'So?'

'Well, the church is always lookin' out fer ways to 'elp the poor. Couldn't you organise a sewin' circle?'

'We 'ad one,' Sara told her.

'Yeah, but that was mainly fer baby clothes an' fings. I was finkin' more o' gloves an' scarves.'

'Who for?'

'Those poor gits on the dole queues, an' that'd include George an' Charlie.'

Sara stroked her chin for a few moments. 'I s'pose I could suggest it,' she replied. 'The trouble is gettin' the wool. It costs money, yer know.'

'Yeah, but the church ain't short of a few bob, an' I'm sure they'd go along wiv the scheme if someone like you was pushin' it. All right, I know the winter's nearly over, but they could get a good supply o' gloves an' scarves ready fer next winter.'

Sara looked smug as she considered the idea. 'Well, I 'ave got some clout on the committee,' she said. 'I'll bring it up next week.'

Lucy dreamed of her sister-in-law spending her weekends at the fellowship and she noticed that Charlie had his fingers crossed too.

During the spring a new face joined the Cooper Street men on the dole queue. 'Mornin', lads,' he said cheerily as he slipped in behind them. 'Tod Franklin's the name, anyfink's me game.'

'What's Tod stand for?' Danny asked.

'Nuffink. I was christened Tod,' the newcomer replied.

Danny did the introductions and patted Charlie on the back. ''E was our ganger,' he said proudly.

Charlie studied the newcomer and felt that his face was familiar. He was short and dapper, with a dark complexion and a full head of grey wavy hair. 'D'you ever get in the Mason's Arms?' Charlie asked.

'Occasionally, but I use the Crown at Dock'ead most times, when the funds allow,' Tod replied.

Danny got into a lengthy conversation with him and George joined in from time to time. Charlie listened, feeling a little puzzled. He had noticed the man standing to one side of the queue as they arrived and knew he had joined them purposely. He was to learn the reason why before too long, but for the moment the chatter was light-hearted and trivial.

With the signing on completed Charlie led the way out of the exchange and stood in the afternoon sunlight debating whether or not to go to the library for an hour or so. Roy had decided to do the rounds of the local builders and he wandered off with his hands in his pockets. Tod Franklin came out and sidled up to Charlie and the others. 'Do you lads fancy a cuppa at Sadie's café?' he asked. 'I got the price.'

Danny nodded. 'I ain't got anyfing better ter do.'

George accepted too and Tod looked at Charlie. 'What about you, big man?'

Guessing that Tod Franklin had a reason for his offer he nodded. 'Yeah, why not?'

They walked round the corner to the steamy café and found a table while Tod ordered his tea, and it was not long before the short man came to the point. 'Tell me, gents,' he began, pushing his mug to one side and resting his arms on the table. 'Do you ever get desperate when yer standin' in that dole queue? I mean desperate enough ter take a chance ter get some money? I know I bloody do.'

'Yer mean like thievin',' Danny said.

'Exactly.'

'Well that depends,' George cut in. 'Yer don't rob yer own, do yer, an' in any case they'd most likely 'elp yer look fer fings werf nickin'.'

'Nah, I was finkin' o' somefing else,' Tod told them.

Charlie frowned. 'Are yer talkin' about ware'ouse breakin'?'

Tod smiled. 'What if I told you gents there was a nice bit o' money ter be earned wiv little trouble an' no danger involved?'

'Are yer tellin' us the gear's just sittin' there waitin' ter be nicked?' Danny said incredulously.

'It's not there yet, but it will be very shortly,' Tod replied, 'an' I'm lookin' fer a team o' lads I reckon I can trust to 'elp me nick it.'

'You reckon you can trust us?' Charlie asked.

'I'm a good judge o' character,' Tod went on. 'I

get the feelin' you can be trusted ter keep yer gobs shut, even if yer don't fancy the little caper.'

Charlie gave him a hard stare. 'I'm still a little puzzled why yer should pick us out fer this caper as yer call it,' he said. 'You could 'ave approached anyone in the queue.'

'That's true,' Tod replied, 'but most of 'em are on their own or in twos. I could see you three were pals an' I can't use anyfing less than a three-man crew. We'll need one more as well unless any o' yous can 'andle hydraulic cranes.'

'I work in the docks,' Charlie told him. 'I can work cranes.'

'Look, 'ear me out an' then go away an' fink about it,' Tod suggested. 'There's no rush. If yer decide ter go in wiv us phone this number. It's me bruvver's – 'e runs a newsagent's.' He handed Charlie a slip of paper with the phone number printed on it. 'If yer don't fancy it, don't bovver to get in touch. I'll understand. If I ain't 'eard from yer by this time next week I'll start lookin' fer anuvver team. OK, lads, now listen in...'

Lucy looked worried as she sat in Mary's parlour on that bright morning, watching her friend pouring the tea with a sly smile on her face.

'I could tell when I brought Susan back the ovver evenin',' Mary told her. 'The atmosphere was electric.'

'Me an' Charlie are just good friends,' Lucy said dismissively.

'Well you could fool me,' Mary replied.

'I know Charlie fancies me, but I got George an' Susan ter consider,' Lucy reminded her.

''Ow long 'ave we known each ovver?' Mary asked.

'Donkey's years.'

'An' are we best friends?'

'Course we are.'

'Well why don't yer come clean?' Mary laughed. 'You an' Charlie are lovers, ain't yer?'

Lucy slumped down in her chair. 'Is it that obvious?'

'Ter me it is,' Mary replied, handing her the tea.

'I didn't want it to 'appen but it did, an' now we can't keep our 'ands off each ovver, when we get the chance,' Lucy said, sighing. 'Don't get me wrong, I still love George, an' yer might find that 'ard ter believe but it's true, as God's my judge it's true. I couldn't even fink o' leavin' 'im, even though our love life's practically dried up, but when Charlie touches me I'm on fire. I can't resist 'im.'

Mary made herself comfortable in an armchair facing her friend. 'We all try ter squeeze the best out of our lives,' she said quietly. 'You get from Charlie what yer can't from George, but you gotta be sure in yer mind about fings. Is it just about 'avin' it off, or could it get like the love you 'ave fer George? If it's goin' that way then I'd say yer've got problems. One day there'll be a choice ter make an' it won't be easy. I fink 'avin' the 'ots fer someone wanes wiv time an' if there's nuffink deeper then it's not too difficult ter finish.'

'You sound like you've bin there,' Lucy remarked with a smile.

Mary shook her head as she smiled back. 'No, I'm only talkin' as I see it,' she replied. 'There's bin times when me an' Roy 'ave turned our backs on each ovver an' we both got irritable, but the love was still there an' it grew, I'm convinced it did. We don't indulge nearly so often as what we did a few years ago, but nevertheless we cuddle an' kiss, an' try ter please each ovver in all sorts o' ways. That's love, ter my way o' finkin', Lucy. I imagine it's what you've got wiv George, in fact I'm sure it is, but yer've found someone who can give you all that George can't or won't, an' yer need ter see it fer what it's werf. Get what yer can out of it but don't burn yer bridges, luv. George'll be there for yer when you an' Charlie are just a memory.'

Lucy shuddered. 'That's somefing I can't come ter terms wiv,' she said. 'If Charlie left me now I'd die, I know I would.'

'Now, yeah, but let it run a course, an' come an' say that ter me then.'

Lucy finished her tea and put the empty cup down on the table. 'I could never keep anyfing from you, could I?' she said quietly.

'That's what friends are for, luv,' Mary told her. 'Yer secret's safe wiv me, but now I know the score I can be there for yer when fings get bad, an' they will, believe me. Live fer terday, take all yer want from the affair, but remember life still goes on in its 'umdrum way an' generally it's comfortable an' stable. We need that too.'

Lucy stood up to go and suddenly she put out her arms and they embraced. Mary patted her back as though comforting a frightened child. 'Be 'appy, luv,' she said quietly.

421

CHAPTER 36

The three friends from Cooper Street had agreed that they should take a couple of days to think about Tod Franklin's plan and that it would have to be a unanimous decision to go ahead. George also suggested that Roy Chubb should be made aware of the possible escapade but when he was approached he immediately shook his head. 'I don't need any time ter fink about it,' he said firmly. 'Count me out. I've got a chance of a start wiv a buildin' firm in Deptford very shortly an' that'll do fer me.'

Danny made his home available for the next get-together, knowing his wife would be visiting her sister that day. 'Besides, it's better than meetin' in some café or pub,' he remarked. 'Yer never know who might be earwiggin'.'

'Well, lads, we've all 'ad time ter fink. 'Ow d'yer feel about it?' Charlie asked as Danny brought in the tea.

'I'm game,' Danny said without hesitation. 'I've given it a lot o' thought. I've never done anyfing like this before, but all my life I've never 'ad two 'a'pennies ter rub tergevver, an' I've come ter the conclusion it don't pay ter be honest these days.'

'What about you, George?' Charlie asked.

'Yeah, count me in,' he replied. 'I dunno 'ow long I can go on linin' up at that labour exchange, an' fer a pittance. It's drivin' me mad. All

423

right, we're takin' a chance, but I fink from what Tod Franklin's told us it's good odds.'

Both Danny and George looked at Charlie, knowing that the go-ahead rested upon his decision.

'Like you lads I spent a lot o' time finkin' about this, an' I was impressed by Franklin's know-'ow,' he told them. ''E's obviously took a lot o' time plannin' fings out, an' the fact that 'e's worked at the firm makes a big difference. So the answer's yes. I'm wiv you.'

Danny grinned broadly as he poured the tea. ''Ere, get that down yer,' he said cheerily. 'I fink fings are finally gonna look up.'

'I'll drink ter that, even if it's only tea,' George said, grinning.

The number 82 bus trundled through Rother-hithe Tunnel and pulled up in Commercial Road, where the three conspirators alighted and made their way through drizzling rain to the nearby Grapes public house. It was fairly busy in the public bar and Tod was waiting for them. 'We'll move inter the saloon,' he said. 'It's quieter in there.'

Having led them to a vacant table in a corner of the bar and got in a round of drinks, he sat quietly rolling a cigarette with a ghost of a smile on his lips, seeming totally calm as he looked from one to another. 'Right, lads, the caper's on fer Friday,' he said, licking the cigarette paper. 'The two drums o' tobacco were delivered yesterday an' my pal tells me that they'll be started on next Monday. So yer see we've gotta act fast. Now, I've got some sketches wiv me an' I'll explain just what everyone 'as ter do. If we digest this properly an' stick ter the letter, everyfing'll go off like a dream. Oh, an' one more fing before we go over it all. The buyer's agreed ter the price I quoted 'im. An' so 'e should. We're talkin' about two drums, each containin' over three 'undredweight o' compressed pipe tobacco of the finest quality.'

The three leaned forward over the table as Tod laid out his first sketch. 'Now this is the point of entry,' he began.

Mary Chubb thought that her husband seemed very preoccupied at teatime and she put it down to his worrying over money. He had told her that there might be a job coming up for him very soon but she had heard it all before and preferred not to build her hopes up too much.

Roy sat staring into the empty grate for a long time after he had finished his tea with the evening newspaper lying forgotten at his feet, and Mary could stand it no longer. 'Look, there's somefing troublin' you, Roy,' she said as she seated herself in the armchair opposite him.

'Nah, I'm just a bit tired.'

'Don't try an' fob me off,' she told him sharply. 'I know you well enough. There's somefing on yer mind.'

He looked at her and saw that there was no use attempting to keep it from her so he leaned forward in his chair and clasped his hands together. 'George, Charlie an' Danny Albury are takin' a gamble,' he said.

'What d'yer mean, takin' a gamble?' she asked with a frown.

'They're gonna do a job.'

'What sort o' job?'

'They're plannin' on breakin' into a ware'ouse,' he told her. 'They're after nickin' some drums o' tobacco.'

'Bloody 'ell!' Mary exclaimed. 'Does Lucy know?'

'No she doesn't an' you mustn' tell 'er. George don't wanna worry 'er.'

'Where did they get this idea from?' she asked, looking shocked.

'A geezer in the dole queue. 'E's planned it all.'

'I would 'ave thought they 'ad a bit more sense,' Mary remarked with an exasperated sigh.

'They asked me ter go in wiv 'em but I turned it down.'

'I should bloody well fink so,' she replied with passion. 'All right, I know fings are bad an' there's no money about, but stealin' ain't the answer. S'posin' they get caught. Imagine what it'd do ter Lucy an' their Sue. It don't bear finkin' about.'

'Now look, I want yer ter promise me yer won't let on ter Lucy,' Roy said firmly.

'I won't say anyfing,' she sighed. 'I just 'ope it goes off OK.'

Roy picked up the paper but he couldn't concentrate on it. Had he done the right thing in turning down the chance of earning a decent few quid, he wondered? Would they think him a coward?

Mary got up and went to him, gently kneading

his shoulders. 'I've bin finkin',' she said. 'I'm proud you 'ad the guts ter say no, even if it made yer look bad in their eyes. You could 'ave jumped at the chance of the money, but no money in the world'll make up fer you bein' locked away fer years. Me an' Gracie need you 'ere wiv us frew these bad times. We can cope if we're tergevver, but I couldn't if you wasn't there wiv us, an' just fink what it'd do ter Gracie.'

Roy felt distinctly better. Mary was right in what she said, he realised. It made no difference what his friends might think of him. Mary and their daughter came first.

Charlie and George had it planned, and Lucy was told that there was to be a darts final at the Star on Friday evening and drinks were to be served free to the team.

'If we win we may be back a bit late so I wouldn't wait up,' George remarked.

Lucy stole a glance at Charlie and he gave her a sly wink. 'Keep yer fingers crossed fer us,' he said with a smile.

Danny was ready and the three men made their way to the bus stop in Jamaica Road. Charlie carried the key which Tod had supplied and he tapped his coat pocket to reassure himself. Nothing must go wrong tonight, he told himself. Come tomorrow they would all be well breeched.

The rain had ceased and the night was clear with a pale crescent moon shining down from a velvet sky. The river mud was bubbling at low tide and its odour lingered in the air along the narrow riverside lane in Wapping as the three

427

neared Conroy's wharfage. They saw Tod waiting in a doorway and he smiled at them. 'The copper's bin frew an' 'e won't be back fer two hours,' he reported. 'I'll be 'ere at exactly nine o'clock. I'll pull up as planned below that crane an' you be ready ter let the drums down. One at a time fer safety. Like I said, I don't want 'em sent down tergevver. I've seen 'em slip out o' slings before when they come down doubled up. OK then, lads, let's get goin'.'

They watched him hurry off to fetch the lorry and George and Danny followed Charlie into the alley that led down to a flight of stone steps known by the locals as Lover's Walk. Charlie took out the key and removed the rusted padlock that secured the reinforced sliding door at the side of the warehouse. He reached through the iron grille of the lift to depress the locking lever, slid the grille to one side and stepped into the lift, repeating the procedure with the other grille which led into the large storage area. Tod had explained that although the lift was robust enough to take the two drums it would be difficult to manhandle them out from the alley and on to the lorry, whereas the crane would drop them into place with no effort.

George joined Charlie in the storage area while Danny slid the door back into place and replaced the padlock. He then made his way to the front of the building and Charlie let him in through the emergency fire door which could only be opened from the inside. The three men hurried up the dusty stone stairs to the third floor where the drums had been stored and Danny's eyes lit up as he spotted them. "Ow we doin' fer time?' he asked.

Charlie took his pocket watch out of his coat pocket. 'Eight forty-five,' he told him. 'We'd better get started.'

Slowly and methodically the two large drums were manoeuvred across the wooden floor towards the front crane door and Charlie slid the bolt, ready to kick the door open and drop the flap into place when Tod drove up.

'Right, let's get this crane workin',' he said quickly.

George and Danny watched as he switched on the power to fill the water tank and in a few minutes the pressure had built up. Charlie tugged sharply on the operating cord and as the crane rope grew taut he gave a sigh of satisfaction. 'Right, it's ready,' he told them. 'Get the slings. Careful now. That's right, roll it over the rope an' take up the slack. Right, loop it an 'old it up while I 'ook it ter the crane.'

Tod Franklin looked at his watch as he reached the transport yard and saw that it was ten minutes to nine. 'They're cuttin' it short,' he growled to himself.

The swish of tyres and the blazing headlights startled him and he stepped to one side as the car drove quickly into the yard. 'Are they on the premises?' the inspector asked.

Tod nodded. 'They were about ter go in when I left 'em,' he replied.

The police inspector gathered his men around him and glanced quickly from one to another.

'Now you all know your positions and I want you to be as quiet as possible,' he began. 'The object of the exercise is to wait until the goods are visible in the loophole and then we go in. All the exits will be manned and Johnson and Skeets will go up with me to make the arrests. Holland, your back-up team will follow us up the stairs in case we need assistance but for God's sake stay well clear of the loophole. Remember we'll be three floors up and I don't want any of you falling from there, understood?' The police operatives nodded and mumbled their replies and the inspector turned to Tod Franklin. 'Right then, get aboard and take it easy. Just act as you've planned.'

Tod started up the five-ton, drop-side Leyland and drove slowly from the yard. It had been a lengthy bit of work for him and he was looking forward to going up to Manchester for a few weeks' rest as soon as it was all over.

Danny leaned on the attached drum. 'What time d'yer make it, Charlie?' he asked.

Charlie glanced at his watch once more. 'It's two minutes ter nine.'

The waiting seemed interminable but now the three men heard the sound of the lorry approaching and it was time to move. Charlie kicked open the crane door and dropped the flap, and as Danny and George leant their weight to the drum he pulled on the crane rope. It took up the slack and he kicked the suspended drum outwards as the lorry drew up below. Suddenly the lane was lit up like a theatre as the police cars turned on their headlights. Charlie could see men running into position and he swore. 'We've bin tumbled!' he shouted. 'Quick! The stairs!'

As they ran up to the top floor they heard the metallic voice of the police loud-hailer. 'Come down quietly and give yourselves up. There's no-where to go.'

George led the way as they hurried on to the flat roof and Charlie brought up the rear. The adjacent warehouse roof looked tantalisingly near yet it was too far away to reach and Danny leaned over the edge. 'We'd never make it if we tried ter jump,' he gasped.

Charlie hurried across towards Danny and suddenly he felt the floor give way beneath him, and he was falling...

CHAPTER 37

November 1952

Sue leaned back in the armchair and blew long and hard through her pursed lips. 'I tell yer, Charlie, if it 'ad bin anyone ovver than you who told me about those days, about me dad an' all that ovver stuff, I'd never 'ave believed 'em,' she said. 'I find it 'ard ter believe anyway.'

Charlie leaned forward in his seat. 'You know I wouldn't lie ter yer, luv,' he replied. 'Sara got it all wrong, but ter be fair she didn't know anyfing. It was all kept from 'er.'

'I fink she must 'ave realised that you an' me mum were lovers,' Susan said quietly, 'though she never actually said it in 'er letter.'

Charlie nodded. 'You know, I really 'ave a soft spot fer Sara, despite 'er vindictiveness, an' 'er troublemakin'.'

Sue smiled at him. 'As she got older she got more 'ateful towards men but she wouldn't 'ave a bad word said against me dad, so that left you.'

'Poor Sara,' Charlie sighed. 'I even feel a bit sorry for 'er.'

The young woman suddenly realised that the rain had stopped and the sun was breaking through. 'I was only five when you got caught in that ware'ouse,' she remarked. 'When you went away I cried buckets. Me mum an' dad told me you 'ad ter go a long way away ter work but I wanted yer there, ter read me those picture books an' tell me those stories about the crunchy giant.'

'You remember those stories,' he said, smiling.

Sue nodded. 'Yeah, I remember, but there's still so many questions I wanna ask yer.'

'Then ask me,' he told her.

She gazed at his calm face for a moment or two. 'When me dad killed Wally Coates did it affect 'im badly? I knew 'im ter be a gentle, kind man. I can't imagine 'im doin' such a terrible fing.'

Charlie took her hands in his and looked into her pale blue eyes. 'Those times changed people, there's no two ways about it,' he answered. 'Imagine yer dad slavin' in that trench hour after hour, day after day fer a pittance, wiv his 'ands raw as meat an' 'is back ready ter break, an' all the time 'e was plagued by Wally Coates who wouldn't leave 'im alone. Yer dad put up wiv the bullyin' an' the bad-mouthin', 'cos, like yer say, 'e was a kind and gentle person an' 'e couldn't find it in 'is 'eart ter retaliate. P'raps if 'e 'ad Wally Coates would 'ave left 'im alone. Anyway, it was only when Coates grabbed 'old o' Danny Albury that 'e picked up the shovel an' swiped 'im. Yer dad never actually killed 'im, 'e was suffocated by the earth on top of 'im, but we 'ad ter keep on at yer dad fer some time tryin' ter make 'im see it as it really was or 'e would 'ave gone out of 'is mind. 'E was adamant too that yer mum mustn't know, but now I think it would 'ave bin better if she 'ad known. It would 'ave surely drawn them closer.'

'I might sound naive an' stupid, but I can't imagine me dad gettin' involved in that break-in neivver,' Sue told him. 'But then yer've explained 'ow desperate fings were an' 'ow tight the money was.'

'Those dole queues, an' constantly 'avin' ter say no when yer wife an' kids wanted somefing, turned a lot o' men's minds,' Charlie said. 'People got desperate an' the possibility of makin' fings easier by takin' a few chances was 'ard to ignore. Yer dad didn't need ter be persuaded, Sue. 'E jumped at the chance, the same as me an' Danny Albury. On reflection we should 'ave bin a bit more patient, sussed the bloke out before we agreed ter go in wiv 'im, but 'e sounded plausible enough an', like I say, we never 'ad a brass farthin' between us at the time.'

'You said me dad an' Danny got away that night,' Sue reminded him. 'Tell me exactly what 'appened.'

'When I went frew the rotted wooden trapdoor I fell feet first an' broke me ankle on landin',' Charlie told her. 'I was soon caught, but from what I could 'ear I knew they 'adn't caught yer dad or Danny. It was only when I was sentenced that I found out what 'appened. Before I was sent down yer mum was allowed a few minutes wiv me an' yer dad 'ad told 'er everyfing. It turned out that 'e'd found a long ladder on the roof an' 'im an' Danny stretched it between the two ware'ouses an' crawled across the gap. They did the same on the next roof an' managed ter shimmy down a drainpipe on ter the top of one o' those box cranes yer see at some wharves. They used the crane's wall ladder ter reach the quay an' waded frew the mud ter some nearby steps.

Yer mum said yer dad come in covered from 'ead ter foot in mud an' shakin' like a leaf. I 'ave ter say they were dead lucky. It took the police a few minutes ter break in the ware'ouse, an' by that time yer dad an' Danny were long gone.'

'An' you got three years,' Sue added.

He smiled sheepishly. 'Unfortunately I got a stern judge an' 'e set out ter make an example o' me. Trouble was there'd bin a lot o' pilferin' goin' on in the docks at the time.'

'It couldn't 'ave 'elped you not lettin' on who was wiv yer.'

Charlie nodded. 'I told the police I'd bin recruited by a couple o' strangers who'd bin told I was a docker an' knew about cranes. I'm sure they didn't believe me an' I don't fink the judge did eivver.'

'Did Mum come an' visit yer while you was away?' Sue asked.

'Once or twice wiv yer dad, but then I got transferred ter Durham prison an' it was too far ter come, an' they couldn't afford the fare anyway.'

'Was it bad, Charlie?'

'Yeah, it was bad enough.'

'I'll never ferget the day you came 'ome,' the young woman said. 'I was eight years old an' I remember showin' yer me gas mask.'

'Yeah, an' you was upset 'cos they never gave yer a Mickey Mouse gas mask,' Charlie grinned.

Sue studied her fingernails for a few moments. 'Did you an' Mum pick up on the affair?'

'Fer a few weeks,' he answered, 'but then war was declared. Yer dad was called up straight away an' Sara took it on 'erself ter be yer mum's unwanted chaperone. She 'ardly left the 'ouse. It went on that way till the Blitz started. Then...' His voice faltered.

'Go on, Charlie,' she urged him. 'I wanna know everyfing.'

He lowered his gaze for a few moments, then his eyes came up to meet hers. 'The Surrey docks were still burnin' from the day raid an' the bombers were back,' he recalled. 'Sara was at the local street shelter an' me an' yer mum were alone. It was the last time we made love. Two weeks later I was transferred ter Bristol ter work in the docks there an' I only got ter see yer mum every so often at weekends, if I could get away. Yer dad was on convoy duty in the Atlantic an' Roy Chubb was in the air force.'

'But you sent those love letters from Bristol,' Sue pointed out. 'The last one was in 1943.'

'That's right, but they were only expressin' the way I felt an' 'ow I wished fings could be back the way they were,' he explained. 'Fer a long time I'd sensed that yer mum was bein' drawn back closer ter yer dad. I truly fink she expected 'im ter be killed an' she was missin' 'im bad. I remember comin' 'ome fer a weekend. It was the summer of '41 an' yer mum an' Sara were sittin' at the front door in the warm sunshine when I walked inter the turnin'. I 'adn't even 'ad time ter say 'ello before the telegram boy drew up on 'is bike an' 'anded yer mum the dreaded buff envelope that told 'er yer dad 'ad bin lost at sea. I tried me best ter comfort 'er but Sara took charge an' I left after a while. I knew then that the affair between us was over. I didn't doubt that we'd stay good friends, but that was all it would ever be from that day on.'

'Did me mum ever write back ter yer?'

Charlie smiled and shook his head. 'Yer mum told me more than once she was the world's worst letter writer,' he replied, and then his face became serious. 'There was one letter, though. It came a few weeks after yer dad was killed. I want yer ter read it, Sue. It might 'elp you understand a bit better.'

Sue watched while he got up and went over to the dresser. He opened a drawer and took the letter out from under a pile of papers. She saw that his hand was shaking as he handed it to her and the sad look on his face made her heart melt.

Dear Charlie,

I know you'll be surprised to get this letter after me telling you how bad I am at writing, but I just had to let you know the way I feel about things. Yes, Charlie, I really love you and I always will, and it was strong enough to overcome my deep sense of guilt. But things are different now. George is no longer with me and I only have the memory of him. I no longer have the chance to make things up to him for the respect I lost. I found the courage to cheat on him during his lifetime, if courage is the right word, but I find I can't cheat on him now that he's dead. I know that you'll find this hard to understand and I'm not sure I fully understand myself, but please try to see it as I see it. You know I loved George and while he lived I was able to use his failings as a reason for the deceit. His death killed something in me and I can't find fault with him any more, and it tears me apart. Loving you is the best thing that ever happened to me and I'll take the love I have for you to my grave. Think well of me, Charlie, and keep warm memories in your heart, as I will surely do of you. Let's stay friends and let's meet without guilt or strangeness. Continue to smile for me as you always do and I'll be happy to remember the whispering years.

May God bless you, Charlie.

My love for ever,

Lucy.

Tears dropped on to the letter and Sue closed her eyes as she handed it back to him. Charlie put it away in the drawer and came over to sit facing her.

'We were good friends, Sue,' he said quietly, 'an' as the years slipped by the friendship blossomed. We could meet as your mum said, wivout guilt or strangeness. She did love yer dad, you can be sure and she loved me too in 'er own way. I can live wiv that, an' I 'ope that letter 'elps you understand an' forgive both of us. I loved George as a bruvver.' Charlie stood up and gathered the used teacups. 'I'll make us anuvver cuppa an' then I want yer to meet someone. It's all right – she only lives along the landin'.'

The red November sun was molten in a clear sky and the pavements were drying out as Charlie led the way along the stone balcony. He knocked on the last door but one and gave Sue a reassuring smile as they waited.

'Well, if it ain't young Sue Parry,' Alice Albury said as she opened the door. 'Come in, come in. Yer'll 'ave ter take me place as yer find it. I can't get about the way I used to, not any more. It's me legs, yer see. I'm plagued wiv arfritis. Sit 'ere, luv. Charlie, pull up that armchair.'

'Sue's engaged ter be married,' Charlie told her. 'She's gettin' married early next year.'

'Tell me somefink I don't know,' Alice snorted. 'Alan Woodley's a fine young man. Credit to 'is family. I've known the Woodleys fer years.'

'Me an' Sue's bin 'avin' a chat about the ole days in Cooper Street,' Charlie remarked. 'Remember that time I broke me ankle?'

Alice shook her head slowly and tutted. 'You was a naughty boy, Charlie, an' if I didn't know you better I'd 'ave sworn you led my Danny on.'

'You know I wouldn't 'ave done that, luv.'

Alice smiled. 'We was just grateful yer didn't let on about who was wiv yer. Danny an' George would 'ave gone away too. Oops! 'Ave I put me foot in it?' she said quickly.

Charlie smiled. 'She knows all about it,' he assured her.

'Charlie was a good friend ter my Danny as well as yer farvver,' Alice went on. 'Did 'e tell yer about Wally Coates?'

Susan nodded. 'I fink 'e's told me just about everyfing,' she replied with a smile.

'Your farvver was protectin' Danny in that trench an' it was Charlie who got it all sorted out,' the old lady said. 'My Danny, Gawd rest 'is soul, thought the world o' Charlie.'

Charlie looked up at the mantelshelf and pointed to the framed photograph. 'That was taken durin' the Blitz,' he remarked.

'Get it down, Charlie,' Alice told him.

He did as she asked and handed it to her.

'Don't yer fink Danny looked 'andsome in 'is ARP uniform?' she said, and then her face grew sad. 'That was taken a few days before Webber Buildin's copped it. Danny was 'elpin' ter get the poor bleeders out an' a main wall fell on 'im. 'E didn't 'ave a chance. They gave 'im a lovely write-up in the local papers. I was pleased about that.'

'Your Danny was an 'ero, Alice,' Charlie told her quietly.

'Yeah, 'e wasn't scared of anybody,' Alice said proudly. She looked at Susan. 'I remember the time your dad got drunk. It was just after Charlie got sent down, an' everyone knew that the Coleys were be'ind it. Anyway, yer dad was goin' off in the pub about it an' those awful gits got to 'ear. They waited on 'im as 'e came out an' steamed into 'im. They would 'ave killed 'im if it wasn't fer Danny an' ole Ron Sloan the beat copper. Danny waded in wiv 'is fists an' Ron Sloan 'appened ter turn the corner just in time. 'E cracked Ben Coley over the crust wiv 'is truncheon an' my Danny knocked Frank Coley out cold wiv a milk bottle. Lucky fer your dad, it was. A few minutes later an' I don't know what would've 'appened. Those Coleys didn't mess about.'

Sue turned to Charlie. 'Didn't you ever try ter get yer own back on 'em?' she asked.

'I thought about nuffing else while I was locked

441

up,' he told her. 'As soon as I got out I made enquiries, but that was as far as it went. Life itself 'ad taken care o' Frank Coley. 'E'd suffered a stroke an' was paralysed down one side, an' Ben 'ad gone missin'. Nobody seemed ter know where 'e was, but I found out later that 'e was contractin' up in Liverpool. 'E did come back ter London, but it was a bad move. 'E was killed when a flyin' bomb landed on a buildin' site in Dock'ead.'

'You spoke about Sharkey Lockwood,' Sue reminded him. 'What 'appened to 'im?'

''E's still about,' Charlie replied. ''Aven't you ever seen that bloke wiv the scales in East Lane on Sunday?'

'The guess-yer-weight man?'

'That's 'im,' Charlie said, smiling. 'It's a bit of a come-down fer Sharkey, but 'e always liked an easy, uncomplicated life.'

Alice eased her position in her armchair and looked at Charlie. 'I'm goin' again this year as usual, even if I 'ave ter be pushed in a wheel-chair,' she said firmly. 'Will you be there?'

'I will,' Charlie told her, 'even if I 'ave ter push yer all the way.' He looked across at Sue. 'Alice visits Danny's grave every November on the anniversary of 'is death. So do I.'

Susan suddenly felt drained and she looked at Charlie appealingly. 'I really must get me shoppin' before everywhere closes,' she said.

The November day was giving way to a chilly evening as Sue Parry saw him coming towards her. She put down her laden shopping bag and hugged him.

'I was gettin' worried,' he said.

'So was I,' she replied. 'I 'aven't seen yer fer hours.'

'Did yer get it all sorted out?' he asked as he picked up her shopping.

'Almost,' she told him. 'There's one more visit I need ter make soon an' I want yer there wiv me.'

'Don't tell me, let me guess,' he replied. 'Aunt Sara.'

'Right first time,' she said, feeling with pleasure his arm tighten round her waist.

EPILOGUE

They were there in St Mark's churchyard, the people of Cooper Street, and they waited patiently in the mild February sunshine.

'I do love a weddin',' Ada Black remarked.

'So do I,' Emmie replied. ''Specially when it's one o' yer ole neighbour's kids.'

'Wouldn't Lucy be proud if she was 'ere terday?' Ada said.

'She is,' Emmie told her. 'She'll be lookin' down on 'er an' young Alan, an' she'll be pleased. 'E's a lovely boy.'

Ada nodded. 'Yeah, they're a good match.'

'I just 'ope they 'ave it a bit easier than we did,' Emmie said.

The Stricklands were standing next to them and Sammy felt the need to say his piece. 'They will, luv,' he said positively. 'There's plenty o' work now an' there's new 'ouses an' buildin's goin' up all round. Kids o' terday 'ave got a chance, where we 'ad ter scratch around fer a pittance.'

Peggy Strickland hid a smile, wondering how Sammy would have fared as a young man in today's world. Someone would have managed to shove a job down his throat, despite his hatful of excuses to make himself unemployable. 'Yeah, it was 'ard fer us in those days,' she said mildly.

There was a murmur of excitement as someone

445

spotted the car and Ada checked that she had her confetti in her handbag.

'Bloody 'ell! See who's just walked in the gates,' Emmie exclaimed.

Ada turned to see Ron Sloan accompanied by his wife, still upright at seventy and still looking every inch the beat bobby.

'I always felt reassured when I saw 'im walk in our turnin',' Emmie told her. 'It's different terday. They're all ridin' round in cars.'

Will Jackson and his wife Paula were standing nearby and Will's mind went back to the day he was apprehended with a pair of wringer rollers. 'Nice ter see yer, Ron. An' you, luv,' he said.

'Nice ter be 'ere,' the ex-policeman replied.

'I bet yer miss the ole turnin',' Will remarked.

Ron nodded with a smile. 'Yeah, I do. The backstreets are all slowly disappearin' now.'

'Ain't much call fer wringers these days eivver,' Will said with a grin.

The bridal car drove into the churchyard and the chauffeur alighted smartly to open the rear door. Charlie stepped out and helped Susan climb out as she nervously hoisted up her long white wedding dress.

Gracie Chubb was chief bridesmaid and she gave her best friend a supportive smile as her mother helped her adjust the folds of her gown. The bystanders entered the church while the photographer took a few snaps of Susan and her escort by the car, and every head inside the church turned as the opening bars of the wedding march boomed out. Charlie felt the young woman's warm hand on his arm and he

446

threw back his shoulders as he led her down the aisle, casting his eyes briefly to the pews on both sides. He couldn't see her, but he heard the soft murmurings and the whispered words of appreciation as he and the beautiful bride in her flowing white dress walked slowly towards the altar.

Beams of early spring sunlight shone through the stained glass window above the altar and fell in pale spangles of colour on the two young people to be wed, and Charlie was happy.

She came late and eased herself quietly into a back-row pew. She was pale and thin, the gossamer veil of her new hat covering her face. She listened to the words being said and the vows being taken and stood with the rest to sing the cheerful hymn, suddenly aware that there was no hymnal on the rack in front of her.

''Ere, luv, share mine,' Mrs Venners said to her.

The congregation stood to watch the bride and groom walk down the aisle as man and wife and Sara shed a tear.

They were gathering outside for the photo call and Charlie eventually walked across to her. 'Will yer join me in a drink at the reception?' he asked.

'I don't fink so,' she replied. 'I just wanted ter see Susan get wed.'

'But she needs you ter be there,' Charlie said quietly. 'We're all she's got, me an' you. Besides, I gotta do a speech an' I'd feel much less nervous if you was there, Sara.'

She looked at him for a few seconds and then something like a tremor passed across her face.

'Can you fergive a wicked ole lady?' she asked him as she looked down at the ground.

'There's nuffink ter fergive,' he told her with a smile.

Sara pressed her frail hand on top of his, and shed another tear.